MADAM PRESIDENT

MADAM PRESIDENT

A Novel

Nicolle Wallace

EMILY BESTLER BOOKS

ATRIA

New York London Toronto Sydney New Delhi

ATRIA BOOKS

An Imprint of Simon & Schuster, Inc.
1230 Avenue of the Americas
New York, NY 10020

First Emily Bestler Books/Atria Books hardcover edition April 2015

EMILY BESTLER BOOKS / ATRIA BOOKS and colophon are trademarks of Simon & Schuster, Inc.

For information about special discounts for bulk purchases, please contact Simon & Schuster Special Sales at 1-866-506-1949 or business@simonandschuster.com.

The Simon & Schuster Speakers Bureau can bring authors to your live event. For more information or to book an event, contact the Simon & Schuster Speakers Bureau at 1-866-248-3049 or visit our website at www.simonspeakers.com.

Interior design by Kyoko Watanabe

Manufactured in the United States of America

10   9   8   7   6   5   4   3   2   1

Library of Congress Cataloging-in-Publication Data

Wallace, Nicolle.
  Madam President : a novel / Nicolle Wallace. — First Emily Bestler Books / Atria Books hardcover edition.
     p. cm.
1. Women presidents—United States—Fiction. 2. Political fiction. I. Title.
  PS3623.A4437M33 2015
  813'.6—dc23
                              2014045975

ISBN 978-1-4767-5689-9
ISBN 978-1-4767-5691-2 (ebook)

For Mark and Liam

MADAM
PRESIDENT

CHAPTER ONE

Melanie

A re my latest changes to the speech in the version that's in the teleprompter?" Charlotte asked as she held up a draft with her edits marked in black ink.

"Yes, Madam President. I input your final revisions myself," Melanie replied in her usual calm manner.

"What time are we doing this?" Charlotte was tapping her perfectly polished fingernails on the desk and swinging one of her legs back and forth underneath it as she reread her remarks. Melanie recognized both behaviors as two of Charlotte's relatively well-disguised nervous tics.

"You'll go on the air at eleven-oh-two to give the anchors a couple of minutes to set things up and announce that you are addressing the nation live from the Oval Office."

"What time is it now?"

"It's ten minutes before eleven, Madam President."

Charlotte nodded and looked down at the text once more. After about twenty seconds, she looked up again.

"I'm sorry, Mel, how much time until we go live?"

"About ten minutes, Madam President. Can I get you something to drink?"

"I'm fine."

For the first time since they'd met nearly six years earlier, Melanie worried about Charlotte's ability to perform her official duties with her trademark steadiness. They were alone in the Oval Office, and it was Melanie's job to get the president through the next twenty-five minutes.

It wasn't Melanie's *actual* job, but this wasn't a typical day. Melanie served as the secretary of defense, a post she'd held for the last eighteen months, ever since Charlotte had been reelected for a second term as the country's forty-fifth president. Melanie's Oval Office assignment was as unexpected as the events of the previous twelve hours.

The sound of jets patrolling the airspace above the White House and the beams of light from the helicopters hovering nearby weren't helping with Charlotte's unusually high levels of agitation and impatience.

"Madam President, I need you to relax a little bit, or you're going to scare people more."

"Jesus Christ, Melanie!" Charlotte exploded.

Maybe it's good that she's blowing off a bit of steam, Melanie thought.

"Without any of our guys having a goddamned clue or hint of warning, terrorists attacked five cities. Hundreds, maybe thousands, of people are dead. And we don't have any idea if there are more plots under way or where the attacks originated. People *should* be scared."

"I crossed that section out of your speech. Thought it might be a little too much straight talk for tonight," Melanie deadpanned.

Charlotte didn't smile. She stared down at the pages of her speech, but Melanie could tell she wasn't reading them. Melanie moved toward one of the sofas in the middle of the Oval Office and ran her hand back and forth across the smooth linen fabric that she'd selected when Charlotte had tasked her with renovating the room at the beginning of her first term. The president hadn't given her any direction other than to stick to one color. She had a thing for monochromatic dressing that extended to her interior-decorating preferences. The fabric was so pale and delicate that the sofas needed to be recovered quarterly, but Charlotte said that they sent a strong signal to everyone to keep their feet off the furniture. She'd thwarted several attempts to recover them in a more practical material.

The down-filled couches were inviting, but Melanie knew that if she sat, her twenty-four-hour day would catch up with her, and she'd never be able to muster the energy to get back up. She glanced down at her BlackBerry. Her executive assistant made fun of her for still carrying the antiquated device, but she'd had a BlackBerry (at times, she'd had two or three of them) since her first days at the White House almost two decades earlier. Now she also carried an iPhone that her husband, Brian, had given her the year before and that she used for personal communications with him and with their friends and family. Melanie scrolled through the e-mail messages on the iPhone and opened a message from Brian. He was in the White House briefing room, about forty feet away from the Oval Office, with the rest of the White House correspondents. His message simply said, "Good luck with the speech. Call when you can. Love you." Melanie skimmed what looked like hundreds of unopened e-mails. They'd have to wait until after Charlotte's address. When she looked up, she was surprised to see the president standing in front of the two televisions in her private dining room. Melanie walked toward the side of the Oval Office that opened into the dining room and watched Charlotte closely for a couple of minutes. She was wearing a perfectly tailored black Armani jacket with matching pants. A pale blue silk blouse peeked out from under the jacket, and the initials of her twins, *P* and *H*, hung from a white-gold chain around her neck. Her thick blond hair was tucked behind her ears. She had stepped out of her black heels, and in her bare feet, she looked diminutive. Her makeup artist was highly skilled, but Melanie thought she'd been a tad heavy-handed with the blush. Charlotte wouldn't tolerate another touch-up on a night like this, though. Melanie shifted her weight from one foot to the other and moved closer to the door so that Charlotte would know she was there.

"You're the one who's not having a normal reaction, Melanie. No one should be as stoic as you are right now. Frankly, it's jarring," Charlotte said without looking away from the carnage on the screens.

"Madam President, you've mistaken my jet lag for tranquillity. I woke up in Iraq this morning, and with the time change, I think that was about twenty-four hours ago."

"That was this morning?" Charlotte's eyes were still glued to the screens.

"Doesn't it seem like a thousand years ago?"

Charlotte muted the televisions and turned to face Melanie.

"I think it's safe to say that everything has changed since then, don't you?"

Before Melanie could conjure up an appropriate response, the network producer who was directing the live coverage of Charlotte's speech knocked on the door of the Oval Office. Melanie had instructed him to do so when they were two minutes out so she could get Charlotte seated and check the camera shot.

The president had insisted that they be left alone in the Oval Office after the hair and makeup people left. It was unheard of to leave the president alone in the Oval Office for a televised address to the nation without someone who was trained in video production, but Melanie had held just about every job in the White House communications and press departments during her decade and a half of service in the executive branch of government.

"That was your two-minute warning, Madam President. You're going to do this just as we rehearsed it. As you requested, it's just you and me in here, so please do not fidget in your seat. I can keep you in focus, but if you move out of the camera shot, there's not much I can do to reframe you with my limited TV-production skills. Don't move your chair or stand up. And try not to do any forced smiling. You want to appear somber but not alarming."

"Anything else?" Charlotte snapped. She took her seat behind the desk and held up one hand to shield her eyes from the glare. Lighting the Oval Office for an evening address was one of the trickier production feats. The production staff had set up freestanding stadium lights on either side of the president's desk to illuminate her properly for the TV audience. As she read through her speech one final time, Melanie thought she looked surly, but she didn't want to stoke her ire with any more instructions.

Melanie checked the shot and confirmed that it looked OK with the professionals by opening the door a crack. The director gave her a thumbs-up, and Melanie shut the door.

"We're all set, Madam President. You look great."

Melanie took a deep breath and smiled reassuringly at her boss. They hadn't been alone in the Oval Office together in months, and until today, Melanie hadn't worked with her on a speech since she'd left her post as White House chief of staff at the end of Charlotte's first term as president. Despite the current tragic, catastrophic circumstances, it wasn't uncomfortable to be with each other like this. Melanie and Charlotte had worked together long enough to take exactly what they needed from one another. Melanie was acting cooler than she felt because she sensed in Charlotte a hotness that would not translate well on camera. For her part, Charlotte was using these few precious moments to process what had happened before packing away her horror and fear and projecting strength and resolve to the entire world.

Melanie suspected that Charlotte had chosen her for this assignment because she was the one person with whom there was no pretending. The extraordinary step had been taken to transport Melanie from Andrews Air Force Base, where she'd landed an hour earlier, to the South Lawn of the White House in one of the helicopters typically designated as Marine One and used to transport Charlotte. Melanie assumed that it also had something to do with the fact that she'd been through something like this before. After all, she'd worked in the press office on September 11, 2001.

"You're sure about the Longfellow poem?" Charlotte asked.

"Most presidents quote from scripture on occasions like this. You said that you didn't want that, so I included the Longfellow quote. We are sixty seconds out, and I can't replace it at this point, but if you want to drop it, the speech works fine without it."

"No. I like it. It's powerful. And you don't think we use the word *toward* too much? It's in here at least three times." They'd chosen every word in the address with care.

"The speech is good, Madam President."

Charlotte nodded. "I've got this," she promised.

"I know you do." Melanie smiled and said a silent prayer.

At that moment, the light on the camera started flashing. When the flashing stopped, Charlotte would be seen instantly by millions of people.

Melanie checked the teleprompter one last time to make sure the speech had loaded properly and then counted down with her fingers.

When the light stopped flashing, Melanie mouthed, "Go."

CHAPTER TWO

Dale

Q uiet, everyone," Dale ordered. She was in the White House briefing room, where the entire White House press corps had crammed in, minus a few of the correspondents who were filming live shots on the North Lawn.

"The president is starting, people. Please stop talking," she urged.

The image of the president sitting at her desk in the Oval Office silenced everyone. Dale turned to watch on a monitor that had been set up next to the podium where she conducted her daily briefing. Dale's deputy turned the volume up as high as it would go.

"Good evening. Today we witnessed five separate and nearly simultaneous attacks on American cities. Together they make up the most brazen terror attack in our country's history. The numbers are still being confirmed, but we know that several hundred people have lost their lives. Others were wounded, many of them while trying to help the victims. At this moment, hundreds of our fellow citizens are searching for news about loved ones and praying for the best while bracing themselves for the unthinkable.

"And just as we did more than a decade and a half ago in New York, Pennsylvania, and Virginia, Americans confronted today's violence with bravery and heroism. In New York, just more than a mile away from the tender scars of September eleventh, the pedestrian parks in Times Square were targeted with bombs. The images of men and women from the surrounding businesses charging toward the explosions to help those who were hurt in the attack were the first ones we saw of a city that knows the devastation of indiscriminate terror all too well.

"In South Florida, where terrorists targeted a passenger ship at the Port of Miami, people abandoned their cars on the freeways and rushed to the burning ships to help people they'd never met. The majority of those victims were families embarking on cruises."

Charlotte stopped for a second, and it looked to Dale like she was getting choked up. *Don't cry,* Dale silently pleaded. Charlotte took a breath and seemed to regain her composure.

"In Los Angeles and Chicago, suicide bombers detonated their explosives in front of crowded ticket counters while passengers checked in for flights. And finally, here in our nation's capital, terrorists placed bombs on the National Mall. For those of you not familiar with the nation's capital, the National Mall is home to the Smithsonian museums, including the Air and Space Museum, which was the target of today's attack."

Charlotte paused again. She appeared to be gathering herself. The itemized recitation of the destruction had a physical impact not just on the president but also on the journalists gathered in the briefing room. Dale glanced around the room and could see that many of the very same reporters who projected toughness, objectivity, and a studied indifference were struggling under the weight of the news.

"In each of these cities, Americans responded in the manner to which we've grown accustomed. They rushed toward danger and did whatever they could to help friends and strangers at an hour of catastrophe and tragedy. The search for survivors will not stop until everyone is accounted for.

"Now all of us are wondering the same thing: who would commit such vicious and brutal attacks, and why? We don't have as many answers tonight as I'd hoped, but we will learn all the facts. We always do. And we will not delude ourselves with a discussion about delivering justice to these barbarians. Today's acts were not crimes; they were acts of war. Sadly, this is not the first battle on our soil in this young century. America has come under attack before by people who hate us because of our freedoms and seek to change our way of life through acts of terror. Let me be clear: nothing will be spared or compromised in our effort to hunt down those responsible for today's devastation. Every American can rest assured that we will answer today's attacks with the full force of the United States government, including our unmatched military, diplomatic, and intelligence capabilities."

Dale thought she could see Charlotte's face redden slightly. A few of the cameramen in the back of the briefing room whistled, and others clapped. Dale watched Charlotte look down at the pages in front of her and then look back into the camera with even greater intensity.

"I speak to you tonight not only as your president and commander in chief but also as a mother and wife with a family of my own. In the coming days, we will learn all of the names of those who perished, and we will hear their stories. To their families, they will not be names or stories. They will be sons and daughters, mothers and fathers, husbands and wives, sisters, brothers, aunts, uncles, and grandparents. We may hear their final voice-mail messages to loved ones or learn about the victims' final days from those who have been left behind. To those of you who are dealing with the immeasurable grief of the sudden loss of a spouse or a parent or, heaven forbid, a child, please know that we all stand with you in your despair. We will all do our part to honor your monumental loss. In this hour of immense sadness, I am reminded of a Henry Wadsworth Longfellow passage that I first read years ago." Charlotte looked down again and took another deep breath. When she looked up, her eyes were glassy.

"'And the mother gave, in tears and pain, the flowers she most did love; she knew she should find them all again in the fields of light above.'"

Dale thought she could hear someone sniffling near where the radio reporters sat.

"May God bless all of you tonight, and may God continue to bless the United States of America."

At the exact instant that Charlotte stopped speaking, the TV correspondents were on their feet, talking to the network anchors back in New York, while pressing their earpieces into their ears with their fingers to hear above the din of other correspondents doing the same thing. Dale found it disorienting to hear only one side of the conversation, so she headed back toward her office to watch the coverage.

"Dale, are you leaving?" shouted an AP reporter.

"Just going to my office," she called over her shoulder.

"Will the briefing room be open all night so we can file our stories from here? Our editors are going to expect that our copy is updated hourly at least through the morning and probably for the next several days."

"Yes, I'm sure we can leave it open all night tonight, but don't expect to get briefed through the night. We will let you know if there are any developments."

"How about the North Lawn? We will need to go live with any breaking news."

The North Lawn was where the TV reporters stood to film their reports from the White House. It provided the iconic background of the White House residence for the journalists who were fortunate enough to cover the president for their respective networks and cable channels. It hadn't dawned on Dale that the networks would want their correspondents to update their coverage through the overnight hours. It was almost midnight, and most of them would be back on the air at seven A.M. or earlier.

"I'll check with the Secret Service," she promised.

Dale rushed back toward what was referred to as "upper press." Marguerite had assembled their small staff in Dale's office. She took a seat at her desk and pulled a Diet Coke out of the small refrigerator behind it.

"How are you guys doing?" Dale asked.

They assured her that they were fine, but it had been a harrowing day. While she had been escorted by the Secret Service to a fortified underground bunker, her staff had been evacuated when the first bombs went off on the Mall. They were called back to the West Wing, only to be evacuated from the complex a second time when the second bomb went off. Edgy Secret Service officers had harassed a few of her deputies while they were escorting the press back into the White House. Dale had walked out to the newly erected perimeter herself to vouch for her staff and the credentialed press. She'd been shocked by the scene. Downtown Washington looked like a war zone. Uniformed military in armored Humvees filled the streets around the White House. Secret Service agents in black jumpsuits held machine guns as they rode in SUVs with the back windows open. Soldiers in fatigues directed all traffic—human and vehicular—away from 1600 Pennsylvania Avenue. Heavy smoke hung in the air from the bombings on the Mall, and the sound of sirens was constant. Men and women dressed mostly in business suits moved like swarms of bees alongside slowly moving lines of cars toward the residential neighborhoods that rimmed downtown Washington.

"You were all tremendously brave and professional today," Dale said. "Thank you for coming back twice after being evacuated and for doing everything that you did to make things run smoothly. I know the president is grateful to you for your service, the press is indebted to you until the end of time, and I am so impressed by how you handled yourselves."

Her deputies were staring at her, unblinking. A couple of them looked like they were in shock. She should have called them into her office sooner.

"If you guys hadn't come back here and helped to fill that briefing room with our press, the people who needed to hear from the president tonight would not have had the opportunity to do so. I'm proud of all of you."

"Dale, what should we do with Richard and Lucy?" a press assistant named Danner asked. Richard and Lucy were the evening anchors from CBS. They'd been preparing to do a sit-down interview with the president earlier that morning as part of a special they'd been filming, but when news broke about the first attack, the interview was postponed.

Dale's staff had taken part in weeks of painstaking preparations for what they all referred to as the "Day in the Life" special, because it was intended to chronicle every detail of a "typical" day in the life of the president of the United States and her staff. Dale had convinced the president to pull back the curtain and reveal the inner workings of the White House to show the public how much thought and effort and collaboration went into an ordinary day at the White House. No one could have anticipated that close to twenty news crews—each including a cameraman, a sound technician, and a producer—would be embedded with the most senior White House staff members when news of the five bombings started to trickle in.

Most of the crews were respectful of the limits the disaster had placed on their access, and they'd simply waited in the lobby areas or in the press briefing room. But the two anchors hadn't taken no for an answer. They felt entitled to the access they'd been promised, regardless of the extraordinary turn of events. Dale and her deputy had determined earlier in the day that throwing them out would confirm that the president was hunkered down, which would send the worst possible message to the public. The decision had been made to try to accommodate the news crews and the anchors without compromising any aspect of the government response, by leaving the press office solely responsible for them and freeing up the rest of the senior staff to respond to the crisis.

"They've been reporting from their cell phones in the West Wing lobby all evening. The other TV correspondents are furious. The bureau chiefs from NBC and ABC are demanding access to the West Wing lobby as well."

Dale had incorrectly assumed that Richard and Lucy would have returned to their network's Washington bureau to anchor its coverage of the president's remarks, but they had decided to take advantage of their unusual access instead.

"Oh, another thing. Richard and Lucy are insisting that all of their crews be permitted to embed again with the senior staff tomorrow because we canceled everything today," Danner added.

"Jesus, those two are unbelievable. Are they in the lobby right now?"

"Yeah, I think they're on the air."

Dale turned her TV to CBS, and sure enough, they were broadcasting from their cell phones from the West Wing lobby about everyone they'd seen come and go since the speech ended minutes earlier.

Dale pressed her thumbs into the bones above her eyes and took a deep breath.

"Do you want me to come with you?" Danner offered.

"I've got it. Stay here and handle our press corps. Tell them that no one is going to be broadcasting from the West Wing lobby. I will get rid of Richard and Lucy," she promised.

Dale reached for her iPhone. She noticed two missed calls from a blocked number that she recognized as the same one that came up when someone placed a call from inside the White House residence. She knew who it was, but she couldn't deal with him now. Dale had resolved to get through the day, and the only way she could pull it off was to ignore anything and anyone unrelated to her official responsibilities.

She walked out to the West Wing lobby to talk to Richard and Lucy. She had to convince them that there was more to gain by leaving than by staying, and she was confident that she was about to make them an offer that would do the trick.

CHAPTER THREE

Charlotte

You're sure I wasn't too hot?" Charlotte asked Melanie as she stepped into her private bathroom to wipe off her makeup. They'd left the Oval Office so that the production crew could remove the lights and camera equipment.

"It was very strong."

"Thanks to you, Mel." Charlotte stood in front of her in the dining room scrubbing her eyes with the makeup remover cloths.

"That was all your doing, Madam President," Melanie assured her.

"All that *I* did was read the speech that *you* wrote. Seriously, thank you for being here and for everything you've done today."

"Where else would I be, Madam President?"

"I mean, after everything that happened last year with Tara and everything, I really appreciate it."

"There are more important things to worry about now. As you said before the speech, everything has changed," Melanie said.

"I hope so," Charlotte replied.

Melanie moved her hands to her hips and started to speak but was interrupted by the sound of the door being pushed open.

"Great job in there, Madam President," Craig, the White House chief of staff, said.

"Thanks, Craig," Charlotte replied.

"And thank you for all of your help, Melanie. The speech was excellent," he added.

Charlotte watched Melanie toss her BlackBerry and iPhone into her purse and open the door separating the dining room from the Oval Office. She and Melanie had shared more meals in the small sanctuary over the years than she could count. They both had the menu memorized, even down to the seasonal soup selections. Charlotte almost always had a Cobb salad with extra dressing, while Melanie rotated between the veggie burger, the tuna sandwich, and the fruit plate with a scoop of cottage cheese, a selection that Charlotte found revolting. She missed those lunches.

"Are you leaving?" Charlotte asked.

"I've got to get back to the Pentagon."

"I'll see you on the next videoconference."

"Absolutely, Madam President."

Charlotte watched Melanie navigate around the crews in the Oval Office. She couldn't pinpoint it, but Melanie looked different. Then Craig positioned himself directly in front of her and started talking about the things he'd "taken care of," as if to prove that things were under control. Charlotte knew that things were far from under control, and she resented the spin he was trying to put on what was clearly a hideous calamity still in its early stages.

"Madam President, from a message and tone perspective, I thought you nailed it in there. You were serious and determined but not overly alarming."

Charlotte was annoyed that no one on her staff wanted her to be alarming. What the hell was wrong with all of them? The country had just been bombed. She looked down at her intelligence briefing from that morning.

"How long until this gets leaked?" she asked.

"Someone from the House or Senate Intelligence Committee will probably do it by the time the morning shows come on tomorrow."

"There's nothing in here about the chatter getting louder, right?" she asked Craig.

"Nothing. You have no exposure along the lines of September

eleventh. No Richard Clarkes are going to come out of the woodwork and say they told you so."

"Does that make it better or worse?" she challenged.

He knew better than to offer an answer.

"What do we have next?"

"Just the final National Security meeting. The FBI is going to do a briefing on the DNA testing from the remains of the suicide bombers at the airports in Chicago and L.A. The director is on his way back over here, ma'am. I spoke to him before your speech," Craig replied.

"We didn't need to drag him back over here. Please make sure he knows that he can participate via videoconference next time. He's going to be the busiest man in D.C."

"Yes, ma'am."

"Those are the only bodies so far?"

"Yes. And the Miami suspects are still in play."

"They won't talk for a while."

"Depends somewhat on your decision on enhanced interrogation measures."

"When am I visiting the cities?"

"We're doing our best with New York and D.C. The others won't want to divert resources from the investigation or recovery efforts to—"

"I know, I know, to escort my goddamned motorcade. I know. Why do we always have to drain everyone's resources? Why can't I just land, drive in an SUV without the whole motorcade to survey the damage, visit with local law enforcement, pay my respects to the families of the victims, and then get the hell out of the way? Can you ask them if they can make that happen?"

"Yes, ma'am."

"What else?"

"Are you up for a few foreign leader calls after the National Security Council meeting?"

"What kind of question is that? If I have to do calls, just give the list to Samantha, and I'll do them." Charlotte couldn't figure out why Craig was asking her if she was "up" to doing the things that needed to be done. She understood that he was being deferential and trying to gauge her stamina for the long list of official to-do's that emerges during a national security crisis, but it still bothered her that he was talking to her as though she might not have the endurance to complete her obligations.

"Why don't you have the vice president do some calls, too?" she suggested.

"She's done a half a dozen. Maureen is also in contact with the leaders on the Hill. I just spoke to her, and she's suggested that we have the chairmen and ranking members of all of the national security committees down here tomorrow to brief them on the investigation."

Maureen McCoughlin, Charlotte's third vice president, was the former Democratic speaker of the House, and she maintained excellent relations with her former colleagues.

"How's the mood on the Hill?"

"I think some of them are still in their undisclosed locations." For the most part, an undisclosed location was just that, an office that was simply undisclosed to the press and public. Only in very rare instances did government officials evacuate to secure government installations.

"Ask Maureen to make a list for me, and I'll add courtesy calls to the senators from New York, Florida, Illinois, and California, plus the leaders and anyone else she suggests tonight."

"Yes, ma'am."

Charlotte could hear people crying on one of her televisions. She turned up the volume and shushed Craig so she could watch. Seeing the scene of mass chaos just blocks away from the White House complex on her TV screen made her feel oddly walled off from what was happening. She contemplated walking out the door and racing to the Mall below to help with the recovery operation. It was incredibly unsatisfying to be cooped up in the White House with the wreckage and suffering so near.

"You know what, Craig?"

"Ma'am?"

"Don't ask."

"Ma'am?

"Don't ask. Please inform the Secret Service that I plan to visit the Mall first thing in the morning, and tell them that this is the compromise you reached with me when I asked to go tonight."

"Yes, ma'am," Craig replied.

She stood watching the TV coverage.

"This isn't the day I thought we were going to have," she said, more to herself than to Craig.

"Twenty embedded news crews filming your every move don't seem like such a bad deal in comparison, do they?"

Charlotte turned away and hoped he'd return to his office. She appreciated Craig's attempt to lighten her mood, but she found herself missing Melanie's quiet intensity. Charlotte did her best thinking when no one was talking to her. Mercifully, Craig fell quiet.

She thought about what she'd been doing before news of the first attack reached her. Her Democratic vice president, Maureen McCoughlin, had asked for a rather large favor in return for delivering enough Democratic votes in the House and the Senate to pass Charlotte's legislative priorities. She'd asked Charlotte—a Republican—to become a vocal supporter of women's health providers, including those that also provide birth control and abortions. In a move that her admirers had called bold and her detractors had called politically suicidal, Charlotte had been delivering a speech at the Women's Museum in Washington, D.C., in which she laid out the "enlightened conservative's" case for reproductive freedom. As the first female Republican president, her decision to stand with her Democratic vice president and voice her support for a woman's right to choose had been the topic of breathless morning-show commentary, large antiabortion protests in front of the White House, and a phone and e-mail campaign from the prolife groups that had jammed the White House comment line for hours. Then, just as she was hitting her stride with the crowd gathered at the Women's Museum, Monty, her lead advance man, had handed her a note saying that New York City had been attacked. She'd excused herself and made her way backstage. In the motorcade back to the White House, she learned about the attacks in Chicago and Los Angeles. She'd just arrived back at the Oval Office and turned on her television when the media first started reporting on the attack at the Port of Miami. The attack outside the Air and Space Museum in Washington had occurred after she'd already been rushed to the underground command center. After the D.C. bombings, the Secret Service wanted to take Charlotte out of the White House, but she'd insisted on staying.

Now she asked Sam to give her five uninterrupted minutes. She dialed Peter in the residence.

"Hi," she said.

"How are you doing?"

"I'm all right."

"Do you want me to come down?"

"No. I've got another NSC meeting and then a few calls to do. I'll be up in a couple of hours. What did you think of the speech?"

"Was the Longfellow poem Melanie's idea?"

"Was it too dark?"

"I don't think that's possible."

Charlotte leaned forward so that her elbows were resting on her knees. "How are the kids?"

"They're fine."

"Do you think they'll still be up in another hour?" Charlotte asked.

"With the time change, I'm sure that they will."

Their twins, Harry and Penelope, had just completed their freshman years in college, Penny at Stanford and Harry at Charlotte's alma mater, U.C. Berkeley. Both had stayed in Northern California for the summer.

"Please tell them that I'll call tonight."

"Will do."

"Are Brooke and Mark awake?" Brooke and Mark were Charlotte's best friends from college. They made frequent trips to Washington to provide Charlotte with a much-needed reality check from her life inside the presidential bubble. They also added comic relief to Charlotte's structured and formal existence. Charlotte suspected that they came as both an act of charity and genuine friendship and to escape the boredom of their suburban existence.

"They tried to get flights home, but everything has been canceled."

"Tell them not to worry. Sam can work on getting them out of here tomorrow."

"Char, don't worry about us. We're worried about you."

"I'm fine," she snapped.

"We'll see you whenever you finish, then."

"Don't wait up," Charlotte insisted.

"Whatever you say, boss."

Charlotte was being passive-aggressive with Peter, but she really couldn't help it at this point. Her emotions were swinging between fury at the terrorists who carried out the attacks, rage at her own advisors who did nothing to prevent the attacks, and desperate frustration at Peter's inability to anticipate what she needed from him, even though she didn't know what it was herself.

"Have you been watching the press coverage?" she asked.

"It's awful," he confirmed.

"That ship was full of young families. And the museums on the Mall are always full of school groups." Charlotte felt a lump forming in her throat, but she didn't want to cry.

"Are you sure you don't want me to come down there, Char? I could wait in the Oval while you have your meeting and then sit with you while you make your calls?"

His voice was so tender. Maybe he did understand. She felt tears forming, and she swallowed hard to stop them. She wanted to accept his offer, but she couldn't bring herself to open up to him and tell him how desperately she needed to be reassured that she was capable of whatever new and unknown responsibilities now fell to her.

"Char, please say something."

She covered the phone with her hand and cleared her throat. She waited until she was sure that her voice would come out steady and strong. "You don't have to do that. I don't know how long the NSC meeting will go—or the calls, for that matter."

"If you change your mind, let me know."

"I will."

Charlotte hung up the phone and stood with her back to her desk. She felt bad about being short with Peter, but other concerns quickly overtook her guilt. She watched the helicopters above make patterns on the South Lawn with their searchlights. How could she convince people that they should go about their lives and not worry about threats if terrorists could hit targets less than half a mile from the West Wing of the White House? The enormity of her failure to protect the country from harm was hitting her in waves. How could she ever make things right? She had made more than her share of mistakes in five and a half years as president, but this one felt unrecoverable. How had this happened? How had she *let* this happen?

CHAPTER FOUR

Melanie

Twenty-four hours earlier

I f I had half a brain or a scrap of integrity, I'd resign. Effective immediately," Melanie grumbled.

"You're in Baghdad, Mel. That seems slightly irrational, especially for my levelheaded wife," Brian gently teased.

"If Charlotte thinks I'm going to let this go on indefinitely, she's out of her mind. Does she seriously think that I'm going to be able to pretend that nothing happened and continue to put my ass on the line for her? I mean, after her White House threw me under the bus and left me for dead?"

"We've had this conversation a thousand times. You have every right to be mad."

"I can hear the 'but' from ten thousand miles away, even on this crappy satellite phone."

"Actually, that was my call-waiting."

"It's after eleven."

"It's probably the *Today* show. I have a piece on Charlotte's abortion speech that's supposed to be leading the show tomorrow. Hang on for one second."

"That speech is a really stupid use of Charlotte's political capital," Melanie griped.

"I know, honey. I'm sure you'd rather see her squander her remaining political capital on your unpopular wars."

"Exactly." She laughed.

As Melanie held for Brian, the White House correspondent for NBC News, she thought about how, for the first time in her life, her personal life was in a relatively blissful state, while her career had careened into the realm of the ridiculously dysfunctional.

Melanie was working out of an office inside the heavily fortified green zone. She would be meeting with troops involved in training the Iraqi army and a handful of local leaders to thank them for their ongoing service and cooperation. Later in the day, she'd host a video town hall between Baghdad and Washington. For the town hall, the Pentagon press folks had been ordered by the White House to round up a diverse group of military trainers, USAID workers, and local elected officials and cabinet members in the new Iraqi government who would illustrate the collaborative effort under way to solidify recent gains in the political and security situation in Iraq. What Melanie understood as a veteran of three White House staffs was that the West Wing had added an event in the war zone to showcase the commander in chief as a strong and competent wartime leader for the benefit of the TV production under way in the White House today.

It was bad enough that she'd been roped into participating in the "Day in the Life" special. She'd persuaded every president she'd ever worked for to do the same thing that Charlotte was attempting. She'd made the case that by allowing a single network to film every detail of life inside the White House over a twenty-four-hour period, viewers would gain a better understanding of the numerous problems the president had to deal with. The "Day in the Life" was a good idea as part of a larger White House effort to refocus the press on Charlotte's agenda, but Melanie had no interest in being part of the West Wing's public relations apparatus anymore. For nearly six years, Charlotte's image had been her central concern. Enhancing and protecting it had been her purpose in life. But as the country's secretary of defense, she felt a far greater obligation to the men and women who served in far-flung places and to their families who raised children, ran households, and nursed their wounded and traumatized soldiers. Melanie made a point to visit Iraq and Afghanistan as often as she could, and it had served her well in her eighteen-month tenure. The appointment capped a decade-and-a-half career in government that spanned three presidents. Melanie had served as Charlotte's first chief of staff and her closest advisor for the entire four years of her first term as president, but on the eve of Charlotte's reelection, she had resigned. Charlotte had enticed her to return to the administration by offering her the Cabinet post commonly referred to as the SECDEF. In her new post, Melanie had earned praise from both sides of the partisan divide for her management acumen and for her understanding of the impact that the never-ending deployments were having on soldiers and their families. At thirty-nine when she was sworn in, she was the youngest secretary of defense in history, but in an era when soldiers took to Twitter, Facebook, and YouTube to communicate with family, friends, and reporters, Melanie's youth wasn't held against her as it might have been a generation earlier.

Now, while Melanie waited for Brian to return to the line, she scanned her page of notes about the increase in benefits for the families of former combat troops that she'd lobbied for on Capitol Hill and tried to calculate what time it would be when she landed in Washington.

"Mel, are you still there?" Brian asked.

"Who was that?"

"The executive producer wanted to go over my piece for the morning."

"They're leading with the speech?"

"Yes, but it was touch-and-go for a while between the speech and Taylor Swift's surprise album drop."

"Did you see Warren tonight?"

Warren was Brian's best friend. They had met four years earlier, when Brian was covering the war in Afghanistan and Warren was the public face of the military's effort to train the Afghans to handle their own security. Even though they were predisposed to view each other with a healthy degree of skepticism, the two had formed an instant bond. Warren had become one of Brian's most helpful military sources, and Brian had become a trusted peer and resource when Warren planned his move to Washington after he left the military.

"Dale agreed to meet him for a drink, so he canceled on me, which is just as well. I had a ton of work to do tonight."

"I can't believe those two are together. Is she treating him well?"

"He seems exceedingly happy."

"We know what that means."

"At least they're compatible in that department."

"It's amazing that Dale manages to stay in Charlotte's good graces while sleeping with every man in her orbit."

Warren also happened to be Charlotte's most senior political counselor, the person she'd turned to the year before when her political "brand" needed rehabilitating. His duties were varied, but he was the person responsible for giving her straight talk when no one else in her inner circle was willing to do so. Melanie had never served as a political advisor, but she'd had the role of delivering unwelcome news to the president, and she knew that Warren was the rare person who wasn't afraid to give Charlotte the unvarnished truth.

Of course, Melanie was suspicious of Dale's motives in seeking out Warren as her first serious relationship after her explosive and disastrous public affair with the president's husband during Charlotte's first term, but Brian insisted that Warren and Dale were good for each other.

"Honey, I don't think Dale is exactly the president's closest confidante."

"She's the goddamned White House press secretary."

"And she knows just enough to keep us idiots in the press corps coming back for more each day, but no one thinks that she's on Charlotte's short list for weekends at Camp David or cocktails on the Truman balcony."

"Whatever. I don't care anymore. Charlotte can get advice from whomever she wants."

"Mel, Dale has not replaced you. Neither has Craig. In fact, Warren said that she always asks him how you're doing."

"I doubt that. Warren is just trying to make me feel good."

"He wouldn't do that."

They both knew that he would.

"You should go to bed, honey," Melanie said.

"Take care of that baby of mine. Drink lots of water, and don't forget to eat," Brian urged.

"I am guzzling water by the gallon and peeing every ten minutes."

"I'll talk to you in the morning, my time. Stay safe."

"You stay safe, too," Melanie said.

"You're the one in a war zone."

"You never know."

Melanie hung up and studied the seating chart for the town hall later in the day. She was almost twenty weeks pregnant. She and Brian hadn't shared the news with anyone. Melanie was excellent at keeping secrets, and this one felt as though it was worth keeping as long as her body would permit. She looked down at her stomach and was pretty sure that it had grown since the day before. The loosest tops in her wardrobe now failed to cover up her rapidly expanding midsection and chest. No one in town would suspect that Melanie had gone for a boob job. For at least a few more weeks, they'd simply conclude that she'd gained weight with all of the travel required for her job. Melanie smiled and turned back to her work.

She liked to do all of her meetings without using notes, but with the delay from the D.C. satellite hookup, the town hall would go smoother if everyone spoke from a couple of notecards. She thought about calling the White House chief of staff to go over the logistics, but since she suspected him of playing a key role in trying to sabotage her with the president the year before, she decided not to. She jotted a few notes for herself and read her briefing materials about the soldiers who would be in her morning meeting. Melanie was always struck by how young they were. She had pictures to accompany the short biographies, and after reading the briefing materials a couple of times, she covered the text and quizzed herself until she had the soldiers' names and the basic facts of their military résumés and personal lives memorized. She felt that knowing their stories was the least she could do.

She glanced at her BlackBerry and saw an e-mail from Dale confirming her participation in the town hall and asking if she wanted to talk about any aspect of the line-by-line before the event. A line-by-line was basically a script that was crafted by the government official responsible for briefing the president and other participants for an event. It didn't preclude spontaneous conversation, but it was designed to ensure that everyone was able to make a different point so that the conversation covered all of the desired topics. Dale had also arranged for a crew to be inside the town hall meeting in Iraq to provide footage from both sides of the conversation for the "Day in the Life" special. Dale was thorough. While Melanie was surprised that Charlotte had tapped her because of their complicated personal history, the selection showed that the president was still shrewd enough to place a candidate's qualifications ahead of her own preferences. If nothing else, the selection of Dale as her official mouthpiece projected bigness, which had always been Charlotte's strong suit as a politician. Melanie had served two of Charlotte's predecessors from the podium as White House press secretary. She still thought it was the most important White House post, other than chief of staff.

She picked up her BlackBerry and typed back: "All set," to Dale. No one could accuse Melanie of not being a team player. She couldn't think of anyone else in Charlotte's Cabinet who would have tolerated the beating that her reputation had taken the year before when someone deep inside the West Wing had run a whisper campaign blaming Melanie for leaks about the mental condition of Charlotte's then vice president, Tara Meyers. Charlotte had placed Meyers on the ticket as her running mate during her reelection campaign a year and a half earlier to shake up the race. She transformed the political landscape by plucking a Democrat out of relative obscurity and running on the first-ever unity ticket, where a president is a member of one political party and the vice president is from the other. While the bipartisan experiment was celebrated as the first truly postpartisan move by a modern president, Charlotte's political advisors had hastily selected an unvetted and untested politician in Tara Meyers. Tara had suffered a mental breakdown soon after she was sworn in and had resigned in disgrace less than a year later.

From the moment Melanie had first met Tara, she had warned the president about her lack of experience and deficient knowledge base. As the vice president's gaffes went from being seen as minor embarrassments for the White House to a serious indictment of the president's judgment, Melanie had grown increasingly concerned.

But she had not been the source of any leaked information. She'd never spoken to anyone other than the president about Tara. Melanie had considered resigning when the rumors about her alleged disloyalty started showing up in the papers. Brian had persuaded her to stay in the job she loved, and the Pentagon was a world away from the gravitational pull at the West Wing. Charlotte had eventually made several public statements of support for Melanie and even urged her to stay on for the duration of her second term in an interview. Charlotte's backing had quieted the sniping, but the real leaker had never been outed.

Now Melanie pulled out her briefing materials one last time. These trips were always built around meetings with the foreign leaders, but Melanie came for the visits with the troops. They were the reason she was still in government at all. She'd promised Brian that she wouldn't travel around Iraq now that she was pregnant, but she planned to spend as much time with the troops inside the green zone as she could. When she was satisfied that she had committed all of their names and faces to memory, she stood and walked into her first meeting.

CHAPTER FIVE

Dale

Put down that BlackBerry and eat something, or I'm going to make a scene that you'll have to read about in *Politico* tomorrow," Warren warned.

Dale flashed him a horrified glare and then finished typing her e-mail as quickly as her fingers would press the keys. She hit send and then shoved the device into her purse. "There. I'm done."

Warren took the purse out of her lap and put it on the ground next to him.

"Take it easy with that bag. It cost more than my monthly mortgage payment." He moved it from the floor to the empty chair next to him. Dale heard her phone ringing.

"Whoever it is can wait a few minutes. I'm going to leave it on this chair for fifteen minutes so you can eat something and tell me about your day, and then I will give it back to you."

"Five minutes," she countered.

"Ten."

Dale acquiesced and took a long sip of her wine. When she looked back at Warren, he was smiling at her and holding up his wineglass. "What?" she asked.

"A toast to your big deal of a day tomorrow. Everyone is already talking about how the press office is the newest power center in the West Wing."

She got a tremendous amount of satisfaction from what he was saying, but she wasn't sure if it was true. The one thing she did know was that she should not have agreed to have a late dinner with Warren on the eve of a make-or-break day for herself and the president. She was staring longingly at her purse, with all of her electronic devices inside, when she realized that Warren's phone, which was on the table between them, had rung several times.

"That's the third call you've had in the last two minutes. Aren't you going to answer it?" Dale asked.

"They will call back."

"What if it's urgent?"

"It can wait."

"For the love of God, please answer your phone."

Warren laughed and answered it. He rolled his eyes immediately. "She's right here," he said, handing Dale the phone.

"For me?"

"Your work husband."

Dale grabbed the phone from Warren and covered her mouth with her hand to speak to the White House chief of staff.

He was calling to pass along Charlotte's request that the camera crews not be allowed to loiter in her reception area in the afternoon, because the Israeli ambassador was stopping by for a social visit and Charlotte didn't want more to be made of it.

"That's fine. I'll let them put an extra crew in my office while I prep for the daily briefing," Dale said to Craig. "I'm not on a date. We're just grabbing a glass of wine. Come meet us," she urged. Warren shook his head in protest. "OK, OK, I will see you bright and early in the morning," Dale said. She hung up and handed Warren his phone.

"You're lucky that I don't mind sharing you with him," he said.

Dale smiled her best "Don't hate me because I work all the time" smile and tried to pay complete attention to what Warren was saying. He'd commissioned a new poll that had Charlotte's approval ratings at an all-time high. The only downside was that her vice president's approval rating was ten points higher. Dale was about to ask a question about the history of vice-presidential approval ratings when waiters placed half a dozen bowls of Spanish tapas on the table in front of her.

"I thought we were just going to have a drink," she said.

"I didn't order the food. I guess they thought we looked hungry."

Dale nibbled at a piece of cheese and looked around at the boisterous young crowd crammed into the dining room at Jaleo in Penn Quarter.

"Are you still up for dinner with my parents tomorrow?" Warren asked.

"Sure."

"Really?"

"Honest answer?"

"Always."

"I'm terrified."

"Why?"

"Because when they look at you, they see their only son as one of the most respected people in all of Washington, D.C. The president of the United States has you on speed dial. And then they'll look over at me and see one of those career-obsessed New York women who freeze their eggs and spend too much money on shoes."

Warren smiled at her adoringly and rubbed one of her shoulders. "They are going to love you. And I promise you that my mother doesn't even know they sell shoes that cost six hundred dollars."

"She's going to hate me."

"I'm worried that you're going to be too tired for dinner after chasing the CBS crews around all day."

"I'll be fine tomorrow. But I'm feeling stressed about being out tonight. I should be in bed."

Warren stood up right away. "I'll go thank them for sending over the food and tell them we'll come back this weekend."

"We just got here."

"It was a bad idea."

"Are you sure you don't mind?"

"Of course not. Let's get you home."

Dale watched the other women in the restaurant stare at Warren as he walked to the bar. He was way too good-looking for Washington,

D.C. He was oblivious, but people noticed him wherever he went. If he were four inches shorter, he'd be mistaken for an actor, and if he were two inches taller, he'd be mistaken for an NFL quarterback. At five-foot-ten, he was simply the most attractive political consultant in town. He possessed a politician's magnetism and a rare ability to remember everyone's name and exactly what he'd discussed with them the last time he'd seen them. There were few people Dale had ever met in her life who were as good-natured and outgoing as Warren. Dale felt positively brooding and antisocial by comparison. She couldn't recall a single instance in which she'd ever seen him down or unhappy in the six months that they'd been dating. The only thing wrong with him was that he liked her too much.

She was relieved when Warren turned back toward their table. She let him pull her through the crowd and out to where his car was waiting.

"I'm sorry about that."

"I didn't realize how nervous I am."

"Tomorrow is going to be perfect."

He closed her door and then walked around to his side. She glanced at him as he buckled his seat belt.

"What?"

"Nothing." She smiled.

"What's that look?"

"It's not a look. I'm trying to figure out if you have any idea how hot-to-trot all those little Hill staffers are for you and if you drag me to places like this because you secretly enjoy showing them you're taken."

Warren laughed a big belly laugh.

"What's so funny?" Dale asked.

"I dragged you there because I get a good table and free snacks. But that's not nearly as funny as you are."

"What exactly did I say that you find so funny?"

"I didn't know you considered me taken."

She looked out the window so he wouldn't see her smile. His exuberance for her was disquieting, and his willingness to declare his affection for her in public was such a dramatic change from her illicit relationship with Peter that she still found herself pulling her hand away from his when he reached for it and turning her face from him when he went to kiss her in public. He either didn't notice or wasn't insulted, because he never pouted or acted like she'd committed a relationship foul. And while he was the sunniest person she'd ever slept with, he wasn't sweet in a sappy or codependent way. He was, by a mile, the most normal, eligible, emotionally available man Dale had ever dated.

Warren was a very sought-after and skilled consultant, but it hadn't been his plan to have the president's ear. He'd started advising politicians on the wars in Iraq and Afghanistan after returning from four combat tours in Iraq. Warren had been a student at Harvard Business School on September 11. When life there returned to normal before the Twin Towers had even stopped smoldering, he'd decided that he didn't belong at Harvard anymore. He enlisted in the Army and attended Ranger school and also learned how to fly helicopters, which he did quite skillfully. Warren returned from Iraq determined to squeeze every dime he could out of Congress to help his fellow soldiers struggling with posttraumatic stress disorder, traumatic brain injuries, and depression. His political skills turned out to be even better than his piloting skills. The Republican campaign committees urged him to run for Congress, but the idea did not appeal to him. He would only be one vote. He could make a bigger difference by changing the minds—and votes—of the hundreds of politicians who already held office.

After the six candidates he advised in the midterm elections all won their races, his services were in demand. Charlotte called soon after the midterms and asked him to advise her reelection campaign. He was credited with masterminding her surprise comeback during her reelection bid, and he'd been her most trusted outside advisor ever since.

Dale had met him at an East Room event at the White House. He'd brought a candidate for the Wisconsin governor's race to an education speech about the power of charter schools. Dale had asked him to move his chair to get out of the camera shot, and he'd feigned offense. She'd been so mortified about insulting one of the guests that she'd offered him a personal White House tour. After mumbling her way through the China Room and the Map Room, she confessed to Warren that she didn't know anything about the history of the East Wing rooms. Warren then confessed to her that he was a consultant who'd worked as an outside advisor to the president for two years and had spent the night in the residence as a guest of the first family. She was so embarrassed that she didn't know who he was and relieved that she hadn't offended an official "guest" that she'd agreed to have a drink with him that night. Dale found him entertaining enough to stay for dinner, and they'd gone home together. Their relationship had consisted almost purely of late-night dates at the bars within walking distance of the White House and sleepovers at her place so that she could get up at four A.M. to get ready for work. They had had their coming out as a Washington power couple when they'd attended the White House Correspondents Dinner in April. It was a designation that may have once meant that two people with power and influence had ended up together. Now it simply meant that two people with occasion to be on television regularly were an item.

Dale enjoyed having someone to take to the countless black-tie events on her schedule, and she loved that he came home with her every night, but she wasn't sure that she could picture herself on the marriage-and-kids track that Warren obviously craved. Dale cared about Warren more than she'd ever cared about anyone, other than Peter, but she never again wanted to experience the heartbreak she'd experienced when her relationship with Peter had come to an abrupt end. Without directly rebuffing Warren's frequent references to a future together, she was careful to keep the focus on how much she was enjoying his company in the moment. Dale was afraid that she'd live to regret agreeing to have dinner with his parents, but they were in town for one night, and he'd begged her to join them.

They pulled up outside the Ritz on 23rd Street, where Dale had purchased a two-bedroom condo when she was named press secretary.

"Do you want to come up?" she asked. She knew he did, but she appreciated that he still waited to be invited.

"Are you sure you're in the mood for company?"

She leaned over and kissed him in a way that left no doubt.

As they rode up on the elevator together, Dale wondered if she could ever get used to being adored by someone who was smart and attractive and who never made her feel emotionally inadequate. It wasn't like he didn't know about her sordid past. In fact, Dale couldn't be sure that Warren hadn't been involved in Charlotte's decision to go public with the revelation that her husband was having an affair with her two years earlier. While Dale knew that Charlotte hadn't considered the circumstance of her husband's affair ideal by any measure, it was undeniable that she'd enhanced her reputation by standing before the public and accepting part of the blame for the decline of her marriage. It was the first of many displays of generosity toward Dale on the president's part.

Immediately following her reelection, Charlotte had allowed Dale to serve on the White House staff as a senior advisor to her then vice president, Tara Meyers. Dale suspected that Charlotte shared her own knack for extreme compartmentalization, but whatever the reason, Charlotte had enabled Dale to have a second act as a White House advisor at a time when she would have had a hard time finding a position as a newswoman. Dale had loved covering the White House, but once her affair with the president's husband was made public, her credibility as a journalist was shattered. Dale was astounded by how quickly she had adapted to life inside the presidential bubble. It was as though she'd never stood on the other side of the reporter-versus-government-official divide. After a tumultuous year as the vice president's counselor, during which Dale and Charlotte had occasion to collaborate on a variety of sensitive topics, Charlotte tapped her to serve as the White House press secretary.

It had further cemented the end of that chapter in Dale's life when the president and Peter had publicly reconciled. To survive the spectacle of the first couple's renewed affection for each other, Dale threw herself into her new job. Serving as the White House press secretary had renewed her in surprising ways, and Warren's attention had also eased the pain of her very public breakup with one of the most well-known married men in the world.

Now it felt to Dale as though her life had changed dramatically in a very short period of time. She'd gone from a network correspondent who covered the White House and was engaged in a clandestine love affair with the president's estranged husband to the White House press secretary in the span of a few short years. In Washington, time moved in dog years. Seven years of chaos and drama could be crammed into one. As far as Washington's ruling class was concerned, Dale's affair with Peter was ancient history. If Charlotte could forgive her and promote her to press secretary, then surely they could welcome her to their cocktail parties and Georgetown dinners.

"Do you want a glass of wine?" Warren asked.

"Sure. I'm going to change. Bring it into the bedroom when you come in."

Dale sat on the edge of the bed and scrolled through her e-mail messages. Everything was on track for the next day. She sent a message to her deputy, who would be at the White House when the senior staff started arriving with their embedded CBS crews in the early-morning hours. Dale would be driving in with a crew herself.

She still couldn't believe that Charlotte had agreed to participate in the "Day in the Life" and that she'd done so with minimal prodding. The network had assigned camera crews to all of the senior staff and the president and vice president. The idea was for the crews to follow each of them through an "ordinary" day in the West Wing. Crews would also be stationed in the president's private kitchen, in the White House Mess where the senior staff ate most of their meals, and at all of the executive assistants' desks to get a sense of the volume of incoming calls, visitors, and problems that the White House staff managed on a daily basis. Dale had even persuaded the Secret Service to participate in the filming. A film crew would be stationed at the Northwest Gate, where the majority of visitors to the White House entered. An additional crew would be embedded at its command post.

The final production would air on *60 Minutes* on two consecutive Sundays and would be teased each morning on the network's morning show and each night on the evening news, guaranteeing maximum exposure. It was part of a broader publicity plan designed to pull back the curtain on the president's second term. It was also designed to showcase the chemistry between the president and vice president, Maureen McCoughlin. Maureen was the former Democratic speaker of the House, and she deserved much of the credit for helping Charlotte regain her political footing so quickly after her predecessor crashed and burned.

Dale believed that part of the reason Charlotte had backed her for the top press job was for her understanding of the need for unprecedented access and transparency in the wake of Tara's brief stint as vice president. Dale had also developed a keen sense of the president's voice on matters large and small. And the president had noticed. She deferred to Dale completely on matters involving White House press strategy. It had further strengthened Dale's hand that Craig, her closest friend in Washington, had ascended to the White House chief of staff position. The post was the single most powerful appointment in all of Washington, aside from the president herself.

Dale plugged her BlackBerry, iPhone, and iPad into chargers next to her nightstand while she contemplated half an Ambien.

"Are you still working?" Warren asked.

"I probably should be."

Warren put the two wineglasses on the nightstand and sat down on the bed. "What's wrong?"

"What if the president hates Lucy and Richard?"

"Who cares if she hates them? She's a big girl, and she understands why you picked them. Relax. It's going to be great."

"You're just saying that to make me feel better."

"Maybe. But it happens to be the truth."

He smiled his irresistible smile, and Dale relaxed. When he leaned over to kiss her, she let him. His enthusiasm for her was limitless. While the world saw him as a perfectly well-adjusted and emotionally and physically unscathed veteran of the war in Iraq, Dale understood that there was no such thing. According to Warren, they all came back altered. His escape was sex, and for the time being, Dale was content to be his therapy. The bedroom was the one place where she felt she could give him everything he needed from her. She stole a sideways glance at her iPhone to check the time and then quickly forgot about alarm clocks, line-by-lines, on-the-record versus off-the-record interviews, briefing books, staff meetings, speech excerpts, protests, and reporters' complaints.

CHAPTER SIX

Charlotte

This is the shot you should have let them get for your CBS taping," Peter said.

Charlotte looked up from the speech text that she was marking with a thick black Sharpie. Her three vizslas were strewn across the bed with them. Cammie, the oldest, was lying between Charlotte's legs, with her head on her thigh and one eye open to keep watch over her mistress. The other two were in various states of undignified repose on the bed. Peter was watching a baseball game and editing a contract for one of his clients. He still worked as a sports agent and represented some of the biggest athletes in professional basketball and football. Charlotte thought he was genius in terms of always keeping his business smaller than the demand for his services. Athletes typically came to him and asked him to consider adding them to his small and exclusive list of clients, instead of the other way around.

"How's the speech?"

"It's not as bad as it looks."

"That's a relief. Aren't you delivering it first thing in the morning?"

"Eleven." Charlotte handed Cammie a piece of her grilled cheese sandwich.

"Do you feel good about it?"

"I feel fine about it. Maureen has been incredible, and this was one of her conditions for getting the tax cuts and the defense-spending bills passed with Democratic votes. It's a tiny thing to do for her after all the stability she's brought to this place."

Peter nodded. "You don't have to convince me, honey, but it sounds like you're still convincing yourself."

"Maybe," Charlotte murmured without looking up.

"Look, if you're having doubts, you should call Warren. He always puts you at ease about these things."

"I spoke to him before I left the Oval Office."

"Is he worried?"

"Of course not. Says that women will appreciate someone other than a white man talking about the issue, regardless of their position."

"That sounds like good advice."

"I guess."

"Call him again if you're still anxious."

"He has better things to do than talk me off the ledge."

"I doubt that."

Charlotte reached for the phone and asked the White House operator to try Warren's cell. When he didn't pick up, she hung up and refused the operator's offer to keep trying.

"I'm sure he'll call you back," Peter assured her.

Charlotte nodded and lifted the speech closer to her face.

"Did Brooke and Mark schedule their visit for this week in hopes of landing cameos in your 'Day in the Life'?" Peter asked.

At this, Charlotte laughed. She'd sent Brooke and Mark off to the Kennedy Center to see a Sondheim play so they wouldn't bother her. "I wouldn't be surprised if they did."

"Thank you for sparing me from participating in your big production."

"You have Dale to thank for that. I didn't even see a request for any filming of us together."

Peter raised an eyebrow and smiled at his wife of twenty years. "That was nice of her."

"I suppose."

"What else does a day in the life of the most powerful woman in the world entail?"

"You mean my made-for-television day?"

"Yes, your perfectly presidential made-for-television day."

"There's this speech, which I'll deliver at the Women's Museum."

"That's what the protest is about out front?"

"Yes." Charlotte sighed. "Warren warned me that it will cost me any remnant of support I had with the base, but I can't expect Maureen to go along with my agenda without doing these sorts of things."

"Look on the bright side, Char. You might even turn your daughter into a supporter. You know, she wanted to march on the mall with NARAL last year on the anniversary of *Roe*. I convinced her that she'd hurt her cause by overshadowing the march with coverage of her participation."

"You never told me that."

"It was the middle of the Tara fiasco, and you had your hands full."

"I still want to feel like a part of this family."

Peter nodded and looked down at his papers.

Over the years, Charlotte had ceded much of the parenting to Peter. She hadn't had a choice. Her career path hadn't left her much flexibility, but that didn't make it any easier when she thought about everything she'd missed. There would never be another chance to be there for soccer games and field hockey matches, the colds and flus, the breakups and dates, or the family dinners and family vacations that she'd either skipped or ruined by being on the phone the entire time. She didn't care what anyone said. Working and being a good mother were mutually exclusive in certain lines of work. Being president was one of them.

Peter had taken it upon himself to be twice the father most men were, and the kids rewarded him with affection and loyalty. She knew the twins had always felt loved, but that didn't make it any less painful when she felt the distance between herself and their children, especially Penelope.

"Honey, please call Penny and tell her not to post anything outrageous on her Facebook page tomorrow."

"She wouldn't do that," he promised.

"Have you seen her Facebook page lately?"

"Not lately, but I happen to know that you aren't one of her Facebook friends, so how would you know what was on it?"

"I get a printout once a week. Are *you* one of her Facebook friends?"

"Of course. She'd be thrilled to know that you're spying on her. Maybe that's part of the problem."

Charlotte wanted to protest that there wasn't a problem with her relationship with her daughter, but she knew he was right. She decided to do what she always did. "If she ends up in the news tomorrow, I'm going to hold you responsible."

Peter was so accustomed to Charlotte's defense mechanisms that he didn't even look up. "I know."

Charlotte sighed loudly. Only Cammie looked at her with concern. "This dog loves me more than my children do," she added.

"The dogs love you a lot," Peter agreed.

"The last point on the Facebook page, Peter, seriously, and I know you agree with this. If she thinks she'll make me squirm, she'll post something provocative tomorrow, just to show me that she isn't under my thumb, and it might be a good strategy for you to gently suggest that she not do that."

Peter finally put down his paperwork and turned to face her. "How about looking at it this way? If she wants to say something about an issue that's very important to her, she may take to Facebook like everyone else her age and write something about your historic speech. Your daughter might act like a socially aware college freshman who cares about issues like abortion rights. That sounds like someone Charlotte Kramer would be proud of. Actually, that sounds like someone I know. Someone I fell in love with more than twenty years ago."

His voice was patient, as always, but his words felt like a reprimand. She scrunched up her face and turned back to her speech, taking out her frustration on the draft in front of her by slashing several pages with large black lines. "You always defend her," she charged.

"Someone has to," he said quietly.

Charlotte decided to let that be the last word on the topic, but she was extremely unsettled by their conversation. She had a strong feeling that she was correct about the likelihood of Penny saying something publicly about the speech, and Peter was correct, too. It was precisely what she would have done.

It was clear where the fault lines had developed in their family when she and Peter had carved out separate lives for themselves years earlier. Going public about his affair with Dale had been the flash point, but Charlotte had always seen it as an inevitable and unavoidable consequence of her long and willful neglect of their marriage during her first run for the White House. Now she was terrified about giving their relationship a second chance, but she also felt hopeful that they were both finally committed to building bridges back to each other. She was more concerned about whether or not she could revive her relationship with Penny.

Since she and Peter had been back together, Penny acted as though she resented Charlotte for diverting Peter's attention away from her. While he was close to both of their kids, he and Penny had a special bond. After Charlotte was first elected president nearly six years earlier, it was Penny who'd asked if they were going to move to D.C. with Charlotte or stay in California with their father. Charlotte and Peter had never even discussed separating the family, but Penny apparently thought that it should be on the table that the kids could stay in school with their friends and their dad would take care of them while their mom went off to D.C. When Charlotte had affirmed that the family would be relocating to Washington, it was Penny who'd argued that it wasn't fair to make Peter move. He'd ultimately convinced the twins that moving to Washington would be a great adventure. But he returned Penny's protectiveness and was not the least bit intimidated by her stubborn streak. He'd had plenty of training in dealing with strong-willed women.

Charlotte, on the other hand, was constantly thrown off by how fiercely independent her daughter had grown after just one year at college. Charlotte saw in Penny the same seriousness that she'd possessed as an eighteen-year-old and fretted that her daughter was growing up too fast. She also suspected that her displays of toughness were a defense mechanism designed to project more maturity than she felt. But Charlotte was running out of time to correct the mistakes that she secretly feared she was making each time she acquiesced to

Penny's requests for more space and independence. She was beginning to think she should be hopping on a plane and planting herself in Penny's dorm until she talked to her about whatever it was that she was so angry about.

Harry, on the other hand, never played games with Charlotte. He was open and affectionate when Charlotte came to visit, and while he seemed to have formed a closer family unit with his new fraternity brothers at college than with his own family, Charlotte was grateful that he had created such a tight-knit support group during his first year. But between Penny's increasingly sarcastic e-mails and comments in their recent calls and Harry's laid-back approach to everything, Charlotte worried all the time that she'd messed up her kids by abandoning them during the years when she actually could have made a difference. Now they were college students and would never live at home again, and she was terrified that she'd screwed them up by never being around.

Charlotte felt a familiar tightening in her stomach and gently pushed Cammie off her legs and stood up to take the dogs out for a final walk.

"I'll come with you," Peter offered.

"Nah, watch your game. I'll be right back. I need the air."

Cammie walked to the elevator and stood outside it, but the two younger dogs had charged down the stairs. Charlotte had to lure Cammie down the stairs with the rest of her sandwich. Charlotte bent down and kissed the dog's soft white nose.

"You're the only one who understands," she whispered.

Cammie licked Charlotte's face and reluctantly followed her down the stairs and out to the South Lawn. Charlotte breathed in the warm air and tipped her head back to look at the sky. Her surroundings were perfectly soothing, but she was on edge. She'd been questioning herself at every turn lately. Charlotte missed her fearless, self-assured self. She also missed having a chief of staff like Melanie, who anticipated her every move and knew when to step in and when to back off. Charlotte threw a couple of balls for the dogs and watched a car approach the security gate. The large metal bolts that protected the street in front of the White House from car traffic disappeared into the ground, and the SUV rolled through the checkpoint.

As it neared the South Lawn, Charlotte noticed that her friend Mark was hanging out the back window, waving enthusiastically in her direction.

"I always forget how dead this town is at night. Do you know where I can get a drink around here?" He stepped out of the Navigator and rushed to give Charlotte a warm embrace.

Around her, Brooke and Mark acted largely unchanged from their days as the social ringleaders in college, but she had figured out a long time ago that their over-the-top antics were designed to distract and entertain Charlotte. In their real lives, they were pillars of their wealthy community. Mark was a venture capitalist who'd funded a handful of Stanford college students with brilliant technological innovations. He'd turned a couple of them into billionaires. Brooke was the most sought-after interior designer in Northern California. Their son, Griffin, was a senior at UCLA, and their daughter, Finley, was a junior at Berkeley. They were the kind of parents that Charlotte liked to think she would have been if she hadn't chosen a career—a life—in politics. Their children actually talked to them. Finley and Griffin had always been like older siblings to the twins. Charlotte hoped that they'd continue to grow closer now that they were all in California. Neither she nor Peter had much extended family the twins had bonded with over the years, so Brooke and Mark served as the closest thing to an aunt and uncle.

"How was the show?" Charlotte asked.

"Boring as hell," he said. "But the seats were awesome."

"It was fabulous," Brooke said, as she teetered in her four-inch Christian Louboutin stilettos on the uneven pavement. She was wearing a leather dress that would have looked ridiculous on anyone else, but with Brooke's Pilates-sculpted body, she managed to pull it off.

"Charlotte, I'm sorry that my wife looks like a hooker. The good news is that I get to go to bed with her, but the bad news is that we sat with your secretary of labor or education or something like that, and I'm sure he thought we were that couple who crashed your state dinner a few years back. I'm surprised that you didn't get a call during intermission."

"Excuse me. This is a four-thousand-dollar Prada dress that I've been waiting for the right occasion to wear. Unfortunately, the right occasion hasn't presented itself in more than a year, so I decided to wear it tonight." Brooke giggled.

"Did I mention that she's drunk?" Mark added.

Charlotte laughed again and let Brooke take her hand. Brooke and Mark were the only people in her life who refused to see her as anyone different from who she'd been when they were all college students at Berkeley. They had been by her side through every personal and professional milestone, and at this point, they enjoyed the fruits of her political success far more than she did. As far as Charlotte was concerned, the very best part of being president these days was being in the company of the few friends she had who got a kick out of the trappings of the presidency. It wasn't as if the kids were around to enjoy riding on Air Force One or spending weekends at Camp David. But Brooke and Mark were thrilled by all of it—weekends at Camp David, state dinners, the White House Correspondents Dinner, the Gridiron Dinner. Nothing made Charlotte happier than watching her friends enjoy themselves at these events that, to her, were only one step above torture.

"Char-Char, thank you for the tickets. We sat with your secretary of education—not the secretary of labor, as my idiotic husband just said. There's a possibility that he will resign after meeting us."

"Is Peter still awake?" Mark asked.

"I think he may have nodded off during the baseball game," Charlotte said.

"Good. We can have girl talk," Brooke said.

"What about me?"

"You can serve us drinks and pretend that you're invisible," Brooke snapped playfully.

Mark feigned offense and led the dogs inside.

"Speaking of girl talk, how's it going with Peter?" Brooke wanted to know.

"Mostly fine," Charlotte said, as they settled into a sofa in the yellow Oval Office on the second floor at the residence.

Brooke leaned in and started whispering in a voice that was louder than Charlotte's speaking voice. "Are you guys getting along? Are you having fun? Are you having sex?"

"Everything is fine."

"You seem tense."

"I have to give a speech tomorrow that's going to create a big political storm, and I'm dreading it."

"I know—the abortion speech. I think it's great, Char, but I've seen you deal with bigger shit storms than that, and you're never like this."

"Well, it's not just an abortion speech. It's broader than that, really. It's going to get at the very nature of what a unity government can do around some of the most polarizing social issues. I'm going to frame the debate about reproductive freedom in terms that I hope will be less divisive."

"Blah, blah, blah. Sounds good to me. You'll come out for the pro-choice side, won't you? I mean, that's why it's such a big deal, right?"

"Yes, it will be clear which side of the divide I come down on, but I'm not pushing any prochoice policies other than reinstating some of the funding for mammograms and Pap smears and things like that, that are done at women's health clinics like Planned Parenthood."

"Can we go back to Peter for a second, Char?"

"Yes, sorry. What was I saying?"

"That things are fine."

"They are."

"But?"

"Nothing. Things are good."

"Is he staying in line?"

"What do you mean?"

"You know."

"I'm not going to spy on him, for Christ's sake."

"Don't make it sound like such a preposterous suggestion. You spy on everyone else," Brooke retorted.

Charlotte ignored the insult and crossed her legs underneath her. Brooke wasn't going to settle for her one-line answers. "Things didn't fall apart overnight, and they aren't going to get put back together overnight—if ever. But I feel like we're both taking baby steps back toward something that feels better than it has in a very long time."

"And Dale?"

"What about Dale?"

"For one, you made her one of the most powerful people in your White House by appointing her press secretary. That is either insane or brilliant, and I'm still deciding which," Brooke remarked.

When Charlotte didn't bite, Brooke continued.

"And if it were me, I'd be dying to know if they're still in contact."

"I have no idea, but I don't care either way. Peter and I are fine, and Dale is dating a wonderful guy who happens to be my pollster. His name is Warren Carmichael."

"The Iraq and Afghan war veteran? I saw him on *Morning Joe* the other day."

"That's him."

Brooke made a face that displayed her dissatisfaction at Charlotte's answers and reached out for the cocktail Mark was handing her. He'd poured three juice-glass-sized drinks. Charlotte took one sip and choked.

"What is this?"

"It's an old-fashioned."

"Without the sugar?"

"Brooke and I are cleansing."

"You're cleansing?"

"Juice cleansing. Don't you cleanse?"

"I do not. Why on earth are you guys cleansing? You both look amazing."

"It's the juice, it's a miracle!" Brooke exclaimed. "By day three or four, you're so hungry you could eat the children, but your skin glows and your skinny clothes fit perfectly again. I am going to sign you up for a weeklong cleanse. The juices show up at your doorstep every morning."

Charlotte wondered if she'd be buying five-day juice cleanses that showed up on her doorstep if she still lived in San Francisco. "They'd come right to my front door?" Charlotte teased.

"Yeah, unless the juice delivery guy gets shot first," Mark joked.

Charlotte stayed up with her friends for another forty-five minutes, catching up on gossip and talking about their kids. When she returned to her room, Peter was sound asleep.

What she'd failed to tell Brooke was that she was worried about

Peter feeling lonely and isolated. It wasn't like he could walk out of the White House complex and head to Starbucks to read the paper, or play pickup basketball games at the gym, or head outside for a run like he did in San Francisco. Those sorts of outings had to be prearranged with the Secret Service. Peter despised the motorcades and the security and the cameras, so he usually stayed home when he was in D.C. and stretched out his visits to the kids and clients on the West Coast. Living in the White House had to feel like a prison. Charlotte resolved to suggest that they take more trips together to California the next time they were alone. She set her alarm for five A.M. and crawled into bed beside him.

CHAPTER SEVEN

Melanie

M elanie finished her morning meetings feeling both inspired
and depressed. On the one hand, she was heartened by the
high morale of the troops she'd met. No matter what was said by
Democrats, Republicans, and the entire spectrum of media pundits
about America's ongoing security role in Iraq, the troops remained
loyal to one another and committed to the mission. Being in their
midst always clarified things for Melanie and reminded her what she
was fighting for day in and day out in the offices of well-meaning
but clueless senators and congressmen. On the other hand, she was
discouraged by what she knew would translate as minuscule progress
on the ground. The public had long since moved on, but thousands of
troops remained in Iraq and Afghanistan. To Melanie, that amounted
to thousands of sons, daughters, fathers, mothers, brothers, and sisters. Additionally, most of the men and women stationed in both
countries had already endured multiple deployments away from their
families. At this point, they returned home to little fanfare. Nothing
frustrated Melanie more than her inability to refocus the country's
attention on their ongoing sacrifice. With prominent voices on the
right and the left clamoring for every last American to get the hell
out of the region, it was difficult to make the case that the effort was
worthwhile. She'd invited some of the local leaders from her meetings

that morning to Washington to brief the members of the House and Senate Armed Services and Foreign Relations Committees. As she was trading personal e-mail addresses with one of the women serving in Parliament, her assistant gave her the signal to wrap things up. She used to ignore cues from aides, but sometimes they were a warning about a sudden change in the security situation on the ground. She ended her conversation and moved toward the door.

"What's up?"

"Brian's on the phone."

"It's three in the morning in D.C."

"That's why I interrupted you."

Melanie rushed to the holding room.

"Honey, is everything OK?"

"Everything is fine. I'm sorry I worried you. I told them to tell you that it wasn't urgent."

"Oh, my God. My heart is beating out of my chest. What are you doing up?"

"I couldn't sleep. I was worried about you and the baby."

"We're fine. I promise."

"When you get back, I think we need to make a plan for you to slow down. I don't think all of the travel is good for the baby, and I know it isn't good for you."

"We'll do that. Don't worry. I'm not straining myself. I slept eight hours, and when I'm not puking, I'm stuffing my face."

"I worry all the time that something is going to happen."

"Me, too, but this little baby is going to be fine."

"I know."

"Get some sleep."

She hung up and touched her stomach. Brian was overly concerned, but Melanie had to give some thought to her travel schedule and the hectic pace she'd always maintained. She had spent her entire adult life working harder and longer than everyone around her. She couldn't imagine doing these jobs any other way. She finally understood why so many women felt forced to choose between their careers and their families. Melanie couldn't comprehend what full-time motherhood entailed. She only had a few friends who were mothers, mostly former White House colleagues who dropped out of politics and talked about being swallowed whole by the production of taking care of a newborn and then by the playdates and toddler classes that followed. It sounded daunting, but after everything they'd been through to get pregnant, she couldn't envision handing her precious little baby over to a stranger.

Melanie also felt the baby might provide a graceful transition out of government. Surely no one would fault her for stepping away from public service after nearly two decades to raise her child? Melanie rubbed her stomach again and realized that she was famished. She pushed herself up from the table and headed back toward the conference room in search of the cheese tray.

CHAPTER EIGHT

Dale

Dale slid her iPhone out from under her pillow and watched the time change from 3:59 to 4:00 A.M. She gave up on sleep and thought about how she would have given anything to magically transport Warren across the river to his own bed so she wouldn't have to get dressed in the dark. After carefully extricating herself from his embrace, she balanced her iPhone and BlackBerry on top of her iPad and tiptoed to the bathroom. Once inside, she scanned the e-mails that had come in during the four hours she'd been unplugged. While she waited for an attachment from one of her deputies to open, she glanced at her reflection. *Marie Claire* magazine had flown in a colorist and a hairstylist to give her a new haircut and highlights for the photo shoot they'd done of her the week before. Her dark brown hair had a great bouncy shape, and a fresh batch of chestnut-colored strands made her skin look less pale. As the face of the administration, she was getting plenty of attention for her appearance, but it wasn't the kind of attention that did her any good at all at the podium. She hoped the "Day in the Life" production would be the catalyst for people seeing her as more than a spokesperson; she wanted to be viewed as an influential presidential advisor.

Dale thought she heard Warren stirring. She stuck her head out the bathroom door to check. He'd rolled onto his back and was snoring. She closed the door and finished her hair and makeup with more care than usual and then padded into her closet to get dressed. She selected a black Jil Sander dress that her personal shopper from New York had sent down the week before. Its exquisitely cut shape, fabric, and construction would be lost on the Ann Taylor enthusiasts on the White House staff, but she felt more like herself when she adhered to her fashion-addicted New York ways.

Lucy would appreciate the dress. Lucy Edinburg and Richard Thompson, CBS's hot new evening anchor team, had been Dale's pick for the "Day in the Life" special.

She had selected Richard and Lucy over the other network anchors she knew better because everything they did these days was generating tons of buzz. They were being hailed as the saviors of network news for figuring out how to make the evening newscast the most-watched twenty-four minutes of television again.

The rise of Lucy and Richard at CBS represented a final nail in the coffin of Old Journalism. Lucy was a former Fox News anchor, and Richard a beloved fixture at ESPN over the previous three decades. Neither one of them had ever reported from a combat zone, covered a presidential campaign, or done a turn as a White House correspondent. They were skilled conversationalists who managed to endear themselves to viewers by sharing just enough of the details of their personal lives to prove that their challenges and headaches were the same ones that everyone else faced. Their guiding philosophy was that viewers wanted the news delivered by people who managed to inform them without talking down to them. When Lucy underwent invasive fertility treatments at the age of forty-two, she did so with a camera crew in the room. Similarly, Richard did a weeklong special on difficult-to-diagnose ailments that focused on his own symptoms of low energy and weight gain. He subjected himself to several different medical exams, and the series culminated in a visit to an endocrinologist who diagnosed him with "low T" on the air. The reality-television aspect of their newscasts was only one part of their successful formula. Despite a twenty-year age difference, they had the kind of chemistry that made you feel you were peering into someone's breakfast room on a Sunday morning to listen to them read the best parts of the newspaper to each other. Whether or not their off-air relationship was as cozy as their on-air presentation suggested was a topic of endless debate, but most people in the news business figured that they were simply maximizing every tool at their disposal to attract viewers.

While at Fox, Lucy had built a loyal audience by railing against the mainstream media and conducting tough interviews with politicians and so-called experts. Like most of the women who appeared on Fox News, Lucy was blond and looked more like a beauty queen from the South than a woman who'd lived in New York City for more than a decade. Since she'd made the move to CBS, she'd traded sleeveless teal and fuchsia mini-dresses that looked like they'd been sewn onto her for sophisticated suits in black, navy, and off-white that were expertly tailored. She'd also cut back on the Botox injections and stopped wearing false eyelashes.

Richard added whatever gravitas the team possessed. He was the one who was most likely to apologize to a policy expert or a foreign leader if Lucy asked a question about twerking. With a thick head of silvery blond hair and a permanent suntan, Richard was one of the most likable people on television Dale had ever seen in her life.

Their path to success started a little more than a year earlier, when they were paired up for a weeklong pilot at the third-place morning show. Management was throwing everything against the wall to see if anything would stick, and Lucy and Richard were instructed to be themselves. What happened was pure TV magic. Lucy was irreverent and feisty, and Richard was funny and relaxed. Together, they interviewed celebrities, senators and congressmen, victims of a tornado, and other journalists. Since they'd never covered any official government beats, they leaned heavily on the network's correspondents at the White House, the State Department, and the Defense Department and, at times, kept them on for an entire newscast. If a celebrity meltdown or weather story was dominating the news, they talked about that and ignored the network correspondents at the White House, State, and DOD. Their approach had plenty of detractors, particularly among the Washington, D.C., circles of elite journalists and pundits, but it attracted viewers from every important demographic. Richard and Lucy quickly turned their show into the hottest thing in television news. After a nine-month streak on the morning show, they'd taken their freewheeling, teleprompter-free gabfest to the evening news hour, and that program had moved from dead last to second place in only a few short months.

Dale had taken a sizable risk by selecting Lucy and Richard for the "Day in the Life" special, but she wanted to do everything in her power to extend Charlotte's second honeymoon with the press, and that included courting the journalists who were getting the most attention.

The vice president had also been a strong advocate for doing the "Day in the Life" with Lucy and Richard. Maureen had a very positive impact on Charlotte when it came to her approach with the media. She was generating a lot of goodwill herself through her "open-door" policy. There were as many reporters in and out of the vice president's office as there were in and out of the press office. Dale privately worried that the vice president's open-door policy would eventually clash with Charlotte's preference for keeping the media at arm's length, but so far, it had only served to enhance reporters' understanding of the close partnership Maureen had forged with Charlotte. As long-time politicians who'd largely sacrificed their mothering years for their careers, both women shared a bond of wistful acceptance of the trade-offs they'd made to arrive at their positions of immense power. They'd also both endured messy chapters in their personal lives that had played out publicly because of their high-profile positions and unfaithful husbands.

Dale liked to think that Craig's ascent to chief of staff and her promotion to press secretary contributed to the positivity that the press felt toward the administration. History suggested that Charlotte was wise to shake things up in her second term; successful second-term presidents almost always demanded staff turnover, and Charlotte was an astute student of the pitfalls of the modern American presidency.

Dale glanced at herself one last time in the mirror, and then, with her BlackBerry screen as her flashlight, she made her way toward the front door, picked up her heavy purse, threw a black cashmere sweater across her shoulders to keep herself warm inside the over-air-conditioned West Wing, and shut the door behind her. As soon as she stepped into her building's lobby, she noticed the van parked in front. The plan was for a CBS crew to drive in with each member of the senior staff. She tucked her hair behind her ears and went out to retrieve the crew.

"Good morning, everyone." Dale wasn't good at forced cheer, especially in the morning. The crew piled into her car and positioned a camera in the front seat. When they turned the camera light on, Dale was temporarily blinded.

"Do you usually stop for coffee?" one of the production assistants asked from the backseat, where he'd settled in amid the dry cleaning she kept forgetting to drop off and two gym bags that she'd packed and had never used.

"Nothing is open before five." She tried to make eye contact with him in her mirror, but he was focusing intently on holding her pile of black suits off his lap as he jotted notes in a spiral notebook. She'd been meaning to stop at the cleaner's for weeks.

"Do you want me to pull over and put that stuff in the trunk?"

"No, I'm fine. Will any of the other senior staff be there when we arrive?"

"Probably not, but I'm supposed to meet with Craig to go over the final line-by-line for the day," she said, glancing in the rearview mirror again to get a better look at her questioner. He looked twenty years old.

"Are you an intern?" she asked.

"No, ma'am."

He'd called her *ma'am*. She sighed and shook her head slightly. It served her right for asking. She stayed quiet for the rest of the drive, except to answer the twenty-year-old's questions. Dale thought about how thankful she was that Craig was her boss. At least they could laugh about this at the end of the day. Dale knew exactly what he'd say. "The things we do for love of country and Charlotte Kramer," he'd joke. She smiled thinking about it as she pulled into the entrance on E Street and flashed her hard pass. The guard greeted her with a nod and waved her onto the pad where the canine unit would examine her car for explosives. When the dogs were satisfied, the large steel gate would disappear into the ground, and Dale would be free to drive slowly toward the next gate. She cherished the lengthy process and treated it as her last moment of peace before the workday commenced.

"Ma'am? Excuse me?"

"Yes?"

"Who is allowed to park in there?" The producer was pointing at West Executive Drive, the strip of coveted parking spots between the West Wing and the Old Executive Office Building that separated the most senior advisors from the rest of the presidential staffers. Dale had pulled up to the third and final entrance and was waiting for the large wrought-iron gates to swing open.

"Only assistants to the president may park in here," she replied. His face didn't register any comprehension, so she explained the White House hierarchy that allowed her one of the best parking spots on the White House complex.

"Assistants to the president are the most senior staffers. They have what we refer to as walk-in privileges. That means that they can walk into the Oval Office without an appointment. I mean, most of us call ahead. It's not like we just barge into the Oval Office." Dale laughed. She was afraid she sounded like a jerk.

Dale heard the alert on her phone that signified a new text message had come through. Relieved by the distraction, she fished her iPhone out of her giant bag. Dale smiled as she read Craig's message. "They lit my block with stadium lights to film me walking from my front door to the SUV. You owe me many drinks," he wrote.

She quickly typed back: "I'm driving in with Doogie Howser. Don't complain."

Craig shared her sense of humor, and the two of them were often described by other members of the White House senior staff as being "in cahoots" on matters large and small. And while they often sat together on long flights and at staff dinners and meetings, their relationship was purely platonic. Craig was gay. He was only partly out of the closet, but it was not enough to quell suspicions from some corners of oblivious Washington about his relationship with Dale. Privately, they laughed about the knowing winks from congressmen and members of Charlotte's cabinet who suspected that the two were an item. Dale wished Craig would come out more publicly, but it was something he wasn't ready to do.

As she pulled into her regular parking spot, she thought about how wrong the reporters had been about Craig's role in the Tara Meyers scandal. A couple of the most aggressive investigative reporters had sniffed around months earlier about whether he had played a role in leaking information to Congress and the media about the former vice president's instability and questionable competence. Dale had felt torn about whether to take the inquiries to Craig or the White House counsel or even the president. The rumors about Craig unfairly painting Melanie as the leaker had posed a giant moral dilemma for Dale, as Melanie was the one who'd made sure that Dale had a top-notch lawyer to defend her from charges from Congress that she'd played a role in covering up the vice president's condition. Melanie was also the one who had warned her about how ugly the West Wing would become once an investigation was under way. Ultimately, Dale had decided not to confront Craig with the allegations. She could not fathom that he was capable of what the reporters suggested. He was her closest friend in Washington and her steadfast ally. Craig had also waged an aggressive campaign to help Dale secure the press secretary job. Surely he was entitled to the benefit of doubt from her. Dale was interrupted from her thoughts again by the sound of the production assistant tapping on her window.

He had hopped out of the car to help the crew set up to shoot her walking into the West Wing.

"Are you guys ready?" she asked him.

"Yes, ma'am. Whenever you are."

CHAPTER NINE

Charlotte

C harlotte reached over and turned off her alarm before it went off.

"Are you getting up?" Peter asked.

"I'm going to get some reading done. I'll go into the study so you can go back to sleep," she whispered.

"It's the middle of the night," he protested.

She leaned over and kissed him on the cheek. "It's almost five, and I'm about to walk into an ambush. CBS is going to be embedded with me all day. I'm not going to get any real work done. You'll call Penny?"

"As soon as the sun comes up on the West Coast."

"Before that, please."

"Yes, ma'am."

Charlotte scratched Cammie's ears, gathered her pile of papers from the nightstand, and walked down the hall to her study.

The White House staff secretary had placed a copy of her briefing book for the day in the center of her desk. The White House office of the staff secretary—a little-known and utterly indispensible group of West Wing employees—was responsible for assembling the briefing book and setting it on her desk at whatever hour it was completed the night before. The book contained detailed minute-by-minute schedules, briefing papers, final versions of speeches, and any sensitive background material for every meeting and event on her schedule. Even seemingly spontaneous drop-by meetings on her schedule were carefully researched, vetted, and scripted to avoid any potential for embarrassment.

The actual newspapers wouldn't be brought up until about 5:45 A.M., but there was a set of news clips still warm from the copy machine that had been placed next to the briefing book on her desk. A junior staffer in the White House press office came in at two A.M. and printed off the major stories from the Web sites of all the major newspapers. The "clips" were then photocopied for the senior White House staff and also placed on their desks.

The White House butlers had placed a pot of coffee, a pitcher of warm milk, and a cup and saucer on a tray on the side of her desk. In a few minutes, one of the butlers would come in and ask her if she wanted anything to eat. She'd say "Not yet," as she always did, and they'd come back every thirty minutes to see if she'd changed her mind, until she finally agreed to a smoothie, her one concession to Maureen's evangelism for clean living. Charlotte made a mental note to tell Maureen about Brooke and Mark's fondness for juice cleanses. It seemed everyone her age was resorting to extreme measures to beat back the forces of nature. Charlotte found it amusing. Self-improvement was her generation's obsession. She just wanted to be able to sleep past five A.M. again. Maureen was always carrying around a bottle of green juice, and if she didn't have to entertain a lawmaker or a foreign dignitary, she preferred drinking her green potions for breakfast, lunch, and dinner. Charlotte could barely choke down one salad a day. Maureen also frequented spinning classes at Washington's first "Soul Cycle" spinning club with members of her staff. Charlotte learned from Craig that Maureen had been asked to climb onto the instructor's bike in the front of the darkened room to lead the group. Apparently, the class of sixty had gone wild. Maureen's commitment to healthy living paid off. At five foot two and about one hundred and ten pounds, she had the body of a female gymnast. The deep lines around her eyes and mouth were the only clues to her age. At sixty-one, she had ten times the energy Charlotte had at fifty, and she seemed to outpace most of her twenty- and thirty-something staff members, too.

Charlotte tried to remember the last time she'd worked out. She made a mental note to start hiking with the dogs again on the weekends, at least. Then she pulled out her speech and scanned her edits from the night before. After underlining the sections she planned to emphasize when she delivered the address, Charlotte set the speech aside until the speechwriters came in to make her final changes. Her hope was to highlight the areas of consensus, but there was no chance the press would amplify those parts of her speech. She could already envision the breathless live shots from her press corps as they reported from in front of the antiabortion protesters all day long. If she had any power at all, she'd use it to cure the press of its conflict addiction.

Charlotte turned to a memo from her economic advisors. No one had been able to crack the code on the right combination of spending cuts, tax relief, and government support for the unemployed, but she was determined to figure it out without alienating her own party any more than she already had. Charlotte was still in a strong position with most conservatives on national security issues. Until recently, they respected her decision to leave sufficient troops on the ground in Iraq and Afghanistan to secure the gains they'd made over the last decade and a half and to combat the violent flare-ups in both places.

Charlotte had misgivings about taking a visible role in the abortion debate after forcing her remaining Republican allies to accept a progressive Democrat as her vice president, but it wasn't as if she'd had much of a choice. She leaned back in her chair and thought about all that had transpired since her reelection less than two years earlier. She'd had such high hopes for her second vice president, Tara Meyers, but it had unraveled amid revelations that she'd been hiding serious mental-health issues for the majority of her political career. In a behind-closed-doors deal, designed by Craig, who'd served as her chief legislative affairs advisor at the time, Charlotte had agreed to appoint the wildly popular and experienced Democratic speaker of the House of Representatives as Tara's replacement. The deal halted the impeachment proceedings against her and allowed her to regain her political footing.

Charlotte still felt guilty about subjecting Tara to the type of scrutiny that exacerbated her stress and brought her mental-health issues into public view. She hoped that someday they could speak about everything that had transpired, but her advisors had urged Charlotte to pour all of her energy into moving forward with whatever she could still accomplish in her remaining years as president.

For the first time in a very long time, that included having someone to come home to. She and Peter were both doing their best to be a couple again, but she was concerned that the time they'd spent apart had rewired both of them from the people they'd been when they'd first married more than two decades earlier. They were no longer trusting individuals who made good partners. When she was completely honest with herself, she worried that they'd both become wholly self-sufficient adults with unlimited capacity for taking care of others but severely limited ability to be vulnerable with each other. Most of the time, she pushed those concerns aside and recognized that getting back together wasn't a second chance so much as it was a last chance to be a family again. It was less romantic but more urgent, and Charlotte was committed to getting it right this time.

She looked up at the clock and contemplated crawling back into bed for a few minutes. The sun wasn't up, and already she was looking forward to dinner with Peter, Brooke, and Mark. She remembered that Craig would be in the office early because of the "Day in the Life" shoot. She picked up the phone on her desk and asked the White House operator to connect her to his direct line.

"Top of the morning, Madam President," he chirped.

"Obviously, you're being filmed right now. You never sound that happy to hear from me without half a dozen cappuccinos in you."

"I started caffeinating early, Madam President."

"Call me when you shake the television crew."

"Yes, ma'am. About five minutes."

"In the meantime, can you send someone up to my study in the residence to pick up the final edits to this morning's speech?"

"I'll pick them up myself, Madam President."

"That isn't necessary."

"On the contrary, it's completely necessary."

The film crews were not allowed into her private living quarters.

"See you in a minute."

"Thank you, Madam President. I owe you."

CHAPTER TEN

Melanie

Melanie paced the conference room and tried not to look as impatient as she felt. The videoconference between Baghdad and the White House was supposed to have started at six-thirty A.M. Washington time. It was almost seven, and the president still hadn't arrived in the Situation Room. Melanie looked around for her travel aide. He appeared instantly.

"What's going on?"

"The president made an off-the-record stop in the cafeteria in the Old Executive Office Building with the CBS film crew and was delayed by a group of summer interns who wanted pictures with her."

Melanie nodded and turned to the group of military trainers, state embassy staff, and local political officials. They didn't seem particularly bothered by the delay, but it irritated Melanie that the White House had kept them waiting. She waved her hand to get everyone's attention.

"I'm sorry, again, for the late start. As you all know, the president has a lot of demands on her time, and even with the help of an army of staff, you can't always make the trains run on time." This was precisely the sort of thing that furthered the impression of America as an arrogant superpower. It sent a clear signal that Charlotte's time was more valuable than theirs. Melanie was embarrassed for herself and for the White House.

Seconds later, the TV screen at the front of the room came to life. There was Charlotte smiling warmly from the White House Situation Room.

"Good morning—actually, it's afternoon for all of you, so good afternoon to you all, and I apologize for being late. It's entirely my fault that we're running behind on our end."

Melanie remembered that the camera in the room was beaming her face back into the situation room in D.C., so she returned the president's smile and waited a second to speak so that she wouldn't get cut off in the delay.

"Thank you, Madam President. We are looking forward to our discussion today. We are honored by the participation of several of the very best partners we've had since our efforts here began many years ago."

Melanie scrutinized the shot of the Situation Room and noticed the vice president, the secretary of state, the president's national security advisor, the White House chief of staff, and a few other policy advisors seated around the conference table. She almost gasped when she saw that Richard and Lucy were sitting directly across from the president *at the table*. A few of the participants in Baghdad noticed the look of surprise on Melanie's face and looked around nervously.

Melanie was supposed to open the call with an overview of the goals that the group had settled on for the year ahead. She glanced down at her notecards and started to speak.

"We have assembled a group that includes some of Iraq's brightest new leaders. These men and women are on the front lines in terms of making sure their country is in the hands of true patriots and modern thinkers and not those who wish to see Iraq descend into violence. Today, Madam President, we're looking forward to hearing from them about the status of the fight against ISIS, which security and political measures have been productive, and the opportunities for greater collaboration on the security front and the political front. I think we'll all be able to make better-informed decisions after our discussion today, and many more like it."

"Thank you, Madam Secretary. I'd like to direct the conversation to your associates in the room and ask all of you what you're seeing that concerns you and what you're seeing that gives you confidence about the path ahead. Melanie, perhaps you can make sure that everyone gets a chance to share their observations with us," Charlotte offered.

Melanie and the group had done a run-through, and they were prepared for Charlotte's invitation. Melanie introduced the first participant, Azeeza Maloof, the head of Iraq's Women's Affairs department. Her predecessors were assassinated, and before Azeeza accepted the appointment, the position had been unfilled for nearly a year and a half.

Charlotte listened intently as Azeeza spoke about the threats that had been made against her and her family. When she was finished, the president praised her for her courage and determination. Melanie could see that Charlotte was completely focused on Azeeza, but she noticed that Lucy had passed the president a note in the middle of Azeeza's recounting of having to move her family from their home because ISIS terrorists lit their house on fire one night while she and her children slept inside.

It took Charlotte a couple of minutes to see the folded piece of paper in front of her, but once she did, she read it and then folded it up again and placed it under her notepad. Melanie started to introduce the second participant, but Charlotte interrupted.

"Madam Secretary, do you mind if our friends from CBS News ask a few questions before we move on? Azeeza, would that be all right? Your story is compelling, and you are so brave. It's important for the American public to know that there are strong leaders like you guiding your country."

"I don't mind," Azeeza said.

I mind, Melanie fumed.

"Azeeza, you must be aware of how eager the American public and our elected officials are to disentangle ourselves from your affairs, and I wonder how you feel about our ongoing presence in your country. Is it helpful, or does it do more harm than good?"

Azeeza was ready for the question and offered an eloquent defense of the American-Iraqi partnership. She also discussed the need for international investment in education and infrastructure.

"Thank you, Azeeza," Melanie said.

"Azeeza? This is Richard. I'm Lucy's lesser half. Well, not in real life, just on television. That was a joke. Is any of this translating?"

"You're not being translated, Richard. Everyone here speaks English," Melanie corrected. She was annoyed that they were trying to turn the town hall meeting into a CBS News interview.

"Oh, right. Sorry. Azeeza, does your husband have any role in creating a new generation of male leaders who see women as their equals? Because it seems to me that all of the courageous women in the world will fail at changing society if you can't teach young boys to grow up believing that their sisters and daughters are their equals and deserve respect."

Melanie knew exactly how Azeeza was going to answer Richard's question, and if Richard had read more than the first paragraph of the briefing materials that had been provided to the Washington participants, he would, too.

"My husband was murdered for working with the Americans in the early years of the war. He was a translator and he was killed. That's why I serve now."

"Oh, God. I'm sorry. You're even more impressive to me now. Jeez. Thank you for what you're doing over there."

"Over here is my country, sir. It is my home."

"Of course," Richard mumbled.

Melanie summoned her travel aide. "Get Dale on the phone, and tell her to cut off Richard and Lucy. We can't use our partners as props in a White House infomercial," she whispered into his ear.

He nodded.

"Tell her that if Lucy or Richard speak again, I'm going to pull the plug. They were supposed to observe. They were not supposed to interrogate our participants."

"Yes, ma'am. I'll call Dale right now."

Melanie had a hard time staying focused on the rest of the conversation, because she was so irritated that the president had allowed Lucy and Richard to participate. The deal was that they could film an event that would otherwise have been closed to the press. As soon as the videoconference ended, she asked her travel aide to get Dale on the phone again. He tracked her down immediately.

"Dale?"

"Yes, ma'am. I understand that you're upset, and I'm sorry about that. Lucy passed the president a note, and I didn't have any idea that she'd asked to speak until I heard her ask a question."

"Listen, Dale, I've been in your shoes, and one thing you will learn very soon is that your success or failure in that position has a lot more to do with the bad occurrences that you prevent from happening than the good things that you make happen and take credit for. This whole goddamned 'Day in the Life' is going to be a distant memory twenty-four hours after it airs, but Azeeza is going to go home tonight and wonder if she was asked to be here today because we understand and appreciate her contributions or if she was invited to serve as a prop in a cartoonish American propaganda production. You probably think that you're doing things that haven't been done before, but I presided over five 'Days in the Life,' and every one of them went off without the journalists hijacking a presidential event."

"I'm really sorry, and you're right. It's my fault, entirely, Madam Secretary."

"Let me finish. It is your job to protect the president from herself with the press. Do you know where she is right now? Is she in the hallway still talking to those idiots?"

"I don't believe so, Madam Secretary, but I can't be sure at the moment."

"You should probably go find out."

Melanie slammed the phone down and looked around the conference room to make sure that no one was there to witness her outburst. She reached for a bottle of water, and as she drank it, she knew that she shouldn't have been so hard on Dale. She could hardly afford to alienate anyone else in Charlotte's inner circle. Melanie packed up her papers for the long flight home. As she headed for the door to participate in the final photo op of her trip, a departure photo with the commanders and a few of the top trainers, she wondered how much longer she could tolerate her outsider status with the West Wing. It was one thing to have shaky relations with a White House chief of staff. It made the job of any cabinet secretary difficult but not impossible. But once the people around a president sense that the president has lost confidence in a Cabinet secretary, that official plunges to persona non grata in a nanosecond. It wasn't clear that this had occurred yet, but Melanie sensed that she was viewed as an advisor with diminishing importance to the success of Charlotte's second term. Melanie knew from decades of experience in D.C. that it was best to seek out other opportunities before her stock dropped too much further and exchanges like the one that had just transpired with Dale ended up in the press.

CHAPTER ELEVEN

Dale

Dale took the stairs back up to her office two at a time and tried to shake off Melanie's tongue-lashing. Sure, they hadn't planned for Lucy and Richard to question the Iraqis, but the point of these interactions was twofold: to make the Iraqis feel invested in the American partnership and to show the American public that there were credible partners who would eventually take control of their own country's security.

Dale was eager to get back to her office and check on the coverage of the speech. She was afraid that they were losing the "spin war," with Republicans and prolife advocates filling the airwaves with their heated complaints. With the CBS crew huddled in the corner capturing B-roll, Dale looked up at the wall of televisions in her office. The abortion protests were still going strong. Dale turned the volume up on one of the stations and listened to a couple of the speakers. They were so loud that even with the televisions muted, Dale could hear the crowd's cheers from inside her West Wing office. She looked around her desk for her morning coffee.

"Clare?" she called.

Her assistant appeared in the doorway. "Another coffee?"

"Please."

Clare disappeared, and Dale started going through her e-mail messages. After returning everything with "urgent" in the subject line, she leaned back in her chair and drank a few sips of the extra-large coffee that Clare had placed on her desk. She felt like she'd been awake for ten hours already, but it wasn't even eight A.M. She shared a wall with her deputy, but she didn't want the film crew to put together a montage of Dale sitting in her chair yelling for her staff. Dale dialed Marguerite's direct line and asked her to come in.

"Don't worry about Secretary Kingston," Marguerite remarked, before she even made it through the doorway. Dale eyed the camera crew and then looked back at Marguerite to make clear that they should not speak openly with the cameras rolling. Marguerite was wearing a tight black skirt and jacket with a lacy camisole underneath and open-toe heels.

Marguerite smiled warmly at the camera crew. "Please don't use that, guys."

They nodded their heads and assured her that they would not.

"Do you mind if I talk to Dale alone for two seconds? I promise I'll let you back in for the good stuff."

Miraculously, they exited the room without objection. Dale shook her head in amazement. Marguerite had a magic touch with the press.

It helped that she was a beautiful Cuban from Miami who dressed like one of the female stars of a Spanish-language soap opera. She was smart and unflappable, and when she was angry, she swore in Spanish. Half of the press was in love with her, and the other half wanted to look like her. More important, she was hardworking and shameless when it came to advancing the president's agenda. Dale found her indispensible. When Dale was first appointed press secretary, she'd elevated Marguerite, who'd worked in the press office as a spokesperson for the two major Spanish-language networks.

"What did you hear about Melanie?" Dale asked.

"That she was furious that Lucy and Richard asked questions."

"It was the president who turned over the floor to them."

"I know. Don't worry about it."

"Whatever. Did all of the morning shows lead with today's speech?" Dale asked.

"The speech-slash-protests."

"Right."

"The other nets are feeling left out today, so I thought I'd get the vice president to do a round robin and talk to ABC, NBC, Fox, and CNN."

"Good thinking. Five minutes with each of the White House correspondents, right?"

"Yes."

"Good. What else?"

"Do you think we should have the president call in to Rush or Hannity or one of the other conservative talkers, to show that she still cares about the base and understands they won't agree with today's speech, but she honors all points of view, or something like that?"

"It might make things worse. Maybe Melanie can do those. DOD could pitch it as an update from her visit to the troops."

"I'll wait a couple of hours before I put in that request with the DOD press office. Oh, and the *New York Times* wants to know if their request for their own 'Day in the Life' is still alive."

"I've said no three times. What is wrong with them?"

"They are the *New. York. Times,*" Marguerite said, with feigned indignation that made Dale laugh out loud.

"I will call them again today," Marguerite promised.

"Anything else breaking?"

"We have a stack of requests for San Francisco that we need to go through. The local press thinks that the president should talk to them while she's out there this summer."

"She's going there for vacation," Dale objected.

"I know, I know, I will handle it," Marguerite soothed.

"Did anything important happen in senior staff?"

"Does anything important ever happen in senior staff?"

"Did anyone complain about the camera?"

"Everyone seemed to like it. Larry gave an extra-long presentation on the expectations for Friday's job number, and Bonnie gave the longest report from the White House counsel's office that I've heard since I've been attending senior staff meetings."

Dale laughed.

"You have dinner with the parents tonight, right?" Marguerite asked.

"I'm sure they already hate me. Midwesterners don't usually approve of commitment-phobic New York women as mates for their only sons."

"Warren knows that he is a lucky man. That's all that matters."

"I work all the time, I can't cook or make a bed, and my idea of getting serious is sharing frequent flier miles. He won the girlfriend lottery with me," Dale quipped.

At that moment, Clare burst into Dale's office.

"Excuse me, I'm sorry, but Sam called to see if either of you were planning to join them in the Oval."

"Join who in the Oval?" Dale asked.

"Apparently, the president invited Lucy and Richard up to the Oval Office after the videoconference, and she's waved Sam away every time she's tried to break it up."

"Crap. That wasn't on the schedule. How long have they been in there?"

"According to Sam, they all came up from the videoconference together."

"Jesus. I'll go get them. Why didn't anyone tell me?"

"I thought they were in their hold," Marguerite said.

"Gather the entire staff, please, and find out how it is that we lost a network anchor team inside the West Wing," Dale ordered.

CHAPTER TWELVE

Charlotte

After the meeting in the Situation Room, Charlotte invited Richard and Lucy to the Oval Office to visit with her for a few minutes. She thought it would help the piece if she spent some off-the-record time with them. Even Charlotte had to admit that Richard and Lucy knew how to stage a clever charm offensive.

Lucy would say something outrageous, and Richard would fall all over himself to apologize for her crassness. They'd talk among themselves for a minute or so, and she'd promise him that she wouldn't offend their guest again. Then Lucy would ask the same probing question in a more polite and politically correct way. Richard would feign outrage, as if to suggest that he simply couldn't control her even if he'd wanted to, but it was clear that their routine yielded the exact results they were after.

Charlotte watched them put on a fairly entertaining show for the waiter from the White House Mess who came in to take their coffee order. Lucy pretended to be insulted by something Richard had said, and Richard kept apologizing to the waiter for Lucy's bad manners (she'd stuffed a stack of cocktail napkins into her purse and was asking about taking home a coffee cup and saucer). Charlotte could see how it could all become a little too much, but she was impressed that they didn't seem to take themselves too seriously. So far, they seemed genuinely interested in her views about presiding over a bipartisan

White House staff. They'd likened it to *The Brady Bunch*, and the comparison wasn't too far off. Maureen had brought her "kids" to the family, and Charlotte had hers. They couldn't supervise all of their interactions, but they both hoped that everyone would learn to get along. Dale had proven, once again, that she had excellent judgment when it came to doling out Charlotte's interviews.

Charlotte sat across from them and asked Lucy about her twenty-month-old twins. She spoke enthusiastically about juggling motherhood and a high-pressure job. While she was talking, it was clear to Charlotte that Lucy didn't suffer from the sort of guilt that Charlotte had struggled with for nearly two decades for abandoning her young children and her husband to pursue elected office. It was at once impressive and startling.

Charlotte wouldn't admit it to anyone on her staff, but she was actually enjoying herself.

"That's the private dining room and your private bathroom over there, right?" Richard asked.

"Ooh, can I use it? I have had to pee since before the meeting in the Sit Room."

Before Charlotte could answer, Richard stood to block Lucy's path to the bathroom.

"I can't take you anywhere," he scolded. "Madam President, I'm sorry. I bought her one of those books about acceptable social behavior, but she refuses to read it," Richard joked.

Charlotte told Lucy to go ahead.

The president's assistant, Samantha, wasn't accustomed to seeing her boss hold court with reporters, so she poked her head in every few minutes to see if anyone needed anything. On her fourth attempt, she flung open the door and cleared her throat to get Charlotte's attention.

"Madam President, you have a call with the president of Brazil in ten minutes. The translators are here to set up." It was a lie. The call was in thirty minutes, but Sam was trying to protect her from the anchors. Charlotte smiled.

"Yes, of course. Richard, Lucy, I'm sorry. You'll have to excuse me, but I will see you shortly at the Women's Museum, and I am looking forward to our interview afterward."

Richard and Lucy reluctantly stood to go. Dale appeared suddenly in the doorway to the Oval Office with a look of alarm on her face.

"There you are, Dale." The president smiled.

"Yes, ma'am. I'm sorry I'm late. I had an urgent call from Secretary Kingston after the teleconference."

"Is everything all right?" Charlotte asked. She suspected that Melanie was peeved about Richard and Lucy's participation. It wasn't that Melanie wouldn't appreciate the gesture. It would have more to do with the fact that she hated surprises and liked to be the one doling out favors to the press.

"Yes, ma'am," Dale assured her.

"Good to hear. I'll see all of you later."

Charlotte stood in front of Samantha's desk and listened as Dale quizzed the anchors about how they had ended up in the Oval Office. When Charlotte was confident that Dale had herded Richard and Lucy far enough along toward the press office that they were out of earshot, she sat down in the chair next to Sam's desk.

"Sometimes it makes perfect sense to me that the public thinks everyone in government is an incompetent boob," Charlotte said, more to herself than to her assistant.

"Ma'am?"

"Do you think anyone in the press office had any idea that they were in here?"

Sam stared at her keyboard and tried to conceal a smile. She never ratted out the staff, but the president was pretty good at figuring things out for herself.

"I couldn't tell if you really wanted them to stay, ma'am."

"Usually, I don't want anyone to stay, but they were amusing. And you were equally amusing with your persistent efforts to free me," Charlotte teased.

"I am, if nothing else, persistent, ma'am."

"I realized after ten minutes went by without Dale or Marguerite bursting in that no one had any clue that they were in there alone with me."

"I'm sure they just thought it was good for everyone. You know, to let the reporters feel like they have unfettered access, and it's not like you need press handlers around all the time, ma'am."

Charlotte smiled. Sam was too good at her job sometimes. "Sam?"

"Yes, ma'am?"

"Do I have time to walk over to the residence?"

"Yes, ma'am. The translators need time to set up anyway. Is twenty minutes enough time, or do you want me to move the call back?"

"That's perfect. I'll be right back."

Charlotte walked out through the door behind Sam's desk and nodded at the Secret Service agent who met her on the colonnade to walk the short distance to the residence with her. They passed the Rose Garden, and Charlotte noticed that all the flowers she'd seen the day before were gone. That happened all the time. Just a few weeks earlier, the park service pulled up hundreds of gigantic red tulips. Dinner-plate-sized blue hydrangeas had replaced the tulips, and now they were gone, too. A dizzying mixture of multicolored sunflowers had been installed in their place. The roses, which were the mainstay of the garden, were in bloom. The entire South Lawn smelled almost sickeningly sweet. Charlotte wondered what they did with all the perfectly good plants they ripped out.

She waved at the nurse who stood up to greet her when she passed the medical unit. Charlotte preferred the stairs, but she didn't have much time, so she popped into the elevator. She slipped out of her heels and walked toward the Lincoln Bedroom, which Peter used as an office. She didn't intend to eavesdrop, but what she heard stopped her in her tracks.

"I don't talk to Dale on a regular basis anymore, sweetheart."

Charlotte couldn't have moved if she'd wanted to.

"I know she works here. I watch the news, and I see her on television . . . Look, it wasn't my decision, it was your mother's, and I have to believe that she chose her because she was the best person for the job . . . She's your mother's press secretary. I'm sure she talks to Mom every day . . . No, Penny. They have more important things to talk about than me . . . Dale would love to get an e-mail from you. Her old e-mail address should still work. Are we done with this subject for now? I am calling with an important message from your mom about her speech today . . . No she didn't ask me to do her dirty work.

I need you to keep a low profile today, for my sake, kiddo, got it? . . . You know exactly what I'm talking about . . . Yes, I will get Dale's new e-mail address, but repeat after me: I will not step out of line today after my mother's brave and important speech."

For the first time since Charlotte had been standing there, Peter laughed.

"Yes. Yes. I know, I know. She's a little uptight about that stuff." He laughed again and listened to something Penny was saying.

"Oh, God, that's a terrible thing to say about your mother. She was actually a lot of fun when she was in college. Yes, I'm serious. I don't know what happened. I guess she decided that what the public thinks of her is more important than what we think, and as much of an imposition as that might feel like sometimes, we need to keep in mind that this time in all of our lives will come to an end. In a couple of years, she'll just be your neurotic mother again."

Penny said something else, and Peter laughed again.

She felt ill. They were commiserating about how miserable she was. She knew she should turn around and head straight back to the Oval Office, but she was frozen in place. She'd never asked Peter if he stayed in touch with Dale. Her assumption was that he'd cut all ties to her, but she had no idea if that was the case. They could still e-mail or talk on the phone. She was pretty sure he never saw her. How could they get together without her knowing? The moment the question crossed her mind, she wanted to smack herself in the head. Peter and Dale had carried on an affair for more than two years behind her back. Not entirely behind her back. She'd known about it, but that had been different.

And Charlotte understood that Peter had a special relationship with Penny, but she didn't know that complaining about what a drag she was and discussing his ex-mistress with his college-age daughter were among the topics over which they bonded. Charlotte was so hurt. She needed to get out of the residence immediately.

"What are you doing here?"

It was Mark. He was wearing Lululemon workout clothes and looked as though he'd just run several miles in the humidity.

"I came over to change my shoes," she explained, pointing at the heels in her hands.

"Did you see Brooke?"

"No. Is she up?"

"I doubt it. She said she had to sleep off my shitty cocktails."

"I need to sneak back to the office for a call with the president of Brazil. I will catch up with you guys at dinner."

"I'd kiss you good-bye, but I'm a little sweaty."

"Please don't."

"Hey, Char, what are you doing up here?" Peter asked from the doorway to the Lincoln Bedroom.

"I came up to change my shoes," she repeated.

"I caught Penny on her way to the gym. She isn't going to do anything to embarrass you."

Charlotte was speechless. "Great," she practically whispered. She had trouble maintaining eye contact with Peter. "All right, then, I'll see all of you tonight." She started walking back toward the elevator.

"Char?" Peter called after her.

"What?"

"Weren't you going to change your shoes?"

"What?"

"Aren't those the ones you wore when you left this morning?"

She looked down at the shoes in her hand. She hadn't changed them for others, and she didn't want to. The ones she had went perfectly with what she was wearing.

"I changed my mind."

She put the shoes down and stepped into them and then walked straight toward the elevator. Once inside, she reminded herself to breathe. Charlotte could handle political upheaval, public disapproval, and the ire of her staff. But it stung terribly to realize that her husband and daughter had developed a greater capacity for intimate conversation with each other than she had with either one of them. When she got off the elevator, her agent reminded her that the CBS film crew would be setting up on the South Lawn to film her departure to the Women's Museum. She thanked him and pasted on a smile as she walked back down the colonnade toward the Oval Office for her call with the Brazilian president.

CHAPTER THIRTEEN

Melanie

After spending forty-five minutes longer than her schedule had allotted on good-byes to troops, Melanie boarded the giant C-17 aircraft that would transport her and her entourage of press, handlers, and military aides the nearly seven thousand miles back to Washington, D.C. She settled into what was referred to by Pentagon insiders as the "silver bullet" for the first leg of the thirteen-hour journey. The silver bullet was a giant trailer that had been inserted into the middle of the plane to ensure that the secretary of defense rode in relative comfort. Members of the press and a handful of policy advisors and other staff sat in seats surrounding the giant installation. The plane was built for function, not comfort, but she'd managed to make her private cabin a sanctuary. She had a bathroom and a comfortable bed that she found herself using more and more. As soon as one of the military aides dropped off her lunch—tuna salad with crudité, Wheat Thins, and a large bottle of water—Melanie closed the door and collapsed into the oversized chair behind the desk. The bed was inviting, but she had a few calls to make while it was still early in Washington. She piled a forkful of tuna salad onto a Wheat Thin and was about to take a bite when she remembered that tuna had mercury in it, and mercury was to be avoided during pregnancy. She was starving, so she ate it anyway. As she wondered just how much mercury was in canned tuna, she thought about the teensy being inside her. Most of the time, she refused to believe that she was actually growing a baby that she'd ever get to hold and kiss and love. She'd had two miscarriages, and they'd both devastated her. One had occurred at seven and a half weeks and the other at eight weeks. It sounded like such a short time, but to believe for two months that you were pregnant and then to find out suddenly and without warning that you were not was like having your heart ripped apart. Twice. Melanie had once been described as Washington's version of an "iron lady," but the two miscarriages had reduced her to dust. The first time, she'd just begun to tell a few close friends and family that the invasive IVF procedures she'd endured had finally worked when she learned that she'd lost the baby. People who were otherwise kind and intelligent had said the most idiotic things. Things like "Oh, you're so lucky it happened so early," and "It's God's way." She vowed not to tell anyone ever again until she absolutely had to. She and Brian had muddled through the disappointment and sadness of the second miscarriage privately. Melanie had refused any further IVF treatments, and any discussion of pregnancy, fertility, and motherhood was strictly banned. Nearly six months went by, and Melanie was just starting to feel normal again. She tried to rationalize that perhaps motherhood was one blessing too many. Perhaps God only handed out a finite number of blessings to each person, and Melanie had used all of hers up on her charmed career and the sweet, handsome man she'd found to spend her life with. Maybe motherhood was a dream that would go unfulfilled.

Then, after a grueling trip to Asia in which she could barely stay awake for her bilateral meetings with defense ministers and foreign heads of state, she came home to Washington with what she was certain was the Avian flu. She was in bed for five days before Brian dared to ask if she could possibly be pregnant.

"Only if I was raped by a stork," she'd retorted.

He'd actually winced at her remark.

Nevertheless, she'd dragged herself from the bed and pulled a leftover home-pregnancy test out of her medicine cabinet. She'd peed on the stick and waited for the test to show that she was not pregnant so she could show Brian. When it came out positive, she threw it away and took another. And then she took another. After five pregnancy tests all said the same thing, she crumpled into a ball on the bathroom floor. When Brian came in and found her, she'd held up all five of the tests. He took them from her and placed them on top of the toilet bowl. He'd wiped her tear-stained face and carried her back to the bed. She couldn't look at him. She wasn't sure that either one of them could handle another loss. Brian lay next to her and wrapped his arms around her tightly. They stayed like that until the sun went down, and then he called in sick for both of them in the morning. They made an appointment to see Melanie's fertility doctor at eleven. She didn't even have an obstetrician, because she'd never stayed pregnant long enough to need one. They sat in the lobby with all of the other couples, who probably had very little in common with Melanie and Brian other than the desire to have a child regardless of the cost— monetary, physical, emotional, and otherwise. Melanie was afraid of every possible outcome that morning. She feared that between the five pregnancy tests she'd taken the day before and her morning appointment, she'd miscarried this pregnancy, too. She was also afraid that perhaps the tests were wrong, and she wasn't even pregnant. But most of all, she feared that she was pregnant with another baby that wouldn't survive. She was afraid to hope for anything other than heartbreaking news. She knew exactly what the doctor would say if she wasn't pregnant.

"Melanie, we know you can get pregnant. Keep trying."

She had decided that they were selling the cruelest kind of false hope she had ever encountered. Brian never complained, but she knew it was also taking a toll on him.

"You should have married someone with younger ovaries," she'd said to him on several occasions.

The nurse who'd seen them for all of their appointments came out to retrieve them.

"Dr. Fishbourne wants to visit with you first," she said.

Brian had nodded and pulled Melanie up by the hand. She felt like she was sleepwalking. The doctor was waiting for them in his office.

"What's going on, guys?"

Brian spoke. "Melanie thought she had the flu, but after five days in bed, she took a pregnancy test."

"This was yesterday?" he asked.

"Yes. And it was positive. Actually, there were five, and they were all positive."

"Do you remember when your last period was?"

Melanie shook her head. "No idea. A while ago. I figured everything was still screwed up from the fertility treatments."

He jotted some note in her file and then looked up. "I'll have a nurse take some blood from you, Melanie, and then I'll be in to examine you."

Melanie had tried to numb herself against everything that would happen next. The nurse had her make a fist while she took blood. Then she undressed from the waist down and squeezed her eyes shut so she wouldn't be tempted to look at the monitor while the doctor performed the ultrasound. She didn't hear anything, and that alone was a bad sign. She felt a lump forming in her throat. She turned to look at Brian, and he was staring intently at the monitor.

She shifted her gaze to Dr. Fishbourne's face. He was smiling. "Melanie, I'd say you're about thirteen and a half weeks pregnant."

Then he had turned up the volume on the giant ultrasound machine. The sound of a very fast heartbeat filled the room. The sound filled her with hope. Tears spilled from the corners of her eyes, and when she looked over at Brian, he was choked up, too.

"How do we know that everything is OK?" she'd whispered.

"It's a good sign that you're this far along. We'll do all of the testing you want to do. There's an early test that's as accurate as an amnio. It will give you peace of mind. I can schedule it with some of my colleagues for later this week."

"Tomorrow," Brian had insisted.

"Tomorrow," the doctor promised. "Congratulations," he added.

"Don't say that yet," Melanie pleaded.

When the results came back one week later, the doctor assured her that everything was fine. He also asked if she wanted to know the sex. Melanie still refused to believe that she was having a baby, but when he'd said, "You're having a son," something inside her shifted. She realized at that moment that the whole undertaking was an exercise in losing control. She'd decided to do her best to be brave—for her son's benefit.

More than a month had passed, and the nausea and exhaustion were giving way to indigestion and a more general fatigue. She finished her lunch and pulled a blanket over herself. She had plenty of hours of travel ahead of her. No one would notice if she snuck in a short nap.

CHAPTER FOURTEEN

Dale

Dale ducked into Marguerite's office so she could have a conversation without being filmed by the CBS crew.

"Marguerite, I'm going to go to the Women's Museum with the president so I can be there for the interview with Richard and Lucy, unless you want to go?"

"No, you go. I'll get the VP interviews set up so she can do those as soon as you guys are back."

"Is there anything breaking that I need to prepare the president for before the interview?"

"Everyone is covering the speech and the trouble it's causing for the president with conservatives. Fox is running a banner that says 'busting the base.'"

"That's not surprising. She can handle that. I like her language on the generational divide on social issues. She'll broaden the discussion and call for tolerance of the entire spectrum of views on the life-versus-choice debate. Warren said that the polls show that every time she's forced to defend herself against the Republican base, her numbers go up among women and independents."

"The deciders," Marguerite joked. Whenever they wanted to make the case for the president or the vice president to do an interview or a media avail, they appealed to everyone's desire to see the president's political capital remain intact. Women tended to be the biggest group of swing voters, and not simply in general elections. They watched the most news and were the most persuadable on nearly every major policy debate. Dale and Marguerite had taken to simply calling them the "deciders."

"The president will do fine. Take a deep breath, Dale."

Dale smiled appreciatively at her deputy. "I've been called an idiot by the secretary of defense, and I've lost an anchor team in the West Wing only to find them in the Oval Office. There really isn't too much more that can go wrong, is there?"

"Don't say that. You're going to jinx us!"

As if on cue, Dale's assistant knocked on Marguerite's door.

"Adam Leary from Buzzfeed said that you'd want to take his call," Clare said.

"When have I ever wanted to talk to Buzzfeed?" Dale scoffed.

Marguerite picked up the phone. "This better be good," she demanded. Dale watched Marguerite's face morph from annoyed to concerned. "I haven't seen it. Send it to me. Isn't her Facebook page private? How do you know it's legit? OK, OK, fine. I'll check it out as soon as you send it to me. I don't know how long it will take me. I'll call you back when I know something."

"What was that?" Dale asked.

"Hang on."

"Marguerite, I have to get in the motorcade in ten minutes."

"I'm waiting for his e-mail."

"What did he say?"

"Buzzfeed is claiming that Penelope Kramer posted something snarky on her Facebook page about how today is the first time in her life she's been proud to be Charlotte Kramer's daughter."

"You are kidding me, right?"

"Let's see if it's real before we freak out. I don't think kids her age use Facebook anymore, anyway."

"It might be the only social medium she's allowed to use."

The Secret Service was uncomfortable with the twins using social media. When the twins put up a fight and enlisted their parents' support, the head of the Secret Service had argued that Twitter and

Instagram offered too many details about the twins' exact locations and could reveal security vulnerabilities. After extensive negotiations between the president, Peter, and the Secret Service, they'd finally agreed to let the twins use Facebook.

Clare stuck her head into Marguerite's office again.

"Dale, Craig is holding for you, and Marguerite, I have CNN, AP, and *Politico* holding. Do you want any of them?"

"No!" shouted Dale.

"No to Craig?"

"No, yes to Craig. I'll get it in here. No to the others until we know what the hell is going on."

"Hi," Dale said to Craig, trying to sound calm.

"How's it going with CBS?" he asked.

"Why?"

"Just checking."

"How does the president think it's going?"

"She's having more fun than she'll admit."

"That's good." Dale was peering over Marguerite's chair to catch a glimpse of the e-mail from Adam.

"I heard you lost Lucy and Richard."

"Not exactly. The president brought them up from the Situation Room with her, and we temporarily misplaced them."

"In the Oval?"

"Was she upset?"

"I assured her that it wouldn't happen again."

"It won't."

"Dale?"

"What?" She could barely hide her impatience.

"Is there anything else cooking?"

"Not that I know of. Why?"

"Just checking."

Dale considered telling Craig about the possibility of a social media crisis with the first daughter, but she'd learned to gather all of the information before she broke bad news to the White House chief of staff. She hung up before Craig detected anything else in her voice.

"Marguerite, come on, come on. What do we know? I have to get in the motorcade in five minutes now."

"Here it is. It looks legit. I'm verifying with the Secret Service that this is actually her Facebook page."

They both stood behind Marguerite's desk and read from her computer screen.

"Everyone wants to know how it feels to be the president's daughter and whether she's inspired me like she's inspired countless other young women and girls who will grow up thinking that they can be the president. The truth is that I never feel that way. But today she'll take a stand on an issue that affects every woman in this country. My mom has always believed in a woman's right to choose, but she never had the courage to speak up before. When she does so today, she'll be doing something far more important than any other speech she's given to date. Today, for the first time in my life, I'm proud to be Charlotte Kramer's daughter."

Dale read it a second time and then a third. She picked up a notepad and a pen. "Let's go," she ordered.

Marguerite followed. They went straight into the chief of staff's office and flashed fake smiles at the CBS crew in his waiting area.

"We need to talk to Craig about something that's still classified—it's for a speech next week. We'll be in there for less than two minutes," Dale promised.

Craig was working at his standing desk in the corner of the room. He finished typing an e-mail on the MacBook Pro that Dale recognized as his personal computer before he looked up.

"Ladies?"

"We have a situation with Penelope Kramer," Dale announced.

"And this arose between the time I spoke to you two minutes ago and now?"

"Yes," Dale promised.

She handed Craig the page that Marguerite had printed in her office. He read it quickly and then glanced at his watch. He buzzed his assistant.

"Pick up, please. Ben, please tell Sam that Dale, Marguerite, and

I are coming down to see the president, and we need five minutes before we leave for the speech," Craig instructed.

He slipped into his jacket as they walked the fifteen paces to the Oval Office.

The door was open, and Charlotte was skimming her speech when the three of them appeared in her doorway.

"Madam President, we have a situation. It's something we need to discuss with you before we depart for the Women's Museum."

"What is it?" she asked.

"We're getting press calls about this, and we wanted you to be aware."

Craig handed her the printout, and Dale watched the color drain from the president's face as she read Penny's post.

CHAPTER FIFTEEN

Charlotte

Charlotte finished reading Penny's Facebook post and folded the paper in half and then in half again. She looked up at where Craig, Dale, and Marguerite hovered near the door.

"Madam President?" Craig offered.

"How much time until we leave for the Women's Museum?" she asked.

"I can push the speech back half an hour, Madam President."

"I think that's a good idea. Can you all give me a minute, please?"

They exited her office.

She walked to her desk and dialed Peter's extension in the residence. She forced herself to remain calm, but her teeth were clenched, and her overly caffeinated blood was starting to boil.

"Can you come down here?"

"What's going on?" he asked.

"Just come down here, please."

"I'm on my way."

Charlotte was fuming. It was bad enough that she'd overheard her husband and college-age daughter trashing her earlier, but now Penny had made it clear that she didn't have a drop of respect for her. Charlotte was beyond exasperated. She was also embarrassed that Penny had chosen to lash out in such a public way. She paced her office and thought about all the different ways the press would put her on the couch and analyze her relationships with her kids. Penny had opened a Pandora's box. In her petulant eighteen-year-old mind, she'd simply inserted herself into a debate about abortion while taking a jab at her mother. But the press would quickly forget the narrow context of her Facebook statement. Everything she posted on Facebook and said in public or to her friends would now be fair game for press scrutiny. Penny was a summer intern at Google, and Charlotte wondered if her supervisor would consider her a distraction from the rest of the intern class and dismiss her. It would serve her right, Charlotte decided.

"What's going on?" Peter asked, stepping into the Oval Office. Charlotte handed him the folded-up piece of paper. Peter pulled out his phone and started to punch in Penny's number as soon as he'd read it.

"Don't," Charlotte protested.

"Why not? She needs to fix this, Char."

"Fix it? She can't 'fix' this, Peter. *This* will be the news today. The fact that Penny is proud to be our daughter for the first time in her life—sorry, *my* daughter—will be the *only* story today. I've spent eighteen years protecting her from the prying eyes of the press, and now, in one bitchy post on Facebook, she has exposed herself to every critical, petty, and unforgiving reporter and pundit in the country, not to mention changing the topic from women's rights to herself."

"Maybe then she'll have a better understanding of everything you put up with."

Charlotte turned away from Peter so that he couldn't see how undone she was. She took a deep breath and lowered her voice to a near whisper.

"I thought you had a conversation with her specifically about this."

"I did, but I don't control her. She's her own person. She's practically an adult."

"She's going to feel like one tonight when she leads the network news."

"I'm sorry, Char. I told you I would handle her."

"I thought she was smarter than this."

"She made a mistake," Peter insisted.

Charlotte spun around and faced him with all the fury that had been building since Craig had handed her Penny's statement.

"Are you seriously defending this stunt? Because if you are, we have even bigger problems than I'd thought."

"I'm not defending her at all. I think you should send her to Gitmo if you want. But when the press no longer gives a damn about anything you say or do, she will still be our daughter," he said tightly.

"She is trying to punish me, and she knew that it would have the effect of driving us farther apart. You can let her know that she accomplished both missions."

Peter was about to say something when Brooke and Mark barged into the Oval Office. Sam followed close behind and tried to redirect them into the Cabinet Room next door.

"It's fine," Charlotte assured Sam. Brooke and Mark wouldn't have stayed out even if she'd asked them to.

"Char, it's not that bad," Brooke offered.

"You saw it?"

"It's on the Internet," Mark confirmed.

"Anyone who has ever had a teenage daughter will totally sympathize with you," Brooke added.

Charlotte smiled ruefully at her friends and recognized that their arrival had guaranteed that the simmering tensions between her and Peter would have to be addressed another time.

"Sam?" she called.

"Yes, ma'am?"

"Please ask Craig, Dale, and Marguerite to come back in here."

They appeared instantly, and Charlotte wondered if they'd heard everything that had transpired.

"Madam President?"

"Craig, I think we should be as blasé as possible about Penny's statement. Say that she's a young adult with her own opinions about politics and policy and everything else. Maybe we wrap it into a larger statement about just how difficult it is to be the child of a president. We could touch on the fact that the debate around reproductive rights can divide, and sometimes unite, families. Have the press office say something about how I appreciate Penny's feelings about this issue and the other issues she raised on Facebook."

Dale and Craig looked at each other.

"What's wrong? That covers everything, doesn't it?" Charlotte asked.

"Madam President, the first thing the press is going to want to know is whether you've spoken to Penny," Dale said.

"Oh. Right." She glared at Peter.

"We'll call her now," he said.

"I need to do this alone," Charlotte told him.

She walked into her private dining room. The call went straight to voice mail, and Charlotte dialed again. This time, Penny picked up.

"Dad?"

"It's your mom," Charlotte said calmly.

"Before you say anything, I didn't mean for this to happen. I thought the Secret Service would keep my page private. I didn't think that anyone other than my friends would see it."

Charlotte resisted the temptation to scold her for blaming the Secret Service. It was something a ten-year-old would say, not a college student.

"Are you ready for the media attention that's about to come your way?"

"What? No. That's not why I did it!"

"Well, you should turn on MSNBC or CNN in a few minutes, because it will be all over the news. You will be the big story today."

"That's not what I wanted."

"Really?"

"No!"

She sounded panicked, and Charlotte was starting to feel sorry for her. She rubbed her forehead and listened to Penny's pathetic excuses as her mind played through all the instances in which she'd ignored her responsibilities to the twins to do one more thing at the office. She felt a hundred years old all of a sudden.

"Listen, Penny, the press will move on to something else by tomorrow so let's not lose perspective."

"I'm really sorry, Mom."

"I am, too, for whatever I did to deserve this."

"It's been building up," Penny confessed.

"Obviously."

They were both quiet for a moment, and it sounded like Penny had started to cry. Charlotte felt herself soften a bit.

"Do me a favor, and stay off Facebook today."

"I will."

Charlotte felt her heart twist into a different shape inside her chest. She desperately wanted to rewind the last ten years and get a do-over with Penny. Charlotte would change everything. She'd be there each day when Penny got home from school to hear about her day. She'd be the mom who drove the carpools so she could listen to Penny and her friends talk. She'd be the mom who took all of the kids skiing or to the beach. She'd be the mom who all the other kids knew they could talk to. She wondered which mom had been there for her daughter when she wasn't. Despite her anger at Penny for taking her hostilities public, she felt a dam break inside her chest.

"Mom?"

"I'm here."

"Don't blame Dad. He asked me not to write anything."

"I know."

"It's not his fault."

"I'm not mad at Dad. I'm still mad at you."

"I'm really sorry," Penny said.

"You're not a little kid anymore. You can't just say sorry and move on."

"What do you want me to do?"

"For starters, a lot of reporters are going to write stories about what you wrote, and they are going to want to talk to you about it. They will find your e-mail address, and they will figure out how to reach you through your friends. Some might even show up at Google or outside your apartment. I'd really appreciate it if you didn't talk to any of them."

"I won't."

"I'm going to have someone from the press office call you in a few minutes. I'd like for you to do exactly what they tell you to do."

As she uttered the words, Charlotte realized that Penny must have suspected that it was possible her post would receive attention from the press. Most likely, it was also why she'd overheard Peter explaining to Penny earlier that morning that Dale's e-mail address was the same as it had been. It made Charlotte wonder: Had Dale had an e-mail relationship with her daughter while she'd been romantically involved with Peter?" The thought had never entered her mind, but upon reflection, it was possible. Charlotte felt nauseated by the thought, but she did her best to sound the perfect combination of disappointed and forgiving as she hung up with Penny. Even though she was already late for her speech, she allowed herself to wallow for an extra moment about the fact that Penny had become so distant. She wondered exactly when and how it had happened.

Charlotte was racked with guilt about the huge chunks of her children's lives that she'd missed. Where had all the years gone? It felt like just yesterday that she'd brought the twins home from the hospital. They'd been so tiny, but even as a newborn, Penny had demanded so much of Charlotte's attention. She would use her teeny fingers to grab onto Charlotte's hand, and she'd cry whenever Charlotte put her down to take care of Harry. Penny did everything before Harry. She walked first. She talked first. She was the first to join in with other kids at the playground. Harry liked to watch his sister. He watched Penelope walk around their small Pacific Heights apartment for weeks before he took his first steps. And he let her do all of his talking for months before he opened his mouth to say "Mama."

Where in God's name had eighteen and a half years gone? Charlotte wondered.

She was already late for her speech at the Women's Museum, but she wanted to make one more call. She dialed Harry's cell phone. He was probably still asleep.

"Hi, sweetie," she said.

"Hi, Mom," he said groggily.

"Can you call your sister today?"

"What did she do?"

"Go online when you wake up."

"OK." He yawned.

"I'm going to be out there in a few weeks. We'll have lots of time to visit, if you can make time for your boring old mom."

"Of course."

"Go back to sleep. I love you."

"You, too."

He was still sweet. He didn't get straight As like his sister, and he didn't do a dozen extracurricular activities like Penny did, but everyone loved him.

Charlotte retouched her lipstick and smoothed her hair with her fingers before she returned to the Oval Office. Peter was sitting on the sofa with Brooke and Mark, and Craig, Dale, and Marguerite were huddled near her desk.

"How'd it go?" Peter asked.

"Fine." She didn't want to rehash the conversation in front of her staff.

"Dale, you can tell the press that Penny and I spoke and everything is fine. We plan to spend some time talking politics when I visit later this month. I also spoke to Harry."

Dale was scribbling furiously in her notepad. "Do you want us to address whether she intended for the post to be made public?" Dale asked.

Charlotte thought for a moment. Penny had said that she intended the post for her friends, but certainly, she must have known that it would get out. "You'd better not," Charlotte said.

"Madam President, would it be all right with you if we touched base with her to make sure that she and her friends know how to send every inquiry from the press to us, no matter where it comes from?" Craig asked.

"Yes. I told her to expect a call from the press office. Peter, maybe you can hold her hand through the process?" Charlotte asked.

"Sure," he said.

"Mr. Kramer, we'll need you to make clear to her that she needs to be highly suspicious of every e-mail, text, and Facebook message she gets today. The press will be relentless in their efforts to engage her. Perhaps Dale can jump on the line for a quick second just to assure her that the press office is here to field all of the calls on this today," Craig suggested.

Peter nodded and looked at Charlotte.

"That's fine," she said.

"Madam President, Marguerite and I will come with you to the speech. We should leave as soon as possible," Craig said.

"I'm ready."

Sam handed Charlotte a fresh copy of her speech, and a Secret Service agent held the door open. Brooke and Mark headed straight to the president's limo, affectionately called the Beast, for its size and weight.

As Charlotte walked toward where her motorcade had been idling for the last forty-five minutes, she resisted the temptation to look over her shoulder at Peter and Dale. She couldn't believe that an eighteen-year-old with an overactive social media habit and a grudge against her mother had managed to screw up the most carefully scripted day on Charlotte's schedule in months *and* reunite her father and his mistress. Charlotte would have laughed if the thought didn't sicken her.

CHAPTER SIXTEEN

Melanie

M elanie was in a deep, dreamless slumber when the sound of a gentle but persistent knocking and a vaguely familiar voice calling her name woke her.

"I'm coming. Give me one second," Melanie mumbled. They'd be landing in Turkey soon. It was difficult to fly straight home without making a stop to either change planes or refuel. She popped a mint into her mouth and wrapped her favorite long sweater coat tightly around her body before cracking the door open.

"Sorry to bother you, ma'am. We'll be taking off for Washington from the other plane in about twenty minutes," her military aide reported.

"Thank you."

That would mean they'd already been on the ground for close to an hour. The C-17 was what she preferred to fly into Iraq, but they'd be making the trip home to Washington on the "Doomsday plane," a flying command center that could refuel in flight if it needed to. She wondered who'd suggested that no one interrupt her while they made the switch. Perhaps she wasn't keeping her pregnancy as secret as she thought.

Melanie brushed her teeth, dabbed concealer under her eyes, and applied lip gloss before tossing her personal items into a large canvas tote bag that her aide would move from her private quarters on the

C-17 to her more comfortable cabin aboard the modified 747. She proceeded out to the air base's lounge, where the press and a few members of her staff were assembled. Most of the reporters had their laptops in front of them, either to file stories or check the latest news. A few of them were chatting on cell phones.

"Did you see the first daughter's f-you to her mother?" Sandy Malkin, the AP reporter who always traveled with them, asked.

"I missed that. What happened?" Melanie reached for an oatmeal cookie from an oversized tray of baked goods.

"I'd send my kids to one of those boot camps in Utah if they pulled this crap," she added.

"I don't think you can send college kids to boot camp. What did she do?"

"She took to Facebook to point out that her mom's pro-choice speech today is the first thing she's ever been proud of and a bunch of other snarky crap about how Kramer has always backed choice but never had the guts to say so," Malkin reported.

Melanie grimaced. "That doesn't sound like Penelope Kramer."

"Do you want to put that on the record?"

"Of course not. I was tied up on calls about the Pentagon budget for the entire flight. I haven't seen any news out of Washington."

"Here it is, if you want to read it."

Sandy moved her laptop in front of Melanie. The Huffington Post had posted the story under the headline "President Takes Incoming Fire from First Daughter." Melanie's heart sank as she read the story. Despite the fact that their relationship had chilled, she and Charlotte had been close enough to talk about nearly everything during the years Melanie had served as Charlotte's chief of staff. Charlotte had often confided that her greatest regret in life was putting a political career into motion that she knew would leave all of the parenting of her then very young children to Peter and the small army of nannies, tutors, and housekeepers they'd employed.

"I knew that I could be in this place if I said yes to running for governor of California. I knew it was possible, Mel," Charlotte had said during one of their late-night talks during the first year of her first term.

It had struck Melanie as supremely confident at the time, but Charlotte hadn't said it in a boastful manner. In fact, it was the first time Charlotte had ever opened up to Melanie about her decision to take the leap from the governor's office to the race for the Republican nomination for president.

"I knew that the national media would focus on our tax reforms and our budget overhaul, and not just because California has the sixth-largest economy in the world but because we were doing it faster and with bipartisan support," she'd said. "And I knew that if I picked my issues carefully and made sure to keep my foot on the gas in terms of rebooting California's economy, I could get away with being more liberal, or, as I liked to say to the press, 'aligned with the party's libertarian wing' on issues like gay marriage and choice."

Melanie had been fascinated by Charlotte's bluntness in discussing her political calculations. It went against everything Melanie had ever heard or read about Charlotte Kramer. Melanie realized that the narrative about how Charlotte had reluctantly agreed to dip her toe into the presidential waters simply for the good of the party, out of a sense of obligation to the party elders who had supported her and permitted her to break barriers, had been carefully manufactured.

"Here was my mistake, Mel. Here's where I was just as arrogant as every other human who thinks he or she can be president: I actually thought that I would be strong enough to take the trips to New Hampshire, Iowa, and Michigan and attend the Gridiron and Alfalfa dinners and revel in all of that adulation without taking the next obvious step. I thought that I could just flirt with the idea of running for president and that I would be the *one* person who could pull back and turn it down to be a better parent than that path allows," she'd said during one of those late-night chats with Melanie more than five years earlier.

Melanie remembered thinking at the time that if she could be a good enough friend, a good enough chief of staff, she could unburden Charlotte from what was obviously a mountain of guilt.

"You know what, Mel?" Charlotte had continued that night. "I was like every other ambitious big-state governor. I fell for the whole thing—the praise from the press and the pundits, the excitement of the crowds, the meaningless polls in the early states. And at that point, the kids had been too little to know what was happening, and if Peter understood what was happening, he didn't let on. He was my biggest supporter in those days, my partner. Can you even imagine that now?"

"Excuse me, Madam Secretary, are you done reading?" Sandy Malkin snapped Melanie out of her nostalgia. The AP reporter looked desperate to get her laptop back from Melanie before they had to board the plane for Washington.

"I was just thinking back to when the president's twins were younger. They grew up so fast."

"It happens. Listen, if you decide to comment, you know, as the former White House chief of staff or something, you'll come back on the plane, right?"

"Don't hold your breath. I'm out of the Kramer family psychoanalyst business."

Melanie boarded the bigger plane and settled into her cabin. She picked up the phone and asked to be connected to her personal assistant at the Pentagon, Annie. Annie had been with her since her days as White House chief of staff.

"Hi, Annie."

"You saw the news about Penny?"

"Sandy Malkin just showed it to me. Is the press making a big deal out of it?"

"It has knocked all the abortion protests off the air."

"Can you see if you can get the president on the phone for me?"

"Sure. Hang on. Do you want me to tell her it's urgent?"

"No, it's not urgent. But I don't want my call returned by the chief of staff or the national security advisor. Just tell Sam that I called to check in about Penelope. Actually, don't say that. Just tell Sam I called about a personal matter. Not personal related to me, just personal. No, not personal. You know what? Just tell Sam I called, and the president can call me back anytime if she's busy right now."

"Yes, ma'am."

While she held for the president, Melanie returned to her memories of the conversations she used to have with Charlotte late at night in the residence. She remembered one night when Charlotte spoke about the move from the governor's mansion in Sacramento to the White House.

"I was such an idiot, Mel. I thought that we could turn the move to Washington into an exciting new chapter for our family. Of course, that idea was squashed once we decided to send the kids to boarding school in Connecticut. God, the house was so empty. Peter missed them so much, and I was never around, and it was all so devastatingly quiet. Peter blamed me for dismantling the family he'd always wanted. And after that, the whole thing fell apart. Peter did what he had to do to survive. I really believe that. I think he almost died of loneliness."

Melanie shivered at the memory of Charlotte's pain and realized that soon she'd have a family of her own that could inflict that much pain on her.

"Melanie, are you still there?"

"I'm here."

"Sam said that the president is en route to her speech at the Women's Museum, but she'll have her call you as soon as she's back."

"Thanks, Annie. Please be sure to tell Sam that it's nothing important."

CHAPTER SEVENTEEN

Dale

As Dale watched Craig, Marguerite, Brooke, and Mark follow the president out the door of the Oval Office and into the motorcade, she had the unnerving feeling that Peter could read her mind. Despite the fact that she had spent almost two years trying to get over him, she was certain that she could slip back into love with him in sixty seconds if he offered the slightest hint that he still had feelings for her. She closed her eyes briefly and reminded herself that she was in a relationship with a wonderful, available man who adored her. When she opened her eyes, Peter was staring back at her without any of the intensity or lust that Dale was feeling. In fact, he was looking at her with an ambivalence that suggested either that he'd forgotten the most passionate moments of their affair—the ones Dale replayed in her mind over and over again—or that he was so completely in love with his wife again that he regarded his relationship with Dale as one that had helped him pass the time while he and Charlotte sorted through their complicated union. Either way, it was clear that he wasn't eager to relive any of it. Dale, on the other hand, had spent hours upon hours during the first lonely months after their breakup committing to memory every detail of their romance. The one thing she'd never been able to recall was their last kiss. Dale couldn't remember where or when it took place and whether she'd had any idea that it would be the last time they were that close. Now, with only a touch of self-awareness about the lunacy of her thought process, she wondered whether he might kiss her right there in the Oval Office.

"Do you want to do this in here or in the private dining room?"

Peter's voice jolted Dale from her deranged fantasy. "What?"

"Would you prefer to talk in here, or would you rather go into Charlotte's private dining room?"

Peter was standing as far away from her as was physically possible inside the Oval Office. He was probably appalled that he had to spend any time with her at all.

What is wrong with you? Dale asked herself.

She told herself that *nothing* was going to happen between them. He was with his wife now, and his wife was Dale's boss.

Her boyfriend was one of the most sought-after bachelors in Washington, and for reasons she didn't entirely grasp, he wanted her.

Most important, it was Dale's job to help the first family through their first major political crisis involving one of their children.

As soon as the assignment to stay behind and work with Peter had escaped Craig's lips, he had looked as though he wanted to take it back. The president's face betrayed nothing, but her best friends, Brooke and Mark, had nearly gasped.

She hadn't been alone in a room with him since the day they'd broken up at his home in Pacific Heights almost two years earlier. She remembered the day the way people often describe their memories of a car crash. The frostiness that she'd created between them by complaining all morning about the lack of cell-phone coverage had turned what was supposed to be a romantic weekend reunion into a tense standoff. She'd been working for the vice president at the time, and she was under constant pressure from the West Wing and from the vice president's husband to shield the vice president from mounting scrutiny from the press. Peter had picked her up from the airport and taken her for a hike at Stinson Beach, one of her favorite places. After their hike, he'd surprised her by taking her to a beach house he'd purchased and renovated as a retreat for their rare weekends together in California. Dale had reacted like a spoiled two-year-old. She'd complained about him putting too much pressure on their relationship by buying a home without discussing it with her first. Her reaction had caused the fraying ties between them to come undone once and for all. In an instant, the most passionate love affair of her life came to a crushing end. They spoke a few times afterward, but she'd hurt him too deeply for him ever to reconsider any of her efforts at reconciliation. Less than a year after his breakup with Dale, Peter and Charlotte had reunited. Peter moved back into the White House to give his marriage to Charlotte another try.

Dale knew from the newspapers and from the East Wing staff members, who gossiped to the point of near treason, that he still divided his time between his office in California and Washington, but Dale was surprised that she had never run into him at the White House. Now Dale was doing everything in her power to focus on the task at hand when she desperately wanted to know if he'd struggled as much as she had to move on and if he ever thought about her or missed her.

"Dale?"

"I'm sorry. I was trying to figure out how long we had until someone had to go on the record, but I just realized that the president will be the first to comment when she does the CBS interview before her speech."

"Does that mean that we have more time or less time?"

"It means that I need to make sure I get her exact language from Marguerite before my daily briefing with the press. And, between us, we have very little time, though we'll make Penny feel like we have all the time in the world."

"Thanks. I appreciate that. I know that Charlotte will, too."

Peter looked so distraught Dale wanted to hug him. She didn't dare.

"You don't have to thank me," Dale said softly.

For the first time that morning, he smiled at her. And it was that crinkly-eyed smile that had sparked the most intense love affair of her life the very first time she'd seen it five and a half years earlier.

God, she wanted to touch his face so badly.

"So, what's the plan, Madam Press Secretary?"

"We'll need to make sure Penny knows how to redirect all the press inquiries. The phone calls are easy, but a lot of reporters will try to reach her on social media. She's interning at Google, right?"

"Yes."

"We need to contact the press office at Google to see if we can help them with a statement that says that this is a family matter."

Peter nodded in agreement as they sat down across from each other. Peter was facing the flat-screen TVs on the wall.

"Let me know when the president starts speaking. I'm supposed to allow the CBS crew to film me watching her deliver the speech so they can capture my reaction—as though I don't know what's in the speech."

Peter raised an eyebrow. "That sounds like pretty complicated stagecraft."

"Too complicated. I don't know why I thought it was a good idea to invite two dozen film crews inside this place for twenty-four hours," Dale complained.

"It's a great idea. Charlotte was excited about it. I'm sorry Penny messed it up."

"The president was excited? If that's the case, and I'm skeptical that it is, then I'm even more sorry that she has to deal with this today."

"If there's one thing Charlotte is accustomed to, it is living her life under the white-hot glare of the media spotlight."

"Speaking of the white-hot glare, how do you think she would feel about us sending someone from the press office out to Menlo Park? We would have them out there by this evening, and they could tag along with Penny's Secret Service agents to intercept any reporters who try to ambush Penny or her friends or anyone from her internship program. They'd also be there in case Penny has any questions about how we're handling inquiries about her post."

"If you can spare someone, Charlotte will be fine with it. I will make sure Penny is on board."

"Of course, I can spare someone. I'd send Marguerite if we weren't stuck with the CBS crews," Dale replied.

"What else?"

Dale laid out a plan to spin Penny's Facebook post and Charlotte's reaction to it as a "teachable moment." It was a cliché, but it represented the best option for the circumstances. The White House would suggest that parents remember to engage their kids in conversations about the debates that dominate the news headlines and seek out their opinions about big decisions they have to make in the workplace. Dale took a few more notes and then looked up at Peter.

"Did we forget anything?" he asked.

"I don't think so. I'll get Monica from my office on a flight right away. It's a good possibility that the nets and cables will send their West Coast correspondents to do live shots from outside her apartment or at Google. They may just have their White House correspondents do the story from here, but some of them might want to report from out there."

"I'd rather the world not see where Penny lives."

"Me, too. I'm just warning you that it's possible that some of them will stake her out."

"Incredible that they'd do that. She's a kid."

"Peter, can I ask you something?"

His eyes looked slightly wary, but his face remained relaxed. "Sure."

"How are you doing? Is everything going well? Are you happy? Because I really, really hope that you're happy—that you're always happy. That's something I always want to know that you have. Happiness."

Why, of all days, was today the day that she'd lost the ability to speak in sentences?

She smiled awkwardly. Peter's head tilted to the side while she was speaking, but when she stopped rambling, he looked at her with his crinkly-eyed smile again.

"We're doing great. How are you doing? How's that young boyfriend of yours? Charlotte says he's a tremendous guy. I'm really pleased for you."

"Yeah, he's a great guy. He's probably too good for me, but everything is good. It's really good. I'm great. We're great. It's good that you're so good, too, of course."

It was like she was speaking in Pig Latin. Dale found herself wishing for an urgent press call or, better yet, seven thousand urgent press calls that would distract her for the next ten years so she wouldn't have to relive the day she was having. Peter was so over her that he actually seemed happy for her and Warren.

"Thanks for your help with Penny," he repeated.

"Peter, look, before you go, I want to say something, and I don't want you to take it the wrong way," Dale said carefully. She'd badly botched every attempt she'd made in the last fifteen minutes to create some moment in which they connected. While she didn't want to jam her foot into her mouth again, she was sure she could still make him see that she understood him and cared about him.

"Shoot."

"I know how close you and Penny are. The thing I always admired most about you was that she came first. Think about it; she has grown up knowing that she was—and is—your top priority. For a kid, that's got to be everything you ever want and need in life. And I know it means a lot to you, too, to be there for her. What I wanted to say before you leave was that I hope you know that what she did today isn't your fault."

Dale saw the flash of pain cross his face. She held her breath and willed herself not to reach out and touch him while he looked at her with his beautiful blue eyes that were sadder and more lined than she remembered them. She sat across from him, suspended in time by the look on his face.

And then, as quickly as his face had seemed to register her words as an opening to talk to her, it closed back up. He regarded her with a look that Dale recognized as his polite face. His cell phone rang, and he stood to take the call.

Dale knew that whatever opportunity she had had to break through to Peter had passed. She gathered her papers and waved good-bye with a whispered promise to be in touch with regular updates about Penny-related press coverage.

Clare greeted her as soon as she walked back into her office.

"Coffee?" she asked.

"No more coffee. Maybe a bottle of water?"

"Right there." Clare pointed at the side of Dale's desk, where three unopened bottles of water were lined up.

"And there are cold ones in the fridge," Clare added.

"Thanks, Clare. Has the president started speaking yet?"

"Not yet."

"How late are we?"

"About forty-five minutes. Listen, I need to send the CBS crew in to film you watching the coverage of Charlotte's speech, which is going to start any minute. They said you promised them they could be in here all day."

"Give me five minutes."

"Two," Clare offered.

"Three."

"They will be in here in three minutes or as soon as the president starts talking, whichever comes first. They are really mad. They keep reminding me that you are in violation of the ground rules that you negotiated with them, which was round-the-clock, unfettered access."

"Fine. But it's ridiculous that they're angry. Sometimes things come up that require privacy."

Clare shrugged, and Dale knew she was thinking that she wasn't the one who'd made the deal with the network, but she needed to direct her frustrations at someone.

Dale sat down and started typing an e-mail to Peter. She wanted to apologize for being tongue-tied and awkward and thank him for being so normal. She also wanted to tell him, once again, how happy she was that he was happy. Her iPhone vibrated on her desk.

Dale looked down and saw Warren's office number. She hit ignore and looked down at the e-mail message she'd started drafting to Peter. Then it hit her. She was acting like one of those delusional women she always rooted against in chick flicks. She deleted the message to Peter from her compose window and stood up. She looked out the window at the cameramen outside the door to the briefing room. They were smoking and laughing about something. Dale wished she could escape the confines of her office and sit outside in the morning sun. She picked up her phone to return Warren's call, but before he picked up, Clare barged in with the camera crew in tow, and Dale hung up.

CHAPTER EIGHTEEN

Charlotte

As they rolled through downtown D.C. in the giant armored limo, Charlotte tried to pinpoint the exact moment she'd started treating Penny like another disenchanted stakeholder. Whatever mothering instincts she'd once possessed had been replaced along the way by her desire to neutralize and contain Penny's hostility. She couldn't remember the last time she'd tried talking to her about anything other than the logistics of her life.

"Riding in this thing is like being trapped in a rolling meat locker. Aren't you two freezing?" Brooke complained.

"It keeps the mind sharp, darling. Maybe we should lower the temperature in our house to keep *your* head clear, like Char's." Mark snapped his fingers in front of Brooke's face while she swatted him away.

"How badly do you think I've screwed Penny up?" Charlotte asked her friends.

"Oh, Christ, everyone ends up in therapy, Char. If Mother Teresa had kids, even they would be screwed up in this day and age. It's the goddamned Internet. These kids can't do anything without everyone in the world seeing it. Can you imagine if things like Twitter and Instagram had been around when we were in college? Oh, my God. They'd never allow little Brookie here into the White House complex."

Brooke gave Mark a dirty look and rubbed her goose-bump-covered arms.

"You weren't exactly running a 'Just say no' campaign from deep inside that pot den disguised as a fraternity," she jabbed.

"Ignore her. She's extra-nasty when she's cleansing," he explained.

The limo stopped in front of the Women's Museum. Brooke and Mark were ushered to their seats in the front row, while Charlotte waited for Monty, her lead advance man, to brief her. She could live for weeks without ever seeing most of her policy advisors, but she was fairly certain she couldn't get through an afternoon without Monty's skilled, near-invisible hand guiding her smoothly through every official interaction and event. It fell to Monty to remind her of the names of foreign dignitaries, small-state governors, and big-state congresspeople. He always remembered to bring the gift, the coat, the umbrella, or anything else that Charlotte might request. And while he had an answer to almost every question she posed, he never tried to spin her or make a situation appear more appealing than it actually was.

She liked that Monty had managed to hang on to some of his pre-Washington identity. Monty was a former professional surfer from Santa Cruz, and while he'd adopted the D.C. uniform of blue suit, white dress shirt, Vineyard Vines tie, and loafers, he'd refused to trim his wavy blond hair. He wore it in a neat ponytail at the base of his neck. Monty had a dry sense of humor and never made idle chitchat. Charlotte had thought, on more than one occasion, that if Peter were able to read her moods half as well as Monty could, their relationship would be on firmer ground.

Once Brooke and Mark were out of the car, Monty nodded at the Secret Service agent holding Charlotte's door shut. The door opened, and Monty kneeled down so he was at eye level with her.

"CBS is probably filming us now, so as soon as you get out of the car, you're going to head toward Lucy and Richard and greet them. They'll be rolling on that. Then you go straight into the walk-and-talk, which starts where they're standing right now and ends backstage."

He pointed down at a map of the venue and ran his finger along the route she'd walk with the reporters.

"Richard and Lucy will break away after the interview and watch the speech from backstage, and then you'll do a longer, sit-down interview with them afterward."

"Don't they need to mic me?" Charlotte asked.

"No, we're too late. They agreed to do it with a boom, so everything you say as soon as you get out of the car will be picked up."

"How long do we have for this?"

"Five minutes, but we've kept them waiting, so we will let them go a couple minutes longer if you are in mid-sentence. They've agreed to keep it short."

Marguerite had appeared while Monty was talking to Charlotte.

"How are we doing, Marguerite?" Charlotte asked.

"They're going to ask you one question about Penny and then turn to the speech and all the controversy surrounding it."

Charlotte nodded and got out of the car.

Lucy greeted Charlotte with a smile that was oozing with phony sympathy, and Richard put his arm around her like she was a wounded bird. Charlotte was instantly annoyed. All of the good feelings she'd had about them earlier in the day evaporated.

"You've had a busy morning," Lucy said.

Mindful of the cameras, Charlotte smiled politely. "Never a dull moment."

"I need to ask you about Penny and her Facebook comments, but I can do it after the speech."

"Let's get it out of the way. I just spoke to her."

"How was that?"

"Being the commander in chief is just a title, and not one that holds much weight inside your family. In the Kramer family, I'm obviously just the mother of two college freshmen." Charlotte smiled.

"It must have slayed you to see her take to Facebook instead of picking up the phone and calling you."

"A call would have been better," Charlotte admitted.

"But at least we all know how proud of you she is," Lucy said, winking.

Charlotte thought it was a cheap shot, but she fought the urge to cut off the interview.

"Did you punish her in any way?"

"I didn't, Lucy. Your kids are still in diapers, so I wouldn't expect you to understand, but at some point, you just hope that your children learn from their mistakes."

"So, in your view, obviously, Penny made a big mistake, but prochoice activists are saying she's brave beyond her years."

"Maybe they'll pay the rest of her tuition at Stanford," Charlotte said with a tight smile.

Charlotte was feeling ambushed by the interview. She saw Marguerite make a *wrap it up* sign with her fingers while she maintained a stoic gaze at Lucy. The reporters pretended that they didn't see Marguerite.

"All right, Madam President. I know you're already late. What can you tell us about the speech you're about to deliver? Is the political price you're paying worth the relief of finally sharing your true thoughts about reproductive rights with the public? And do you think your side can really advance a prochoice agenda if politicians wait until they don't face any further elections before they speak out on this issue?"

It had been a long time since Charlotte had been asked so many questions in a row that she found offensive, but Lucy had managed to press her buttons in a way no one had for as long as she remembered. Lucy had essentially called her a fraud. Charlotte turned to Richard, who was standing silently next to Lucy.

He shrugged his shoulders as if to say, *Don't look at me; I can't control her, either.*

"Lucy, I'm looking forward to listening to the women who have come here today. Many of them are working hard to make sure that women and girls at all income levels have access to quality health care. As to the question about any political price I might pay, let me assure you that at this point in my presidency, I don't give a damn about the political price to be paid for anything my administration does, as long as we're all doing what we believe to be in the best interest of the American people. As far as your other question about waiting until I didn't face any other elections, I think that if you look back at my record, you'll see that I typically did the most politically difficult thing, not the politically beneficial one, so I resent your suggestion. But I thank you for this opportunity to speak to you. To be continued. I need to get into the reception now."

Monty appeared by her side the moment Charlotte turned away from Lucy.

Charlotte was steaming.

"We're going to head into the hold for about two minutes of down time, and then you have photos and brief off-the-cuff remarks at the VIP reception," Monty said.

Charlotte nodded and followed him into a small office that had obviously been commandeered from someone on the museum staff.

"Where's Marguerite?" Charlotte demanded.

"She stayed behind to talk to Lucy."

"Ask her to come in here right now."

Monty covered his mouth and spoke into his sleeve. Seconds later, Marguerite appeared.

"What the hell was that? I sure as hell don't plan to do another interview with them after the speech now."

"I understand, Madam President."

"I don't know why I agreed to do this. Call Dale, and tell her she's going to have to come up with something else, because I am not sitting down with them after the speech."

"Yes, ma'am."

While Charlotte was venting, Craig had entered the room. He was still talking on his cell phone when Charlotte turned from Marguerite and glared at him.

"Are we keeping you from something?" she snapped.

"Sorry about that, Madam President. I heard the interview was nasty. And short." He slid his phone into his pocket.

"I told Marguerite to cancel the next one."

"Let's discuss it after the speech," he soothed.

"There's nothing to talk about."

Monty handed her a cup of coffee and a bottle of water. As Charlotte reached for the coffee, she noticed that Craig gave Marguerite a knowing look. Charlotte felt handled.

"I saw that. For the record, I'm not simply venting. I'm dead serious. I am not talking to them after the speech. Period. Let the geniuses in the press office come up with someone else for Lucy and Richard to harass. Maybe the vice president can take them to spin class, where they will inadvertently spin themselves into cardiac arrest."

Charlotte saw Monty's face break into a smile.

"Monty, is there something you'd like to say?" she asked.

"No, ma'am."

"No? At least share with us what it is that you find funny."

"I was trying to figure out if Richard would die faster from the spinning or from being henpecked to death by Lucy during the class. I can picture her yelling at him the whole time to spin faster and faster until his heart simply quits from the stress of it all."

"You are one dark dude," Craig remarked.

Charlotte turned away from all of them and pretended to study a painting on the wall so no one would see her smile.

"Thank you for that, Monty. I will bring that image with me as I head into the most important speech of my presidency. It's all on you if I screw it up," Charlotte said, with her back still to the group.

"Yes, ma'am."

A few minutes later, Monty led her into the VIP reception. After a quick hello to the museum director, Charlotte was positioned at the head of the photo line, where she'd pose for one hundred photos in about fifteen minutes. She was dreading it. Before she greeted the first VIP, Monty pulled out an official-looking briefing paper to show her the diagram of the stage one last time. She peered over to look and heard him whisper, "Faster, Richard, spin faster, God damn it," under his breath in his best impersonation of Lucy. Charlotte greeted the president of Planned Parenthood with a huge grin.

CHAPTER NINETEEN

Melanie

H i, honey, are you busy?" Melanie asked.

"I'm just waiting for Charlotte's speech to start," Brian replied.

"Where are you?"

"I'm standing on the press riser at the Women's Museum. Don't you follow me on Twitter?"

"You know the answer to that."

"I do."

"You're not covering the Penny stuff, are you?"

"Of course I'm covering it. Not with any vitriol or schadenfreude, like some of my esteemed colleagues, but I have to cover it."

"Her relationship with Penny is tortured."

"You're talking to me as my wife right now, not the former White House chief of staff?"

"Of course."

"Anything you want me to include as the White House correspondent for NBC News, you know, the job that pays our mortgage?"

"Why does everyone keep asking me that?"

"I'll let you figure it out for yourself." He laughed.

"Thanks."

"Listen, I just got a two-minute warning from the press advance folks. How are you feeling?"

"Fat, tired, starving, and nauseated. Aren't you glad you asked?"

"I will see you tonight when you get home."

"Go easy on her today."

"Who?"

"Charlotte."

"I will pretend that I didn't hear that."

"Call me back when you're done. I'll be in the air for a while."

Melanie hung up with Brian and tried to think of someone else she could call for a read on how the Penny news was playing. She considered calling Dale to offer her assistance with the White House response. She knew exactly how Charlotte would want this handled. If she hadn't screamed at Dale earlier in the day over the "Day in the Life" filming, it would be easier to weigh in. Instead, Melanie asked the operator to place a call to Warren. Melanie could register her suggestions with him and be sure that they'd make their way to Dale and the president.

"Hello there, Madam Secretary. What a pleasant surprise. How was your trip?"

"We're making some progress with the military but I'm afraid that the police are being infiltrated by thugs—same old struggles."

"I understand exactly what you're saying, and I want to hear about it this weekend. We're having dinner together at your place on Saturday."

"With you and Dale?"

"That's the plan."

"I can't wait."

"Is that sarcasm I detect in your voice, Madam Secretary?"

"Not even a touch of sarcasm. We haven't seen you in weeks. What the hell do you and Dale do with yourselves? Actually, I don't want to know the answer to that. Listen, I need a favor. Have you talked to Charlotte?"

"Not since yesterday, when we went over the polling on her speech."

"You did polling on her speech?"

"We do polling on all of her major speeches."

"I forgot that."

"If it makes you feel any better, I do the polling after the speech text has gone final. We find out what language resonates and all that stuff. God, Mel, you make me feel so dirty about it!"

"I didn't mean to do that. Can you please make sure that Dale knows not to try to brush Penny's post under the rug with any sort of shrug of the shoulders or glib comment like 'Teenagers will be teenagers.' That would drive Charlotte crazy. She'd want Penny to be treated like an adult. She doesn't care about how it looks to anyone but Penny, so tell the press folks not to do any apologizing for Penny's behavior. Besides, I'm sure that Penny knew exactly what she was doing."

"You're right, of course. Look, I think this is a good moment for the president. Most people I know with kids in college feel like human ATMs. This show of disrespect from her eighteen-year-old daughter is something that will rally everyone with kids to her side, especially if she is able to reveal some of her angst over being a working mother."

"That's always been something that she talks about in private but not in public," Melanie said.

"It would be great if she could do some hand-wringing in full view of the public, but you are probably the only person who could have persuaded her to do that."

"Not anymore," Melanie reminded him.

"You'd be surprised. She still talks about the advice you used to give her about letting people see enough of her to empathize with her even when they don't agree with her."

"She does?"

"All the time. I can't believe Charlotte let you go to DOD."

"She'd tap me to be ambassador to Siberia at this point, but for the time being, I'm staying put."

"How long until you have to stop traveling?"

Warren was one of five people, including their doctors, who knew she was pregnant. Brian had told him. At first, Melanie was upset that he'd shared the news, but she realized that he'd needed someone to talk to about everything they'd been through.

"I don't have any idea. I guess a couple more months, right?"

"I think they let you travel up to six months these days."

"Good to know. I hear Dale is going to meet the parents tonight. Good luck with that."

"Thanks. You don't like her very much, do you?"

"Warren, I love that she makes you happy, and I think she does a nice job from the podium for Charlotte. I just think she's one of those women who are never happy with what they have or who they are with."

"I hear you, Mel. I worry about that, too."

"Brian would kill me for saying this, but I don't see her wanting the same things you want in life. Women like Dale don't have a biological clock or an internal compass that points them toward a settled life with a home and a husband and kids."

"Mel, you're probably right, as usual, but I have to play it out. I'm crazy about her."

"I know. I'm sorry to be such a downer. I'm probably wrong. Listen, your parents are going to love her."

"I think so, too, but you know how easily Dale spooks. I hope she doesn't think an engagement ring is imminent or anything. That would totally freak her out."

"Yes, a diamond ring from a handsome, smart, interesting guy with fabulous friends and a steady job. That's every girl's nightmare."

Warren laughed. "Have a safe flight home, Mel. You're spot-on about the White House response. I'll track Dale down as soon as we hang up."

Warren was the only person Melanie knew who appreciated her intimate history with Charlotte's "interior landscape," as they jokingly called it when they were trying to game out how a particular intra-Cabinet debate or power struggle would unfold. Warren hadn't been on the scene as an advisor to Charlotte yet, but he'd listened patiently one night when he'd been over for dinner to Melanie's stories of being wooed by Charlotte six and a half years earlier, when she was the president-elect and Melanie was one of the most well-respected White House press secretaries in modern presidential history.

"I told her no way, no how, when she first asked me to stay on," Melanie had recounted. At the time, Melanie had been the seasoned

Washington insider who'd served two presidents and had her pick of plum post–West Wing job opportunities. There were lucrative paid speeches to be given, invitations to appear on network television shows as a White House expert, and offers from investment banks, defense contractors, and the former presidents she'd served. But she'd been intrigued by the notion of serving as the first female White House chief of staff. While it was well known that the country had never elected a female president, it was a matter of slightly more consternation to Melanie and a small circle of high-powered women in Washington that no president had ever selected a woman to serve as his chief of staff. That was the case until Charlotte had asked Melanie to take the job and Melanie had accepted.

Now Warren was the only person who sought out Melanie's judgment on sensitive political and policy issues. Warren looked out for her and made sure she was never blindsided by anything coming out of the West Wing, particularly when it pertained to national security. But going from Charlotte's closest ally and most trusted counsel to a Cabinet official with waning influence was more than a blow to Melanie's self-esteem. It had forced her to examine all of her own motives for serving in the government. She was forced to confront her own ego and the blows it had suffered when she was cut out of the tight circle around the president. This, in turn, forced her and Brian to have a more practical discussion about whether she could even carry out her responsibilities as the secretary of defense. Ultimately, they'd read Charlotte's public statements of admiration for Melanie's commitment to the troops and the Pentagon as a strong enough show of support for her to stay in the post, but Melanie privately hoped that some sort of reconciliation with the president was in the cards in the very near future. It was something she planned to discuss with Warren the next time she saw him alone.

CHAPTER TWENTY

Dale

The vice president had the crowd whipped into a frenzy. The veep was hitting every applause line and ad-libbing in all the right places. The vice president had also added a very funny joke about her and the president that would get picked up everywhere. Dale was smiling for the cameras in her office, and it wasn't staged. She felt her phone vibrate. She'd missed the last call from Warren, so this time, she picked it up.

"Are you watching?" she asked.

"Dale?" It was Peter.

"I thought you were someone else. Hang on."

She covered the phone with her hand.

"Sorry, guys, can you excuse me?"

"We were supposed to be allowed to shadow you all day, Dale. We won't put every call you get on TV."

She was getting tired of being reminded that it was part of the agreement *she'd* made with the network to allow the cameras to be stationed in her office all day. She sighed and walked out of her office and into the hallway.

"Did something happen with Penny?" she whispered.

"That's not why I'm calling."

"Oh?"

"You were obviously uncomfortable in the Oval Office, and I'm sorry that I didn't do anything to make you feel more at ease. I was pretty damn uncomfortable myself."

"You were?"

"I don't know if *uncomfortable* is the right word."

Dale didn't say anything. She heard Peter sigh the way he did when he was choosing his words carefully.

"I think it's easier this way," he said.

"What way?"

"Not having any contact. Leaving you and Charlotte to have a professional relationship that has nothing to do with me."

"Is that what you want?"

Peter sighed again. "It's not exactly like the two of us could meet in Georgetown for lunch, Dale."

Dale didn't disagree. The only way they'd all been able to settle into what was once an unthinkable scenario—the president's husband's former mistress serving on the White House senior staff—was that they'd all erected firewalls around their past entanglements. Everyone, including the president, had become a master at projecting an air of amnesia when it came to everything that had transpired. What few people outside of the three of them would ever know was that it had been Charlotte who had done the unthinkable. She'd treated Dale with extraordinary kindness. She'd offered her a prized interview at a time when Dale had been on the ropes professionally at the network. Charlotte had always kept her disagreements and disappointments with Peter separate from her dealings with Dale. It suggested to Dale that Charlotte was very much in control of the relationship with Peter.

Dale realized that neither one of them had spoken for nearly a minute. "Peter?"

"She asked about you this morning."

"Charlotte?"

"Penny."

"Why?"

"I called her very early this morning at Charlotte's behest to ask her not to do anything outrageous today, and she asked me for your e-mail address. I didn't know yet what she'd written on Facebook when I spoke to her, but it all makes sense now."

"Peter, I can tell that you're beating yourself up over this. I meant it when I said that it was not your fault."

"Listen, Dale, I can't see you or talk to you or be around you, because I can't keep moving forward with Charlotte if I have any reminders of the past—of our past. Can you understand that?"

"Of course." She wanted to tell him that she had never stopped loving him.

"I really am glad that you're happy. Charlotte would definitely say that you've made an upgrade with Warren."

Dale forced herself to laugh, but she wanted desperately to seize this window to tell him how much she still wanted him. "You set the bar very high."

"Don't expect me to toast you at the wedding. I'll leave that to Charlotte."

The thought of getting married to Warren in front of Peter made her insides ache. Of course, if they ever were to get married, Charlotte would probably attend.

"I don't know if things between Warren and me are heading in that direction."

"Really? Well, that's too bad for Warren, if that's the case."

Oh, God. This was starting to feel like a nightmare. "Peter, do you ever wonder what would have happened if things hadn't fallen apart in Stinson that weekend?" she asked.

He was quiet. "I try not to."

"I can't *not* think about it. I think about it all the time. I was such an idiot."

"It's not worth rehashing."

"But it is. Can I see you for five minutes? I want to explain and apologize, properly. Can I do that?"

Peter didn't say anything, but she knew he was still on the line.

"Peter?"

"I don't think it's a good idea."

"I will take five minutes of your time. Please. I will leave you alone forever after this."

"It's a busy day."

"Five minutes."

"OK."

"When?"

"Now. Family theater."

"I'm on my way."

CHAPTER TWENTY-ONE

Charlotte

Charlotte stood on the side of the stage during Maureen's lengthy introduction and laughed at her quips while silently willing her to wrap it up. When Maureen finally started to wind down, she moved closer to the microphone and spoke so loudly that Charlotte had to resist the urge to cover her ears.

"I give to all of you my boss, the best Republican friend of a woman's right to choose that any of us will ever know, President Charlotte Kramer."

Charlotte cringed inwardly while the vice president led a lengthy standing ovation for her. Once everyone stopped clapping and sat down, Charlotte started speaking quietly and without looking at the text in front of her or at either of the teleprompter panels.

"I am one of three women in my family, and what I'm about to tell you is something that I was not aware of until I was an adult. My sisters are beautiful and talented. They have always been creative and successful in ways that I could never compete with. But they haven't always had jobs that provided health care. My older sister is a writer. Until she was thirty-three, the only medical attention she received came from doctors and nurses and counselors at the Planned Parenthood Clinic in her Berkeley, California, neighborhood. My younger sister is a musician, and she, too, turned to Planned Parenthood for all of her health-care needs until she got married at the age of thirty-one and was able to join her husband's health insurance policy. When she was twenty-nine, she had an abnormal result from one of her routine exams. That test led to others that led to a diagnosis of precancerous conditions in her uterus. She had a lifesaving surgery, and she is cancer-free. If she hadn't been able to turn to Planned Parenthood, her story might have ended differently. We are here to discuss issues far broader than Planned Parenthood, but at its core, both of my sisters taught me that the debates in Washington, particularly around women's health, are so far detached from women's lives that they barely make sense to people living outside the ideological combat zone.

"I know that the following two things are true. Men and women who are committed to advancing a culture of life are good, decent, and honorable, and they deserve our respect.

"And this is also true: men and women who champion reproductive freedoms also value life, but they believe that the freedom to make decisions about a pregnancy should rest with a woman, her partner, and her doctor—not with politicians in Washington, D.C., or any state legislature."

The crowd rose in thunderous applause. Charlotte waited for it to end before she glanced down at her speech text and continued.

"This disagreement has gone on for decades, and it will continue after all of us have left the political arena. My wish for you is that you speak from your hearts and fight for your sisters and mothers and daughters. Remember that the debate is waged from the hearts of not just those who champion choice, but from the hearts of those who champion a culture of life."

Charlotte had really hit her groove. She wondered why she hadn't delivered this speech years ago. This was the kind of president she had wanted to be. Penny was right. She really wasn't worthy of her children being proud of her for much of her first term. But everything was different now. She had things mostly squared away at home; her new vice president was opinionated and demanding, but at least she knew how to govern; and as Lucy had just pointed out, Charlotte would never face election again, so she was finally free to speak her mind.

She was so caught up in the crowd's enthusiastic response that she didn't notice Craig and Monty huddled on the side of the stage. She didn't see Craig scribble something on a piece of paper and fold it in half. And she didn't notice when Monty approached the podium with the folded piece of paper in his hand.

CHAPTER TWENTY-TWO

Melanie

I understand someone back here is celebrating a birthday," Melanie said.

She walked toward the back of the press cabin on her plane, carrying a small chocolate cake to Sandy's seat. A dozen candles were quickly melting on top of it.

"Sandy, you'd better blow out those candles before we have to crash-land the plane," one of the other reporters teased.

Sandy looked pleased. She blew out the candles and sat through an off-key rendition of "Happy Birthday." Melanie couldn't think of a trip she'd taken as secretary of defense that Sandy hadn't covered. They made a practice of celebrating birthdays on the plane, one of the many ways Melanie had set out to tame the Pentagon press corps.

During more than a decade of service at the White House, Melanie had always appreciated the White House press corps, and she counted a few of them as good friends. But the Pentagon press corps was made up of an entirely different breed. While White House reporters were often on their way up the ladder to be network anchors or cable news hosts, the Pentagon reporters would rather die than trade in their flak jackets and satellite phones for a news-reading gig.

This was something that Melanie knew all too well. She'd met Brian while he was transitioning from covering the wars in Iraq and Afghanistan to a job stateside. He'd been given the White House beat on a temporary basis, and he'd hated it. He and Melanie had begun to date during this period—a situation that presented both of them with more conflicts of interest than anyone could enumerate. She'd ultimately quit as White House chief of staff. Four years in the job was enough to burn anyone out. But Melanie had also had Brian's career in mind when she'd done so. Fortunately for both of them, she'd returned to government as the secretary of defense, allowing his bosses to promote him to the permanent White House correspondent position, which he ultimately made peace with. He still complained about the beat and worried that he was simply "drinking the sand," as he liked to say—a reference to his favorite scene in *The American President*. They'd watched the movie together one night, and he'd stopped the "drink the sand" scene and played it for Melanie a second time after announcing, "This is what you do, right? You make people drink the sand?"

Melanie had nodded and laughed until she watched it a second time. It had led to one of their first fights.

In the scene, Michael J. Fox's character, an idealistic political staffer, was urging the president to get into the ring and defend himself against character attacks. Fox's character, Lewis, explained: "People want leadership. They are so thirsty for it they will crawl through the desert toward a mirage, and when they discover there's no water, they'll drink the sand."

It had set Melanie off that night. She'd stood up and started gathering her things. "You know what? You're an asshole," she'd said to Brian.

"What?"

"And you should insist that they don't ram the White House beat down your throat. You should demand that they send you back to Iraq, where you can do real journalism," she'd added angrily.

"Are you seriously mad at me because I like this movie? It's from 1995, and it's just a corny movie about a president who falls in love with a lobbyist."

"Don't try to make me feel stupid for being insulted. You suggested that my entire existence is about selling people a pile of bullshit. You said that it's my job to make people drink the sand, right?"

"I was mostly trying to figure out which character you would be in this movie."

"Don't make a joke of it now."

"Come on, Mel, please don't be like this. Don't be this person who is so sensitive about her job that she freaks out at some offhand comment her idiotic boyfriend makes at eleven-thirty at night when we should both be going to bed."

"Unfortunately for you, I am that person. I'm also the person who makes people drink sand for a living. I'm sorry it doesn't rise to your high-minded standards. Maybe you'll meet a nice girl in Baghdad."

She'd stormed out that night. Now the memory made her laugh out loud.

"What?" The *Washington Post* reporter wanted to know why she was laughing.

She handed him a piece of cake that was covered with wax from the candles.

"I assume this is nontoxic wax?"

"I'd call that a known unknown," Melanie joked, quoting one of her predecessors.

He smiled. "Is that why you're laughing? You finally found a way to get rid of us?"

"I was remembering a fight I'd had with Brian when we first started dating. He accused me of making people drink the sand, a reference to—"

"*The American President*," Sandy and the *Washington Post* reporter said in unison before Melanie could finish her sentence.

"Exactly. Anyway, he accused me of being the person on the White House staff in charge of making people drink the sand, and I flew off the handle. I was laughing just now because that was exactly what I did, and on days like today, I'm so damn relieved not to have those responsibilities anymore."

"It's ironic that he's the one drinking the sand these days," Sandy said.

"It's funny how things turn out," Melanie agreed.

Melanie always rewarded her press corps for traveling to the far-away locations that summon a secretary of defense with off-the-record candor on long flights. In her eighteen months as secretary of defense, no one had ever violated the off-the-record ground rules of these conversations. It was not in either side's interests to see these exchanges chilled or cut off by a leak.

Besides, Melanie understood how powerful the relationships could be. She had worked in government long enough to understand not just how to work with the press instead of against them but also how to co-opt some of their most explosive reports to further her own policy objectives. She'd harnessed the momentum created by a five-part newspaper series on the staggering suicide rates of former service members by hosting town hall meetings across the country on the topic. With Warren's assistance, she mobilized Congress, the business community, and mental health professionals to fund a massive public awareness campaign about the early warning signs of PTSD and depression. Melanie had also hijacked an investigative report on conditions at the schools on military bases by announcing the creation of a blue-ribbon panel made up of civilian and military leaders to develop a set of recommendations for on-base education reform the day before the report was published. She appointed the journalist who'd done the reporting to the panel. She understood that without them, her work and, more important, the wars themselves would go unnoticed.

"My kids would be in deep shit if they pulled a stunt like what Penelope Kramer pulled today," Sandy remarked.

"Penny and Charlotte have always had a love-hate relationship," Melanie said.

Her press was obsessed with the behind-the-curtain details about the Kramer family. Despite Melanie's best attempts to redirect the conversation to the trip to Iraq, her reporters wanted to gossip about the president.

"Why did she take her husband back after he carried on for years with a White House reporter?" another reporter asked.

"And why the hell did she hire his former mistress as her spokesperson?"

Melanie shook her head. "Come on, guys. We've beaten these issues to death. And it's not as if President Kramer is the first politician to experience challenges in her personal life. There are more power couples in marriage counseling in Washington, D.C., than anywhere else in the world. It's unavoidable when people work in jobs that force them to spend so much time with their colleagues and on the road with the likes of you guys."

"Madam Secretary, we're off the record here, right?"

"I hope so."

"You're a high-profile woman working at the highest levels of government."

"Why, thank you."

"I know we've discussed it before, but I'm curious what you think it says to other women that she takes her husband back, acts like a doormat when her teenage daughter rebels against her, and invites her husband's former girlfriend onto the White House staff?"

Melanie shook her head with mock exasperation. She knew they would never tire of asking these sorts of questions, but she refused to divulge any information about the inner workings of Charlotte's tortured soul.

"It says that she is a glutton for punishment," Sandy remarked.

Melanie's theory wasn't too far off from Sandy's observation. Melanie believed that Charlotte felt she deserved to be treated badly by Peter and Penny as punishment for having a job that took her away from them when she felt that they'd needed her most. The truth was more complicated than that. Charlotte had a right to pursue her career. Melanie wished that she'd stop accepting responsibility for everything that went wrong in the lives of her husband and children.

"One thing I observed that makes Kramer unique is that she doesn't blame anyone else for the things that transpire in her life. She sees herself as the only person who determines the outcome of her relationships. I'm certain that she didn't call Penny and yell at her this morning. In fact, she probably called Penny and had a pretty adult conversation with her."

"I don't get it. It doesn't say anything good about female leadership if they have to put up with this kind of crap," Sandy added.

"Charlotte doesn't offer herself up as an example for anyone. To her credit, she's honest about her shortcomings and doesn't spend a lot of time thinking about how her decisions about her personal life are viewed by others."

"I bet she thinks about it more than she lets on. I've heard that her closest staffer these days is Warren. *Politico* ran a story last week saying that he does focus groups for everything. Did you guys do that when you were chief of staff?"

"In the interest of disclosure, Warren is my husband's best friend, and I am quite fond of him myself."

"Do you accept these new polls that show the president and vice president hovering above sixty-percent job approval, or do you think those are honeymoon numbers?" Sandy asked.

Before Melanie could answer, the three-star general who served as her senior military assistant entered the press cabin.

"Madam Secretary, there's a call for you up front."

"I'll be right there."

"I'm sorry, Madam Secretary, it's urgent."

Melanie stood up and excused herself. As she left the press cabin, she heard one of the radio reporters make a mock announcement.

"This is CNN Breaking News. The White House announced today that it has shut down the Internet indefinitely, or at least until the first children are out of college."

Melanie turned and waved as she headed toward the front of the plane. "Happy birthday, Sandy. I hope you always remember celebrating it at thirty thousand feet with your closest friends." Melanie winked.

CHAPTER TWENTY-THREE

Dale

Before she even hung up the phone, Dale knew exactly what she wanted to happen once she was alone with Peter. It had been almost two years since they'd stood face-to-face, and all of the feelings that she'd worked overtime to squash had rushed to the surface when they'd been together earlier. The timing was terrible. She had CBS trailing her, and the first daughter's Facebook crisis had added to her already nearly unmanageable workload. But she'd replayed the fantasy in her mind too many times to pass up an opportunity to make it come true. She'd imagined that they would simply run into each other and that they'd both realize that there was much left unsaid between them. The knowledge that this emotional reunion could never take place while Peter was with Charlotte, and Dale was with Warren, never dimmed Dale's hopes that a chance meeting would bring them back together. She'd long hoped that he had as many unresolved feelings about her as she had about him, but he'd regarded her with such indifference in the Oval Office that she'd been convinced he had finally moved on. It had been surprising and satisfying that he'd been the one to call her after their awkward conversation in the Oval Office and that he'd agreed to meet her in the place they'd once rendezvoused during a state dinner years earlier.

That encounter had taken place during the first state dinner Dale had ever attended. She would have done anything not to be at the dinner that night, since she was secretly sleeping with the husband of the woman she covered for the network. Dale had come through the photo line, and Peter had asked her to meet him in the theater. Against all of her better instincts, she'd traveled down the flight of stairs from the grand rooms of the White House residence to the ground level. She'd looked around to make sure that no one was looking, and then she'd pushed the door to the theater open to find Peter waiting inside. He'd had to convince her that they wouldn't get caught. Dale's date had been waiting for her upstairs; Peter's Secret Service agent had been right outside the door; and ultimately, Charlotte had ended up in the hallway outside the theater speaking to her cabinet member. They hadn't been caught, but it had revealed to Dale just how reckless Peter had become. In hindsight, it was clear that he'd wanted Charlotte to find out about the affair. Dale wondered sometimes if their entire relationship had been an elaborate scheme to get Charlotte's attention.

This time, she entered the family theater determined to explain her reaction on the day nearly two years earlier when Peter had surprised her by purchasing and refurbishing the house in Stinson Beach. When he'd proudly shown her around, pointing out all the little details of the house that he'd hoped would please her, she could barely muster any enthusiasm. Instead of seeing the house as their haven, she'd felt too disconnected from the round-the-clock demands of her job, and she'd lashed out at him for buying it without consulting her. Now she had an opportunity to tell him how much she regretted everything that had happened that day. Even if he couldn't forgive her, he'd know that she was sorry and that she still had feelings for him.

"I should have been appreciative of the effort you put into making such a beautiful home for us. I'm still so sorry," she blurted as soon as she saw him.

He was leaning against the back of one of the oversized theater chairs. Dale's eyes were still adjusting to the dim light. She couldn't make out the look on his face. When he spoke, she could tell that he wasn't interested in her apologies.

"I don't care anymore, Dale. It was just a house."

"It was supposed to be *our* house. A place for us to spend time together when I visited," she said.

"The house was a bad idea. You were getting pulled in too many different directions. I shouldn't have added another one."

"No, the house would have been perfect. I was there, you know. When you and Charlotte went there after the impeachment stuff. I was down on the beach in the staff trailer, and I looked up, and all I could think of was that Charlotte was in my house."

Peter moved closer to her. "It was just a house," he said again.

"Stop saying that."

"Dale, we don't have to do this."

"Yes, we do. It was my house, and I want my house back."

There. She'd said it. Dale was certain that the little smile on his face was an invitation. Their physical attraction to each other had always been the central pillar of their relationship. While it hadn't proven sufficient to keep their relationship together, Dale was sure that it was too strong to keep them apart. She moved closer to him and waited for the familiar feel of his lips on hers.

When she looked up at him, he shook his head. "Dale, come on."

"I thought . . . when you called, I thought that you . . ."

"You thought that I wanted to have sex with you in the family theater while Charlotte delivers a speech a mile away?"

Dale's shock at being rejected was turning into anger about being led on. "You make it sound so implausible. Have you forgotten what happened here?"

"Unfortunately, I remember everything. Do you?"

"Of course."

"Then you'll excuse me for not feeling sentimental."

"Why did you call me, then?" She was fighting the impulse to raise her voice.

"I thought we could have a normal conversation. I don't have too many of those." He said it with enough of an edge to blunt Dale's anger. She'd been so focused on what she wanted from him that it never dawned on her that he might need something from her, something as simple as someone to talk to.

She was still reeling from his rejection, but there was something sad about him. He had snuck down to the family theater to see her with no intention of being intimate with her. He simply wanted to talk. He was either screwing with her as payback for her near-inhumane treatment of him at the end of their relationship, or he was back at square one with Charlotte and feeling emotionally isolated, which was where he'd been when they'd first met nearly six years earlier. Her mind was spinning, and while she was mortified that she'd misread his signs and awash with guilt that she was being so hideous to her own boyfriend, she was intrigued that he had gone through so much effort to be alone with her. It was still something that would get both of them into mountains of trouble if anyone found out. Dale took a deep breath and glanced down at her phone. It had been going crazy since she'd walked in. She'd noticed the red light flashing on her BlackBerry and had felt the phone vibrate several times.

When she finally looked down at her devices, she noticed that Marguerite had texted her "911" and that the missed calls were from the Situation Room operator. It was ringing again.

"I'm sorry, but I have to get this."

"Go ahead." Peter looked down at his phone, too.

"Hello?"

"Miss Smith, the national security advisor has been trying to reach you for the last ten minutes."

"You can put him through."

"He's on another call, but he asked that you come directly to the Situation Room."

"I'm on my way."

She looked at Peter and felt like crying. After nearly two years of no contact, he'd called her because he needed someone to talk to, and now she had to go.

"Go," he said.

"I don't want to. Not like this. I can't seem to avoid acting like a psycho when I'm around you."

"I seem to have that effect on women," he joked.

"Can I call you?"

"I don't think that's a good idea."

"So this was, like, a one-time thing? One opportunity to make it right, and because the goddamned Sit Room is calling me like the friggin' world is ending, I miss out?"

"Dale, don't."

"Don't?"

"Please. If you care about me at all, or about Charlotte, please just let it all go."

Dale looked down at her phones again and felt like throwing the blinking, vibrating devices against the ornate paneled theater walls. "Right. Because I'm the one who fucked everything up, I have to do this one thing for you. Again. Whatever you want, but you agreed to meet me here, too. I didn't force you here."

He barely made eye contact with her. "You'd better go," he said quietly.

"Yeah," she agreed. She was suddenly more concerned about why the Situation Room would have called five times.

CHAPTER TWENTY-FOUR

Charlotte

I t wasn't until the faces on some of the guests in the front row started to register discomfort that Charlotte looked around and saw Monty standing next to her onstage. Her first thought was that something awful had happened to one of the twins. She held her breath as Monty unfolded the note and handed it to her. Before she looked down, Charlotte noticed that the reporters standing on the riser in the back of the room were studying their devices and whispering among themselves and into their phones. She also noticed that her Secret Service agents had started to move onto the stage. Charlotte forced her eyes to focus on the piece of paper.

"There's been an attack in New York City. We need to get back to the White House." That was clear enough, but there were no instructions about what she was supposed to say to the audience. Her staff picked one hell of a time for her to start ad-libbing. She was temporarily frozen in place, uncertain what she should say to the crowd and cognizant that the entire press corps was watching and broadcasting her speech live. Monty hadn't moved, which made resuming her remarks impossible. But it seemed abrupt to simply say that she had to go. She remembered all of the controversy surrounding her predecessor who had learned of the September 11 attacks while reading to elementary-school children. Her eyes moved over the words a second time, and her brain took over.

"Ladies and gentlemen, I'm so sorry, but there's an emergency that requires my attention at the White House, and I need to leave you right away. As soon as we can share the details, we will. I'm going to return this podium to its rightful owner, my vice president, who will also be needed back at the White House in a few minutes. Thank you for your hospitality. I will be back, and this important conversation is to be continued."

Charlotte followed Monty offstage and was rushed to the motorcade by her agents, who all but lifted her off her feet. The limo took off with a screech of the tires. She heard sirens blaring and noticed the motorcycle escorts on either side of her limo. They hadn't been there for the ride over. Craig and Marguerite were sitting across from her.

"What's going on?"

"There were two explosions in Times Square. We don't have any numbers on casualties, but it looks bad. The second bomb went off two minutes after the first, so all of the people rushing to help the victims of the first explosion were hurt by the second."

"Jesus Christ."

"We've got unconfirmed reports about an explosion outside the check-in counter at O'Hare, and a similar report was coming out of LAX as we were leaving. Both airports were packed. No word on casualties there, either. The FBI thinks there could be more attacks under way. We're getting you back to the White House, but they may want to relocate you to a base somewhere outside of D.C. until things settle down."

"That's out of the question. I'm staying at the White House. Where are the twins?"

"Mr. Kramer is in touch with their Secret Service details. They're fine. The agents are with them and awaiting your direction. It's up to you and Mr. Kramer, but the Secret Service thinks that it's unnecessary to relocate them to Washington or Camp David at this point."

The limo sped the three-quarter-mile distance between the museum and the White House. The return to the White House took about a minute and a half. Charlotte heard the sound of helicopters overhead as the Secret Service whisked her from where the car parked on the South Lawn into the closest entrance. Peter was waiting for her, along with Sam and her national security advisor.

"Char, are you all right?" Peter asked.

"I'm fine. Have you talked to the twins?"

"I've spoken to both of them. The Secret Service thinks they're safest where they are. I can try to get out there to be with them if you want."

"Sam, let's see if we can get Peter to California."

"Yes, ma'am."

"Can one of you make sure that Brooke and Mark get back to the residence? I don't want them wandering around D.C."

"They were in the motorcade, ma'am. We put them in the guest van," Monty assured her.

Charlotte nodded and glanced over her shoulder. Cars from the motorcade were still pulling onto the driveway.

"Where are we meeting?"

"Madam President, we are assembling the entire national security team. Some folks are here already, and others will join by teleconference. We can move the meeting to the PEOC if the Secret Service deems it necessary."

PEOC was short for the Presidential Emergency Operations Center, an underground bunker that could protect the president and staff during a nuclear attack. More recently, the White House staff had worked from the PEOC during the attacks of September 11.

"What do we know?" Charlotte asked as they moved quickly down the colonnade.

"Three separate attacks—New York, Chicago, and L.A. There are confirmed reports now that there were two explosions in New York. It's unclear how many devices were detonated in Chicago and L.A. There are some early reports that suggest a possible suicide bomber in Chicago. We've grounded all flights, but that doesn't seem to be their mode of attack. We'll go through all of it downstairs for you, ma'am."

"How many people do you think we've lost?"

"Not sure yet, but we'll tell you everything we know."

They entered the Situation Room and proceeded to the conference room, where Charlotte took her seat at the head of the table. The attorney general, FBI director, treasury secretary, homeland security advisor, and various deputy secretaries were already seated at the table. When they rose to greet her with the standard formality granted to a president, she motioned for them to sit. The faces of her secretaries of defense, homeland security, and state were being beamed into the conference room on screens directly in front of her. On a large flat-screen to her left, members of the New York and Washington JTTF, or Joint Terrorism Task Force, had also joined the meeting. The screen next to theirs was broadcasting live split-screen coverage of CNN, Fox, MSNBC, and ABC.

Her national security director started the meeting. "Hello, everyone. Madam President, events are obviously unfolding in real time, so we're going to be updating you as we learn new information. We will be getting this raw, so everything we discuss in here should be considered unconfirmed until we verify and approve something for public release. I'm going to let the FBI director start, because he's going to leave in a few minutes to join his team at FBI Headquarters. Go ahead, Mr. Director."

"Madam President, at about ten-forty-five this morning, the NYPD responded to calls about an explosion in the pedestrian park area of Times Square. People were rushing to help the wounded when witnesses described a second, larger explosion. I believe that this is what we're watching on CNN and ABC right now. They are broadcasting the local ABC footage of the second explosion, which took place as they were pulling up. They were the first news crew on the scene. Frankly, it's the footage that we're analyzing ourselves, in addition to security-camera footage, which is coming in a little more slowly."

"How many casualties?"

"We don't have any hard numbers yet, Madam President."

"Give me a soft number."

"I don't want to guess."

"Dozens? Hundreds?"

"We'll have numbers soon."

"CNN is reporting an explosion at the Port of Miami," Dale interjected from the back row. Charlotte hadn't noticed Dale when she'd entered the Situation Room.

"Put CNN on the full screen," Charlotte ordered.

They all stared at an image that was obviously being filmed from a helicopter. A large ship was visible at the bottom of the screen. Dark smoke seemed to be pouring from one side of it.

"They're asking us to confirm the attack. Mr. Director, is the FBI there?"

"They're on their way, Dale. I'd rather not confirm it until our folks are able to assess the scene."

"Are we not able to get our people there before CNN gets its crews there?" Charlotte asked pointedly.

"In some cases, we're learning things at the same time as the media."

"What do we know about Chicago and L.A.?"

"Very similar scenes that appear to have been closely coordinated in terms of timing—the explosions were nearly simultaneous. Witnesses have reported seeing a man in a vest at O'Hare. No such reporting in Los Angeles, but we're checking the security footage. In both instances, there were large explosions outside the ticket check-in area."

"Casualties?"

"No numbers yet, ma'am."

"NBC is reporting hundreds could be dead in New York and unknown numbers of victims taken to all area hospitals in Chicago and L.A.," Dale read from her BlackBerry.

"Four attacks if Miami is what it appears to be. Hundreds, maybe thousands of people could be dead. More attacks are possible. This is a full-fledged multicity terror offensive. Melanie, where are you on this? Are you considering moving our forces to DEFCON Three?" Charlotte asked.

"That would not be an overreaction, Madam President. At your order, we will do so."

The last time the nation's strategic nuclear forces were placed in a "ready" position for worldwide military engagement was on September 11, 2001.

"Do it," the president ordered.

Everyone in the room was quiet while Melanie addressed the National Military Command Center.

"I'm on it," Melanie confirmed.

The gravity of what had just transpired took a moment to sink in. Either Dale didn't understand that Charlotte had just moved the country's nuclear arsenal to a ready-to-use position, or she didn't care. She was suddenly standing and pointing at the TV screen.

"Oh, my God. Oh, my God. It's a huge cruise ship that's burning. CNN is reporting that it's a Carnival cruise ship and they had just finished boarding more than eight hundred passengers," Dale exclaimed.

"Are those people jumping off the ship?"

"Yes. Just like the towers on September eleventh. They're jumping off the ship to get away from the fire," Melanie said from the monitor on the wall.

"God help us," Charlotte murmured.

"Madam President, the Secret Service would like to relocate you to the PEOC immediately," Craig announced.

"Is that necessary?"

"There's an unconfirmed report of an explosion on the National Mall."

Charlotte looked down at her hands and took a deep breath. "Anything on that, folks?"

"We're checking, Madam President," the FBI director said.

"We should be able to look out our windows to verify that one, shouldn't we, people?" Charlotte said as she rose from the table. "Melanie, how long do we have until I have to make a public statement?"

"Events are too fluid right now, Madam President, but as soon as the public is able to see the scenes of devastation, they're going to start wondering where their president is. They will need to be reassured that their government is working to protect them, and they're going to want to know that someone knows what the hell is going on."

"I'm sorry to put you on the spot, but I think everyone here needs to work against a deadline. How much time until I need to make a statement, Melanie?"

"Madam President, we need to move you into the PEOC right now," Craig repeated.

"Melanie?" Charlotte asked.

"Considering the attacks seem to be ongoing, I'd say you have until dinnertime," Melanie responded.

"Thank you. Let's plan on an address to the public at six P.M. We'll rejoin you all from the PEOC in twenty minutes."

CHAPTER TWENTY-FIVE

Melanie

M elanie muted her line and calculated how far from Washington she would be at six P.M. She'd still be at least three hours away, and she'd still be monitoring the videoconference that had been convened so that the various government agencies tasked with responding to the attacks could share information in real time. One of the failures of the response to the attacks of September 11 was the government's limited capacity for coordination and communication during the first few hours after the attacks. What that meant for Melanie was that she would be participating in the videoconference until the moment she landed at Andrews Air Force Base.

"What time do we land, exactly?" Melanie asked.

"Around nine-fifteen this evening."

"I assume that's the fastest we can get there?"

"We're pushing it at that."

She unmuted the line. "Who is taking the lead on the president's remarks?" she asked the group assembled in the Situation Room.

"Melanie, we're going to have the speechwriters take the first stab, but we'll circulate the remarks as soon as there's a working draft. Dale will take the point on getting the remarks around to everyone in here," Craig said.

"Madam Secretary, if you'd like for me to send the speechwriters any guidance from your office, I'm happy to do so," Dale offered.

"I'll wait until remarks are circulated," Melanie replied curtly. She would have to find a way to get her guidance for the president's remarks directly to the president.

The deputy national security advisor addressed the group next: "Folks, if you need to be in touch with your agencies, please use the next fifteen minutes to do so. The line will remain open, and most of us are going to be assembled in here until the Secret Service advises against it. The Cabinet secretaries who are here will relocate down to the PEOC with the president and vice president. As the president indicated, we'll do a formal update in twenty minutes."

Melanie directed her aide to monitor the videoconference. She moved out of the camera shot and called Brian. He picked up immediately.

"I can't believe this is happening again," he said.

"I know."

"Are you feeling OK?"

"I'm fine. We're going to try to get back by nine. I assume I'll go straight to the Pentagon. Where are you?"

"I'm stuck at the Women's Museum. All of the networks have gone to wall-to-wall live coverage, so I haven't been able to get off the air for long enough to move back to the White House. Everyone seems to have been left here."

"The press office should be moving you all back."

"They're working on it. There's an unconfirmed report of an attack on the Mall, so I'm not sure we'll be moving anytime soon."

"I think that report is real."

"Do you have anything on it that I can use?"

"No, but between us, they just moved Charlotte down to the PEOC."

"Jesus. They haven't done that since September eleventh, right?"

"Not that I can recall."

"Listen, they're coming back to me in about thirty seconds, and now I have no idea what I'm going to say."

"Don't report anything I just told you."

"I never do, Mel."

Next, Melanie dialed Annie to ask her to place a call to her parents. She didn't really have time to talk to them, but one call would spare them a day of anxiety. Her dad picked up on the first ring.

"Are you and Mom watching the news?" She knew they were. Her father slept with the remote in one hand and usually turned on Fox News before his eyes opened. He was on a first-name basis with all of the anchors, and one of his favorite conversation starters was to quiz Melanie about the college education of the various female Fox News anchors and pundits. Melanie always failed his quizzes.

"Where are you, Mel? Are you safe? Did you get out of that godforsaken country?" Her father's politics were an odd mix of libertarian isolationism and right-wing lunacy, but he was staunchly opposed to any war that would place his daughter in harm's way.

"Yes, Dad. I'm fine. I'm on my way back to Washington."

"Thank God. Marion, she's on her way back to D.C.," he yelled to her mom.

"Is Mom there?"

"She's just getting out of the shower."

"Tell her I'm fine and that I'll call her later."

"Do we know who the sons of bitches are who did this?"

"Not yet, Dad. We're working on it."

"Tell the president to bomb the entire Middle East to pieces."

"I'm pretty sure that isn't on her menu of options, but I will pass it along."

"It's the only way to protect ourselves at this point."

"Dad, I want you and Mom to stay home today."

"Mom just canceled her book club, and I canceled my golf game. Those bastards targeted innocent families and children. When are we going to realize that they exist on this planet for the sole purpose of doing us harm? It doesn't matter what we do. We should stop trying to rebuild their goddamned schools, and we should stop pouring money we don't have into their corrupt economies. Do you think it's done us any good? All the money we spend?"

"Listen, I've got to go, but if you need to reach me, you can call Annie."

"What am I going to call Annie for? Fox News knows what's happening before the goddamned government."

"Just tell Mom that she can call Annie if she needs anything or if she wants to talk to me."

"Darren, stop harassing your daughter." Melanie could hear her mother yelling.

"Tell your mother that you are safe." Her father handed the phone to Melanie's mother.

"Where are you, honey?"

"I'm on my way back. I'm fine, Mom. Don't worry."

Melanie had waved in her press aide while she was talking to her parents.

"How's our press?" she asked him as soon as she hung up.

"They want to file from the plane about your meetings and calls. Can I read out anything from your videoconference?"

"Only read out the call if the White House is doing the same thing. It's easy to get ahead of the White House on a day like this. Be sure that Dale is reading out the same meetings to her press, so that it doesn't feel like we're all on different pages."

"Got it."

"And tell the press to thank you for insisting that the plane has Wi-Fi. You should sit in for the next videoconference and make sure you and Dale are talking to all of your counterparts at CIA, FBI, State, and DOJ. Tell Dale she needs to set up an hourly interagency press call."

He took down Melanie's orders and excused himself.

Next, Melanie placed a call to the chairman of the joint chiefs and confirmed that NORAD had taken over North American air space as they had done on September 11. Then she pulled out her laptop and started typing a few notes for the president's speech. She knew exactly what Charlotte would need to communicate that night.

CHAPTER TWENTY-SIX

Dale

"Should I stay here, or do you need me in the PEOC?" Dale asked.

"You are going to have to read out the president's meetings and phone calls to our press," Craig noted.

"I know, but I figured you'd want to keep it very small in the PEOC."

"I have room for you. Come on," Craig urged.

Dale wished she'd attended one of the half dozen emergency drills that had taken place since she'd joined the White House staff. She didn't even know where the PEOC was. She always sent Marguerite to the Saturday disaster drills. She never thought she would witness something so dire that it required the Secret Service to evacuate the president to the PEOC. Dale followed Craig up the stairs from the Situation Room. He stopped in his office and told his assistant to heed the evacuation orders.

"Yes, sir," his assistant, Ben, replied nervously. Half a dozen executive assistants from the West Wing were hovering around the television on Ben's desk, which was normally on mute if it was on at all.

"There's a rumor that the State Department was attacked. Is that true?" Ben asked.

Dale glanced at the TV. They were airing a shot of the street that ran alongside the Old Executive Office Building. The OEOB was the largest building in the White House complex. It housed all but the most senior presidential advisors and their staffs. Smoke was billowing up the street from the direction of the Washington Monument.

"As far as we know, the explosion was down on the Mall. We're not hearing anything about an attack or evacuation at the State Department," Craig reassured him.

The administrative assistants were mesmerized by the coverage.

"Do you know that people are jumping off the burning ships in Miami and into the water?" one of them remarked.

Craig was quiet for a second and then nodded. Dale couldn't tell if any of them had even looked away from the TV for long enough to notice.

Dale moved closer and stared at the image of the black cloud moving toward the White House complex. The day had taken a surreal turn. When they were dealing with attacks in New York, Miami, L.A., and Chicago, they were doing what they always did: managing a crisis. Once the report had come in about an explosion in D.C., the sense of security that Dale had always felt as a senior staffer with a hard pin and easy access to armed Secret Service agents evaporated. She was on her way to an underground bunker, but she still felt vulnerable.

"Where does everyone else go if the entire White House gets evacuated? Is there an office building or a safe house downtown or something?" Dale asked Craig.

Craig shook his head and picked up the phone on Ben's desk. He punched in a number that Dale didn't recognize.

"Hey, listen, I'm going to give your address to my assistant and some of his colleagues. If they evacuate the West Wing, I'm going to send them to your offices to work. You'll set them up with phones and computers and some lunch, right? Thanks, man. I'll call when I can." He hung up. "Listen up, everyone. If you get evacuated, I want you to head to Main Street Strategies. Ben has the address," Craig ordered.

"Yes, sir."

As Craig started to move toward the door, Dale wondered how her own staff was faring. Dale and Craig hadn't taken two steps toward the East Wing when they encountered the CBS crew that was supposed to be embedded with Dale all day. The light on the camera was on, and Dale recognized the associate producer who had driven in with her that morning.

"Here we are with the White House press secretary and chief of staff. What can you tell us about what's happening? Can you confirm the D.C. attack? Has the president been relocated to an undisclosed location, or is she still on the premises? When will she address the nation?"

The producer was holding a microphone two inches from Dale's face. She held her arm out to push the microphone a little farther away, and then she stood squarely in front of the camera and tried to project calm.

"We'll have a statement for you shortly. We appreciate all of your questions, and we're working on answers. Obviously, there are things we can't share with you for security reasons, but we'll get you all of the information we can. Now, can you guys please wait in the briefing room with the rest of the press?"

"We were supposed to be embedded with you all day, ma'am."

"That was before the country was attacked, and you're going to have to stop calling me ma'am."

The camera was about ten inches from Dale's face, and she was certain that her "ma'am" comment was snippy enough to make the highlight reel. She silently cursed herself for losing her cool. There was no news that spread faster than a sense of panic exhibited by a senior White House official, and there was no mission more critical for someone in Dale's position than exhibiting otherworldly tranquillity in the midst of a national security event.

"I'm sorry about that, guys. It's a tense time. As I said, the nation has been attacked."

"A terrorist attack?"

"I'm sorry?"

"Is there a reason no one in the government has called it a terrorist attack yet?"

Dale didn't want to get ahead of the president, but she felt boxed in by the question. She understood why celebrities punched paparazzi in the face and smashed their cameras. "I'm really sorry, but we are rushing to a national security briefing. I'll ask Marguerite to walk you through everything we know."

"Can we remain embedded with you?" they yelled after her.

"I'll be in touch after this next briefing," she replied.

Dale squirmed past the crew and stormed away. Craig held the door to the colonnade open for her. Once it had closed behind her, she exploded. "Those little pieces of shit."

Craig put an arm on her shoulder to calm her down. "Let it go. You know better than I do that the minute we start restricting press access, they start broadcasting that the end of the world is upon us, and the public really freaks out. We can't do that to the president. She needs more time to get her arms around the situation. We all need more time. Just go through the motions with the press. We can always limit access as the day goes on, but I'm guessing it wouldn't be worth it. The press has a way of making everything about them."

"You're right. What a bunch of jerks," Dale complained.

Craig and Dale had barely made it halfway down the colonnade toward the East Wing when Marguerite came running after them.

"Whoa, hold up. I need you for two seconds before you disappear underground not to be heard from for hours."

Craig glanced at his watch. "We have a briefing in two minutes."

"I'm dealing with total chaos at the moment. Our press is scattered everywhere. Most of them are stuck at the Women's Museum," Marguerite reported.

"Can we send the staff vans back for them? They will kill us if they can't be on the air from here," Dale asked.

"I'm working on it."

"We just got ambushed by CBS. Can you send someone to round up all of the crews? They are literally wandering around the East Wing."

"I don't have anyone to spare, but as soon as Molly gets back from the museum, I'll have her park them in your office."

"Thanks, Marguerite. I'll call you as soon as there's something to read out from the president's meetings."

"Wait, wait. I need to give them something now. Can I say that the president has been in meetings with her national security team since she returned from the museum?"

"Yes. Tell them she's met with the entire national security team in the Situation Room and via videoconference. She's been briefed on all five of the attacks, and her prayers are with the victims of this senseless violence."

"Senseless violence sounds like a mass shooting. Can we call it a terrorist attack?"

"I just danced on that myself with CBS. Craig?"

"I think so. Let me just check with Tim."

"We have to check with the national security advisor to find out if five bombings constitute a terrorist attack? Seriously?" Marguerite put one hand on her hip and glared at her colleagues.

"Marguerite is right. We should be able to tell them that the president condemns today's act of terror and her prayers are with the victims," Dale corrected.

"You'd better let me run it by the president," Craig warned.

"For Christ's sake," Marguerite muttered.

"I'll settle it right now. Come downstairs with us," Craig ordered.

As they marched toward the East Wing, Dale took out her iPhone and sent off a quick text to Warren. "I'm heading underground. If I don't have service, will call you in a couple of hours."

He wrote back immediately: "Stay in PEOC and be tough for POTUS."

She didn't bother to ask him if he could see the smoke from his office, which was just a couple of blocks from the D.C. blast site.

They descended into the PEOC, and the first thing Dale noticed was the elaborate lunch spread. A tray of sandwiches lay next to a vegetable tray in the center of the table. There was a fruit bowl, a plate of cookies, and a fresh bucket of ice next to a neat display of diet sodas. On a console table behind the conference table were a carafe of coffee and two small pitchers holding milk and cream. Dale stared at the sugar bowl and the container holding four types of fake sugar and wondered who had requested all this food.

Peter was standing in the corner talking on a landline. Dale glanced down at her iPhone and BlackBerry and noticed that neither was getting reception. She only heard snippets of Peter's conversation, but it sounded like he was talking to one of the twins' Secret Service agents about whether they should travel to Washington.

"What does he think?" Charlotte asked Peter.

She glanced over her shoulder and saw Dale staring at them. Dale averted her eyes and felt like she'd just violated their privacy. She hadn't seen Peter in two years, and now she was going on her third encounter in one day.

Dale took out a pad and started jotting down notes about who was in the PEOC, what it looked like, and what people were doing. It wasn't anything like what Dale had expected. There weren't any screaming aides or loud debates. The television on the wall provided the only noise other than the various military aides picking up incoming calls and directing them to the officials in the room. Someone was setting up the speakerphone in the middle of the table for the interagency briefing that was about to start.

"Madam President, we'd like to tell our press that you're heading into a second briefing on today's attacks. We'd also like to issue a statement saying that you condemn today's terror attacks and that your prayers are with the victims. Do you have any problem with that?" Craig asked.

"That's fine. Get it out. I don't want to look like I'm hiding in a cave. Should I deliver the statement on camera and announce that I will address the nation with more extensive remarks this evening?"

"That would be ideal, Madam President," Marguerite urged.

"Dale?" Craig asked.

Dale looked around the room and thought for longer than usual. "It might be too early to put you out there. You can't take any questions. I think we should wait until the address."

"I agree with Dale. We don't know for sure that there aren't more attacks under way. We need to get some more information before we put you out there," said Tim, the president's national security advisor.

Marguerite glared at Dale again. Craig shrugged at Marguerite. Dale thought she saw Craig mouth, "I tried," to a clearly exasperated Marguerite. Dale was annoyed with Marguerite. The president had approved the written statement, and to put her in front of the cameras was premature. Sometimes Marguerite was *too* focused on what the press wanted.

"I'm going back upstairs, boss," Marguerite called from the doorway.

"I'll call you after the briefing," Dale promised.

Dale poured herself a cup of coffee and tried to shake the cobwebs out of her brain. Ever since she'd first entered the Situation Room and learned about the attacks, she'd felt she was taking more time than those around her to react to what she was seeing.

"Dale, who is working on my remarks for tonight?" the president asked.

Dale hadn't had a chance to call the speechwriters yet. "I thought I'd draft a few message points based on this briefing and then let the speechwriters flesh them out."

The president nodded.

The same faces that had surrounded them in the Situation Room were suddenly arrayed around them on the screens. Plus, now there was a feed from the Situation Room above.

The FBI director started the briefing by confirming the attack on the Mall in Washington. He reconfirmed the attacks in Miami, Los Angeles, Chicago, and New York. He didn't have very much new information, other than a mounting death toll. About ten minutes into his briefing, everyone around the table in the PEOC suddenly turned to watch the TV coverage. The screens were filled with images of terrified White House staffers streaming out of the Northwest Gate of the White House complex. Dale searched the crowds for members of her own staff. She didn't see any. She wondered if everyone gathered in the nuclear-blast-safe bunker knew that the mid-level and junior staffers had nowhere safe to go once evacuated.

"I assume they are being evacuated to an alternative location or something along those lines?" Charlotte asked.

Dale spun around to see how Craig and Tim would answer. The evacuation policy was haphazard at best. Staffers were told that evacuation was mandatory unless their functions were essential. While the most senior officials were ensconced in the security of a nuclear-safe bunker, Dale suspected that there were dozens of twenty-four-year-olds upstairs faithfully manning the desks of the White House senior staff. Dale presumed from her last conversation with Marguerite that she was upstairs with most of their staff trying to get the press back onto the premises so they could cover the president.

"No, Madam President, but most of them can walk home with colleagues or friends, and we'll be in touch with them as soon as it's safe to come back to the White House complex," Craig offered.

Charlotte's look made clear that she didn't approve of the response. She pursed her lips and extended her disapproval to the lavish spread of food.

"We may be here for a very long time," Craig explained quietly.

Dale was staring at her notepad and furiously trying to capture everything everyone was saying. She asked one of the military aides when the order had been given to evacuate the White House.

"About two minutes ago."

Dale nodded and turned her attention back to the conversation around the table. The national security advisor had engaged the attorney general in a conversation about whether the Posse Comitatus Act of 1878 prohibited the military from taking over the U.S. cities that had been attacked.

Dale noticed that one of the networks was now airing a split screen of the White House evacuation on one side and the burning ship in Miami on the other. The shots of the burning ship were being interspersed with interviews of sobbing family members who had just waved good-bye to loved ones. On another screen, the anchor of NBC News was standing in front of the yellow police tape that now rimmed the site of the explosions in Times Square. On another, Dale watched first responders with rescue dogs search for survivors at the airport in Los Angeles. The fourth feed was CNN's coverage of the White House evacuation.

"Dale? Dale?"

"I'm sorry, Madam President."

"Do you have enough from everyone in here to get the speechwriters started?"

Dale hadn't been listening for the last sixty seconds or so, but the speech would go through a million different iterations. She looked down at her notepad and then up at the president. "Yes, ma'am, I have plenty."

CHAPTER TWENTY-SEVEN

Charlotte

Charlotte's eyes met Craig's, and they both knew that Dale was going to have to snap out of whatever state of shock she was in, or she'd need to be replaced for the day by her deputy, Marguerite, who was firing on all cylinders. Craig took a seat next to Dale, as if to convey to the president that he would personally supervise his protégée. When the FBI director rose to take a call from his deputy, the national security advisor took over the briefing.

"Madam President, we're going to take you through each of the sites that were targeted this morning, starting with New York. The mayor is joining us now by phone. He's still down at the site. Mr. Mayor?"

"Yes, hello?"

"Mr. Mayor, I have the president on the line."

"Mr. Mayor, this is Charlotte Kramer. I am calling to see if there is anything we can do for you right now and to assure you that as the day goes on, we will be in constant contact with your staff to provide any resources that you might need."

"Thank you, Madam President. It looks like a war zone right now. I've never seen anything like it."

"How are the first responders holding up?"

"They're doing exactly what they're trained to do. We don't have a count on casualties, but since I got down here, I've seen about two dozen ambulances speed off from the site."

"I won't take up too much more of your time, but please call me directly if there's anything we can do to help the victims and their families or to support the first responders."

"Thank you, Madam President. The carnage is unbelievable. I can't believe they did this here again."

"Mr. Mayor, I know your focus is on the rescue-and-recovery effort, but as soon as you will have us, I will be there."

"That would mean a lot."

"Please pick up the phone and call me directly if you need anything."

"The investigation?"

"Yes, of course. We'll coordinate with the JTTF and keep your office in the loop at every step."

The phone clicked, and Charlotte repeated a similar conversation with the mayors of Los Angeles and Chicago. She pledged the full support of the federal government and promised that the federal government would be there with an open checkbook. The mayor of Miami was still at the site and was not available to speak to her, but the FBI director was tracking down the special agent in charge of Miami when they all heard another explosion from one of the televisions.

"What was that?" Charlotte asked.

Dale grabbed a remote off the table and turned up the volume. All of the networks suddenly switched to a live shot of the area outside the Air and Space Museum in Washington. The first explosion had shattered the glass façade of the building. Everyone feared that schoolchildren would be among the victims.

The military aide fielding all incoming calls to the PEOC handed the phone to the national security advisor. "It's the Situation Room, sir," he said.

Tim stood to take the call. As he listened to the report from the Situation Room, his face turned gray. He hung up and turned to address the room.

"The FBI is confirming that the D.C. site was hit again. There was a second explosion where they were staging the recovery efforts. We have FBI assets, victims of the first explosion, and members of the media down. They don't want to rush more first responders in until they can secure the site."

"Why the hell didn't they secure the site the first time?" Craig demanded.

"They thought they had."

Charlotte's hands flew to her mouth to stifle a gasp. These types of sequenced bombings were the most lethal. She wasn't sure why they hadn't been more prepared, considering that the attackers had used sequenced bombs in New York in the first attacks of the day.

"Why were they staging the rescue effort so close to the site of the first bombing?" Craig asked.

"I don't know. I guess they thought the site was secure. They've got confirmed casualties among the first responders. I'm waiting for an update. At least half a dozen journalists are down."

Charlotte looked up at the screen and registered Melanie's flash of concern.

"Dale, please run upstairs and make sure all of the White House correspondents are in the briefing room."

"Madam President, most of them are stuck at the Women's Museum. They haven't been able to get back here."

Charlotte tilted her head to one side and tried to convey her concern for Melanie's husband to Dale without saying it. Melanie caught on before Dale did.

"I spoke to Brian a few minutes ago. He was at the Women's Museum. I'm sure he's fine," Melanie offered, her face betraying nothing.

"Let's make sure," the president ordered.

CHAPTER TWENTY-EIGHT

Melanie

Melanie excused herself from the videoconference and moved quickly toward her cabin. Once inside, she dialed Brian's cell-phone number. When the call didn't go through, she placed it again.

"Mel?" he answered.

"Oh, thank God. Thank God."

"What?"

"I thought maybe you'd gone down there."

"Where?"

"To the Air and Space Museum. I thought maybe you'd walked down there to help cover the recovery effort."

"No. I'm still at the Women's Museum. Have you guys confirmed a second explosion there?"

"Yes. They said that a bunch of journalists and first responders were hit."

"Can I report that?"

"What?"

"I don't have any information yet on the second blast. Can I go on the air with that?"

"I don't know. I was calling to make sure it wasn't you."

"It wasn't me. I'm fine. I've got to try to get on the air with something, though, Mel. Can I call you back?"

"Of course. Call me back."

Melanie rubbed her stomach and stood up slowly. She was feeling dizzy and tired. She guzzled a bottle of water and sat back down. She hadn't allowed herself to think about any of the victims yet, but she understood something that Charlotte's other advisors did not. The blanket of grief that had smothered the country for months and years after September 11, 2001 was about to return. It would color the president's decision making and influence her ability to think clearly about anything.

Melanie remembered every instant of September 11, but the day that was seared in her consciousness was the day she'd stood alongside her White House colleagues in the East Room to honor the family members of those lost on Flight 93. They'd visited the White House a week after the plane carrying their husbands, wives, fathers and mothers, sons and daughters had crashed into a field in Pennsylvania. While the president had heralded the bravery of these first soldiers in the war against terror, Melanie remembered holding the outstretched hand of one woman who'd lost her brother and thinking, *How is she standing here right now?*

In hindsight, Melanie realized that the family members' shock and pride had mixed with their grief that day, affording them the resolve to accept the president's invitation, even during their darkest hours.

Melanie had been unable to sleep or eat for weeks after that. While many of her colleagues plunged back into twelve-hour workdays, early-morning trips to the gym, and the occasional Friday-night cocktail hour, Melanie had struggled to adapt to the new normal.

For weeks after September 11, Melanie couldn't tear herself away from the round-the-clock news coverage. She watched the victims' family members hang on to every scrap of information about the remains recovered at the World Trade Center. Each time the first responders appeared on television to offer grim updates about the recovery effort, Melanie wept with relatives holding photos of their missing loved ones. She grew familiar with the stories of the victims and the families they'd left behind: the father of three who'd left final voice-mail messages for his wife and young children; the summer intern who called her parents to tell them not to worry because she was on her way downstairs; the families of the firemen and police officers who were asked to feel consoled by the fact that their family members died as heroes; the pregnant wives of Pentagon employees whose children would never know their fathers' touch. She couldn't comprehend how her friends on the White House staff were carrying on with scheduling meetings, event planning, press calls, and nights out. Melanie isolated herself and became paralyzed by her grief.

Counselors were made available to the White House staff, and after passing the basement office in the OEOB where they were housed a dozen times, Melanie finally decided to go inside. She remembered walking into the waiting room, where a friendly woman in her late thirties greeted her and asked her to fill out a questionnaire. Melanie took the clipboard from her and sat in one of the folding chairs. Before she was able to answer a single question, all of the fear and anger and sadness she'd been carrying around came spilling out. The counselor gently led her into a private room and handed her a box of tissues and a plastic cup of water. Melanie had left two hours later with a prescription for Ambien and an order to watch less news. She was drained, but she began to see herself as the one who was having a normal reaction to the tragedy and the robots around her as the ones who were in denial. The counselor had suggested that Melanie view her White House responsibilities as a way to give back to those who had lost everything. It felt like a reach, but Melanie complied.

It would be years before Melanie could look at a plane in the sky above downtown D.C. and not worry that it might have the White House as its target.

Now, as she made her way back to the conference room on the plane, she wondered if the president had yet grasped how dramatically her presidency was about to change.

CHAPTER TWENTY-NINE

Dale

After learning of the second D.C. blast, Dale called Margue-rite, who was able to quickly confirm that Brian was still on the air from the Women's Museum, something Dale could have done herself if she'd simply changed the channel to NBC. Dale delivered the news to the group in the PEOC and then excused herself.

She stepped into the bathroom and heaved into the toilet for what felt like forever. There was nothing in her stomach except coffee and, when she was done, not even any of that anymore. She looked at herself in the mirror as she wiped her mouth and swished mouth-wash through her teeth. Dale was a hardened former newswoman who thrived on chaos, but something about the scale of the attacks and the sudden loss of so many innocent people had her feeling unhinged.

Pull yourself together, she said to herself. She washed her hands again to make sure she didn't smell like what she'd just thrown up and then took a deep breath and walked back to the PEOC. The president appraised her with a look Dale recognized as concern. Dale poured herself a Fresca and sat down in one of the chairs in the back row.

She focused on the various briefings from the different agencies and soon fell into a routine. She alternated between taking notes from the briefings; passing the information on to Marguerite in the press office; convening conference calls with her counterparts at DOD, State, and the FBI; and then taking more notes and passing more details about the president's participation to Marguerite. She was careful to instruct her staff to direct calls about the military to the DOD press office, calls about the investigation to the FBI, and calls about intelligence to the CIA. Dale doled out minuscule nuggets of information to the press and approved the release of three photos taken inside the PEOC.

She looked up at the televisions when she heard a correspondent comment that more than four hours had gone by since the first attacks. She'd lost all sense of time.

"Dale, how quickly could we assemble a press pool?" the president asked from across the room.

"I need to check with Marguerite, but I imagine we can do that in as little as twenty minutes."

"We need to tell the public that we're responding, and I don't see my address to the nation coming together in time for a six P.M. delivery. I can do it, or Maureen can, but we need to get in front of the American people with some reassuring facts. All they are seeing is horror; all they feel is fear. We need to draft a short statement about all of the agencies that are collaborating to respond to the crisis, and then we'll touch on a few points that preview the address tonight."

"Yes, ma'am. I'll call the speechwriters now."

Dale stepped into the small conference room and called Marguerite again to inform her of the president's desire for someone to make a statement to the press.

She let the phone ring twenty times, but no one answered. Dale put the phone back in its cradle and sat for a few seconds. She was about to head up to the press office to assemble the press pool herself when Craig walked in.

"Come sit in for the next briefing. We're not going to put the president out until after this, anyway."

"I told the president I'd assemble a pool so that she or the veep could make a statement about the government's response. I need to at least pass the order on to Marguerite."

"Leave it for now. You can call Marguerite after this update, and I'll help you wrangle the press if I have to."

Dale hated to ignore a direct order from the president, but she didn't want to miss the update on the recovery effort. She followed Craig back into the conference room and grabbed another can of Fresca.

CHAPTER THIRTY

Charlotte

Madam President, we're about four and a half hours out from the first attacks at Times Square. We're proceeding with the rescue-and-recovery effort under the theory that the attackers have carried out their mission for the day. We don't have reason to believe that there are any further attacks under way. Regardless, our law-enforcement agencies will remain in a posture of preparedness for ongoing attacks for at least another seventy-two hours. The rescue-and-recovery missions are under way at all five locations, with Miami being the biggest question mark at this point. The explosion started a fire on the ship, and we understand that the ship is now sinking. The ship was full at the moment of impact, so the fire has complicated the evacuation and rescue missions," the FBI director reported.

"People who survived the terror attack may now die in a fire or drown because they are trapped on a sinking ship?" the president asked.

"Madam President, we have offered the first responders every asset available to the federal government to assist in the rescue operation."

Charlotte felt her chest tighten. The horror of what was happening in Miami was overtaking the situations at the other sites. "What about the attacks on the Mall?"

"We have investigators on the scene now. They should be reporting back before our next briefing."

"How many dead?"

"I don't know yet. I'd say close to twenty from the first and probably more than that from the second, but I wouldn't use those numbers publicly. There are twenty-six confirmed dead in New York, with about two hundred and fifty taken to area hospitals. The numbers out of L.A. and Chicago fluctuate, but we know there are twenty-one dead in Chicago, with about a hundred taken to area hospitals. In Los Angeles, we have eighteen dead and about seventy-five taken to area hospitals."

"Any information about the bombers?"

"They've recovered the bodies of the suspected bombers at LAX and O'Hare. We should have some preliminary reports by our next briefing. There's some evidence that the bomber at LAX was wearing a vest, but at O'Hare, they think the bomber may have been trying to board a plane with an implanted device. One of the early investigative theories is that the bomber was running late, so he detonated it in front of the counter. It was probably his second-choice target. The ship in Miami was clearly the target. There are some eyewitnesses who saw a boat speeding away from the scene. We are interviewing eyewitnesses."

"It wasn't a suicide attack like the one launched against the U.S.S. *Cole*?"

"We don't know yet, but we're pursuing the eyewitness lead about a boat fleeing the scene."

"What sort of explosive device could they have launched from a speedboat onto a cruise ship?" Charlotte asked.

"We're working on that now, Madam President. As soon as we develop any useful information, we'll brief it."

Charlotte thought that the FBI director had a decent amount of information for so early in the investigation. She felt reassured that they'd be able to catch those responsible. Her mind raced to the next step.

"Was there any intelligence at all that something big was coming? Anything that maybe a low-level analyst dismissed as too far-fetched or too unrealistic?"

Charlotte could see the CIA director unmute his line and move to the speakerphone in his office at CIA Headquarters.

"We're still running that down, ma'am. Nothing that a cursory look has revealed as of yet, but as you know, things have a way of getting out, so we're going to run this down for you."

"Not for me—I don't care about recriminations directed at me at this point. I'm wondering if perhaps there's a lead about who did this, and how they did this, that might be buried in some low-level report or recorded call at an NSA facility or something, somewhere, that would point toward today's attacks."

"Yes, ma'am. We're checking."

Charlotte turned to her secretary of transportation, who was in the PEOC.

"Madam President, as you know, the airspace is closed. Amtrak will remain shut down. All public transportation has been suspended in New York City, Chicago, Los Angeles, Miami, and everywhere else. All bus and ferry service is suspended everywhere, too."

"People will be terrified *and* stranded," Charlotte remarked.

"ABC just reported that a suspect has been apprehended in Miami," Dale interjected.

"Turn that up," Charlotte ordered.

The network's chief investigative reporter was sitting at the anchor desk in New York. "ABC has learned that the Coast Guard has apprehended two suspects hiding in a thick clump of mangroves on a small island off the coast of Miami. They've been taken into police custody, and they will be turned over to the FBI for questioning. Something to keep in mind here is that the president of the United States will have to make a very quick and difficult decision about enhanced interrogation measures if these suspects aren't talking, because it's clear that the attacks against America are very much ongoing."

"Dale, is there anything in the news about how the Coast Guard found them?" the attorney general asked.

"According to the *Miami Herald* Web site, these suspects were the same ones seen by eyewitnesses speeding away from the scene in a speedboat this morning."

"Mr. Attorney General, do we have a current legal opinion on the use of enhanced interrogation methods?" Craig asked.

"I'll get that for you," the attorney general replied.

"And anything on the extraordinary powers of the executive branch during a time of war," Craig added.

"I'll have the deputy attorney general brief the guidelines himself at the next briefing."

"We may not have that long," the vice president said. "My predecessor had contemplated the shoot-down of passenger jets by this point on September eleventh," she added.

"The vice president makes a good point. Let's get some information about where the suspects are at this moment. And why are we hearing about this from the media and not through our own people?" the national security advisor complained.

"Tim, the Coast Guard probably tipped off the media before they reported it through the chain of command," the FBI director explained.

"Who is going to interrogate them?" the president asked.

"Madam President, it will be the FBI antiterror task force. They are trained in these sorts of interrogations."

"Madam President, we'd like to break for about forty-five minutes to give the interrogators clear direction legally and operationally. Additionally, we're working to organize the first briefing on the intelligence. The CIA director, the director of national intelligence, and the head of the NSA will all be here."

"Fine. That's fine. I'll go upstairs," Charlotte said.

"Madam President, the White House is completely evacuated except for the essential personnel and the folks in the Situation Room," Craig noted.

Charlotte was starting to feel exasperated. If the White House were actually to be attacked, the only people who would be killed were the staffers deemed essential and those manning the Situation Room. It was completely illogical. Her exasperation quickly shifted to anger as she pushed herself away from the table. The staccato pace of the briefing was distorting the reality of what had happened. This wasn't simply a matter of connecting the dots from five disparate attacks on distinct targets in five different cities. The entire nation had been terrorized. Every citizen had been victimized. She took a deep breath and turned back to the group.

"Melanie, are you still there?"

"Yes, Madam President."

"I'd like for you to convene a group tonight when you get back to discuss how we get this country back on a war footing."

"Yes, ma'am."

"Thank you, Melanie. Folks, whatever war footing this country was once on has slipped. These guys didn't find us to be on war footing at all, and they took full advantage of it," Charlotte said.

She looked around at the faces in the room and felt like firing everyone, but she was just as much to blame as they were—more so. They had all been plodding along, not challenging any of the conventional thinking on preventing something like this. For as long as she'd been president, they'd been walking on eggshells around Congress when it came to the country's domestic surveillance programs. Screw civil liberties. She wasn't to blame for doing away with any semblance of privacy. The terrorists were. God damn it.

"How did we let this happen, team? When did we stop listening? Stop watching? What did we miss? Five goddamned attacks? I want to know what we missed and why we missed it."

"Madam President, it's probably not a good idea to head upstairs right now. The Secret Service called about an hour ago to say that they'd like to move you and Mr. Kramer to a more secure location."

"Where would they like me to go?"

"Either Central Command in Tampa or Offutt in Nebraska," Craig said.

"Send the director down here so I can tell him for the last time today that I'm not leaving the White House. The last time they sent the president hopscotching around the country, he had one hell of a time getting back here. He was up in the sky chasing information all day while his vice president called the shots. With all due respect to my eminently qualified vice president, I have no intention of leaving the White House. There must be some occasions when my word is the last word," she fumed.

"Charlotte, maybe we should hear them out," Peter gently remarked.

She gave him a look that clearly said, *Stay out of this.*

Everyone in the room looked away from the two of them.

Charlotte was so frustrated with everyone that she wanted to throw the entire plate of sandwiches against the wall. Instead, she turned and walked out of the PEOC. A single Secret Service agent followed her silently as she walked up the stairs and headed straight to the West Wing. The sight of Samantha sitting quietly at her desk and Monty waiting in the office across from Sam soothed her. She walked into the Oval Office and sat behind her desk. She figured that Craig and the others would give her about five minutes to cool off before they demanded that she return to the safety of the PEOC.

Sam came in with a glass of ice and a bottle of water.

"Can I order you something for lunch, Madam President?"

"No, thanks, Sam. Did you call your parents?"

"Yes, ma'am."

"Tell them not to be worried."

"Yes, ma'am."

Sam returned to her desk, and Charlotte moved into her private dining room. She turned on the flat-screen TV on the wall and watched a CNN reporter interview a woman who was in such a state of shock that the responsible thing to do would have been to end the interview. The woman became hysterical describing how she had dropped off her parents and her children at the Port of Miami early that morning. Her parents were taking their grandchildren, her son and daughter, on their first cruise. They were all unaccounted for. Charlotte shuddered and fought the urge to punch a wall. On September 11, it was easy enough to say that they could never have imagined attacks so brazen, so coordinated, so far-reaching, and so lethal. But what was her excuse? She knew exactly what Al Qaeda and their more monstrous offshoots like ISIS and ISIL were capable of. And everyone in her administration knew exactly where and how they operated. They had just stopped being audacious enough to do what was necessary to stay a step ahead. Charlotte glanced at her watch and knew she only had another minute or so before Craig or Tim lured her back down to the PEOC.

"Sam, get Melanie on the phone, please."

"Yes, ma'am."

CHAPTER THIRTY-ONE

Melanie

Please attribute this to a senior military official. Earlier today, I directed the nation's armed forces to Defense Condition Three, an increased state of military readiness."

"Other than September eleventh, when have we been at DEFCON Three before?"

"Sandy, the press office will put all of this into historical context for you after I head back to the front of the plane to resume my briefings."

"Yes, ma'am, sorry about that."

"Don't apologize. I have five minutes before I need to get back up there, and I wanted to speak to what we've done on the military side. I'm not going to be able to speak to any of the response or recovery efforts. You're going to have to get that from your colleagues who cover the FBI."

"Madam Secretary, you have a call," Melanie's military aide announced from the front of the press cabin.

"Can I return it in two minutes?"

"I believe it's urgent."

"I'm coming."

Melanie left the press cabin and traveled to the front of the plane.

"It's the president," her aide said once they were out of earshot of the press.

"Madam President."

"Melanie. You're not on speaker. I'm in the Oval Office."

"I sincerely hope that isn't the case, Madam President." Melanie panted. She was out of breath from the walk to her cabin. The baby was already robbing her of some of her lung capacity.

"Calm down. I'll get back down to the PEOC in a minute," Charlotte said.

"Madam President, you need to get back down there immediately. If it gets out that you violated the continuity-of-government protocols, there will be hell to pay."

"Jesus, Melanie, you sound like the rest of them. I *am* the continuity of government."

"Not if something happens to you. Please call me back from downstairs. I'm more concerned about the press reaction than I am about anything actually happening to you."

"Thanks a lot."

"I didn't mean it that way. But you know that they'll hammer you for losing your cool in the middle of the crisis and for making emotional decisions—all of the crap they've been waiting to pin on you for being a woman, all of the criticism that you've worked tirelessly to avoid for six years, will come raining down on you if it gets out that you simply walked out of the PEOC in the middle of the attacks."

"Try not to worry about my reputation for five minutes so I can ask you something."

Melanie sighed. "What can I do for you, Madam President?"

"We took our foot off the gas, didn't we, Mel? *I* took my foot off the gas. We got distracted and lazy, and they hit us. They never take their foot off the gas, do they?"

"No, ma'am. They do not."

"What do I say to them?"

"To whom?"

"The families. The ones who had loved ones who were embarking on cruises or visiting New York City and got blown up this morning? How do we make this right?"

Melanie had seen a president rise to the occasion of comforting the families after September 11. She had seen him changed by it, and she'd watched the president turn the families' healing process into the nation's purpose. Melanie wasn't sure that Charlotte had the same capacity for communal grief.

"You'll do what you have to do to make it right. It will become the entire purpose of the rest of your presidency. It will go on after you're no longer president. You won't worry about your poll numbers or the stupid spats with Congress. Your purpose will be singular. You won't let it happen again."

She could hear the president tapping her pen against her desk.

"I know what you're not saying, Mel."

"I'm sorry?"

"You're afraid that I'm incapable of comforting people in a public, cathartic way."

"I didn't say that."

"You didn't have to. And I didn't miss your jab about focus groups and polls."

"Madam President, I—"

"No, you're right. We lean on Warren too much."

"He can actually be very helpful to you now, though not as a pollster. You could put him in charge of recovery efforts in New York or Miami. He's infinitely optimistic."

"When do we start talking about recovery as opposed to rescue?"

"The FBI director will make an official designation in consultation with each city, but I think you need to let people keep hope alive for a while longer."

"Is that a kind thing to do or a cruel thing to do?"

"Madam President, you're about to discover just what a fine line there is between the two."

CHAPTER THIRTY-TWO

Dale

D ale, I have Marguerite calling for you." The military aide who was fielding all incoming calls to the PEOC pointed at a blinking line, and Dale picked up.

"What's going on?" Dale asked.

"I have an insurrection on my hands. CBS is going completely batshit; half of our press is stuck outside the gate; all of our interns were evacuated with the rest of the White House staff, and the Secret Service won't let them back in; and I'm sitting here by myself trying to answer the phones. Can you please come up here for a few minutes?" Marguerite sounded uncharacteristically hysterical.

"I tried calling you before the last briefing, and no one picked up. You should have called me sooner. I'm on my way."

Dale allowed herself a sideways glance at Peter, who looked up briefly. She smiled sympathetically in his direction and then turned to go. When he stood, Dale thought for a moment that he was going to follow her out. She waited in the hallway for a few seconds and then saw him pour himself a cup of coffee. Dale walked quickly to the press office. When she entered the hallway outside the offices that she and Marguerite shared, she could hear her deputy screaming into the phone.

"Get me your supervisor. Please. I need all of the credentialed press and all of the press interns allowed back inside the White House complex now!"

"Who is that?" Dale asked.

"Some jerk from the Waves office who refuses to let our press back in."

The Waves office was responsible for clearing staff and visitors into the White House complex. Dale took the phone from Marguerite and hung it up.

She dialed the PEOC and asked Craig for a favor. Two minutes later, the deputy director of the Secret Service walked into the press office.

"How can I be of assistance?" he asked.

"Thank you so much for coming up. We need your help getting our press and our interns back into the complex."

"Happy to help," he said.

The three of them walked out the door of the West Wing lobby. It was the first time Dale had been outside all day. She placed both hands around her eyes to shield them from the bright light.

The sky above her was hazy from the smoke on the Mall. The sirens from fire engines and emergency vehicles competed with the whirring of the helicopters patrolling the airspace above the White House. Dale knew from her time in the PEOC that those helicopters were the only aircraft allowed to fly in the now-closed airspace. Dale noticed that there was a burning smell in the air. To her right, the White House fountains were running as they always did, a bizarre nod to the automated grandeur of the White House complex. As Dale, Marguerite, and the deputy director of the Secret Service strode purposefully down the driveway, Dale noticed that about half a dozen White House correspondents were filming live shots from their designated spots in front of the White House's West Wing. The press location was called the North Lawn, but it was actually a patch of gravel wired for live broadcasts so that the White House correspondents could air their news reports to the country and the world with the White House residence as the backdrop. As soon as all of the White House correspondents arrived back from the Women's Museum, they would stand shoulder-to-shoulder on that patch of gravel with hot lights shining down on them. They'd provide minute-to-minute updates about the president's actions. Between live shots, they'd frantically call, text, and e-mail their White House sources for nuggets of news that hadn't aired anywhere else. Dale didn't miss that gravel at all.

She glanced over her shoulder to get another look at the North Lawn and was surprised that so few of them had returned from the museum. She should have offered to help Marguerite sooner. They approached the Northwest Gate, the entrance most commonly used by visitors, staff, and the press assigned to cover the White House briefings. Dale spotted the well-known faces of the network correspondents at the front of the crowd waiting impatiently behind a temporary perimeter that had been set up twenty feet beyond the gate.

"Dale, come on, get us out of here!" one shouted.

"If we go out there, you'll make sure we all get back in, right?" Marguerite confirmed with the Secret Service.

"Yes, ma'am."

Dale and Marguerite stood outside the Northwest Gate rounding up their staff and reporters. The deputy director of the Secret Service worked his magic, and a guard held the gate open for everyone wearing a hard pass, the official photo ID that, on a normal day, meant that you could walk into the White House complex without inviting more than a glance at the pass from a guard. Marguerite stepped back out for a moment to shout at a reporter from the Huffington Post who was taking video of the chaos at the gate.

"You're either a cameraman or a White House reporter. Can't do both, Stanley. You coming or staying out here?"

"I'm coming," he replied.

Dale watched Marguerite pull the White House reporters through the rope line and push them toward the gate. Marguerite scanned the crowd one last time and then walked to where Dale and the Secret Service officer were standing.

"Is that everyone?" Dale asked.

"Everyone I could see."

True to form, some of the reporters started shouting questions at Dale as soon as they stepped through the gate.

"I'm not out here to brief. I came out to get everyone back inside. I'll come down to the briefing room as soon as everyone is back on the White House grounds."

"Can you bring the national security advisor to the briefing room?"

"I'll make the request."

Dale turned back toward the West Wing and noticed that Lucy and Richard were watching the entire ordeal. Two of their crews were filming the activity at the gate. Dale wasn't the least bit surprised that they'd ignored the evacuation order. Dale reminded herself that as a journalist, she never would have evacuated the White House on a day like this, either. For a reporter, there was something honorable about putting yourself in danger to cover the president. It was a mutually beneficial, if irrational, calculation, but from the perspective of the White House, there was a benefit to allowing the public to see the decisive actions that their leaders were taking in the face of grave danger through the press coverage. It was a dynamic that ensured that the press would always be underfoot even when dealing with them felt like an unnecessary burden.

"Hello, Lucy, Richard. How are you guys doing?" Dale asked.

"How is the president holding up? How are you doing? I hope she's cooking up plans to obliterate whoever did this. Is she going to stay out of the PEOC for the rest of the day?"

Dale smiled at the anchors and glanced at the four cameras filming their interaction. "She's doing fine. I'll try to come up and brief off-camera as soon as we get everyone back in the briefing room. Some people got stuck at the Women's Museum."

"We sent a crew over to film it all."

Dale smiled again. "Are you going to be broadcasting from the North Lawn or back at the D.C. bureau?" she asked.

"Wherever they send us." Richard shrugged as though they had no say, which Dale knew was not the case.

Dale turned and walked quickly back toward the West Wing. Something was bothering her. She turned back around.

"Lucy?"

"Yes?"

"Can I talk to you off-camera for a second?"

Lucy walked to where Dale was standing and held her hand over her microphone. When Dale didn't say anything, Lucy unclipped the microphone pack from her belt and handed it to Dale. Dale flipped the power switch to off and handed it back to her.

"Who told you that the president had left the PEOC?"

"What? Oh, no one. I just assumed that if you were out here, you guys had maybe cleared out of the PEOC and she was back in the Oval Office because the security situation had stabilized."

"I wouldn't go so far as to say it's stabilized. It's been what? Five or six hours? I think we're a long way from stable."

Dale always knew when a reporter was covering for a source. She pressed her lips together and stared at Lucy. Dale felt like her shrewd, skeptical self again.

"And the president is still working out of the PEOC," she said icily.

CHAPTER THIRTY-THREE

Charlotte

Charlotte had called off the continuity-of-government planning that would have required her and the vice president to separate. She'd also excused herself from the PEOC this time with the permission of the Secret Service.

She was staring at the draft of her remarks from the speechwriters for later that night.

"Sam, can you get Melanie on the phone again?"

"She's on the line," Sam replied a minute later.

"Where are you?" Charlotte asked.

"Somewhere over the Atlantic Ocean," Melanie replied.

"Do you have a copy of the remarks?" Charlotte asked.

"I don't, but I started working on something for you a few hours ago. I know sometimes the speechwriters are kept out of the loop, and they spend all their time chasing meaningless details, so I thought it might be helpful to frame something out."

"Send it to me, because I can't stand what I have."

"I just sent it to Sam."

"Thanks."

"What time are you going to do this?"

"Not at six, seeing as how it's five-thirty now. There's some talk about trying to assemble a joint session of Congress tonight, but I think that's going to be impossible to pull off. We may just bump it to eight or nine P.M. Is it terrible to wait that long?"

"It's not ideal, but I understand that these things take a while to sift through. You'll put the FBI director out before that, right?"

"Yes. Dale and Marguerite are prepping him now. He's going to head down to the White House briefing room with Tim."

"Good. That's good. That will buy you some time."

"The FBI thinks that more than two hundred people may be dead in Miami, Mel."

"I heard."

"How do you retaliate against someone who targets innocent families? What possible military action can come close to evening the score in the eyes of their loved ones?"

Melanie didn't say anything.

"What was he like on September eleventh?"

"The president?"

"Yes, Melanie. The president. What was he like? Did he feel like he was in control? Because I don't feel like I'm in control of anything."

"I was a junior staffer. I didn't see him on that day."

"But you were around people who did."

"I don't think he felt like he had any control. But he knew right away that the country was at war. Just as you did, and after making sure that his family was safe, he wanted to be in the loop with his national security team. Unfortunately, he was stymied by technological breakdowns. Air Force One didn't have the same video teleconference ability, and the phones kept cutting out. It was incredibly frustrating. He wanted to get back to the White House, but the vice president and the national security advisor kept urging him to stay away from Washington. You were wise to push back when they wanted to get you out of D.C."

"Sam just handed me a note from Tim that says the second D.C. blast took out two FBI agents, a reporter from a local TV station here in D.C., two members of a CNN crew, and some volunteers who were helping the wounded."

"It's awful."

"People are going to need to feel like someone will be punished."

"Everything will be on the table, Madam President."

"The country doesn't have the stomach for a war. Any response will have to be surgical."

Melanie was quiet. Charlotte wasn't telling her anything she didn't already know, but Charlotte knew Melanie would not appreciate being told what kind of strike was needed before they had all of the information about the attackers.

"We should have a clearer sense of our options in the next couple of days."

Sam walked in again and handed Charlotte an outline and introduction that Melanie had drafted. She paused to read them.

"Mel?"

"Yes?"

"This is exactly what I had in mind."

"Madam President?"

"The remarks."

"They still need a lot of work."

"I'm going to tell Dale and Craig to scrap the earlier version. We will wait for your next draft."

"Yes, ma'am."

"Melanie?"

"Madam President?"

"I'd like for you to come straight here when you land at Andrews."

"Yes, ma'am. In the meantime, I will work on the remarks. I'll send you something in about an hour."

"Thanks, Mel."

CHAPTER THIRTY-FOUR

Melanie

Melanie was thankful to be working on the president's speech instead of monitoring the videoconference. The situation remained fluid, but the next significant briefing, as far as Melanie was concerned, would come after the attackers' bodies were identified or when the interrogations started yielding information. Melanie had access to all of the official sources of information, but being cut off from the media coverage made her feel strangely detached from the human reaction. She hoped that it wouldn't hinder her ability to write a speech that struck a chord with the public. It would be a couple of hours before the satellite on her plane started picking up U.S. TV channels.

On September 11, watching the day's events unfold on live TV had been a crucial part of the collective experience for Melanie and her White House colleagues. She remembered when she first saw the image of the World Trade Center tower with smoke billowing from its side. She had just returned from the daily meeting of press staffers in the West Wing. She had taken a seat behind her desk to listen as Katie Couric and Matt Lauer calmly discussed the different possibilities for the disconcerting spectacle. One of them suggested that a commuter plane could have made a tragic miscalculation. Incapable of looking away, Melanie had been staring at the screen when the second plane, a large jet, had careened into the second tower. She'd felt a physical jolt at the moment of impact. One of her colleagues ran in to see if Melanie had seen the shocking images. A few minutes later, Melanie had been on the phone with the White House chief of staff, who was traveling with the president that day. The senior press officers were all on the road with the president, he explained. He needed her and her team to research when and how previous presidents had addressed the public and the press in the wake of terror attacks that had occurred on their watches. The chief of staff was doing what Charlotte had been doing earlier in the day: He was trying to figure out how much time they had before the president needed to speak to the nation.

Now Melanie directed her thoughts back to Charlotte's speech. Drafting the sentences that the president would utter to the nation was a familiar exercise. She knew exactly how far to push Charlotte without making her uncomfortable. The president would want to be resolute, but Melanie would make sure that she also expressed tenderness and compassion toward those who'd endured unspeakable losses. The trick would be finding the right words to accomplish all of those things. Melanie rubbed her stomach and stretched her neck from side to side. She wasn't sure how long she'd been sitting in front of her laptop, but she had the main section of the speech in good shape. She needed to come back and work on the second half of the address. The way she closed the speech would determine its success or failure. What was missing from the current draft was an element that would allow Charlotte to present herself as fully in touch with the profound suffering of the day. Melanie racked her brain for an appropriate passage to provide a literary entry point for Charlotte to transition into something heartfelt. Nothing came to mind. Melanie let her mind wander to all of her favorite writers and their lesser-known works for something unexpected but profound. She sat perfectly still and looked up at the ceiling. She missed the collaborative process of working with the speechwriting team, but it was probably better that she work alone.

Melanie's speech-crafting methods used to drive the president's official speechwriters crazy when she was at the White House. She would sit in front of her computer and bang out several sentences in a burst of creativity. Then she would stare at the screen intently for a few seconds, rereading the words she'd just typed. Just as quickly as she'd typed them, Melanie would delete most of what she'd written. She would think for a minute with her hands perched just above the keyboard, as though she didn't want to waste time reaching for the computer when inspiration hit her again. She'd repeat the process over and over again. It appeared tedious to onlookers, but in all the years that Melanie had overseen Charlotte's speeches, there was never a single instance in which a speech was delivered that didn't completely embody the president's thoughts and persuasions on a certain issue. While assuming responsibility for the presidential speechwriting office had been well outside the typical role of a White House chief of staff, it had allowed Melanie to get to know her new boss on a deeply personal level. It also dovetailed into Melanie's area of expertise: communicating on behalf of the most powerful people on earth.

In her years as press secretary for Charlotte's predecessors, she'd always felt that the ability to speak from the White House podium was about understanding your bosses' potential and presenting an image of the person that he or she most wanted to be. Most of the time, it was a foolproof strategy. By constantly reaching for that virtue that Melanie knew to be a slight exaggeration of the actual person she worked for, she was able to manipulate internal deliberations to force an outcome consistent with the image she'd helped create. Writing for Charlotte had presented different challenges.

Charlotte's inability or unwillingness to open up to anyone on her newly minted White House staff about what she wanted to prioritize and how far she was willing to push to get what she wanted from lawmakers had made it next to impossible to get a workable first draft for most policy addresses into the approval process. Like a lot of politicians, Charlotte usually didn't know what she wanted to say until she saw what others thought she'd want to say on paper. Her reactions to some of the first speeches drafted for her were so visceral that several policy and personnel announcements had been scuttled at the last minute. More than a few opening statements at press conferences had been rewritten at the last possible second. After a few dramatic speechwriting crises, Melanie had taken over.

Now Melanie printed out the current draft of the speech for later that evening and asked her military aide to fact-check the details of the five attacks with the FBI director. She dialed the CIA director to see if he was hearing anything overseas that Charlotte could work into a section about early leads. While she was waiting for him, she typed in "passage TK" to remind herself to add something powerful and memorable as a closer.

CHAPTER THIRTY-FIVE

Dale

Dale looked around her West Wing office and tried to figure out how to restore some semblance of order so that she
could prepare for the on-camera briefing she'd scheduled to update
the press and the public on the attacks. The TV correspondents were
sitting hip-to-hip on Dale's couch speaking into BlackBerrys and
iPhones with their hands over their mouths. Several print reporters were typing on laptops on the floor of her office, and a scrum of
wire reporters and bloggers were standing three bodies deep in her
doorway. The wire reporters held notepads and BlackBerrys, and the
bloggers held iPads with keyboards attached. Lucy and Richard were
doing a phone interview from the small conference table in Dale's
office, where they'd spread out their makeup bag, several bottles of
cold-pressed juices, and an assortment of personal electronics. Two
nearly identical beige dresses and a white dress shirt were hanging
on the back of an empty chair which neither one of them thought to
move, despite the fact that more than a dozen reporters were standing
or sitting on the floor. One of Lucy's high heels had landed next to
a *New York Times* reporter sitting cross-legged on the ground when
she'd kicked it off. Dale watched the reporter appraise the shoe and
then return his attention to his laptop.

Dale caught Brian's eye and shook her head slightly. He smiled, and they shared a moment of mutual disgust at Lucy and Richard's behavior. Dale returned her gaze to her desktop computer and tried to focus on an e-mail message from the public affairs officer at DOT. The Department of Transportation had been slowly reopening various public transportation systems around the country, and Dale hoped to be able to offer an update about New York City's subway system by the time she briefed.

Hours ago, Dale had suggested that the national security advisor, the FBI director, and the homeland security secretary conduct a joint briefing, but the FBI director had insisted that his time would be better spent overseeing the investigation, and Tim was holed up with the president. The current plan was for Dale to brief the press alongside the homeland security secretary.

"Dale, sorry, are you going to release a transcript of the briefing that the NYPD just did?"

Dale had asked them to hold their questions until the briefing, but some of them simply couldn't help themselves.

"Why would we do that, Evan? We don't have any better access to the audio from the New York Police Department than you do."

"Sorry."

"Dale?"

"Yes?"

"Any chance we'll hear from the president or vice president before the address to the nation?"

"Not likely, but we will keep you posted. No more questions, guys, or you're going to have to clear out. I will brief in half an hour. Feel free to start heading downstairs."

The press had been staked out in her office ever since she'd invited them upstairs for a short "gaggle," an informal briefing for the press that wasn't "on camera." It served as an opportunity for both sides to prepare for the more theatrical on-camera briefing later in the day. Dale had been in their shoes, and she understood the pressure they were under to break news and keep up with their colleagues.

Dale looked up and saw Lucy shush a reporter and point at Richard, who was speaking in a booming voice about how he was sitting deep inside the West Wing, where he had a front-row seat to all of the latest information about the attack.

"President Kramer is, at this moment, steps away from us, working on her address to the nation and monitoring the recovery efforts in the five cities that were terrorized today," he bellowed. The *Politico* reporter snapped a picture of Lucy and Richard with his iPhone. Dale secretly hoped that he would write something awful about them.

Lucy and Richard were getting on Dale's nerves. She'd asked them to do their live shots from the North Lawn or the briefing room like everyone else, but they were under the impression that they could run roughshod over Dale's staff and the rest of the reporters. Now Lucy was standing in her bare feet and smoothing Richard's hair down with her hand, which she'd licked.

Dale was about to order everyone to get out when she heard a commotion at the door. She prayed that it was Marguerite with one of her clever jujitsu strategies for getting the press to do something they didn't want to do. She peered hopefully toward the small parting of reporters and jumped up when she saw Craig.

Some of the reporters stood. Others started shouting questions.

"Hello, everyone. Thanks for all of your hard work today. I need to borrow Dale for a few minutes."

Dale and Craig walked out of the press offices and ducked into the Roosevelt Room across the hall.

"What's up?"

"The FBI director just called with the names of the CNN crew injured in the second blast on the Mall. They're notifying families now, so make sure these names don't get released from here. Let CNN go public if and when they want."

"Did they—?"

"The cameraman died on the way to the hospital. The other two are in critical condition."

Dale studied the piece of paper he'd handed her and felt her chest tighten. The correspondent was a seasoned journalist who'd made multiple trips to Iraq and Afghanistan.

"Such a tragedy, isn't it?"

Dale spun around and was surprised to see Lucy and Richard

standing in the hallway. She couldn't believe they'd followed her out of her office. They clearly believed that the rules that governed inter-actions between the press and the White House staff did not apply to them. On an ordinary day, this would be annoying, but on *this* day, it represented a shocking degree of arrogance and insensitivity.

"What are you doing out here?" Dale demanded.

"We just heard about Carla. She was one hell of a reporter," Lucy said.

"She *is* one hell of a reporter. She's in the hospital."

"Right."

Dale realized the trap she'd just fallen into. They were fishing. And she'd given them more information than they probably had. Dale of-ficially hated them.

"I don't know if they've tracked her family down yet, so please don't report that she's been hurt. She has a husband and kids," Dale urged.

"We wouldn't do that," Richard promised.

Dale thought she saw him nod in Craig's direction.

"I'm sorry—did you guys need something?" Dale asked the an-chors.

"Just stretching our legs," Lucy said.

"Can you do that in the briefing room or out on the North Lawn? I have something else I need to speak to Craig about."

Dale watched Lucy turn her back toward them and assumed that she and Richard were making their way to the West Wing lobby. She leaned in closer to Craig and lowered her voice so that Lucy and Rich-ard wouldn't hear her.

"I'm getting ready to brief our press on the rescue-and-recovery efforts. I have the interagency notes. Is there anything that I can say about the president's speech? Do we have a new time for the address to the nation yet?"

"Not right now. She hated the first draft the speechwriters sent her. She cleared everyone out and said she wanted to work on it by herself," Craig said.

"And how's the speech shaping up?" Lucy interrupted from a few feet away.

Dale couldn't believe that they were still hovering close enough to eavesdrop. She was out of patience with them and ready to throw them out of the West Wing.

"Everything is going fine," Craig said. He put an arm on Dale's shoulder to calm her.

"Craig, can we speak to you off the record for two minutes about the mood as the president prepares for her address to the nation? We can do it off the record if you want, but we're still going to broadcast the 'Day in the Life,' and it will just be so much better if we have a sense of the dramatic turn this day has taken," Lucy said.

Dale was incredulous.

"It's up to Dale," Craig offered.

Dale faced him to see if he was serious.

He shrugged his shoulders, as if to say *I thought this was what you wanted.*

"Whatever!" Dale said. Her attempt at indifference had come out as irritation.

"What's going on out here?" Marguerite asked, appearing in their now-crowded hallway.

"Good news, Marguerite. We're going to get out of your hair for a little bit. Craig has been generous enough to agree to spend a few minutes with us," Lucy chirped.

The look on Marguerite's face was priceless. "But Dale is briefing in fifteen minutes."

"We'll be back for that."

Marguerite put a hand on her hip and started to protest, but Dale stopped her.

"Come on. Let's go back inside and finish our prep in your office. I've got the entire press corps sprawled out in mine."

Lucy and Richard followed Craig down the hall toward his office. Dale and Marguerite watched them go.

"Did you have any idea that they were such pains in the ass?"

"I'd heard from half a dozen of their colleagues, but I figured it was sour grapes."

"They are definitely more trouble than they are worth," Marguerite muttered.

"Before we go back inside, I need to show you something. I just got the names of the CNN crew who were hurt in the second Mall attack. Let's pull the CNN White House unit out and tell them so they don't hear it while they're sitting in the briefing room in front of the rest of the press corps when it breaks. I don't want them to see it on Twitter or on another network."

Dale handed Marguerite the piece of paper that she'd folded into a tiny square. Marguerite unfolded it and read the names. She covered her mouth with one hand and stared at the list.

"These two are in the hospital," Dale said quietly, pointing at the names of the reporter and producer. She stood there with Marguerite for a moment to allow the shock to wear off.

"Come on, let's go get them before it leaks. Lucy and Richard knew about it," Dale said gently.

They took two steps toward the press office, and Marguerite seemed to crumble. Dale could see that her whole body was trembling. She reached out and pulled Marguerite toward her. Dale wasn't accustomed to comforting female friends, but she patted her deputy's back and stood as still as possible in an awkward embrace. She wasn't sure if she was providing any comfort at all. Dale had never seen Marguerite upset about anything.

"Sorry," Marguerite said through her tears.

"I'm relieved to learn that you're human," Dale gently teased.

Marguerite pulled away and wiped the tears from her face. "It's all catching up with me."

"You're doing great."

"I'm going to freshen up in the ladies' room, and I'll meet you in my office."

Dale nodded and walked slowly back toward the press office.

CHAPTER THIRTY-SIX

Charlotte

Charlotte couldn't remember the last time she'd spoken to Peter. It felt like it had been a while, and she wondered how the kids were doing. She picked up the phone and dialed his number in the residence. Before he picked up, the national security advisor appeared in her doorway.

Charlotte hung up the phone.

"Madam President?"

"Come in."

"I thought I'd check in before the next NSC meeting to see if you needed anything before we head down to the Situation Room."

"No, but come sit for a moment. Anything new?"

"They've identified the body of the Chicago bomber. The FBI director is on his way over."

"I'm here." The FBI director had appeared in the doorway to the Oval Office.

"Come in and sit down," Charlotte invited.

He entered the Oval Office but remained standing.

"Madam President, there's something I want to tell you both before we go downstairs. It's going to be very upsetting to a whole bunch of people here, so I wanted to tell you in person and before the meeting downstairs."

"What is it?"

"We have identified one of the volunteers killed in the second attack on the Mall as Warren Carmichael."

Charlotte felt the blood drain from her arms and legs. She steadied herself by placing both hands on her desk. "Who knows about this?"

"No one yet, Madam President. I know he works for you—worked for you. I wanted to tell you myself. We've been trying to notify the family, but they're not picking up the home phone numbers that we have on file from DOD. We're trying to locate cell numbers for Mr. and Mrs. Carmichael from Warren's phone."

Charlotte's throat tightened. "How?" she rasped.

But she knew how. And she knew why. He wasn't like most people who worked for her. He didn't stay in his lane like typical political operatives. He went where he could make a difference. Of course, he'd rushed down to the site of the explosion. If only Charlotte had called him and summoned him to the White House. She'd considered it but was afraid of the blowback she'd get for bringing in a political advisor in the middle of a national security crisis. The FBI director was still talking.

"Apparently, he'd gone down to help with the rescue operation. He was helping the first responders comfort the victims when the second explosion went off. A witness said he threw his body on top of a young boy who'd already been injured when the second bomb went off. No normal person would have had the reflexes—or the time—to do that. No doubt that he saved the kid's life."

Charlotte was having a hard time containing her emotions. "I'll be right back." She nodded at the FBI director and the national security advisor and walked into her private dining room. She closed the door and leaned against it. She didn't have time to cry. Instead, she took deep breaths and shook her arms out next to her body. She sat down at the table and started to dial Peter's number again but hung up more quickly than before. Peter wouldn't say the right thing. And Peter wouldn't understand why Warren would have walked into such a dangerous situation. Where Peter was cautious and deliberate, Warren was fearless and impulsive. Charlotte took one last deep breath and then walked back into the Oval. They had to tell Dale before it leaked.

"Gentlemen, please postpone the meeting downstairs for thirty minutes. We'll get started around six-thirty. And when you get the number for Warren's parents from his cell phone, I'd like to make the call to them myself."

"It's a horrible shame, Madam President," Tim said.

Charlotte nodded and walked over to Sam's desk.

"Sam, can you find out where Dale is right now?"

"She's right there," Sam replied, pointing at the small television on her desk.

"Where?"

"Walking up to the podium in the White House briefing room to do her first briefing of the day with the secretary of homeland security."

CHAPTER THIRTY-SEVEN

Melanie

M adam Secretary, I have the president for you," Sam said. Melanie thought she was calling with feedback on the speech. Maybe Charlotte had felt that it was too morose.

"Are we close, Madam President?"

"I'm not calling about the speech, Mel."

"No?"

"Are you sitting down?"

"No."

"Please sit down."

"You're making me nervous."

"Are you sitting down?"

"Yes, I'm sitting."

"I have to tell you something upsetting. I want you to be prepared for some bad news."

"What is it?"

"Warren went down to the site of the bombing on the Mall."

"Why am I not surprised to hear that?"

"Melanie, he got hurt by the second blast."

"Is it serious?"

"God damn it. I hate being the one to tell you this."

"Tell me what?"

"When the second bomb went off, he threw his body on top of a kid who'd been injured in the first blast. He saved his life, but his injuries were fatal."

"What?"

"I'm sorry, Mel. I know how close you and Brian are to him."

Melanie couldn't believe what she was hearing. "Are you sure? Who told you? Maybe it's a mistake? Maybe he's at the hospital?"

"No, Melanie. The FBI director was here. I'm so sorry."

Melanie couldn't form words. How could this happen? How could he survive four tours in Iraq and get killed a block away from the White House? Melanie looked around the cabin and knew that she would always remember every single detail about where she was and what she was doing and exactly how Charlotte had told her that her friend had died.

"Does Dale know?" Melanie whispered.

"No. She just started briefing the press."

"You have to tell her before it gets out."

"How do you suggest I do that?"

"I don't know, but you need to make sure she isn't standing up there when she finds out."

Melanie heard Charlotte sigh deeply. She felt her throat tighten, but she was determined not to cry until she hung up with Charlotte. Something about being pregnant had rendered her less capable of controlling her emotions. Melanie worked hard to steady her voice.

"Madam President, Warren was Brian's best friend. I need to tell Brian."

"Isn't he in the briefing room right now, too?"

"Yes, I suppose he is."

"Please do me a favor and give me a few minutes to figure out how to tell Dale, and then you can call Brian as soon as I've broken the news to her. I'd like to call his parents, too."

Melanie wanted to scream. It was so unfair. She did her best to quell her emotions so that she could help Charlotte with the logistics of sharing the worst news of the day.

"Madam President, I have an idea."

CHAPTER THIRTY-EIGHT

Dale

E van, this is the last question on this topic, and then we're moving on," Dale warned. They'd been taking questions for about ten minutes, and it wasn't going well. She had underestimated her press corps's level of agitation and overestimated the secretary of homeland security's ability to field rapid-fire questions about an ongoing crisis.

"Madam Secretary, one more time on this, can you clarify when the threat level was elevated and if it was after at least four of the attacks had already occurred—maybe even after the second D.C. bombing—can you explain what value the warning system has at this point, if any?"

"Evan, the decision to elevate the threat level is a complicated one—"

"Madam Secretary, with all due respect, what's complicated about four cities getting bombed by terrorists?"

"Evan! She's answered the question. We are moving on. Next question?" Dale urged.

"No!" Evan protested. "Answer the goddamned question with something other than a platitude. Why the hell do we have a warning system if it goes off after all of the attacks are complete? How does that warning system protect anyone? And if it doesn't, why the hell does the government bother?"

"Evan, we'll put together a briefing for you and anyone else who wants to be educated at a more granular level than what we've gone into here about the various factors involved in elevating the country's threat level."

Dale tried to move on to friendlier territory for the secretary of homeland security, who was usually one of the administration's most effective spokespeople.

"Madam Secretary, was there ever any consideration given to separating the president and the vice president, particularly in the early hours, when, as you said, it was unclear how many cities had been targeted?"

"Frank, we're not going to address every precaution that was considered, mostly because we've spent the last few hours gathering information about the specific actions that were taken. I can tell you that at no time were the president and the vice president separated, other than in the first minutes after we learned of the attack when they returned from the Women's Museum in separate motorcades," Dale interrupted.

The secretary of homeland security looked relieved. Dale glanced down at her notes to see if she could move the briefing in another direction. She looked up quickly when she heard the reporters shift in their seats. A few of them rose to their feet. Dale glanced over her right shoulder and was more than a little surprised to see the president walking toward the podium.

She'd changed into a knee-length black skirt with a matching belted jacket. Her hair was pulled back, and while she didn't look as though she'd had her makeup redone since the morning, her face looked fresh and focused. Craig and a single Secret Service agent had accompanied her to the briefing room.

"Madam President, welcome."

The president joined Dale at the podium. Dale removed her binder and bottle of water and stepped aside.

"Thank you, Dale. Thank you, Madam Secretary. May I?"

"Of course."

Dale moved toward where Marguerite was standing and leaned against the wall. The secretary of homeland security sank into a chair along the side of the room with relief. The press remained standing. Charlotte adjusted the microphone and folded and then unfolded her hands on top of the podium.

"Please be seated," she said. "I came down to answer a few questions, but first I want to announce that I plan to address the nation this evening at eleven P.M. At that time, we will share everything we know about the terror attacks that struck five American cities this morning. I want to add my thoughts and prayers to those of every citizen of our shaken but determined nation. We send those prayers out to every family that has lost a loved one in today's attacks. To those families who are still waiting for word about your loved ones, we wait with you, and we pray with you. To the first responders in Miami, New York, Los Angeles, Chicago, and here in D.C., we are grateful to you, and we hold you up today as the bravest among us. And to all of you in here today, and to the brave journalists who risk everything to bring important information to their readers and viewers, we appreciate and honor all of you and your families, too. As I said, we'll have a more complete report about what we know about the attacks and the evidence we've gathered today when we meet again at eleven P.M., but I'm happy to take a few of your questions now."

Dale knew that the briefing had been going badly, but she didn't think it had been disastrous enough to justify a presidential intervention. She wondered if they'd caught one of the attackers or wanted to ask for the public's assistance in a manhunt.

"Psst." Someone had opened the pocket door that separated the briefing room from the press office. Dale looked and saw a Secret Service agent she recognized as one of Peter's.

"Miss Smith, please come inside," he urged. Dale looked around. No one else noticed him. She stared at Craig until he looked over at her. She motioned toward the press office. Craig nodded and mouthed, "Go ahead."

Dale slipped through the door. The agent disappeared into the hallway, and Peter stood alone in the press office.

"Walk with me," he said.

"What's going on?"

"Let's walk."

"I can't."

"I need to tell you something."

"I need to listen to the president."

"It was Charlotte's idea for me to talk to you now. Please come with me."

Dale's stomach sank, and her heart felt like it was beating outside of her body. Peter walked quickly down the colonnade toward the East Wing.

"You're scaring me. What's going on?"

"Come on." His voice was stern.

He held the door to the East Wing open for her and then led her into the medical unit, which occupied the first office on the ground level of the East Wing.

The nurse who was watching the press briefing on television smiled at them. When Peter failed to return the smile, she gathered her things and left. Peter nodded his appreciation.

"Please tell me what's going on," Dale begged.

"Dale, you probably know this part already, but Warren went down to the site of the D.C. bombing to help with the recovery."

The last time she'd spoken to him was when she was on her way to the PEOC. He hadn't said anything about helping with the recovery. Dale stopped breathing. Warren was hurt. She needed to get to the hospital. They'd come in to tell her that he was hurt and calling for her. Charlotte would want that for Warren.

"Dale?" Peter was standing in front of her, talking to her, but she couldn't focus on what he was saying.

"Where is he? Can I see him?"

"I'm trying to tell you. He went down there to help with the rescue-and-recovery effort. And he was there helping the victims. When the second bomb went off, he threw his body on top of a young boy and probably saved his life by doing so. But he was badly injured."

"How badly?"

"Dale, I'm so, so sorry."

"Why are you sorry? What happened to Warren?"

"I'm so sorry, Dale. I would give anything for it not to be true."

"I don't believe you!"

"His injuries were fatal. He died on the way to the hospital."

"No!" She shook her head so hard she grew dizzy.

"Dale, breathe."

She felt like she was going to pass out. Peter tried to comfort her by placing an arm around her shoulders. She pushed him away roughly.

Dale felt like she was falling. Warren was the best person she knew. He couldn't be dead. The harder she tried to stop crying, the more out of control she felt. Dale leaned against the wall and tried to catch her breath. Peter moved closer to her and embraced her. Dale raised her head slowly to look at his face.

She prayed that he was telling her a cruel joke or that she was imagining the whole thing. Anything would be better than this. Her eyes met his, and she knew from his helpless look that he was telling her the truth. Warren was dead.

"I'm so sorry, Dale."

She looked at him and felt the weight of his words strike her again. She pounded his chest with her fists until the crush of his arms around her was too much to resist. When she was finally drained, she collapsed into him. She decided that if she never moved from there, she would never have to face the fact that the most extraordinary person who would ever love her was dead.

Peter had stopped saying he was sorry, and Dale had stopped crying, but they hadn't moved. Dale's back and neck ached, but she was too afraid to face whatever came next.

What did come next? It wasn't like she could go home. That was the only thing that sounded worse than being here. But what was she supposed to do? Whatever it was, she wasn't ready to face it.

CHAPTER THIRTY-NINE

Charlotte

As she neared the medical unit, the nurse sitting on a chair outside looked at her with such discomfort that Charlotte knew she should turn around and walk away. Instead, she nodded in the nurse's direction and walked slowly toward the door. She pushed it gently and saw Dale and Peter sitting on the floor. Dale had her head cradled in her arms, and Peter was sitting as close to her as was possible. He was gently rubbing her back with one hand. They weren't speaking, but his head was close to hers. It looked like their heads were touching. Charlotte couldn't remember the last time she'd sat that close to Peter.

She forced herself to look away. Charlotte was thankful that the nurse hadn't said anything. She could escape undetected.

"Char, your press conference was tremendous. You were strong and compassionate and informative, and you didn't try to bullshit people. It was a phenomenal performance," Mark called out from the direction of the Diplomatic Room.

Charlotte had stayed in the hallway a moment too long. Brooke and Mark had entered the East Wing from the South Lawn with the three dogs a few steps ahead. She tried to smile at them.

When Charlotte turned back to the medical unit, she saw Peter rush to his feet. He pulled the door shut to offer Dale privacy and came out to stand in the hallway. Charlotte was irritated by the gesture. She knew she was being irrational. Looking after Dale had been the one thing she'd asked him to do all day, but he was *her* husband. That had to count for something. It had been Melanie's idea for him to break the news to Dale while Charlotte addressed the press, and she'd agreed to it without hesitation. But Warren was her friend, too. She'd known him longer than Dale had. Why was Peter acting as though Dale's reaction was the only one that concerned him? Shouldn't it at least cross his mind to ask her how *she* was holding up?

"How are you doing, Char?" Mark asked.

"Can I get you anything?" Brooke offered.

"I'm fine. What are you guys doing down here?"

"We took the dogs out as soon as the Secret Service would let us out of the residence. They've been inside all day," Mark said.

"Thank you."

"Isn't it a relief that all of the kids are together? Griffin and Finley are at the house with the twins and about two dozen Secret Service agents. They're watching everything on TV."

She couldn't remember if Peter had told her that the twins were going to Brooke and Mark's house in Atherton. If he had, she didn't remember. The last update she'd heard was that Harry was still in Berkeley and Penny was in her apartment near Stanford.

"I'm so glad they're all at the house," Charlotte said.

She allowed Mark to put a protective arm around her shoulder. It was the first time anyone had offered her any physical comfort all day, and she was afraid she might start to cry.

"Please tell the twins that I'll call them as soon as I get out of the next NSC meeting."

Brooke and Mark turned their gaze to Peter.

"Are you sick?" Brooke asked him.

"No."

Brooke looked from Peter to Charlotte and then to Peter again. Mark sensed the tension and pulled Brooke gently toward the residence.

"Char, we'll be upstairs if you need anything," Mark said. He snapped his fingers to summon the dogs. The two younger ones followed him, but Cammie remained at Charlotte's feet.

"I'll take her to the Oval with me," Charlotte said.

When she heard the elevator door close, she looked back at Peter. He looked agonized.

"How is she?" Charlotte asked.

"In shock."

Charlotte couldn't remember a time when Peter had been as distressed about her as he appeared to be about Dale.

"Do whatever you have to do to get her through the rest of the day. If she needs to go home, I understand, but it would be helpful to have a press secretary tonight," she said coolly.

Peter nodded.

Charlotte contemplated telling him that her heart was breaking into so many pieces she wasn't sure she could get through the next ten minutes, not to mention the next two hours. She considered pulling him further into the hallway and clinging to him tearfully simply to experience his embrace. Part of her wanted to know what it would feel like to let go of the ball of pain she'd been holding on to so tightly all day. She couldn't remember a time when she'd allowed him to see her in pain. She wasn't even sure that she still knew how to show him that side of her or to lean on him if he had thought to offer. She stood there for a moment longer, waiting for him to ask her how she was or touch her or say something to her about how brave she was and how proud he was of her. He didn't do any of those things. Eventually, she murmured something about keeping her posted about Dale and then turned around and walked slowly back toward the Oval Office with Cammie underfoot.

CHAPTER FORTY

Melanie

"Brian, can you hear me?"

"Barely. I've got another live shot on Charlotte's press conference in five minutes. Can I call you back?"

"I need to talk to you."

"Can it wait five minutes?"

"I don't think it can wait. Brian, walk outside for me."

"Mel, what's going on?"

"Just tell me when you're in a place where no one can hear you."

"Hang on."

Melanie heard him explain to his producer that he had to take a call outside. It sounded like she asked him if he'd be back for his live shot.

"I'll be back," Melanie heard him say. "I'm walking out the door. I'm passing the smokers. A sniper might mistake me for an intruder, but I am alone and out of earshot now. What's going on?"

Melanie was scared to tell Brian. She didn't know how he'd take the news, and she was afraid that he wouldn't be able to do his job afterward.

"Do you have a break after this live shot? A longer break?"

"No. I don't have any breaks, Mel. I am on the air every five minutes with whatever scrap of information I can get." He sounded stressed.

"Brian, listen to me. I have to tell you something terrible."

"What?"

"It's Warren. He went down to the Mall after the first explosion. He was helping the first responders, and he was right there when the second bomb exploded."

"Where? He was right where? Mel, why are you crying? What happened to Warren? I can't understand you."

"He died. He died in the second explosion. Warren died." Melanie was choking on her own sobs now.

"Oh, my God, my poor wife. I'm so sorry that I'm not there, honey."

"Did you hear me?"

"I heard you, honey. Dammit. I wish I was with you. Try to calm down."

"What was he even doing down there?" Melanie couldn't stop crying.

"I don't know, sweets, I don't know. Knowing him, he probably found it unbearable to sit and watch all of the carnage on television, so he went down to help."

"I'm so mad at him. I wish he'd just stayed in his office. Why couldn't he just have stayed in his office like everyone else?"

"Mel, listen to me. Warren would be so pissed if he knew that you were this upset."

Melanie cried harder.

"Mel, is there a doctor on the trip? Did you tell the doctor? Let me talk to the doctor. I want you to lie down. Do you promise me that you'll lie down for a few minutes?"

"I'm OK. I was scared about telling you."

"I'm fine, Mel. I want you to take care of yourself."

"I will. I promise. Are you sure you're all right?"

"I'm going to try not to think about it until we're together, Mel. This is going to sink in for both of us over the next few days, and we'll deal with it then. I don't want you to worry about me. Will you promise me that you will not worry about me? Just get home and take care of yourself, and don't get too upset. We'll deal with this together."

Melanie sniffled.

"Do his parents know yet?" Brian asked.

"Charlotte is calling them now."

"They're here. They came to see Warren. They were going to meet Dale tonight. Does Dale know?"

"Peter just told her."

"When?"

"While the president was briefing you guys."

"Was that your idea?"

"Yeah."

They were quiet for a couple of minutes. Melanie blew her nose.

"Don't you have another live shot?" she asked.

"I have a few minutes," Brian assured her.

"I worked on Charlotte's speech for tonight."

"Charlotte's lucky to have you."

"How's the mood there?"

"Safe to say that it's about to get worse."

"Because of Warren?"

"And the CNN crew."

"Right."

"Listen, there's something else that Warren would want."

"What?"

"Warren would want you to focus on Charlotte today."

"I know."

"Wait a minute. Is she waiting for you to get back?"

"What do you mean?"

"She announced that she was addressing the nation at eleven. Is that so you'll be there?"

"I don't think so."

"I'm sure it is."

"I can't imagine that's why she delayed the address."

"I'm willing to bet you it is."

"Are you sure you're all right?"

"You promised not to worry about me. I'll see you in a couple of hours."

Melanie hung up and felt relieved. She'd get through the rest of the day. But did Charlotte really schedule the speech so that she would be there?

CHAPTER FORTY-ONE

Dale

Dale could hear people around her speaking in low voices, but she couldn't make out what they were saying. It was as if she was underwater and they were standing at the edge of a pool or bathtub waiting for her to lift her head above its surface. Every time she tried to focus on the conversations around her, Peter's words replayed in her mind, and she was plunged deeper underwater.

He didn't make it, Peter had said.

That was the part of the story that still felt like a lie.

She understood that shortly after she last spoke to him, Warren had gone down to the site of the bombing. It didn't surprise her that he'd wanted to help with the recovery effort; Dale could even picture him rushing to help the victims. And she couldn't help but wonder if the universe was exacting its revenge on her for her attempted infidelity.

But the rest of it was incomprehensible. Warren had survived the wars. He'd come home from Iraq and Afghanistan and had thrived in D.C. He wasn't one of those people who rose to professional and social heights for the purpose of reveling in access or status. Warren was oblivious to those sorts of things. Warren was bright and warm, and everyone flourished in his presence. And he'd loved Dale in a way that made her feel normal. Every other relationship she'd ever been in had left her feeling broken. Being loved by Warren had made her feel like she could have a happily ever after just like everyone else.

He didn't make it.

She knew that Warren had wanted their relationship to grow more serious. He'd never pushed, but he made it no secret that he imagined a future with her in it. When they encountered couples with young children, Warren could barely contain his longing to have a family of his own. His face would grow serious, and he'd pull her in for a kiss and whisper something about how beautiful her children would be. She always kissed him back, but she usually made a joke about what a horrible mother she'd make. No one else had ever made her feel like she could bring another life into the world and take care of it and love it.

He didn't make it.

Dale had often worried that Warren loved her too much. She shouldn't have. Warren had made clear over and over again that he was happy to be with her in whatever kind of relationship she was ready for. He told her that she was the one he'd been waiting for.

He didn't make it.

Dale noticed that the conversations had stopped, and everyone was looking at her. Had someone asked her a question? She looked at Peter for guidance. He placed an arm on her shoulders and leaned closer to her.

"How are you doing?"

"I'm OK."

"You know Violet, Charlotte's makeup artist?" Peter offered.

"Hiya, darlin', how are you doing?" Violet had a pleasant accent. It wasn't quite a Southern accent, but it definitely had a twang.

"I'm a mess," Dale acknowledged.

"We're gonna fix you up, sugar." Dale watched as Violet unpacked her makeup bag on the counter in the medical unit next to the bright orange box marked "biohazard."

"Sugar, can I put this cape on you so I don't get makeup on your pretty dress?"

Dale nodded. Violet worked methodically. First, she poured makeup remover onto a Q-tip and wiped it under Dale's eyes.

"We're gonna start with a clean slate," Violet said, more to herself than to Dale. She opened a bottle of clear liquid and poured a quarter-sized dollop onto her palm. "This serum is gonna calm your skin down so it looks nice again," she soothed.

Next, Dale watched Violet open three different tubes of undereye concealer and examine them closely. She scraped off a chunk from each stick and mixed the chunks together on the back of her hand. With an egg-shaped sponge, Violet started working the makeup onto Dale's face. When she was done with the concealer, she moved on to foundation. She poured dime-sized dollops from two bottles onto a small mirror and mixed them with a fresh sponge. Then she dabbed the beige lotion onto Dale's face until her entire face was one color. Violet lined Dale's eyes with black liquid eyeliner and covered her eyelids with four different shades of brown. She brushed mascara onto Dale's upper and lower lashes and then stood back to admire her work.

"You have eyes again, my dear."

Dale forced a smile. "Thanks, Violet."

"All you need now are cheeks and lips, and then you're good as new."

Dale sat quietly and watched Violet apply several different shades of pink to her cheeks. She used a different brush to sweep bronzer under her cheekbones and above her brows.

"Smile for me, sugar."

Dale forced the corners of her lips upward while Violet expertly applied lip liner.

She added a gooey drop of lip gloss in the center of her lower lip and ordered Dale to rub her lips together.

"You look gorgeous!" she exclaimed.

"Thank you, Violet," Peter said.

"Thank you," Dale said again.

"I'm just gonna blow out your hair a little bit, and then we're done."

Dale sat silently while Violet folded sections of her hair over a round brush and blew hot and then cold air over them until her strands yielded to Violet's will.

"Just a touch of shine, and you're set."

"Thank you," Dale repeated.

"My pleasure, sugar. Call me if you need a touch-up."

While Violet was packing up her supplies, the president's physician sat down in a chair next to Dale.

"Do you feel like you can go back to the press office, or would you rather rest here a little longer?"

"I think it will be helpful to get back to work," Dale said.

The doctor stared intently at Dale's now-made-up face. "I'd like to suggest that you make contact with your parents and ask them to come here if that's possible so that you have an around-the-clock support network as the news sinks in," he added.

Dale nodded. She had no plans to ask her parents to come stay with her. "If I start to feel like it's more than I can handle to be out there, I'll come back here."

The doctor's eyes took in her shaky hands. "I think it's possible that you're still in shock. And what I'm concerned about is that the stress of your job could expedite the process of the shock wearing off. When it does, it's likely that it will be replaced by the sort of grief that most of us like to experience in the privacy of our own homes, surrounded by loved ones."

He looked at Peter. Peter looked uncomfortable.

"I know what you're saying, but it's not like I'm going to be too far away from all of you. If I walk out there and start to lose it, you have my permission to remove me from the premises." She tried to joke.

Peter didn't smile.

Dale was trying to show them that fragments of her sense of humor were still intact. It was almost eight P.M., and the press would be crawling the walls of the briefing room by now. She was sure Marguerite was at her wits' end.

"Do his parents know?" Dale asked Peter.

"Charlotte was calling them right after the press briefing, so I assume they know by now."

Dale nodded.

"If you're up for it, I thought I'd invite Marguerite over, and she could bring you up to speed. The press has been told that you were tapped to work on a very small team to draft the president's speech for tonight," Peter explained.

"Whose idea was that?"

"I think it was Melanie's."

"Does Marguerite know about Warren?"

Peter nodded and dialed her number from the landline in the medical unit. "She'll be right over," he reported.

"Great." Dale tried to smile.

"Do you want something to eat?" Peter asked.

Dale made a face and shook her head.

"I'd like you to try to drink some water," the doctor urged.

Dale took a sip from the bottle he handed her and patted her pockets for her BlackBerry and iPhone.

"You were briefing, remember?" Peter reminded her.

"Right."

A minute later, Marguerite rushed in and handed Dale her Black-Berry and iPhone.

"Are you OK?"

"Yeah. I'm OK."

"I'm so sorry."

"Let's not do this," Dale begged.

"Fine with me," Marguerite said, looking up at Peter and the White House doctor for guidance.

"Why don't you bring Dale up to speed here and then make your way back to the press office? Call us in an hour, and let us know how everything is going," the doctor suggested.

Marguerite nodded.

"Maybe we should plan to touch base when the news breaks in the press about Warren," Peter suggested.

Dale smiled weakly. "Yes," she agreed.

"Call me if you need anything before that," he offered.

"Marguerite, let's catch up in my office," Dale proposed.

She stood for the first time in what felt like hours and felt so light-headed that she had to grab Marguerite for balance.

"Do you want to sit back down?" Peter asked.

"No. I just felt dizzy for a second. I think I need some fresh air."

Dale held on to Marguerite as they moved slowly toward the press office.

"Marguerite, fill me in. Are our guys driving you crazy?"

"Evan wrote a nasty hit piece on his blog about the homeland security secretary being clueless after the briefing. She sat in my office crying for half an hour."

"Jesus, I'm so sorry you had to deal with them by yourself."

Marguerite spoke without stopping to breathe as they walked back toward their offices. Dale felt reassured about her decision to return to work. The sheer volume of requests for information and interviews would help numb her from her own pain for a while.

It wasn't until she was settled at her desk, catching up on the latest news articles, that she realized she hadn't thanked Peter for breaking the news to her and taking care of her afterward.

CHAPTER FORTY-TWO

Charlotte

M adam President, we need to reach a consensus in here about how we manage the news about the Chicago and LAX bombers being U.S. citizens," the FBI director implored. "We are in the process of moving the alleged attackers' families into custody for questioning and protection," he added.

Charlotte nodded. They'd gone around and around the question of whether and when to release the identities of the bombers for the last forty-five minutes. The early theory on the attacks from the intelligence community was that all of the attackers were living in the United States and were coached by someone from ISIS or Al Qaeda to launch a lethal multicity attack on soft targets.

Now the suspects' apartments would be searched, computer hard drives would be examined, e-mail and text records would be reviewed, and the story would probably be a familiar one. The difference between this investigation and the others that had occurred on Charlotte's watch was that this group had managed to elude law-enforcement and intelligence agencies during the planning and implementation phases. One of the theories presented to her in the meeting was that they'd communicated on the "secret Internet." A senior intelligence analyst had recently done an entire presentation on secret Internet messages and transactions at one of the recent national security meetings. He'd explained that it was of particular concern because of the difficulty of monitoring the encrypted material. Charlotte wondered if that analyst would be on television the following morning claiming to have been waving a red flag at her national security team.

One thing was clear to Charlotte. The bombers had innovated beyond the government's ability to watch and protect and prevent. The suspects detained in Miami offered the greatest opportunity for intelligence gathering, but it could be weeks before they talked.

"Where are we on the Miami suspects?" Charlotte asked.

"They're being moved to a federal facility."

"Gitmo?"

"That's TBD. Most likely Gitmo for security purposes and a host of other legal and logistical reasons."

Charlotte had requested a private briefing with the attorney general for nine P.M. to revisit the enhanced interrogations that had been utilized by previous administrations. She remembered being asked about torture during the presidential campaign. At the time, Charlotte had said she'd take a careful look at the issue and had assured the interviewer that she'd never do anything to endanger the lives of American soldiers fighting abroad. But now the debate about enhanced interrogations seemed ludicrous. She'd do anything to find out who was behind the deadly attacks and to make sure no other attacks were planned.

"If there are no security issues, I leave it to Craig and the lawyers and communications folks to make the determination about when we release the bombers' IDs." Charlotte stood to leave.

"Madam President, is it something you'd like us to save for your speech to the nation?" the CIA director asked.

"I don't want anyone to do anything when it comes to releasing information to the public for the purpose of my speech. Understood?"

Heads nodded. Charlotte walked out of the Situation Room alone and rushed upstairs.

She hadn't been able to reach the Carmichaels yet. Sam had tried several times before the NSC meeting, and the calls went directly to voice mail. Charlotte didn't want Sam to leave a voice message asking them to return the call. She couldn't imagine receiving a message like that about one of her children, and she wasn't about to put them through any more anguish than what they were about to endure.

"Sam, let's try both of their numbers again," Charlotte called from inside the Oval Office.

She heard Sam pick up her phone and was surprised to hear her say, "Mrs. Carmichael, please hold for President Kramer."

Even though she'd been thinking about it since the moment she learned that Warren had been killed, she still didn't know what she was going to say to his parents. Charlotte wanted them to know that their son was a hero and that she'd found him indispensable. She'd tell his mother and father that their son was kind, humble, funny, and wise beyond his years and loved by all—especially her. Charlotte would make sure that they knew that he died helping others and that she would make sure that the individuals behind the attack were brought to justice. But those things seemed inconsequential. In Charlotte's eyes, Warren was a man in the prime of his life, but Charlotte knew that if the news were being delivered to her about Harry or Penny, her thoughts would be on the baby she'd brought home from the hospital. She would think about the first steps Penny and Harry had taken, the first words they'd uttered, and the way she'd celebrated their first days of school, Christmas mornings, and birthdays. How did you tell a mother that the boy she raised to do the right thing and help others and live a life of service had died in the line of duty? How did you tell a mother that the son she prayed for every day while he served his country in Iraq and Afghanistan had died in an attack in Washington, D.C.?

Charlotte took a deep breath and walked around her desk. She picked up the phone slowly.

"Mrs. Carmichael?"

CHAPTER FORTY-THREE

Melanie

The plane was starting to feel claustrophobic, and Melanie worried that her perspective on the attacks might be too insular for her to be guiding so much of the president's decision making and shaping her public posture. She hadn't seen an instant of news coverage yet, and she wasn't sitting in the room with the rest of the president's national security team. She was stuck at forty thousand feet.

"Sit," Melanie mouthed at her communications advisor, who had appeared in the doorway while she was holding for the chairman of the joint chiefs. She wanted to give the chairman direction about the plans that Charlotte would expect from them. He came on the line and listened quietly while Melanie outlined what she needed. When she finished, he launched into a long response about the fruitlessness of drafting plans that he couldn't recommend in good conscience to the president.

"Bud, of course you can put your finger on the scale in terms of the final outcome, but she is going to want to understand her choices at a very detailed level. She'll want to know what each option would involve regarding troop strength, coalition possibilities, and logistical pros and cons. She will not rule out the harbor-and-support doctrine, and she will not want to rule out some extremely targeted military strikes."

Melanie listened as the chairman laid out a handful of reasons why the sort of war planning that she was looking for was complicated by the fact that Congress had been balancing the federal budget on the back of the military for the last five years. She listened patiently and then reiterated her request.

Something in his voice made Melanie pause.

"Bud, is there something that you're worried about that we haven't discussed?"

"Madam Secretary, folks around here are shaken. The last time this happened, we were pulling bodies out of our offices. This brings all of it back."

Melanie prided herself on being in touch with the morale in her building, but in this instance, she'd underestimated the emotional trauma that another attack on the capital would cause for everyone working at the Pentagon.

"I'm sorry. I shouldn't need you to tell me that. Being trapped on the plane is impairing my capacity to appreciate how everyone there must be experiencing this day."

"No apology necessary, Madame Secretary. People understand that they have a job to do. I'll get a team together right away to start tweaking the plans that exist already for your review later tonight."

Melanie hung up and turned her full attention to her spokesman. "What are you hearing?" she asked.

"We're starting to get calls about our coordination with allies and intelligence sharing."

"Send all of that to State and CIA today."

"I did."

"What else?"

"Our press is asking if you will come to the back of the plane and read out some of your meetings and calls."

"Not now. I'm crashing on the president's speech, and I have something that I need your help with."

She wanted her spokesman to be prepared to release the statement she'd worked up from her and on behalf of the Pentagon that could be released as soon as the news broke about Warren's death.

He took out a pen and a pad. "Madam Secretary, there's something sensitive that I'm going to need your guidance on."

"In that case, you go first."

"The first thing you need to know is that this didn't come from our traveling press. It came from the CBS Pentagon producer back in D.C. My deputy passed it along."

"What is it?"

"Patty Siebel, the off-air, said that she is hearing that the president, quote, stormed out of the PEOC earlier today against the advice of the Secret Service, end quote, and *while* the continuity-of-government plans and procedures were still in place."

Melanie nodded.

"And that she refused to relocate to a more secure location even after the Secret Service and her husband urged her to do so," he added.

"That's it?"

"Yeah."

"OK."

"How do you want me to handle this?"

"Don't do anything. Let me make a couple of calls."

The leak would be extremely damaging to the president. As Melanie had warned Charlotte hours earlier, it would make her look emotional and unprofessional. While it was debatable that what she'd done constituted storming away, it was a fact that she'd left the bunker at a time when the Secret Service would have preferred her to stay in the PEOC or relocate to a more secure place than the White House.

"How did Patty describe her source?"

"'A senior administration official familiar with the goings-on in the PEOC,'" he read from his notepad.

"The source isn't claiming to be a witness?"

"Not explicitly. She just said 'familiar with the goings-on.'"

"Give me a minute."

"Thanks. What did you have for me?" he asked.

"It can wait."

He turned to leave, but Melanie stopped him and closed the door to her cabin.

"The president did leave the PEOC for a few minutes early in the day. No attacks were under way, but it was premature for her to leave the safety of the PEOC. She returned after spending about ten minutes in the Oval Office."

"Thank you for telling me," he replied.

As soon as he left her cabin, Melanie called Sam. "Is she there?"

The president picked up immediately. "I was about to call you. The Carmichaels were unbelievable."

"I need to ask you about something first. The CBS Pentagon producer just got a tip from a senior administration official that would suggest that we need to tighten the circle of participants for future NSC meetings."

"What kind of tip?"

"A senior administration official told someone at CBS that you may have violated security protocols by leaving the PEOC while the continuity-of-government plans were still in place."

"Why would someone discuss my movements with the press today, of all days?"

"I'm not sure. It's probably some deputy assistant secretary trying to show a reporter how in the loop he is. Why don't you have Sam send me a list of all of the participants, and we'll get the agencies to submit participant lists, too. Maybe some jackass at the State Department is trying to become famous."

"I thought the call came from a Pentagon reporter?"

"It did, but it's a rookie-leaking tactic to call a reporter who doesn't cover your principal."

"What do you really think is going on?"

"I'm not sure, but I'd like your permission to limit the number of people who get a draft of the speech and who participate in the next NSC meeting."

"Yes, of course. Is there any way to figure out who it was?"

"It's more important that it doesn't happen again."

"I agree."

"I'm going to handle it, Madam President. Don't worry. I'm going to call Dale now to enlist her help."

"Is she up for it?"

"I'm about to find out. I wanted your permission to take the lead."

"Permission granted."

"Thank you, Madam President. I'll call you back in a few minutes. I want to hear about the Carmichaels."

CHAPTER FORTY-FOUR

Dale

M arguerite!" Dale called from her office.

Marguerite appeared in her doorway.

"Where are Lucy and Richard?"

"They were broadcasting from the North Lawn about forty-five minutes ago."

Dale flipped through all of the stations to make sure she hadn't missed them. "They're not there now."

Dale and Marguerite stood together and watched the CBS White House correspondent deliver a live report about the small group of aides who had been tapped to draft the president's remarks for later that evening.

"I hate that they keep reporting that I've been working on the speech all evening long. I haven't even seen it," Dale complained.

"I wouldn't worry about it," Marguerite said.

"When they find out about Warren, am I supposed to confess that I didn't work on the speech after all?"

"I'll ask Sam if I can get a copy for you," Marguerite offered. She understood that it was better to make the story true than to go about setting the record straight.

Dale stood.

"Where are you going?" Marguerite asked.

"If Richard and Lucy aren't on the air or in our office, they're getting into trouble somewhere. I'm going to look for them."

"Do you want me to come?"

"No. I don't want them to think we're more concerned than we actually are about their whereabouts."

As she walked toward the briefing room, Dale contemplated how she'd deal with the condolences that everyone would offer about Warren. Just thinking about it made her feel like a fraud. She hadn't deserved someone like Warren.

She shook her head from side to side to expel those thoughts from her mind. If she only managed to do one thing to contribute to the day, she would salvage the "Day in the Life" production.

"Have you seen Lucy or Richard?" Dale asked one of the deputy spokesmen.

He glanced up at the television on his desk airing the three networks and shook his head.

"I haven't seen them since the briefing."

"Please send them up to my office if they turn up."

"Will do, boss."

Dale walked quickly past the Oval Office and down the hall toward Craig's office. His assistant, Ben, stood up when she entered. *He must know about Warren*, Dale thought.

She tried to act normal. "Is he free?" she asked, looking at Craig's closed door.

"He's not in there."

"Is he with the president?"

"He's with the vice president," Ben replied.

"Thanks."

He had such a pained look on his face that she felt compelled to say something else to him.

"I haven't seen you since before they evacuated the West Wing. Were you guys all right today? Did you have to leave the building?"

"A bunch of us just hung out in the mess."

"And the Secret Service didn't mind?"

"They didn't say anything."

"At least you didn't have to deal with getting back in. We had to escort our press back into the complex. It was a zoo."

He nodded politely at Dale and then turned back to the TV on his desk. Dale followed his gaze. On one side of the screen, the mayor of New York City was holding a news conference with the police chief, and on the other side of the screen, they were running live footage of Times Square. It looked like a scene from a movie. Emergency vehicles were parked haphazardly in the empty streets. Crowds were gathered at the police perimeter, but the area was otherwise empty except for police and investigators.

Dale shivered and glanced at the bottom of the screen, where the news crawl was spitting out tragic data points like they were sports statistics. Dale read along for a minute and then looked away.

"Ben, I'm sorry to keep bothering you, but those reporters, Lucy and Richard from CBS, have they been hanging around here?"

He shifted in his seat and glanced nervously from the TV to Dale and then to the TV again. She wasn't imagining his discomfort.

"Did something happen with them?" she probed.

"Not that I know of."

"You don't happen to know where they are?" Dale asked.

His eyes darted to the hallway that led to the vice president's office. "Uh, no," he said.

"It's not your job to keep tabs on the press. That's our job. Thanks for everything. Please ask Craig to call me when he has a free moment."

Dale walked down the short hallway that separated the chief of staff's office from the vice president's office. The hallway dead-ended into two separate suites. To the left, the national security advisor and his assistant shared a large office. Dale nodded at Tim's assistant, who was watching the small TV on her desk. Tim was probably in with the president. To the right, the vice president's secretary had a small desk behind which the vice president's large West Wing office was located. The remaining members of the vice president's staff were housed in the Old Executive Office Building, where the vice president had a ceremonial office that was mostly used for photo ops and bill signings. Several members of the vice president's security detail were gathered around a second desk that had been squeezed into the corner of the reception area. When Dale entered the suite, the vice president's secretary looked up. The look on her face said everything. It was as if she'd been caught committing a crime. Even the Secret Service agents looked as if they were anticipating something interesting in terms of a confrontation. Dale held her finger to her lips to silence the vice president's secretary and stood there without speaking long enough to hear several loud voices speaking in an animated fashion inside. She was certain that the female voice she heard belonged to Lucy, and she thought she'd heard Craig shush her when the conversation grew too loud. A million red flags went off in her mind, but she forced herself to think before she acted. Why was Craig in there instead of in the Oval Office with the president? Why were Lucy and Richard in with the vice president? Why would the vice president be talking to reporters? If Dale hadn't been so exasperated, she might have laughed at the absurdity of the rogue news anchors finagling their way into the vice president's office on the day of a terror attack. Dale had her hand on the doorknob and was about to barge in when Marguerite appeared in the doorway and pulled her away.

"I have an emergency call for you from the SECDEF."

"From Melanie?"

"Yes. She said to find you and get you on the phone immediately."

Dale watched the vice president's secretary breathe a sigh of relief as Dale turned to follow Marguerite back to her office.

CHAPTER FORTY-FIVE

Charlotte

Shouldn't we place the teleprompter exactly where it will be later tonight?" Charlotte asked.

"They're working on it, Madam President," Sam said calmly.

Staffers from the White House event production office were frantically rearranging the furniture in the Oval Office to make room for the camera equipment and lights. Charlotte's national security advisor had convened the deputy director of the FBI, the White House counterterrorism advisor, and the two presidential speechwriters Melanie had deputized to make any of Charlotte's edits to the speech after her first formal read-through.

"Should we have some normal people in here?" Charlotte asked.

"Ma'am?"

"You know, people who can listen to the speech the way normal Americans will hear it later tonight."

Her advisors looked at her blankly.

"Sam!" Charlotte called.

"Yes, ma'am?"

"Can you ask Brooke and Mark to come down here?" Charlotte requested.

"Yes, ma'am. What about Mr. Kramer?"

Charlotte paused. "He can come, if he wants," she concluded.

Sam reentered the Oval Office a minute later. "Madam President, I have the Miami mayor on the phone. His assistant said that he just returned from the site, and he's heading back to the port in a few minutes, but if you'd like to speak to him now, he has time."

"Yes, of course I'll talk to him," she said, and picked up the call. "Mr. Mayor, this is Charlotte Kramer. I'm sorry to take you away from more important duties, but I wanted to express my condolences and assure you that the entire federal government is at your disposal today, and in the days and weeks to come."

"Thank you, Madam President. I'm sure we'll be taking you up on that offer. It's an unspeakable scene and one that I never thought I'd see in my lifetime."

"We are standing by and ready to assist in any way you need."

"I don't even know what to ask for, ma'am. I've been watching them pull bodies out of the water since I arrived at the port a few minutes after the explosion—all ages, and I tell you, there's nothing that prepares you to see a child in that sort of situation."

"I am praying for all of you. I will do everything I can for the victims and for their families. Please tell your first responders that the White House is prepared to send down any additional resources they need. I understand there's an elite dive unit assisting with the rescue operation."

"Yes, ma'am. I'm afraid that what they're really helping with is more recovery than rescue, but we're grateful for the help."

"Is there anything else you need at this moment?"

"Madam President, our police chief is having a tough time getting much information out of the FBI about the suspects that were picked up down here."

"I'll direct the FBI to place a call to your police chief as soon as you and I hang up."

"Thank you, ma'am."

"Thank you, Mr. Mayor. We'll be in touch."

Charlotte closed her eyes for a moment and took a deep breath. To go from thinking about the details of a heavily scripted speech to the nation from deep inside the fortified presidential complex to hearing about the grisly details of the human suffering that was taking place outside made her question every decision she'd made that day.

"Do you need a minute, Madam President?" Sam asked.

"No," she replied brusquely.

"Would you like to rehearse the speech a couple of times in the family theater or in your private dining room while they finish setting up in there?" Sam asked quietly.

"No. I would not. The point was to simulate what I'm going to have to do tonight, which is to deliver the speech from behind my desk, and at the moment, I'm not sure what the hell I'm doing here at all. Shouldn't I be at one of the sites? Comforting these people?"

"Do you want me to ask Tim to come in?"

"No!" she yelled.

Sam remained calm.

"Why can't I rehearse in the Oval?" Charlotte asked after a minute had passed.

"The staff needs a couple of hours alone in the Oval Office to set it up for tonight. They are not accustomed to doing this while the president of the United States is hovering over them," Sam explained patiently.

Charlotte peered into the Oval Office and noticed two heavy-set men in suits straining to move one of the sofas. One of them had beads of sweat pouring off his forehead. Both of their faces were bright red.

"Fine. We'll practice in the family theater."

Sam looked relieved when she went to deliver the news to Monty and the speechwriters. The group followed her down the hall from the Oval Office to the theater in the East Wing.

Charlotte had taken Melanie's advice to close ranks after the leak from the PEOC, and only a small group of advisors sat in the front row of the theater a couple of feet away from her. Charlotte fidgeted with the pages in front of her and squinted at the teleprompter screens.

"Can you see the panels?" Monty asked quietly.

"Not really."

Monty handed her three pairs of glasses. She selected one and looked at the panels again.

"The letters are smaller. Can someone adjust the font size?"

"It's the same as always, Madam President," one of the speech-writers replied.

"Then my eyes have deteriorated since the last time I used that thing," she said, pointing at the teleprompter.

While Monty kneeled next to the teleprompter operator to instruct him to increase the font size, Charlotte remembered that also she hadn't been able to see the teleprompter six months earlier, when they'd practiced the State of the Union address.

"Madam President, the press office needs a length on the speech for the nets, so when you're ready, we'll start timing. Feel free to stop, but before you start again, just give me a second to get the timer back on," one of the speechwriters requested.

She scanned the familiar faces in the front row. It was maddening to be tucked away in the soundproof, windowless movie theater while cities burned.

"Ready, Madam President?"

"One second— Tim, you'll do a final interagency-check with the CIA, FBI, and DOD?"

"Yes, ma'am. It's under way right now."

"And you guys will coordinate with Melanie on any changes to the speech?" she asked.

The speechwriters nodded.

"We'll wait one more minute for our ordinary Americans, and then we'll get started."

While they were waiting, Tim approached the president at the podium. "You spoke to the Carmichaels?"

"I did."

"That must have been extremely difficult."

"They were unbelievable. They asked if there was anything they could do for *me*. They asked how *I* was holding up. Can you imagine?"

Tim shook his head. "I'm sure they appreciated your call, Madam President."

"I invited them to come to the White House tomorrow. I told them I'd like to express my condolences in person."

"Yes, ma'am."

"Tim, is anyone working on a day of remembrance? We should have a memorial service somewhere in Washington or in the East Room for all the victims and their families. Maybe we should do it at the National Cathedral? And I'd like to travel to all of the sites as soon as possible."

"Yes, ma'am. I'll make sure someone is working on that."

"My preference is to visit the sites before the memorial service. In fact, I'd like to go down to the Mall first thing in the morning or tonight after the address and travel to the four sites tomorrow. Is that doable?"

"We'll work on it."

"I'm already tired of that answer."

Tim turned to greet Brooke and Mark. "Our ordinary people have arrived," he said.

Brooke was wearing navy slacks and a crisp white blouse. Mark had on dark jeans, a dress shirt, and a sportcoat and was carrying a yellow legal pad and a fancy pen. They took the last two seats in the front row.

"Just listen to the speech, and let me know what you think. Be honest," Charlotte urged.

Mark saluted her and removed the cap from his pen.

"Whenever you're ready, Madam President," Monty prompted.

Charlotte started reading the words displayed on the panels in front of her, but inside her, rage was building. She kept replaying the Miami mayor's words over and over: *I've been watching them pull bodies out of the water.* Her thoughts turned to revenge.

CHAPTER FORTY-SIX

Melanie

Melanie didn't want to involve Brian in her trap, but she didn't have many options. She let his phone ring five times. When it went to voice mail, she hung up and called her assistant, Annie.

"Can you get Brian on the line, please? And tell him that nothing is wrong; I have a work question."

Annie had him on the line in less than a minute.

"Was that you calling?" he asked.

"Yes, were you doing a live shot?"

"Yeah, and they're coming back to me in two minutes. What's up?"

"I'll be quick. Someone leaked to CBS's Pentagon unit that Charlotte stormed out of the PEOC this morning and violated security protocols."

"Did she?"

"That isn't the point."

"Of course it isn't."

"I need to figure out who's leaking."

"Jesus, Melanie, is this seriously the best use of your time right now?"

Melanie was incredulous. "I'd say that making sure the president can make decisions about our national security without worrying that one of your colleagues in the press is going to broadcast her decisions to the enemy is of utmost importance, wouldn't you?" She sounded shriller than she'd intended.

"Mel, you don't have to spin me or convince me. I don't give a damn about the president or your leaker. I am on your side, no matter how wild your caper. I am simply pointing out that it sounds a bit detached from reality right now to be launching a leak investigation from thirty thousand feet while five cities burn."

Melanie silently seethed.

"Your heavy breathing suggests that I've pissed you off, but I will say one last thing, and then I will follow you down Alice's rabbit hole in search of your leaker, real or imagined. Is it possible that being trapped on that plane all day has you acting a little desperate to find ways to remain critical to the president?"

Melanie was certain that this was *not* the case. She wasn't imagining her restored connection with Charlotte. Why would Brian doubt the first positive development in her relationship with the president in nearly a year? Why would he make her doubt herself? Melanie fought back tears of frustration. Pregnancy made it much more difficult to swallow her emotions. She gathered herself and cleared her throat. "The leader of the free world doesn't seem to think that I'm grasping at straws to remain relevant."

"You weren't even speaking to her twelve hours ago."

"I'm going to hang up before I say something I'll regret."

"Mel, come on. I'm sorry. It just sounded like you'd swung from one extreme to the other where Charlotte was concerned. This morning, you were talking about quitting."

"I know."

"And I didn't mean to upset you. Tell me what I can do to help."

"Nothing. I'll figure it out."

"I'm not going to beg you, but if you need me to do something, I will do it."

"Let's just talk about something else," Melanie urged.

"What's the White House plan for when the news breaks about Warren?"

"I don't know."

"Everyone has quietly confirmed it over the last hour, and it isn't going to hold for much longer."

"Please don't report it yet," she asked.

"It's going to get out soon."

"I still can't believe it."

"Listen, not to add any pressure, but between Warren and the finger-pointing going on from Capitol Hill, there will be very high expectations tonight for the president."

"Who is pointing fingers?"

"Republicans. It's pretty muted, but they're still pissed about her prochoice speech, and right-wing radio and Fox News will be merciless on her. They'll say that she lost her nerve when it came time to stand up to Congress on her drone policy and surveillance measures. It won't take two days for members to conclude that it came down to a staring contest between us and them, and they won. We blinked."

"That's not fair. The world blinked."

"The world didn't get bombed to shit today," Brian remarked.

"Not yet, at least."

"You sound like the old Charlotte protector you were when I first met you."

"Old habits die hard."

"I've got to go, Mel. I'll call you back."

As soon as she hung up, her aide pointed at the phone. "Madam Secretary, I tracked down Dale Smith for you. She's been holding for five minutes already."

"Dale?"

"Something strange is going on around here," Dale reported.

"What do you mean?"

"Lucy and Richard are in with the vice president. I think Craig is in there, too."

"Where are they?"

"In the vice president's West Wing office."

"What makes you think Craig is in there? Did you see him in there?"

"No, but his assistant said he was with the veep, and he had invited

Lucy and Richard to his office for some off-the-record time earlier today, so I have this sick feeling that it's been a rolling background briefing with CBS ever since I went off the grid."

"Do you think the vice president has been spending time with them, too?"

"She's in with them right now."

"Maybe she thought that was what you would want since you didn't pull the plug on the 'Day in the Life.'"

"It's not what I want. I think Craig is leaking a little too much color to Lucy and Richard."

"What sort of things?"

"They knew about the CNN crew earlier today, and they asked if the president was in the Oval Office earlier while she was still supposed to be in the PEOC."

"What time did they ask you about the president being in the Oval?"

"I don't remember."

"I know you've been through a lot today, but can you try to piece together when Lucy and Richard asked you about the president being in the Oval when she should have been in the PEOC?"

"It was when I was out on the North Lawn escorting our press back into the complex. I'll get with Marguerite and figure out exactly when we were out there."

"Have you had any press calls from anyone else about information that shouldn't be out there?"

"Other than those two from Lucy and Richard, no."

"Nothing?"

"I don't think so. Why?"

"We just got one."

"What was it?"

"The CBS Pentagon producer called our press office and asked about the president storming out of the PEOC while the attacks were still under way."

"You think Lucy and Richard passed the information to their Pentagon reporters so she could get another source?"

"That's one theory."

"The attacks weren't technically under way anymore."

"The president didn't know that at the time."

"What did you guys say to CBS?"

"We haven't said anything yet."

"We can't lie."

"Of course not."

"What do we do?"

"We can't lie, but we can do things that are in the interest of national security to make sure that the president is surrounded by people she can trust."

"Right."

"Do you understand?"

Dale knew exactly what she was being asked to do. Melanie was finally collecting her payback for her generosity to her the year before. She was asking her to bury her best friend and closest ally in the White House if he was indeed the one who leaked the information about the president leaving the PEOC to CBS.

"I understand. We give someone bad information and see where it ends up?"

"We give our suspects some slightly off-base information and see what happens with it. It needs to be very sensitive, and it needs to be delivered by people who are normally their trusted colleagues."

"You keep referring to suspects, but you only have one suspect, right?"

"At the moment, yes."

Dale took a deep breath and pressed her fingers into the bones around her eye sockets. She had a searing headache. She prayed that Craig wasn't the source of the leak. She would love to prove Melanie wrong about him. "Tell me what you want me to do, Melanie."

CHAPTER FORTY-SEVEN

Dale

C raig wants to see you in his office."

"Tell him I'm on my way," Dale replied to her assistant.

Dale knew that she was playing with fire, but she also knew that earlier in the day, Melanie and the president had carried out the most elaborate act of charity that anyone would likely ever do on her behalf. They'd staged a presidential news conference so that Peter could tell Dale about Warren's death in private. In return, she'd been asked to help determine the extent of Craig's involvement in leaking information to the press. If he was guilty of sharing information that shouldn't be made public, then he deserved whatever happened to him. But if he wasn't, then she was most certainly ending her own career.

Dale was grateful that Melanie hadn't offered her condolences about Warren. In an odd way, it made Dale feel closer to him to be collaborating with Melanie. He would understand that protecting Charlotte from a traitorous advisor was the priority, and he would be pleased that Melanie trusted Dale enough to enlist her support. It eased some of Dale's anxiety about the act of disloyalty to Craig that she was about to carry out.

"He's waiting for you," Ben said as soon as Dale entered his office suite.

"Thanks."

Craig greeted Dale with an embrace. "Are you holding up?"

"I'm on autopilot."

"The president is worried about you. I know she's grateful that you came back to work after you found out."

"It's difficult to feel sorry for myself with all of this." Dale gestured toward the wall of TVs in Craig's office. When she looked back at him, he was transfixed by something on one of them.

"Jesus Christ, the ship is almost completely underwater now."

Dale wasn't even sure what she was looking at until she heard the reporter practically scream into her microphone that the entire cruise ship was now submerged. The network cut away from her hysteria and went to a grim-faced search-and-rescue "expert," who said that it was very unlikely that anyone else would be rescued from the Miami site. Dale listened for a couple of minutes and then walked to the window in Craig's office.

"I'm sorry." Craig muted the TV.

"Don't be. We need to watch the news. I'm just trying to keep it together."

"Dale, I want to make something clear. We'll get through the rest of today, and then I want you to take some time off, understood?"

Dale nodded.

She was trying her hardest to sound normal. If Melanie was wrong about Craig being the leaker, this stunt would destroy her closest friendship in Washington. She reminded herself that the president had approved their effort and went back to the script that Melanie had suggested.

"I came to see you because the press is starting to ask for excerpts from the speech. Do you have any that stand out for you that I could release?"

"I didn't pick up my copy yet. I was about to go get it from Samantha," Craig said.

"I have it."

He looked surprised. "That's good, Dale. You should have it. I'm sure that Ben just forgot to pick mine up. Ben?" Craig yelled at his assistant.

"Yes, sir?"

"Can you call Sam and ask her for a copy of the president's speech?"

"Yes, sir."

"Sam gave me your copy when I picked up mine," Dale said carefully. She pulled out a brown envelope with a staffing sheet stapled to it. It was the typical way sensitive speeches were shared with senior staff. Only hard copies were circulated, and edits were made by hand and input by the speechwriters.

Craig looked relieved to see it. "Ben, forget it!" he yelled.

Craig opened the envelope and pulled the sheets of paper out.

"Have you read it? How is it?" he asked.

"It's very Melanie," Dale replied.

Craig rolled his eyes. "I'd better read this right away and send back my comments. Let me call you after I get through it, and we can select a couple of excerpts and go through the plan for morning shows and the rest of the interviews for CBS."

"Sounds good. Everything going smoothly with Richard and Lucy?"

Craig raised an eyebrow. "I think so. Why?"

"I was planning on babysitting them all afternoon, and I wasn't able to, so I just wanted to make sure they hadn't caused any incidents."

"Not that I'm aware of."

"Not yet, anyway, right?" Dale tried to make a joke.

"Dale, I'm serious. If you think of anything that I can do for you, please let me know."

"I will."

Dale walked out of his office and closed the door behind her.

CHAPTER FORTY-EIGHT

Charlotte

On days when the CIA director didn't travel to the White House to brief Charlotte personally and on all of the days when she was on the road, she received her daily intelligence briefing from a woman named Sydney Travers. Charlotte and Sydney had spent countless hours together discussing the threats facing the United States from the various Al Qaeda networks and their more lethal affiliates in Iraq and Syria, ISIS and ISIL. Not once had Sydney suggested that an attack on the U.S. was imminent. But not once had Sydney failed to mention the groups' ongoing desire and intent to strike America again, in the same way and with similar effect as it had done on September 11, 2001. Even her shortest briefings and those delivered by classified top-secret white papers included Sydney's reminder that Al Qaeda and the Islamic State remained committed to planning and carrying out another attack on the homeland. Now Sydney was sitting across from the president, and they were discussing the identities of the bodies found in Chicago and Los Angeles.

Sydney handed the president the two-pager she'd quickly compiled on the Chicago bomber. Charlotte read it carefully.

"Madam President," Sydney interrupted.

"I'm almost done, Sydney."

"I just wanted to say that I'm sorry," Sydney whispered.

"For what?"

"Madam President, I was twenty-six years old on September eleventh. I remember watching the towers fall a couple of hours after the planes hit them and swearing that I would spend the rest of my career making sure it never happened again."

Charlotte smiled sympathetically at her briefer. They'd all missed something, but the members of the CIA would face harsh recriminations from their critics on Capitol Hill, given the legacy of September 11 and the growing list of intelligence lapses. Charlotte suspected that these attacks would embolden the agency's harshest detractors, who would call for investigations into the counterterrorism units that were supposedly strengthened and augmented after September 11.

"Sydney, the failure is ultimately mine, and I will make sure that everyone who needs to understand that hears it from me. You are going to have your hands full in the coming weeks, and you need to tell your colleagues that I have their backs. I'll take the blame, but I want everyone focused on the task at hand."

Sydney nodded and returned to her file of notes about the suicide bombers.

Charlotte looked up again when she saw Sam standing in front of her desk.

"He's here," Sam whispered.

Charlotte had reluctantly filled Sam in on the details of their strategy to find out if Craig was leaking to CBS.

"Sydney, give me a minute?"

Charlotte watched as Sydney exited and Craig entered the Oval.

"Craig, did the national security advisor talk to you?"

"Yes, Madam President. That's why I'm here. I want to talk to you about this assignment. You have an entire advance operation that is designed to plan days like this. I don't have the first clue about how to move you to five cities and get you back in time for a memorial service. I'm really, honestly not the best guy to oversee the planning and advance work for your trip tomorrow."

"Craig, I was afraid you'd feel that way, but this is the most sensitive and important day of my entire presidency. Someone has to be on the phone with the mayors and first responders and thinking about getting the correct congressional delegations on board Air Force One for the trip. The White House chief of staff is uniquely positioned to move the mountains that are going to need to be moved to make this trip happen."

"With all due respect, Madam President, there are also established lines of communication between the offices of intergovernmental affairs and the local officials. Those are the people who are accustomed to doing these trips. I would add a layer of bureaucracy."

"I doubt that. You are the only person who can actually speak with authority about what I want for a trip like this. That can't fall to a twenty-eight-year-old advance person. I will not put those kids in that position. I would make the calls and set up the trip myself if I could. It's that important to me. But we both know that I can't do that. I need you to lead the countdown meetings and be my eyes and ears and mouthpiece on the ground with these mayors and local officials."

Craig knew he was losing the argument.

"Please," she implored.

"Yes, ma'am."

"Thank you. Did you have a chance to review the speech yet?"

"I sent in my comments. It's a good start."

"You liked it?"

"I liked parts of it."

"Good." Charlotte offered a closed-mouth smile and looked back at the papers in front of her.

Her natural instinct was to smooth things over, but she resisted the urge. She needed him to be angry with her. As soon as he left, she asked Sam to get Melanie on the phone.

"How'd it go?"

"He's not pleased about heading up logistics for my trip tomorrow. He expected to be running the national security meetings, and in asking him to oversee the advance operation, I essentially demoted him in the middle of the most serious crisis of my presidency. I feel sick about having to do this today, but I can't worry about everything I say and do ending up in the press."

"It sounds like you handled it perfectly, Madam President."

They needed Craig to be mad enough to want to do something to show Lucy and Richard that he was still running things.

"Do you really think this will work?" Charlotte asked.

"If he's our man, it will work."

"How will we know if he leaks the speech?"

"Either they will start talking about it on the air at CBS, or CBS reporters and producers will start calling around to get a second source."

"Then what?"

"We'll have to wave them off it by telling them it's an early draft and not the speech that you plan to deliver. The rest of what we do is up to you."

"Thanks a lot."

"You have time to figure that out."

"*We* have time to figure that out," Charlotte corrected.

"Yes, ma'am," Melanie replied.

Charlotte felt reassured. It was unsettling to contemplate that Craig had been leaking information to the press about her actions all day. "How much longer until you're on the ground?"

"About forty minutes," Melanie said.

"See you then."

CHAPTER FORTY-NINE

Melanie

HMX is transporting you from Andrews to the South Lawn of the White House on one of the president's helicopters," Melanie's military aide reported. HMX stood for Marine Helicopter Squadron One and included the elite group of pilots responsible for flying the president.

Melanie nodded.

"We land in ten minutes. Do you need anything?"

"No, thank you."

Melanie buckled her seat belt for landing and made a note to herself to buy a maternity wardrobe as soon as she got a chance. The skirt she'd changed into was so tight she had to leave the top buttons open. She'd stretched her loose sweater over her stomach and chest. Melanie wiggled her toes in the black heels that were squeezing her feet and took a last sip of coffee before one of the flight stewards took it away.

The CNN feed was finally coming in on the TV in her cabin. She watched a female correspondent deliver a live report from in front of the curbside check-in area at the Los Angeles airport. The reporter kept pointing over her shoulder toward the check-in area where the bomb had been detonated. Other than the yellow police tape and the other reporters who were standing close enough to be overheard in her broadcast, there weren't many outward signs of the destruction behind her. But Melanie knew from her classified briefing that twenty-seven people had died, and another forty-nine remained hospitalized with gruesome and mostly critical injuries. It wasn't public yet, but one of the victims was an eight-year-old girl who had been on her way to visit her grandparents in Colorado. Her mother was among the dead. Melanie felt queasy and snapped the rubber band on her wrist that was supposed to help with morning sickness. She forced herself to keep watching.

Anderson Cooper thanked the correspondent in L.A. and turned to a reporter in Chicago who had a similar story from a near-identical location at the airport curb. This reporter had more details than even Melanie's classified briefing a couple of hours earlier had provided. She watched as he reported that thirty-two people had lost their lives, and another sixty-four remained at hospitals in the area. At least seven of the injured were children. Among the dead in Chicago were a couple from Evanston, Illinois, who had been traveling to Orlando with their two young sons to visit Disney World. They'd been unlucky enough to be standing next to the bomber when he detonated his explosives, and they all died. Melanie took out her notepad and jotted down their names. Charlotte would want these details when she drafted letters to the family members of the victims, and she might even want to pay tribute to some of the victims in her address to the nation.

Once the plane landed, Melanie watched a live report from Times Square while she waited for her press corps to unload and set up their cameras so they could film her walking from her plane to Marine One. CNN was reporting that more than a hundred people had died in the attacks there. Melanie knew from her briefings that the second explosion had killed more people than the first, because people had rushed to the victims of the first attack to help. The New York attack was the second most lethal because it took place in the most concentrated area. Melanie stood to leave just as CNN was getting ready to cut to the Miami site. Other than the still images she'd seen as part of the FBI briefing, Melanie hadn't seen any live footage of the ship in Miami, but she knew that it had sunk in the last hour. She wanted to watch the report, but the president was waiting. Melanie walked down the stairs of her aircraft and onto the helicopter that was waiting for her. She recognized the Marine One pilot as one of the president's regulars.

"Good evening, Madam Secretary."

"Good evening. How are you guys doing?"

"All right, all things considered. We're going to get you to the South Lawn as quickly as possible. I understand the president is eagerly awaiting your arrival." He smiled.

"Thank you."

As they neared the White House, one of the crewmembers pointed out the window of the helicopter to the flashing lights below. Melanie looked down and saw the still-smoldering site of the D.C. blast. The museum looked like someone had stomped on it. The entire front of the building was crushed. A perimeter had been erected around the blast sites, and emergency vehicles surrounded an area the size of a baseball diamond. Melanie could see the beginnings of what looked like a crime-scene investigation. The forensic experts would examine every piece of bomb-blast material, glass, and clothing from the victims to determine exactly how a deadly terrorist attack had occurred less than half a mile from the White House. The smell of smoke was making Melanie feel sick again. She closed her eyes and took a deep breath.

"Are you all right, Madam Secretary?" one of the crewmembers asked.

"Yes. Thank you. The travel is catching up with me."

"We'll be on the ground in another minute," he offered.

Melanie returned her gaze to the window to watch as the Truman Balcony appeared in front of her. They descended onto the South Lawn so softly that Dale wasn't sure they'd touched the ground until the helicopter door opened. A press pool had been assembled to film her arrival. She knew from her last conversation with Brian that he wasn't part of the pool, so she didn't bother looking over at them. She saluted the pilot and followed her security detail straight to the Oval Office.

The president stood to greet her. "Thank you for coming," Charlotte said.

"Thank you for the ride."

They'd spent the entire day talking on the phone, but she couldn't remember the last time they'd been alone in the Oval Office together. When the awkward silence that followed their overly polite greetings was finally broken, it was because they both spoke at once.

Charlotte cleared her throat nervously. "Sorry. Go ahead."

"No, you go ahead," Melanie insisted.

"I was going to suggest that maybe we run through the speech on the teleprompter."

"The news about Warren is going to break before your speech. We need to finalize a statement from you. I started working on something on the plane," Melanie said.

Charlotte sat down to read Melanie's draft. "This is good," she said. "Do you want to add anything?"

"Should we say a little more about his military service?"

"Sure. I'll add something about his four tours."

"And maybe something about how he'll rest for all eternity with his fellow soldiers?"

"Let's save that for a memorial service or something," Melanie suggested.

Charlotte frowned. "When do you think this will break?" she asked.

"Any second, Madam President."

"The statement is good."

"I'll give it to Sam to get to Marguerite. I'll instruct her to hold it until the second the news breaks."

"Thanks for taking care of that, Mel."

Melanie stepped out of the Oval Office and reviewed the statement one final time before she handed it to Sam. Writing a statement for the president about the death of one of her most beloved friends was the very last thing she'd expected to do on the flight home from Iraq. Melanie grabbed a peppermint out of the candy dish on Sam's desk.

"Do you want me to order you dinner?" Sam asked.

"I won't have time to eat before the speech."

"Take this. You look pale." Sam handed her a Luna bar, which she finished in three bites before returning to the Oval Office.

CHAPTER FIFTY

Dale

Dale closed her eyes and rested her face in her hands. Clare had been arguing with Lucy for nearly five minutes, and it didn't sound like she was going to come out on the winning side. Reluctantly, Dale opened her office door and motioned for Lucy to come inside. Clare looked relieved and mouthed, "Sorry."

Lucy marched inside and stood in front of Dale's desk, crossing and uncrossing her arms while Dale walked around it and sat down.

"I understand that you are frustrated that we've had to limit your access today, Lucy," Dale started.

"You think I'm frustrated?"

Lucy had one hand on her hip, and the other was supporting a giant purse slung over one shoulder. The bag was so heavy that Lucy couldn't stand up straight. She dropped it to the ground with a thud.

"*Frustrated* is the word I'd use to describe the rest of your press corps, the ones you screwed when you decided that it was acceptable for them to take cabs back to the White House, only to find themselves locked out of the complex by overzealous security goons at the front gate. They pay for those godforsaken workspaces beneath the press office because it is their job to cover your boss when she hands out the Teacher of the Year award. But they come here every day in case the world blows up, and today it did, and you fucked them over.

Frustrated describes their state of mind. I'm enraged. I know that today wasn't a day for us to stay close to the president. I'm not the Fox News bobble-head that you think I am. But I did expect some of the terms of our carefully negotiated access to stay in place when you decided early in the day to allow us to stay."

It was true that Lucy had given Dale an opportunity to pull the plug on the "Day in the Life" production right after the attacks. Dale had decided that it would appear more hysterical to have the entire press corps report that the White House had changed course on a long-planned special. In hindsight, it would have been a much better idea simply to ask Lucy to film the "Day in the Life" on another day.

"Lucy, I'm really sorry. I had not realized the magnitude of the crisis when I said you could stay."

"I'm not done. The fact that you picked us for the interview and then completely abdicated any and all responsibility for us as your carefully scripted day fell apart speaks not only to your profound disrespect for your former peers in the media but also to your complete disregard for making sure that the press has a complete picture of what your boss is going through."

"Lucy—"

"Dale, I know that you were lying to me when I asked you about the president being in the Oval. But I didn't report it. I also know that she did, for a fact, storm out of the PEOC, and I don't blame her. Neither would our viewers. But you didn't deign to level with me, which is fine. That's your choice. And maybe you had all of the access you needed while you were sleeping with the president's husband when you were covering the White House, but some of us still have to work our sources."

"Lucy, I—"

"Let me finish," Lucy demanded. She reached into her oversized purse and pulled out a brown envelope that Dale recognized as the one that contained the copy of the president's speech that Dale had given to Craig. Lucy threw the envelope onto Dale's desk and sat down across from her. "What the hell is this, and why was it handed to me? Are you trying to entrap me so your Justice Department can prosecute me along with your suspected leaker or something?"

Dale opened the envelope and saw inside Craig's copy of the president's address for later that night. Her stomach sank. "What? No. That's ridiculous."

"The last administration prosecuted half a dozen journalists. Ask them how ridiculous it sounds."

"I can explain. Just stop yelling at me. Please?"

Lucy leaned back and crossed her legs and stared at Dale as though daring her to speak.

"You're right about a lot of those things, Lucy. Maybe you can cut me a little bit of slack today?" It was a cheap tactic, but she needed Lucy's help, and she'd get it any way she could.

"Dale, I'm sorry about Warren. I can't imagine what you're going through. But somewhere along the way today, you made a decision to stay here, and you also made a decision to allow us to stay. Even before the news broke about the attacks, or Warren, you've treated us with disdain and hostility. I should be specific. You have treated *me* with disdain. It has felt personal for a while now, and my experience today confirms that. You have a problem, generally speaking, in telling the truth to the people who have the job that you used to have. But you have an extra challenge in treating *me* with respect. Why is that?"

"It's not you."

"Come on. I saw you rolling your eyes at Brian while Richard and I were doing our phone interview from your office."

"You were sprawled out in my office, with your numbered juices on my coffee table, while the rest of the press corps fought for space on the floor."

"And you rolled your eyes at the press about what a pain in the ass I am."

"I rolled my eyes at your lack of self-awareness."

Lucy laughed. "*My* lack of self-awareness?"

Dale worried that she was alienating the person she needed to complete the assignment she'd been given by Melanie and the president. "You can take me out back and shoot me tomorrow, but tonight I need to know where you got that speech."

"I'm guessing that you already know, so before I answer your questions, I need to know that I'm not a pawn in some sting operation."

"Why would you ask that?"

"We're totally and completely off the record here, right? There are no recording devices, and you are not going to report what I say to your colleagues, are you?"

"I swear."

"A very good source gave me the speech. He's someone I've come to know very well in the last three years, and his information is rock-solid."

"But here you are with it, Lucy. Why didn't you go on the air with your big scoop about what the president planned to say tonight?"

"You tell me."

"There must be something that gave you pause. Why didn't you use the speech?"

"Because it isn't the speech, is it?"

"No," Dale admitted.

"God damn it."

"How did you know?"

"I don't know why I'm telling you this. Pity perhaps, but Craig's been a good source for months. He cultivated us during the impeachment scandal a year and a half ago. He took credit for our selection for the 'Day in the Life.'"

"He did?"

"Yes. He said that he told you it was with us or it wouldn't happen."

"That's not remotely true," Dale insisted.

"He gave us a heads-up about the CNN crew earlier today, about the president leaving the PEOC, and about Warren. I told him I'd use anything that I could verify with a second source. He didn't want me to do that, but I passed some of his tips to our Pentagon bureau to see if they could verify them."

"That's why Melanie got the call about the president leaving the PEOC," Dale said.

Lucy nodded.

"And the speech?"

"The speech was too easy," Lucy continued.

"How so?" Dale asked.

"He just called us and said he had something for us, and then he kept calling to see why we hadn't teed it up yet. I told him I was looking for a second source, and he flipped out."

"How did you know that it wasn't the real speech?"

"Because the president isn't stupid enough to give it to someone who would even be thinking about us while dealing with attacks as heinous as today's."

Dale contemplated this. "Was the vice president talking to you today?" she asked.

"She spent five minutes with us. Craig called her and told her that you'd decided to leave us embedded with the staff to record the day's events for history. She spoke glowingly about the president. She said that she saw a human being in there today, someone you'd want to have as a leader. And then she threw us out."

"She said that?"

"Yeah."

"Lucy, I'm not good at this, but I want to apologize."

"That's not an apology," Lucy scoffed.

"I'm getting to it. I am sorry about the way I've treated you guys. I will make it up to you—as in CBS—and I will make it up to you, personally. I promise."

Lucy sighed. "I also know that the president walked into the briefing room so that someone could break the news to you about Warren."

"Craig told you that?" Dale gasped.

"If I'd reported half of what he's told me over the last year, I'd probably have a freaking Emmy."

"Why was he leaking everything to you? I mean, why was he trying to harm the president?"

"You need to ask the White House shrink. People tell us all kinds of stuff, and it's never about us. Usually, it isn't even about the information they're sharing. It's usually about their attempts to manipulate their own circumstances to their advantage. Last year, Craig told us that it was Melanie who'd gone to the special prosecutor during the Tara Meyers scandal."

"Why was he after Melanie?"

"I don't know."

"But you knew he was using you to sabotage Melanie? Why did you let him use you?"

"I understand very clearly now why you have no friends, Dale. Your people skills are shit."

"I didn't mean to suggest that you conspired with him, but you just said that he was telling you things to manipulate the situation. You knew he was lying."

"Now you're twisting my words. You really are cut out for this line of work."

"Lucy, I think we're speaking past each other. I'm trying to get to the bottom of why Craig gave you a bad speech."

"I don't think that's the case, Dale. Once again, you're treating me like a fool. I think that someone, maybe Melanie, has suspected Craig for a long time, and the leaks today were the most glaring clue to date, a sign that the suspected leaker is growing desperate and reckless. So someone decided to give him a bum speech and see what happened to it. Right?"

"I can't say."

"Well, congratulations. You have your leaker, Dale. The day isn't a total loss."

Dale flinched.

"I didn't mean Warren. Shit. I'm sorry. Can we pick this conversation up another time? Obviously, we have some unfinished business between us, but before I say something that I can't repair and before the network replaces me for going AWOL, I need to find Richard and get back on the air. We're going to report the news about Warren before the president's speech. I'm sorry."

Dale nodded and watched Lucy walk toward the door and hoist her massive bag over her shoulder. "Lucy, one more question."

Lucy turned and looked at Dale.

"You had the White House chief of staff as a source, and you said that you knew some of the information was true. Even without a second source, it was news. Why didn't you use any of it?"

Lucy's eyes narrowed. "I really hope that this isn't a lecture about my journalistic obligations. That would be so rich I couldn't take it."

"I'm curious."

Lucy shrugged. "There are other considerations. Being true doesn't sanitize the information from the stench of Craig's nefarious motives. I sat on plenty of things over the last year, and not just from here. I don't expect you to give me a goddamned medal. My viewers don't give a crap about how many scandals I reveal. In case you haven't paid attention to your former profession, there are not a lot of ticker-tape parades being thrown for the great journalists of our times. People are sick of hating their political leaders, and when we give them more reasons to do so, they start to hate us, too. My viewers want someone pleasant who doesn't take herself too seriously to sit with them at the end of their stressful days and make them laugh a little. They already know what happened. They just want to know why they should give a damn."

Dale was speechless.

"You should get back to work on that speech," Lucy remarked. Surely she knew from Craig that Dale hadn't contributed one single word.

"I didn't work on the speech," Dale confessed.

"I know," Lucy said, with the faintest of smiles.

"Thank you," Dale said.

"I didn't do it for you, and I didn't do it for the president, so there's nothing to thank me for."

Dale nodded again.

Lucy closed the door behind her, and Dale reached for her phone.

"Sam, I need to see the president."

CHAPTER FIFTY-ONE

Charlotte

When Dale appeared in the doorway of the Oval Office, Charlotte had to force the image of Peter and Dale sitting side-by-side with their heads touching in the medical unit earlier that afternoon from her mind. She hadn't had a conversation with Peter all day about anything other than the whereabouts of their children. Charlotte examined Dale closely. She appeared thinner and paler than usual. Charlotte was overcome with dueling desires. Part of her wanted to throw a comforting arm around her slim shoulders and assure her that everything would be OK. The other part of her, the one that ultimately prevailed, felt compelled to regard Dale with professional coolness, especially after watching her with Peter earlier.

It was at this moment, however, that she fully understood why Dale served as an inescapable magnetic force for Peter's affections. Dale was in a perpetual cycle of needing to be rescued, and if Charlotte knew one thing about Peter, it was that he desperately needed to be needed. For reasons she didn't entirely understand, Charlotte had never been able to muster any animosity toward Dale. She'd never viewed Dale as her competition for Peter's affections, because she'd always seen herself as the one responsible for pulling him in and pushing him away based on her own limited capacity for intimacy.

Now she focused on the immediate concern, which was Craig's role in spreading confidential information to the press. Charlotte waved Dale toward the sofa.

"Come in and sit down," she urged.

"Can I get you something to drink?" Melanie offered.

"He gave Lucy the speech," Dale blurted.

Charlotte and Melanie exchanged a glance.

"He's been talking to them off the record for more than a year about . . ."

"What?" Melanie asked.

"About a lot of different things," Dale confirmed.

"What sorts of things, Dale?" the president probed.

"She said that going back a year, he was talking to her on deep background about you, Melanie, and how you were the source for the leaks about Tara. She also said that he'd been passing along information all day long—the CNN crew, Warren, the PEOC story."

"Did she say why?" Melanie asked.

"She didn't know why."

"Why didn't she use any of it?" Charlotte asked.

"I'm not sure I buy this part of the story entirely, but she said that it was all tainted by Craig's ill motives and she didn't feel an obligation to use information that was provided by a disgruntled source."

Melanie's face registered disbelief. Despite the fact that she was married to a network correspondent, she set a very low bar for most journalists.

"Should I call her?" Charlotte asked.

"She said that she didn't do it for you and that we should not ever thank her."

"What do you want to do?" Melanie asked Charlotte.

"I want to think about it." Charlotte was annoyed that Melanie expected her to make some sort of snap judgment about her chief of staff on the day of the attacks.

Melanie didn't disguise her disapproval, and Charlotte could tell that Dale suddenly felt uncomfortable.

"I'm sorry to ask this, but what should I do about Craig? He's going to know, or at least suspect, that someone, probably me, waved Lucy off the speech when she doesn't use it in her next live report," Dale said, worried.

"He's going to get a new draft in about fifteen minutes as part of the staffing process. You can say it was an early draft, and you heard from me that the president went in another direction after her last editing session," Melanie suggested.

"Will that work?" Charlotte asked.

Melanie was about to respond when Sam walked in.

"Excuse me. You have an urgent call out here, ma'am."

Charlotte closed the door to the Oval Office, leaving Melanie and Dale alone, and stood at Sam's desk to watch the networks announce that Warren had been killed in the attacks on the Air and Space Museum. She stayed until they read her statement in its entirety and then turned slowly back toward the door to the Oval. She felt wearier than at any other point in her presidency.

"Ma'am." Sam gently touched her arm.

"What?" Charlotte said, more curtly than she'd intended.

"Madam President, your hair and makeup folks are here."

Charlotte sank into the chair next to Sam's desk to catch her breath. "How much time do I have?"

"You have about half an hour until the speech."

"Tell them I'll be with them in five minutes."

CHAPTER FIFTY-TWO

Melanie

Melanie and Dale both watched Charlotte leave the Oval Office. Melanie could tell by Dale's reaction to being left alone with her that she presumed that Charlotte was doing something related to Warren.

"She and I worked on this together," Melanie revealed. She reached into a manila folder and handed Dale a copy of the president's statement. Dale sat down on the sofa and read it. She wiped a couple of tears from her cheeks and then looked at Melanie and smiled.

"Thank you."

"Thank the president," Melanie said.

"Please thank her for me. I've got to get down to the briefing room before her address."

Melanie watched Dale push herself up from the couch as though it were as difficult for her in her one-hundred-and-five-pound body as it was for Melanie in her growing form. She walked toward the door that opened to the hallway between the Roosevelt Room and the Oval Office so that she wouldn't bump into the president, who had exited to the reception area on the other side of the Oval. Dale turned to face Melanie before she left.

"I know that you and Brian knew him better and longer than I did, but I was falling in love with him, and I always knew how important you and Brian were to him. I'm sorry that we didn't all spend time together," Dale said in a near whisper.

"Me, too," Melanie admitted, even though she remained skeptical that Dale and Warren ever would have had the kind of relationship she knew Warren yearned for. Even in her grief, there was something unfeeling about Dale that Melanie couldn't ignore. The news of Warren's sudden death had undoubtedly shaken her, but Dale's sadness seemed more akin to what someone might feel at the news that they'd missed out on something exciting, rather than the loss of one's soul mate.

When Charlotte returned to the Oval Office a few minutes later, it was apparent that the public announcement of Warren's death had added a layer of personal loss to the day for her. While it was important that the president appear emotional and connected to the enormous sense of loss that the victims' families would be experiencing, Melanie worried that she might be feeling too much.

"Have you eaten anything today?" Melanie asked.

"I don't remember. Have you?"

"I had a Luna bar when I got here. Sam gave it to me. Why don't I order you a cheese plate or something?"

"No. Let's run through the speech one more time."

Charlotte clasped a copy of the speech in her hands. When she went for her black Sharpie, Melanie stopped her.

"It's too late for that. If you want to change anything else, I'll do it myself in the teleprompter."

"What time are we doing this?"

"You'll go on the air at eleven-oh-two to give the anchors a couple of minutes to set things up and announce that you're addressing the nation live from the Oval Office."

"What time is it now?"

"It's ten minutes before eleven, Madam President."

There followed a familiar scene in the Oval Office. The president lashed out, and Melanie listened and tried to absorb as much of her negative energy as she could. When the time came for the president to be seated behind her desk in the Oval Office, she seemed to adjust her mind-set and put on a "game face."

Now, as Melanie watched the president deliver the address that she'd carefully crafted, she wondered what would happen in the days to come. Surely their collaboration on this most extraordinary day meant that Charlotte still trusted Melanie more than all of her other advisors. However, it was possible that the president simply needed her too much to leave Melanie on the outside of her inner circle.

One thing was certain: there was no way Melanie would return to the White House if the president allowed Craig to stay on. Other presidents had prosecuted government officials for leaks like the ones he was guilty of. Without an assurance from Charlotte that Craig would face consequences for his actions, Melanie was overcome with an almost urgent desire to flee the Oval Office. But Charlotte had insisted that they be left completely alone for the address to the nation. It was irrational for a president to ask to be left alone without any technical experts, but Melanie had agreed to the assignment. She made sure that everyone she would need if anything went wrong was stationed on the other side of the door.

Melanie was following along by watching the words displayed on the teleprompter. She noticed that Charlotte was nearing the Longfellow excerpt. She touched her stomach lovingly. The passage fit the occasion perfectly. Melanie looked directly at Charlotte as she delivered the final line and smiled. All politicians needed that instant approval at the moment a performance ended, and Charlotte needed it more than most. As soon as Melanie got a signal from the producer speaking in her ear that they were clear, she gave Charlotte a thumbs-up and rose to praise her.

"I couldn't have done it without you," Charlotte replied.

Melanie offered Charlotte more compliments on her performance as they moved into the dining room to allow the crew to break down the lights and other equipment. She wondered where everyone else on Charlotte's staff was. Her entire body ached, and she wanted to see her husband and feel his arms around her for a few minutes before she returned to the Pentagon.

"Madam President, that was very strong!" Craig exclaimed, bursting through the door.

As soon as he arrived, Melanie made her getaway. She stopped briefly in the hallway outside the Oval Office to send Brian a text message. She asked him to meet one of her agents outside the briefing room. After he finished his live shot, the agent led him to her SUV, which was parked on West Exec. It was all she could do not to cry with relief when he opened the door and climbed in next to her. She couldn't remember a time when she'd been more comforted by his presence.

"How's my wife?"

"I'm exhausted."

He put his arm around her, and she leaned into him. Her agents were waiting outside the car.

"I'm sorry about earlier," she said.

"Me, too. How do you feel?"

"Everything hurts."

"You need to tell Charlotte about the baby. She's going to call on you all the time. It's going to be around the clock. I can see it happening already. And you're going to get sucked in. You can't help it. It's what I love about you. You don't even see it; you can't say no to her. You have to tell her you'll be there for her, but it can't be like before," Brian pleaded.

Melanie nodded. She couldn't stop the tears from streaming down her face.

"What's wrong?"

"I'm so sad about Warren. He was trying to help. And all of those people on the ship—do you think they knew they were going to die? And can you even imagine getting a call about your kid getting killed at the Air and Space Museum?"

"Do you have to go back to the Pentagon, or is the next meeting something you can call into? I think you need a couple hours of sleep."

"I can call in. When can you come home?"

"I'll come with you. Let me go grab my bag and tell them I'll be back for *GMA*."

While she waited for Brian and the agent who accompanied him, she rested her forehead against the window. She dozed off and woke up a few minutes later when they were driving up Foxhall Drive toward their home in the Wesley Heights neighborhood of Washington.

"I'm not sure what time I'm going to go in tomorrow, but it will be early," Melanie told the agents as Brian helped her out of the vehicle.

"We will be here all night, Madam Secretary," they assured her.

Brian thanked them and guided Melanie into the house. He led her straight to the bedroom and plugged in all of her devices while she brushed her teeth and then crawled into bed.

They sat up together watching the news coverage. When Melanie saw the early footage from Miami for the first time, tears streamed down her face. She couldn't believe what she was watching. They'd bombed a cruise ship as long as a football field and as tall as a building as though it were a battleship. It lay on the bottom of the bay.

"The first footage that everyone aired had the images of people jumping off the ship—just like the Towers on nine-eleven. We all stopped using it as soon as people figured out what they were looking at, but it's all over the Internet," Brian said.

"Can you imagine what the horror must have been like aboard that ship for a mother and father to look at each other and take their children by the hand and jump into the water? I can't imagine it."

Melanie lay with her head on Brian's chest, watching the coverage. When she woke up a few hours later, Brian was in the shower. She swung her legs around and started to get out of bed but was hit with a wave of nausea and exhaustion so strong that she immediately lay back down. This baby had opinions all of a sudden. Melanie rubbed her stomach and promised him that if he let her get to work for the next few weeks, she'd slow down afterward. He seemed to listen.

CHAPTER FIFTY-THREE

Dale

"Will the briefing room be open all night?"

"Yes," Dale promised.

"How about the North Lawn?"

"I'll check with the Secret Service," she called over her shoulder.

Dale hurried back to her office to avoid having to talk to any of the reporters who were lining up to offer their condolences. Marguerite walked next to her and stopped just before they arrived at Dale's door.

"We need to pull our staff into a meeting. You don't need to say anything about Warren, and they won't, either, but they need to see that you're all right."

Dale agreed.

After the meeting, she went to the West Wing lobby to offer Lucy and Richard the first sit-down interview with the president in exchange for halting their live reports from the West Wing lobby and other off-limits locations. For the first time all day, they were satisfied with Dale's offering. They immediately packed up their things and marched out to the stand-up location on the North Lawn to report on their exclusive. The White House counsel had pulled Dale aside at one point during the day and suggested that she had the legal authority to throw all of the press off the premises under the same set of laws that granted the president of the United States extraordinary powers during times of war.

"The nation has been attacked. If we can justify a national security threat that the press being underfoot creates, we can send them packing," the gray-haired White House lawyer had said.

Before Dale could respond with her full-throated defense of the press's right to cover the president's actions at a time of grave national importance, the president had inserted herself into the conversation.

"Thanks, Bill, but that would be the worst thing that we could do. The press is so accustomed to knowing everything about everyone in their government that if we suddenly shut the doors and turned off the lights, the public would be more terrified than they are watching the same men and women they watch every single day of the year stand in the same exact spot reporting what usually amounts to complete nonsense from out there. Today, of all days, is a day to let them do their jobs."

Dale had been stunned, but she shouldn't have been. Charlotte had always understood the modern presidency better than anyone, especially the rest of her White House staff and the reporters who covered her. It was why Dale had always had such a tremendous amount of respect and admiration for her. It was why today, even after learning about Warren, she pulled herself together and tried to do her job.

She'd promised the president that she wouldn't watch any of the news coverage about Warren, but when she got back to her office after the president's address to the nation, she turned on the televisions. The picture they kept showing of Warren was one that Dale had never seen before. In the photo, he was walking next to the president as they approached the stairs to Air Force One. It had been taken during her reelection campaign. Dale didn't recognize the airport, but there were palm trees in the background. Warren was dressed in khaki slacks and a white button-down shirt. Charlotte was in light gray pants and a sleeveless silk tank the exact same shade of gray. She was holding her hair with one hand and had the other on Warren's shoulder while she spoke to him. He was listening intently to whatever she was saying. It looked like the kind of photo the press snapped after the last campaign event of the day.

Dale hadn't even met Warren yet when the photo had been taken, but there he was with the president. She tried to listen to what the news anchor was saying about him. It was something about how he was one of President Kramer's most trusted advisors and also a personal friend. Dale wondered if perhaps they were reading the statement from the president. She couldn't focus for long enough to make out the words. She wondered what he and Charlotte had been talking about at the instant the photo was snapped. Was she suggesting a new campaign message or soliciting his feedback on her stump speech?

Dale started to feel a sense of panic about all the things she still didn't know about him. She'd rarely asked him about his work for Charlotte. Dale hadn't realized how close they'd been during the campaign. Her chest tightened. She slid to the floor and continued to stare up at the television. She wasn't sure how long she was sitting on the ground before Marguerite came in and found her.

Marguerite barely contained her alarm at finding Dale slumped against her desk. At first, she darted around Dale's office, bringing her water and offering to call her parents. Then she kneeled next to her and tried to coax her to move to the couch. Now she was talking on the phone on Dale's desk. Whoever she was talking to was getting someone else. Marguerite was speaking in a low voice, and Dale couldn't focus on what she was saying. Maybe she was in shock, like the doctor had suggested earlier.

This must be what it feels like to wake up during surgery, Dale thought. You were supposed to be safely anesthetized when they cut through your skin and through your muscle and into whatever sick part of you they needed to remove or repair. Human beings weren't meant to be awake for that kind of searing pain. The brain simply couldn't process what was happening.

Dale was aware of feeling cold and thirsty. There was a bottle of water next to her, but she couldn't send the message to her hand to pick it up.

"How long has she been sitting there?"

The voice was familiar. Dale looked up, and Peter was standing in front of her.

"I found her here about ten minutes ago."

"Dale? What's going on, honey?"

She couldn't speak.

Peter scooped her off the floor and placed her on the couch.

He was looking at her with a kindness that she didn't deserve. She wanted to push him away, but her body still wasn't responding to her brain's commands.

"Marguerite, hand me her sweater, please."

Peter gently pushed Dale's arms through the sleeves and then handed her the bottle of water.

"Take a sip."

Dale did as she was told.

"Do you think you can stand up? We need to get you out of here for some air."

"Where are we going?" Marguerite asked.

Dale didn't hear what Peter said, but she saw alarm register on Marguerite's face again.

"Do you think that's a good idea?"

"We're about to find out."

Peter pulled Dale to her feet and guided her to the West Wing basement, where his SUV was waiting for them. Marguerite climbed in and helped Dale up. The car was freezing. Dale started to shiver.

"Turn off the AC, please," Peter ordered.

Dale didn't look out the window until the car stopped. When she did, there were emergency vehicles everywhere. Dale looked up and saw the shattered façade of the Air and Space Museum. She rolled down her window and stared out.

"I don't think this is a good idea," Marguerite warned.

"Can I get out?" Dale asked.

"Whenever you're ready," Peter answered.

Dale nodded, and Peter opened the door. His Secret Service agent escorted her through the yellow police tape. The agent pointed toward an area that was crowded with investigators.

She stood watching them do their work and tried to picture the scene twelve hours earlier. She remembered her last text from Warren. She'd been heading down to the PEOC. He'd told her to be strong for POTUS. Dale had been a nervous wreck. *He* was the one who'd wanted to be strong for the president, and she should have anticipated that he'd want to head to the place where he could do more than simply watch the horrors unfold on television. Nothing in his DNA would have prepared him simply to observe a tragedy from a distance, and if she'd taken the time to think about what he'd been going through when the attacks had occurred in Washington, she would have known that.

Dale was so angry that she hadn't been enough to make him *not* do something that he must have known could kill him. Surely he knew that the blast was close enough to be lethal. He'd seen combat. He could have grabbed the boy and made a run for it. If only thinking about her and their future together had been enough to force him to make a different choice in the instant the bomb exploded. If only she'd agreed to be more serious, to do more than change the subject every time he mentioned marriage and kids and a life together. If just one time she'd shown some interest in the life that he'd envisioned for them, maybe he would have thought twice about trading his life for the child's. But as she wiped the tears from her face, she knew that even if she'd given him all the things she knew he'd wanted from her, he still would have done what he did. It was who he was. And she was who she was, and he'd loved her anyway. She felt glued to the spot where she stood. It felt good to be this close to where he'd been. She tried to think about what he would have been doing and thinking about in his final moments. He would have been happy that he was doing something for someone else. He would have been happy that he'd be remembered this way. The thought gave her enough comfort to take a deep breath for the first time since she'd heard the awful news. She turned around slowly. Peter was standing on the other side of the yellow tape, just a few feet away. Dale knew from the look on his face that he'd been standing there the whole time. She also realized that Peter had loved her the whole time, ever since they'd first met in the early weeks of Charlotte's first term as president. She realized that she was the one who had devastated him, not the other way around, as she'd convinced herself. She'd been the one to reject him when she'd taken a job on the vice president's staff instead of building a life with him in San Francisco, where they'd moved together after their affair had become public. She was the one who'd refused to carve out the small space in her life that he'd asked for during their long-distance relationship. And it was Dale who had rejected the sanctuary he'd built for their stolen moments together. Even earlier that morning, when they'd met in the family theater, she had belittled his effort at reconnecting with her by acting incredulous that he'd suggest a rendezvous without any intention of sleeping with her. Dale was so ashamed she couldn't bring herself to look him in the eye, but she let him guide her back to the Suburban. Peter quietly directed his driver to Dale's apartment building. When they pulled into the parking lot, he got out of the car with Marguerite and whispered something that caused Marguerite to do a lot of nodding. One of Peter's Secret Service agents accompanied them up the elevator. Once inside, Dale wandered around aimlessly for a few minutes, while Marguerite boiled water for tea.

"Do you want to change?" Peter asked.

Dale shook her head.

"Marguerite is going to stay with you, and if you need me for anything, just call."

Dale's eyes remained glued to the window. When she turned around, Peter had his hand on the door.

"Marguerite has all of my numbers."

She managed to whisper, "Thank you."

Her plan was to stay up all night, but at some point, she fell asleep on the sofa in the living room. When she woke, the sky was just starting to brighten. Marguerite was sleeping on the couch across from her. Dale covered her with a blanket and wandered into the bathroom, where she noticed Warren's T-shirt and shorts on the floor from the morning before. She picked up his shirt and held it to her face. It smelled like him—a mix of Dial soap and Old Spice deodorant. She walked into the bedroom and picked up the pillows and held them to her face. They smelled like him, too. Dale frantically pulled the pillowcases off the pillows and then stripped the sheets off the bed. She surrounded herself with the linens and sank to the floor. Dale sobbed desperate, gulping sobs, careful to weep quietly so as not to wake up Marguerite. She cried for all the things she'd taken for granted until it was too late.

CHAPTER FIFTY-FOUR

Charlotte

Charlotte broke up the final NSC meeting of the night when her most senior Cabinet members started snapping at one another. Tensions had been building between the CIA director and the attorney general all day, and when the AG suggested that the press might pursue a story line about how the law-enforcement community was, once again, left to clean up after a major attack that the CIA had failed to predict, Charlotte had called for an immediate end to the sniping. She'd ordered everyone to get some rest and return at six A.M. Now she was listening to the prime minister of Great Britain offer his condolences. When he stopped for a breath, she took the opportunity to thank him and promised to call again the next day.

"Are there any other calls you need me to do tonight?" she asked her national security advisor.

"No, ma'am. But I have some news that will dispel your belief that we are all hostages of the intractable bureaucracy."

"This sounds promising."

"The advance folks went down to the Mall tonight and walked through a scenario for an off-the-record visit to the D.C. site with the Secret Service for you first thing tomorrow morning. Not an announced stop, but we can take a small press pool, and you can thank the first responders and investigators and lay a wreath for women and the other victims."

"Thank you, Tim."

"And we're working on getting you up to New York tomorrow afternoon and to Miami by the end of the week."

"Good."

"We'll regroup in the morning."

"Call me if there are any developments overnight."

Charlotte couldn't have made any more calls if she'd had to. All she wanted to do was crawl into bed.

She left everything on her desk and closed the door to the Oval Office behind her.

"Samantha, I thought you went home before the calls. That's why I asked Tim to stay for them. Did Monty leave?"

"He went down to the Mall to do a walk-through for your trip in the morning."

"You both need to get home. It's almost two in the morning. Please have them drive you home tonight and pick you up in the morning, and tell Monty I'd like for him to do the same."

"Yes, ma'am."

"Promise me that you'll have a car take you home?"

"Yes, ma'am."

Charlotte walked slowly out the door behind Sam's desk and down the colonnade. When she arrived upstairs, the two younger dogs jumped from the couch in the Yellow Oval to greet her. Cammie opened her eyes and wagged her tail but didn't move from her spot on the sofa.

"Hi, girls," Charlotte cooed. As the dogs licked her face and wiggled in front of her, she felt a lump form in her throat. So many people had died such violent deaths. And not one of them had done a single thing to prepare for such a tragic end. She couldn't shake the images of the burning cruise ship from her mind. She'd watched as it sank into the bay and had nearly cried out when she saw the last of it completely submerged along with any hope of recovering any more victims alive. They were working to raise the ship, but it would take days, possibly weeks.

She let the dogs lick the few tears that had fallen, and then she took a handkerchief out of her pocket and blew her nose.

"Char, how are you doing?"

Mark had entered the room from the Truman Balcony.

"You guys didn't need to wait up for me," she said.

"Can I get you a drink?"

"No, thanks."

He filled two glasses with something from the bar and handed her one anyway.

"Do you want to sit?"

Mark pointed at the balcony. Charlotte followed him out. Brooke was snoring softly on the sofa. Mark sat down next to her and put a small pillow under her head.

"She passed out about half an hour ago. She wanted me to wake her up when you got home," Mark whispered.

"Let her sleep," Charlotte insisted.

They sat sipping scotch and listening to Brooke snore. When Charlotte's eyes started to feel heavy, she forced herself up from the couch.

"I should go check on Peter."

"He's not here, Char."

"Where is he?"

"He got a call from Marguerite a couple of hours ago. Brookie answered the phone, and Marguerite was hysterical. She said Dale was catatonic or something."

Charlotte nodded and sat back down.

"He'll be back," Mark assured her.

Charlotte smiled at him and looked down at her hands. They didn't look like hers—they looked like the hands of a much older woman. She examined them carefully and thought about all the years and all the effort she'd expended trying to be the things that she thought she was supposed to be to all the people around her. She knew that where Peter was concerned, she was finally done trying.

"I don't have the energy for the charade with Peter anymore."

"Every day won't be like today."

"It shouldn't be such an extraordinary effort for two people who were once very much in love to comfort each other."

"You're right about that."

"I asked him to break the news to Dale about Warren. It was Melanie's suggestion, but I thought it was a humane way to inform her that her boyfriend had died. I figured that she and Peter had the only relationship that was separate from work and that with him, she would be able to let her guard down."

"And?"

"Well, what I saw when I stopped by the medical office to check on her was that it was he who had his guard down with her. He looked like he'd been crying, or talking, or sorting through the chaos of the day with her. I don't know. Maybe I imagined that. Maybe he hadn't done any such thing. I don't know what I'm talking about."

"No, Char, I think your intuition is right. He doesn't have to try so hard with her. She isn't you. She's isn't the president. She isn't perfect and smart and funny and beautiful all at once. She's a mess. He needs that."

Charlotte smiled. "I think he's in love with her."

"Maybe, but not for the reasons you think."

"No?"

"I don't think he ever stopped loving you, Char. I think he just saw that you preferred to do things alone."

"It wasn't a choice."

"No? I remember thinking that the last time you guys were really partners was while you were governor. The jump from the governor's office to this place was one that you took all alone, honey. And I remember watching you guys once the presidential campaign got under way. You never really talked through what would happen to the lives you'd built in California. We were there. Peter's head never stopped spinning from the day you won the New Hampshire primary to the morning of your first inauguration."

"I wasn't paying enough attention to him to notice."

"Char, everything isn't your fault."

"But this one is. If I'd been satisfied serving out two terms as governor of California and then riding the wave as a popular former governor, we could have had a great life in San Francisco."

"That never would have been enough for you, Char."

She wanted to protest, but if he were wrong, she never would have left California and uprooted her entire family. Mark reached for her hand.

"Why do I feel so shitty about it all?"

"Because you wanted to have everything, but that's a bullshit fairy tale they tell women to make you dependent on Prozac and therapy. It's a fucking lie."

"What do I do now?"

"Whatever you want to do."

Charlotte hugged her friend and went into her bedroom, where she lay down, fully clothed, on the bed with the dogs huddled around her to wait for Peter.

It was after three A.M. when he finally tiptoed in.

"Where were you?" She shot out of bed to confront him.

"I took Dale to the blast site. I thought she needed to see it."

As they stood facing each other with the three dogs on the bed between them, Charlotte knew that if she ever had to recount the moment that she knew that spending any more time on her broken marriage would be a disservice to them both, it would be this one. Charlotte barely had the energy to say what needed to be said. Sensing this, Peter spoke first.

"I'm sorry that I couldn't be the things you needed me to be, Charlotte."

"Please, don't," she urged.

"What?"

"Don't turn this into a failure that you get to claim as your own. That's horrendously unfair, and I'm tired of being the person you simply can't figure out how to satisfy. I'm the one who's sorry that I couldn't become someone you could talk to. I'm sorry that I dragged you here twice. I know that you never wanted to live here."

"It's not Washington, Char. We stopped being us before we got here, but once you were here and the kids were in Connecticut and I was in California, I couldn't ever figure out how to put it back together."

He was trying to say the right things, but his words felt like an assignment of blame to her for disassembling the family.

"And Dale?"

"You asked me to take care of Dale."

"Yes, today I did do that. But when you guys were together—you were happy, right?"

"I don't understand what you're asking me. I thought you had given up on me and on our marriage before I ever got involved with Dale."

"Peter, stop trying to hold yourself harmless from any responsibility. I'll take the hit for this—don't worry. Everyone will still think you're a great guy. I am trying to figure out if I ever had a shot this time around. Were you ever really invested in our marriage, or was I just conveniently standing there begging for another chance at the very moment things fell apart with Dale?"

"Char, I would have liked nothing more than for us to have become a family again."

She felt like screaming. He was so passive-aggressive he didn't even know how to have an honest conversation with her. "I know, but I need to know if you ever really thought it would work."

"I wanted to think that it would, but everything felt like such an effort."

She almost laughed at his statement, but it answered a lot of questions. Being married to someone with a job like hers most certainly would require an extraordinary effort, but that wasn't something that interested Peter, at least not where the marriage was concerned. Charlotte was hurt and angry, but she knew those feelings would recede.

She surprised herself, and him, by starting to cry. The marriage she'd been toiling away at for two decades was over, and the emotion that overtook all others was relief. Peter pulled her into a hug, and they stood there like that for a long time. When he left, Charlotte fell into a deep, dreamless sleep until she was awoken by a call from Tim.

"We've got a tape, Madam President."

"Who?"

"The guys who launched the attack on the ship taped a celebratory message before the attack. It was uploaded on an Al Qaeda Web site, and Al Jazeera has been airing it for the last twenty minutes. I can bring it up to the residence if you want to see it."

"That's OK. I'll meet you in the Situation Room in fifteen minutes."

Charlotte clicked on the TV and watched a live report from outside the Air and Space Museum. The reporter cited the death toll, twenty-four, and the number of injured, thirty-nine. Charlotte sat on the edge of her bed while they aired a photo of the CNN reporter who'd been injured and her cameraman, who'd died. They aired a photo of Warren, whom they described as a close presidential advisor and friend. The correspondent finished her live report by speculating that the president of the United States might venture the less than half a mile to the site later in the day. Charlotte hoped that her Secret Service director wasn't watching. He'd get nervous if he thought it had been broadcast that she'd be there. Charlotte showered and dressed quickly and made her way to the West Wing.

CHAPTER FIFTY-FIVE

Melanie

One year later

I've made this edit three times. Why is this section still in here?" Melanie grilled the chief White House speechwriter, who was sitting on the other side of her desk.

"She specifically told us to leave it in when we met with her in the Oval last night after you left," he explained.

"And I specifically asked you to take it out. Three times."

The speechwriter rubbed his red-rimmed eyes. He looked like he'd been awake for a week. "Maybe you and the president should discuss it and get back to us."

Melanie raised her eyes from the printout to appraise her favorite speechwriter.

"Why do you want it out, anyway?" he probed.

"Because the president won't be able to get through it."

"What do you mean?"

"She can't talk about her call with the Carmichaels without getting choked up, especially with them sitting in the front row, and that's not what I want for the opening paragraph of her first speech of the day. I don't want the country to see her cry on the one-year anniversary of the attacks. I want them to be touched by the tributes and inspired by the stories of survival and resilience. For that to happen, I need the president to be able to read the entire address, and if you start with the call to the Carmichaels, she won't be able to get through it."

"And in your estimation, she *will* be able to talk about her first trip to Miami the week of the attack without crying? I've never even seen her read through that section of the speech without getting choked up."

"I cut out the whole section of the speech that went into her first visit to the Port of Miami and her private meetings with the family members. She may decide to ad-lib it when she gets down there and stands at the port again, but I don't want to put her in the position of reliving that."

"If you take out the Carmichael section, too, do we have enough of her emotional journey in here? Wasn't that part of what you wanted to accomplish with these speeches?"

"It was, but I just don't want her to fall apart at the first event."

"Fine. Can you do me a favor and tell her that you took it out?"

"I'll handle her."

"You're fine with the rest of it?"

Melanie nodded.

"DOD doesn't want us to describe the attacks as limited in nature."

"I'll deal with them. Is there anything else giving anyone heartburn? CIA is fine with the line about stepping up recruitment efforts? We may as well say that we're hiring spies and have her give out a goddamned eight hundred number for interested applicants. I can't believe they want that in there."

"Yeah, they asked if you could get POTUS to give out the Web site."

"Seriously?"

"No."

"Smart-ass. You're lucky that I happen to think you are brilliant, because you are a huge pain. You creative geniuses are all the same—high-maintenance."

"Right back at you, Mel. Are we done here? My omelet is getting cold."

"One more thing."

"What?"

"The speech is beautiful."

Melanie could see his face break into a smile before he rose and walked slowly toward the door of her West Wing office. "I had money on this, you know."

"On what?"

"That you'd come back."

"Get out of here. And I'm not back. It's a short-term, limited appointment," Melanie insisted.

"Keep telling yourself that, Melanie. I'll see you on the flight back to California on her last day."

"Bite your tongue!" Melanie yelled after him as he walked down the hall and back toward the mess, where the rest of the speechwriters were huddled over hot breakfasts and pots of coffee to fuel their twenty-four-hour days.

Melanie liked to think that she'd held out for a respectable amount of time before agreeing to come back to the White House staff, but Brian had been right. She'd been sucked back in almost immediately following the attacks. Charlotte hadn't made a single move in the last year without discussing it with Melanie.

Two American citizens, an Egyptian on a student visa, and two green card holders from Qatar had carried out the attacks that occurred the previous July. Charlotte couldn't consider military retaliation against Egypt or Qatar, but she had used the occasion to force America's allies to pick a side in the battle raging in the Middle East against extremist groups like ISIS and the Muslim Brotherhood. When the president declared war on the groups that had hijacked the democracy movements of the previous two decades to usher in regimes with close ties to terrorists, she did so with the leaders of France, Germany, Great Britain, China, Jordan, Egypt, and the UAE standing next to her in the Rose Garden. She'd played hardball with the tools at her disposal—by cutting off foreign aid, imposing tough economic sanctions, and bombing targets across the region with the help of Arab allies. Charlotte had also directed the CIA to engage in more aggressive recruitment in the region. The president accepted the public's limited appetite for another military engagement, but she refused to accept that America couldn't make the attackers and their supporters suffer.

Melanie was not surprised by the president's shrewdness or decisiveness, nor was she alarmed by Charlotte's decision to permit the use of enhanced interrogation methods for the two bombers captured in Miami. But she did find Charlotte's capacity to sit still amid the country's grief astonishing. Losing Warren had given all of them, especially the president, a toehold on the grief that the victims' families were experiencing. Melanie had watched the president hold hands with the children and parents of the victims, and instead of losing herself in the retaliatory military and economic measures, she'd remained invested in their healing. It was a remarkable transformation for a woman who had spent her entire political career projecting emotionless strength and control. Melanie felt more proud of Charlotte in those months than she could ever have imagined she would.

For her part, motherhood had rendered her helpless over her emotions. She felt everything these days. She'd been almost five months pregnant at the time of the attacks. The realization that the days of asking other people's sons and daughters to protect the country from harm were far from over had filled her with a grief so profound that even the joy of her perfect, beautiful son's birth four and a half months later hadn't completely erased it.

She lived two lives now. Her joy-filled life was made up of the tight circle of love that she and Brian created with and around their seven-month-old son, Christopher. Her heart expanded every single day, and sometimes she'd watch him sleep at night and wonder how much more love her heart could take before it burst. She wondered if it was possible to love him too much. Melanie would catch Brian's eye, and without speaking, she knew that he was thinking the same thing. She'd never loved Brian so much. It felt as though they could exist as an island unto themselves, sustained by the wonder and joy they felt at each sound and smile and kiss from their magical little boy.

Instead of feeling that Christopher's birth was a reason to retreat from her professional obligations, she'd felt more compelled to serve. After the attacks, she'd reasserted herself as the guardian of Charlotte's deepest confidences. Melanie had also resumed her role as the president's surrogate on Capitol Hill and around the world. The president never had to ask Melanie to do anything—Melanie simply knew what she wanted done and did it without ever seeking credit and without ever discussing it in the press or anywhere else.

After the shock of the attacks started to fade into something that could only be described as the new normal, the president started asking Melanie about her plans for returning to work after the baby was born.

"You aren't going to be able to do all of the traveling required of a SECDEF. The Pentagon is the least family-friendly part of our government," the president had declared.

"I'll be sure to mention that to our hundreds of thousands of men and women in the military."

"You know what I mean," Charlotte had said, laughing.

Just before the baby was born, Melanie had started to suspect that Charlotte might offer her a senior advisor role back at the White House, but she'd been completely unprepared for the president's grand gesture. On a trip to the White House to introduce Christopher to the president and take his picture in the Oval Office, something Melanie thought she'd like someday for his baby book, Charlotte had asked Melanie to take a walk with her.

They'd stopped outside a door between the White House chief of staff's office and the Oval Office. Charlotte pushed it open and stood in the doorway expectantly.

Charlotte had turned a small West Wing office into a nursery. She'd had it painted the palest shade of blue that Melanie had ever seen and carpeted in the same color. There were mobiles with airplanes and trains and circus animals hanging from the sky. A series of original *Curious George* and *Babar* prints were framed and hung along one wall, and a mural of carousel animals had been painted on the other. The windows had been outfitted with blackout shades for naptime, and delicate sheer blue panels were also hanging. A cream-colored wrought-iron crib outfitted with elephant sheets and a matching bumper stood against one wall, and a changing table full of diapers, wipes, and burp cloths was against the other. Under the window was an oversized bookshelf filled with children's picture books and toys. There was also an inviting blue glider and ottoman. A giant plush lion stood in one corner, and a giraffe was in the other.

Melanie noticed a noise machine and a baby monitor resting on the windowsill.

"What is this?" she'd gasped.

"An incentive."

Melanie had been speechless. Christopher had wiggled in her arms. Melanie had walked to the window and looked out at the South Lawn. She didn't want Charlotte to see her face yet. She bounced the baby in her arms as he fell asleep. She looked into the crib and noticed that a soft swaddling blanket had been laid down.

"Everything has been washed with that baby detergent. What's it called? Dreft, right?"

Melanie had nodded and laid the baby down. She'd stood there looking at Charlotte. The woman who never thought that she deserved to have it all was trying to hand it to Melanie. She'd walked over to Charlotte and hugged her.

"Thank you," she'd whispered.

"Thank *you*." Charlotte had hugged her back.

Now Melanie forced herself not to stop at the nursery, where she heard her son cooing at the nanny she'd hired to watch him while she worked steps away. She walked into the Oval Office and sat down in a chair next to where Charlotte was making her own final edits to the speech.

"I put the Carmichael section back in," Charlotte announced.

"I took it back out," Melanie countered. She settled in for what she knew would be a contentious battle of wills.

CHAPTER FIFTY-SIX

Dale

What are you wearing for your final briefing?" Lucy asked.

Dale made a face. "I don't know. Do you think I need a special outfit?"

"It will be on all of the newscasts. You know, 'White House Press Secretary Dale Smith conducted her final briefing from the podium today, ending her reign of terror, blah, blah, blah,'" Lucy taunted.

Dale swatted Lucy with her napkin. "You are so nasty it borders on distasteful."

"Next to you, I'm Mother Teresa," Lucy deadpanned.

Dale made another face and then returned her focus to the plate in front of her. "What is this? I didn't order this."

"It's called a detox salad," Lucy explained.

"Why is it in front of me?"

"I ordered one for each of us. You're going to get scurvy if you don't start eating fruits and vegetables."

Until now, female friendship had proven elusive to Dale, and Lucy was an unlikely gal pal. As with all of the meaningful relationships in Dale's life, she was terrified that she'd do something to screw things up with the person who'd come to occupy a previously uninhabited place in her heart.

Lucy finished her salad and then started stabbing at the radishes on Dale's plate. Dale leaned back and drank her iced coffee with an amused smile on her face. They were having lunch at the Four Seasons in Georgetown.

"Did you turn down the CNBC job yet?" Lucy asked between bites.

"No."

"Why not?"

"Because I don't have any other offers."

"When you get to New York and start talking to people, I'm sure you'll have better options."

"Like what?"

"I don't know. Maybe Fox will hire you."

"I'm not pretty enough to work at Fox—or Republican enough."

"Are you Republican at all?"

"I play a Republican on TV, don't I?"

"That's debatable. Maybe you should take the CNBC thing."

"Does anyone watch CNBC anymore?"

"I have no idea, but they pay for your clothes, not that you need any more clothes."

"You're one to talk," Dale retorted.

Lucy smiled.

Dale had taken the first step toward winning Lucy over when she came through on her promise to grant Lucy and Richard the first interview with the president following the attacks. It had taken longer to schedule than Dale anticipated, but when the president finally sat down for the interview, she had made it worth their wait.

It took place in the Oval Office twelve days after the attack, and Dale had held her breath when Lucy and Richard asked the president how she learned about Warren's death. Instead of clamming up, as they'd all expected her to do, Charlotte had walked around to her desk and pulled out a notepad from the top drawer.

"These are my notes from that call to his parents," she'd revealed.

"Was that the most difficult moment of the day for you?" Lucy had asked.

"I'd thought that it might be, but it was the moment that gave me strength for everything else that followed. Not just that day. I've drawn strength from that call every day since. Mrs. Carmichael read me a passage that I used in my speech that night."

"The Longfellow quote? I thought Melanie found that."

"It was her idea to include it, but Mrs. Carmichael recited it to me. 'And the mother gave, in tears and pain, the flowers she most did love; she knew she should find them all again in the fields of light above,'" Charlotte read from her notes.

"Can you imagine? At the moment you learn that your precious son—your bright, beautiful, strong warrior of a son—has perished, your mind turns to the person on the other end of the phone? I don't understand where that sort of strength, if that's the word, or resolve, or calm, comes from," Charlotte said.

Richard had launched into a line of questioning about whether military action was inevitable. After a few questions that Charlotte mostly dodged, Lucy interrupted.

"Do you believe that quote?"

Charlotte looked surprised by the question. She'd gazed out the window for a long time. It had felt like an eternity to Dale, who was watching from a spot just outside the president's line of sight near the fireplace in the Oval Office.

"I have to believe that, Lucy. I have to believe that for the hundreds of men, women, and children who died in the attacks. I have to believe it for the men and women who die serving their country in Iraq and Afghanistan. I have to believe that as a mother. We all have to believe that, or . . ." Charlotte had returned her eyes to the view out the window again for a few seconds.

"Or what, Madam President?" Lucy pushed.

Charlotte had turned her clear blue eyes directly at Lucy and seemed to consider what she was about to say carefully.

"Otherwise, Lucy, it's unbearable," she had admitted.

Charlotte had conducted the entire interview as though there were no cameras in the room—just the three of them, having a conversation about what the country had endured and about what she had endured. When it was over, the president had left Dale, Lucy, and Richard alone in the Oval Office.

"I can't believe that she spent over an hour with us. She was incredible!" Lucy gushed.

"And very generous with her time," Richard added.

The interview had marked a turning point in Charlotte's presidency. She'd lost something, too. Her friend Warren had died, and she wasn't merely channeling the nation's grief—she felt it, too. Her marriage had ended, and while Lucy didn't know that at the time of the interview, Charlotte had made no attempt to dodge a question from Lucy about the strain on a family that accompanies a career in national politics. People felt they knew her better after the interview, and they trusted her more. She'd needed that trust to muscle through a controversial package of new laws that included unprecedented intrusions into people's electronic lives that made the contentious debates about NSA wiretapping from the previous decade seem quaint. She'd sided with Republicans who'd pushed through an immigration policy that critics claimed amounted to profiling. And she'd demanded that nations with which the United States had had prickly relations for much of her tenure choose a side.

The president had unveiled the legislation in a second address to the nation the night before her sit-down with Lucy and Richard. It was twelve days after the attacks, and divers were still pulling bodies out from the sunken ship in Miami. The country was grieving and racked with anger, and Charlotte spoke to both sentiments in her interview with Lucy and Richard. Many observers had credited the interview with marshaling the public support needed to get her agenda through Congress. Dale was skeptical that Charlotte had gone into the interview having made the calculation ahead of time that she could have her way with Congress if she bared her soul. It had felt like a genuine moment of reflection, but Dale would never know for sure.

"Are you going to miss D.C.?" Lucy asked now, jolting Dale from her memories of the days after the attack.

"I don't know. One minute I can't wait to leave, and the next I'm standing in my bedroom thinking about being here with Warren, and I'm a wreck."

"That's understandable."

Lucy didn't offer advice, but she always made Dale feel as though anything she was going through was normal.

"Did you ever call that shrink?"

"No."

"They're mostly useless, anyway."

Lucy paid the check, and they walked out together. Heads turned as they walked through the lobby. Neither of them noticed.

"I'll see you tonight," Lucy said. Dale didn't respond immediately, so Lucy added, "At your good-bye party."

"I'm still pissed at you for doing that."

"Don't be late," Lucy ordered, before disappearing into a black Suburban.

Dale climbed into her car for the short ride back to the White House. She watched a crew team practice on the Potomac and wondered if any of them ever worried that their loved ones would get killed in a terrorist attack. It was something Dale never would have contemplated, either, but she'd started saying it out loud when she was alone at night. In Washington, everyone knew who she was, and they knew what had happened to Warren. But in New York, she'd undoubtedly meet people who had no idea that her boyfriend had been killed in the attacks the previous summer. She kept reminding herself that that was why she was moving there.

"You're late," Marguerite scolded when she walked back into the press office. Dale was still lost in her thoughts, but she'd promised Marguerite she'd run through the questions and answers for the next day's briefing.

"I thought we were meeting at two-thirty?"

"One-thirty," her deputy corrected.

"I'm sorry."

"I still can't believe you're leaving me," Marguerite complained.

"We both know that you've been running the press office since the day I arrived. No one will notice my absence for days."

"They only like me because I'm the good cop to your bad cop."

"I thought I was the good cop? That actually explains a lot. Give me a minute to check my messages and return a few e-mails."

Her deputy was taking over for her as press secretary and would deliver her first official briefing the following morning. Dale looked out the window of the office she'd inhabited for a year and a half. The view of the North Lawn was the one she'd miss most. She could see everyone who entered the White House complex through the Northwest Gate. She'd watched members of Congress come in for confrontations with the president, heads of state and their unruly delegations unload for meetings with their American counterparts, and family members and friends of White House staff members arrive for after-hours West Wing tours.

She also remembered watching Warren walk down the driveway and into the West Wing lobby once. They'd just started seeing each other. The president and the vice president had invited him to brief them on the most recent public opinion polls before the State of the Union. It was a blustery January day, and he wasn't wearing a coat. Dale had watched him stride down the driveway with a smile on his face. She remembered wanting to know what made him smile so much and wondering—and hoping—that she had something to do with it. As he'd neared the West Wing lobby that day, she'd rushed to greet him.

"Hi," he'd said, bending down to kiss her on the cheek.

"Where's your coat?"

"I left it at the office."

"You're here for the president?"

"Yeah."

"Just a meeting?"

"Actually, we're having dinner," he'd said sheepishly.

Dale had felt a pang of jealousy over the intimate nature of his relationship with her boss. "Must be nice," she'd mused.

"Can I take you out for a drink after?"

"Maybe. Call me when you're done."

He'd spent the next three hours in the White House residence. Dale didn't have a work reason to be at the office, but she had waited for him to finish. When he'd texted her that he was done, she replied that she was still in her office. He'd walked in with his "A" badge around his neck and a smile so warm that Dale remembered being overcome with hope that her dark, tortured relationships with men were finally a thing of the past.

Now, as she listened to Marguerite bang around impatiently outside her door, she thought about how much time she'd spent over the previous twelve months hating herself for spending part of the day that Warren was killed trying to seduce Peter. She wasn't sure which had proven more consuming, the self-flagellation or missing the life she almost had with Warren. Peter had tried to reach out to her on a couple of occasions over the last year. She hadn't spoken to him since the night he took her to the spot where Warren had died, but something about the way he had looked at her when she'd turned back toward the car had shaken her. He still loved her; she was sure of it. There was a time when that would have been enough to pull her back into his orbit, but losing Warren had changed things. Perhaps it was the realization that while Warren was helping people he'd never met and saving a boy he wouldn't live to know, she'd been engaged in her final act of disloyalty. Even though she knew that Warren would want her to be happy, she couldn't bring herself to see or talk to Peter after that night. Warren would probably want her to be with Peter if it made her happy, as long as it didn't make Charlotte *unhappy*. Dale spent a lot of time now trying to do things that she thought would make Warren happy, which was ironic, because when he was alive, she didn't try very hard to do that at all.

Warren was the reason she'd stayed on as press secretary. It made her feel closer to him to be here, and the president had made clear that the job was hers as long as she wanted it. She'd urged Dale to take some time off after the attack, but Dale had refused. The inflexible routine of life in the White House had sustained her during the first weeks after the attacks. She arrived at the office by six A.M. and worked until nine or ten at night. The only hours she found excruciating were the ones she had to occupy on her own.

The president's doctor had kept a close watch on Dale during the first couple of months. He'd suggested therapy and had begrudgingly doled out Zoloft, Xanax, and Ambien. She'd been at her desk tracing the tiny black letters on the business card of the therapist the doctor recommended when her direct line had rung. No one called her on that number.

"Hello?" she'd answered.

"What are you doing right now?"

She'd recognized the voice but couldn't place it. "Who is this?"

"It's Lucy. What are you doing right now?" she'd asked again.

"Reviewing the president's speech for tomorrow."

"Grab your stuff and walk out on the Treasury side. I'm in a black Suburban."

"What is this?"

"It's an intervention. Everyone is on suicide watch, including the president, and she has bombing raids to plan, so you need to get your act together ASAP. You have five minutes to get out here."

"Where are we going?

"We're going to get drunk and pretend that we like each other more than we do. Come on. Hurry up. Your next-best option is a forced vacation at some spa in Arizona, where they'll make you talk about your intimacy issues and ride horses. Trust me, I'm your best option."

The idea of a spa vacation was enough to propel Dale out the door. She and Lucy drank a bottle of red wine at a small table in the bar at Capitol Grille. Lucy returned the following week and forced her out for dinner. Two weeks passed, and she was in town again, bullying her into another night out.

Dale had secretly started to look forward to Lucy's visits. After a couple of months, the dinners were punctuated by e-mails and texts and brief calls while Lucy was in a car on her way to work or when Dale drove home at night. Lucy had listened to Dale's entire confession about her attempt to seduce Peter in the family theater on the day of the attacks one night after they ate at CityZen at the Mandarin Oriental Hotel in D.C., where Lucy was staying. Dale didn't spare any of the details. She'd felt lighter after telling Lucy. It was the first time all of the platitudes about the power of female friendship rang true for Dale. And Lucy had confided that she often felt like she did all the work and secured all the important interviews while Richard happily accepted half of the credit for all their success. She'd also shared her worries that she had the work-life equation dramatically out of balance. Lucy feared that her husband had an emotionally intimate relationship with their nanny that was designed to make her feel like an intruder in her own home. Only Dale knew how devastated she was by the dynamic and how much effort Lucy put into appearing completely satisfied with every aspect of her life to the outside world.

In a plan that Lucy had hatched one night over dinner in George-town, she had suggested that Dale relocate to New York after the one-year anniversary of the attacks. When Dale admitted that the idea appealed to her, Lucy introduced her to a Realtor who'd leased her D.C. condo to a lobbyist. Lucy also found Dale a West Village apartment that was a short cab ride from her own Tribeca loft. The final piece had been the meeting with CNBC, which Lucy's television agent had arranged for Dale.

"Voilà," Lucy had announced when the CNBC offer had come through the week before. "I've officially transformed your life. Now you have to raise my twins, have sex with my husband every night, and carry Richard through every newscast. Deal?"

Dale had laughed and promised her friend that at the very least, she'd buy the drinks from now on.

Craig had also moved to New York after Melanie demanded that he be forced to move on before she'd consider returning to the White House. The president never said anything to Dale about Craig's breach after that night in the Oval Office, and Craig never confronted Dale about her role in the sting that had revealed his actions in leaking sensitive information to Lucy and Richard. He was courteous and professional in his dealings with her, but their friendship had cooled immediately. Dale was astounded that the president kept him in his position for as long as she had. Where staff was concerned, the president seemed to operate in a moral gray area. Dale had benefited from the president's liberal interpretation of what constituted loyalty. But once an aide had crossed her, she had a way of letting him linger beyond a point when most politicians would have shown him the door. It made Dale wonder if perhaps Peter had been in a state of limbo with Charlotte, too, not ever firmly in her good graces but never cut loose, either. The inability to sever ties was not a trait most people would associate with the most powerful woman in the world, but Dale found it reassuring that Charlotte wasn't perfect in all of her relationships either.

Fortunately for the president, Melanie's return had permitted her to disengage entirely from personnel matters. Melanie ushered in an era of stability and order and gave the president a noticeably firmer foundation on which to govern. The two of them communicated in a mystical way. Dale had seen it herself on the night of the attacks. The president was more relaxed and focused than at any other time since Dale had observed her. It made leaving more difficult in ways that were unexpected. Leaving the place—and the people—Warren had loved so much made her feel like she was losing him all over again.

She wiped the tears that had run from the corners of her eyes and dabbed at the eye makeup that had smeared beneath them. Dale thought about Lucy's determination always to put a strong and happy face on every situation. She forced a smile onto her face and opened the door for Marguerite.

CHAPTER FIFTY-SEVEN

Charlotte

Charlotte could hear Brooke and Penny talking in the hallway outside her bedroom. She quickly changed out of her suit and into jeans and a thin white sweater.

"Mom?" Penny called.

"In here," she replied.

The twins were spending more time at the White House and at Camp David than they ever had before. She suspected they were worried that she was lonely, but Brooke and Mark had also managed to manufacture excuses to visit Washington every few weeks, and the house had never been noisier or busier. She loved it. The year since the attacks had ushered in the most painful moments of Charlotte's presidency and the most satisfying times she'd ever spent with Penny and Harry.

"We were talking about those blissful early-morning hours a year ago, when we thought that your bitchy daughter was going to be your biggest problem," Brooke taunted.

"It was a cry for help!" Penny insisted.

"I can't believe you two are making jokes about it. Your father nearly had a heart attack when he read your post, young lady," Charlotte scolded.

"That's true. Your dad was angrier than your mom. She wanted to tell the press that your barb constituted a compliment coming from you, but the West Wing staff wouldn't let her," Brooke added. All three of them laughed.

"Can I borrow something to wear tomorrow?" Penny asked.

"Of course."

Penny made a beeline for the section of clothes in Charlotte's closet with the tags still on them. "What are these?"

"My stylist sent them down last week."

"Can I try them?"

"Sure."

Penny pulled the designer dresses off the hangers and zipped herself into them while Charlotte and Brooke watched. Penny was taller than her mother, but they wore the same size.

"Do you like this?" She had on a black short-sleeved shift dress that looked stunning.

"You look so sophisticated," Brooke said.

"It's gorgeous on you," Charlotte added.

"Can I wear it?"

"Of course." Charlotte smiled. These were the silly mother-daughter moments she felt she'd missed out on. As superficial and materialistic as trying on her dresses might be, it gave her an outsized amount of pleasure.

Penny had started talking to her—really talking—after she'd traveled to California three weeks after the attacks to tell the twins that she and Peter had split for good. They went to lunch in Tiburon, and Charlotte told Penny and Harry all the things that parents think they are supposed to tell children when they decide that despite the gigantic reservoirs of love they have for the children they created together, they no longer love each other enough to try to make a marriage work. Charlotte had underestimated Penny's understanding of their situation.

"I don't know how you did it as long as you did, Mom," Penny had said.

"What do you mean?"

Penny had looked at her mother with such compassion that Charlotte felt embarrassed. Her daughter's pity was not something she was prepared to experience. "It shouldn't be so hard," Penny declared.

Charlotte considered Penny's remark and wondered why she'd never spoken to her daughter like the grown-up she'd become. "You're right."

Harry had returned to campus after lunch to study for a test the next day, and Penny and Charlotte had gone for a hike.

"Do you think Dad and Dale will get back together?" Penny had asked.

"I don't know. Do you?"

"I don't know. Would you care?"

Charlotte sighed. She knew that if she wanted Penny to talk to her, she was going to have to start by being honest with her.

"Of course I would care, honey. I wish it were as simple as wanting Dad to be happy, but it's more complicated than that."

"Why?"

"There are other people involved."

"But Dad and Dale never cared about that before."

"That's true. I don't know if Dale still loves your dad. She was dating Warren."

"I know."

"You know everything."

"Not everything. Just more than you give me credit for."

They'd hiked and talked for more than two hours. When Charlotte returned to Washington, she felt as though the walls between them had finally started to come down. Penny called the following week and asked if she could bring a friend to Camp David for Thanksgiving.

Reaching Penny had been so simple, in hindsight. It made her wonder if she might have saved her marriage if she'd been honest and direct with Peter at an earlier point in their relationship. If she'd ever figured out how to tell him that she'd needed him as much as Dale had needed him, maybe he would have been there for her; maybe they could have been there for each other.

It didn't matter anymore. He'd returned to San Francisco a week after the attacks, and their separation hadn't generated much attention. Charlotte didn't feel that she owed anyone an explanation this time, and aside from a few articles on the *San Francisco Chronicle*

Web site about Peter being spotted around the Bay Area without any Secret Service detail, no one had written much about it.

The first few weeks after the attacks were packed with memorial services and visits to the cities that were bombed, private strategy sessions with her foreign-policy team, briefings on the intelligence they'd gathered with allies and members of Congress, and speeches and press conferences designed to calm the nerves of a jittery and terrified public.

When she finally had time to think about Peter again, she recognized that salvaging her marriage had appealed to her masochistic side. She'd convinced herself that if things between them weren't difficult, they must not be worthwhile. Charlotte and Peter had spent more than a decade growing apart, and she'd naively hoped to bridge all of that distance in a few months. The end hadn't been entirely Peter's fault, but it was clarifying for her that on the day of the attacks—the most horrible day of her presidency—he found his purpose in getting Dale through the shock of losing Warren. Charlotte couldn't square what she'd seen between them with her hopes for a second chance with Peter.

For her part, Charlotte had found someone to save, too. The morning after the attacks, she'd asked Craig to ride with her in the limo to the D.C. site. As soon as the door to the limo slammed shut, she'd turned to him.

"I don't know why you did what you did, and I don't want to know. I need to know what you want to do now."

Craig had reached into his coat pocket. "I drafted a resignation letter last night." He'd handed it to her.

"Is that what you want?"

The car had stopped outside the museum. She heard the Secret Service announce her arrival: "All cars, all stations, Wayfarer arrive."

"Give me a minute," she'd told the agent who'd opened her car door. Then she'd said, "Craig, I believe that you made a mistake—a few mistakes. But before I step out of this car, I need to know if you want to continue to work for me."

"I would like to explain," he'd said.

"No. You don't get to explain why you did it, and I don't have to explain why I didn't accept your resignation. It doesn't matter to me all that much. All that matters to me, today, is that you do your job. Understood?"

"Yes, ma'am."

They'd never spoken about it again, and she had no reason to suspect that he'd ever leaked again. Melanie would never be able to understand, but Charlotte had forgiven Craig as much for her own sake, and in the interest of staff stability, as for his. At this point in her presidency, every action—regardless of how principled or justified—had consequences. To her, purging the White House of a chief of staff who was competent; well-liked by members of Congress, the Cabinet, and the rest of the White House staff; and possessed unmatched influence with her Democratic vice president was unwise. Melanie's strength as an advisor was her clarity and her moral compass, but in some instances, that clarity was blinding. Charlotte saw the decision to keep Craig on for a few months after the revelation of his bad behavior as rooted squarely in the murky area of presidential decision making, where a perfect outcome isn't on the menu, but a leader must make the best choice among less than ideal options.

Now Charlotte walked into the dining room, where Brooke, Mark, and Harry were seated for dinner. Penny had returned to her closet to hunt for shoes to go with the black dress. Harry greeted her with a kiss and confirmed that his new girlfriend would be accompanying them to Camp David the following weekend.

"Smooth move with the Camp David invitation. That must be a magic bullet with the ladies," Mark teased.

"Stop it. Harry is a gentleman, unlike you," Brooke chided.

"I want to know if an invitation to Camp David is the new 'Hey, do you want to check out my aquarium?'" Mark continued.

"What are you talking about?" Brooke challenged.

"Harry knows what I'm talking about." Mark winked at Harry, who rolled his eyes and smirked.

"You guys aren't coming to Camp next weekend, are you?" Harry asked.

"We are now!" Mark exclaimed.

"What girl would be dumb enough to go to some guy's room to

see his fish tank?" Penny asked, as she entered the room with a pair of black heels in her hand.

"I have no idea," Brooke said. Charlotte and Mark laughed.

"Did you seriously have an aquarium?" Penny asked.

"I sure did," Mark boasted.

"There were always dead fish in it," Charlotte remembered.

"It stank," Brooke added.

"But it worked." Mark planted a kiss on Brooke's lips while she pretended to push him away.

Charlotte was grateful for the levity, but she excused herself before dessert to review her speeches for the next day and study the line-by-line schedule. She slept fitfully and took the dogs out to the South Lawn for their walk before sunrise. When she returned to the residence, she dressed carefully in a cream-colored Armani skirt and jacket. She had her hair styled in a low, loose bun and her makeup applied and then left the residence for the West Wing. When she passed the medical unit where Peter had huddled with Dale after she learned of Warren's death, the nurse stood to greet her.

"Good morning, Madam President."

Charlotte smiled and kept walking until she reached the colonnade. She stopped in front of the Rose Garden. Her Secret Service agent said something into his sleeve, and Charlotte walked onto the grass. A podium with a presidential seal had been set at one end of the garden, and several dozen chairs faced it. She would host a ceremony at the end of the day where she would rename the Rose Garden the Warren Carmichael Rose Garden. She had decided that she wanted him close to her, and the Rose Garden was the closest thing she could find. Charlotte ran her finger along the newly etched letters on the plaque she'd had engraved with the Longfellow quote. It had been mounted on a bench that would sit at the far end of the Rose Garden. As she looked around at the enormous blooms in the summer garden, she thought about the last time she'd spoken to Warren. He had called to assure her that the speech she was giving at the Women's Museum would solidify her standing among women and independent voters.

"What about the base?" she'd fretted during their call.

"A wise woman once told me that the base wants to be leveled with more than it wants to be pandered to."

"She was an idiot. They'd rather be pandered to."

"Madam President, is there anything in the speech that you don't believe to be true?"

"No."

"Then stop thinking about it. Stop worrying about it, and give that speech with swagger, or it will be a lose-lose. You'll piss off the base, and the audience will sense your discomfort."

"Swagger, huh? I'll give it my best. How is everything else?"

"Your numbers on national security are strong. Leadership numbers are at an all-time high."

"I didn't mean with my poll numbers. I meant with you. How are you doing?"

"Things have never been better, Madam President. Thanks for asking."

They'd hung up that night, and she had returned to the residence to review her speech. Peter had been watching a baseball game, and Brooke and Mark had been at the Kennedy Center. It felt like an eternity had passed since then, but it had only been one year.

Now she smiled when she remembered their conversations, but for months, she couldn't read his name in the newspaper or listen to detailed accounts of his heroic actions on the day of the attacks without growing emotional. Everyone around a president is capable of giving the boss positive feedback after a solid showing, but Warren was one of a handful of people who never hesitated to provide blunt feedback about her subpar performances. She remembered the first time he'd critiqued her on the campaign trail. Charlotte had completed an interview with a local reporter in Cleveland. She thought it had gone well, and her campaign aides had smiled and told her she'd done a great job. When she got back onto Air Force One to fly to the next campaign rally, Warren had entered her cabin. He'd watched her sign thank-you notes to contributors for a couple of minutes before he said anything.

"That was pitiful."

"Excuse me?" She'd been stunned.

"You acted bored by the questions and annoyed that he asked to take a picture with you afterward. Do you even remember his name?"

"The reporter?"

"That wasn't a reporter. That was Miles Henry. Do you know Miles's claim to fame?"

Charlotte had placed her letters on the table and looked Warren directly in the eye. "You're about to tell me."

"Miles is the longest-serving news anchor in Ohio. He's turned down a dozen offers to move to larger markets. LeBron James tried to get him a job at the Miami affiliate when he moved there in 2010. Do you know what Miles did when he was offered a job in Miami?"

"You're going to tell me that, too."

"You bet I am. As a favor to his friend LeBron, Miles agreed to fly out to Miami Beach for the weekend. He brought his wife and daughter with him. They stayed at the Lowe's Hotel on Miami Beach and shopped and ate in the restaurants on Lincoln Road. They took pictures in front of the house where Versace was killed and lay by the pool until they were sunburned. At the end of the weekend, Miles called LeBron and thanked him for the opportunity, and then he called the station manager and told him that Cleveland was the only place he'd ever wanted to work. Madam President, there wasn't anything more important on your schedule today than making Miles believe that you cared about him and that you cared about Cleveland. And in my humble opinion, you fucked it up royally."

"Your opinions are a lot of things, but I wouldn't call them humble," she'd retorted.

"I'm not one of your staffers. I get paid by the hour, Madam President, and it isn't worth the ridiculous amount you're paying if I suck up to you and tell you how inspired each of your performances is. That, in my humble opinion, would be a waste of your money and my time."

Charlotte had pushed the stack of thank-you notes in his direction. "To be fair, it's their money that's paying your exorbitant rate," she'd said.

"Even those assholes deserve more than a candidate who is simply going through the motions," he'd said.

"What exactly do you suggest I do, campaign Svengali?"

Warren had smiled. "About the interview?"

"Yes, about the interview."

"Well, the interview really isn't the problem. It's a symptom of a larger illness."

"I see."

"There's nothing you can do about the interview except have the press office call them and tell the station that you'll be back next week and you'd like to finish the conversation you started today."

"Are we going to be back next week?"

"I'll add it to the schedule."

"You do have an answer for everything. And what about my illness?"

"Your Svengali would suggest a few more focus groups and some fine-tuning of your campaign message and maybe a few million dollars' worth of new ads. You could even throw in a staff shake-up for good measure and put your old pals Brooke and Mark on the campaign bus to lighten the mood. As your friend, and as someone who is deeply interested in seeing this country remain in your able hands, I would suggest that you get out of your head, get over yourself, and stop worrying about what's going to happen on Election Day. These things have a way of working themselves out if you trust the universe."

At that point, Charlotte had laughed. "I'm really glad that you didn't suggest I trust the universe in your capacity as my campaign Svengali. I would have fired you."

Warren had been her peer and a trusted counselor, but she'd also felt a maternal sense of pride in all that he'd accomplished. She missed his optimism, his humor, and his insights. Most of all, she hated knowing that all of his potential and all of his formidable talent had been cut short by the cruelty of fate.

The boy Warren had saved that day was traveling to the White House from his home outside Philadelphia for the ceremony, and Warren's parents would also be there. The Carmichaels had visited the White House half a dozen times since their first visit the day after the attack. They had created a victims' support network, a national network of charities and mental health professionals that worked primarily to support the children of those killed in the attacks. The twins had also founded a charity to raise scholarship money to pay for college tuition for the victims' children. Brooke and Mark were the cochairs, and Peter had recruited several of the professional athletes he represented to serve on the charity's board. Charlotte would announce at the ceremony that they'd raised more than five million dollars.

But before that, she had to film the first of three short interviews with Lucy and Richard. They were waiting for her in the Oval Office and would travel on Air Force One to cover the events marking the one-year anniversary of the attacks. Their "Day in the Life" special from the year before had won an Emmy and cemented their status as the anchors to beat. Lucy had become an unlikely ally. Charlotte had called her several weeks after the attacks and asked her to reach out to Dale, who was dangerously thin and sleeping on the couch in her office instead of going home most nights. Charlotte couldn't exactly turn to Craig and ask him to look after Dale, and Melanie was too judgmental to become Dale's confidante, so Charlotte had asked Lucy to help. Lucy reported back to Charlotte after their regular dinners, and Charlotte was immensely pleased that they'd developed a real friendship.

Now Sam handed Charlotte a cup of coffee, which she sipped while the technician attached a microphone to her lapel. Sam took the battery pack from the sound tech and attached it to the president's skirt.

"When you're ready, we'll give them the heads-up that you're coming in."

Dale had informed her the day before that Lucy would ask her if there was a particular story or memory about Warren that she liked to think about when she thought of his contributions to her administration. Charlotte had decided to share a slightly edited version of the story from the campaign plane, when Warren had told her she'd done a terrible job with the Cleveland reporter. It encapsulated all of the things she'd loved about him as an advisor, and it made clear that he was brave enough to tell her the truth even if it meant that he risked losing his political clout by offending her with an unflattering review.

From Charlotte's perspective, his honesty had had the opposite effect. From that trip on, Warren's political influence was unrivaled.

Charlotte stood a little straighter and put her coffee cup down on Sam's desk. "I'm ready," she said.

One of her agents pushed open the door to the Oval Office, and Lucy and Richard stood to greet her. Dale and Monty quickly moved to the side of the room to stay out of the camera shot. Charlotte spent the first couple of minutes discussing the ceremonies that would take place over the next two days.

"Madam President, I know that your focus is on the victims and their families today, but I wonder if you can talk about the impact or the toll that this monumental tragedy has had on you personally."

"You're right, Lucy. Today is about the victims and their loved ones, and there's nothing that has made me feel more powerless in my time as president than to stand with a child who has lost her mom or dad or to comfort parents who lost a child or grandparents who lost children and grandchildren. I can't do anything for them in terms of easing their pain, because I can't bring their loved ones back. But I have promised all of them that their loss will always be a part of me. I've spent enough time with the victims' families to understand the character and strength of these individuals."

"Madam President, a lot of people were surprised by your capacity to be so public in your grief. Was some of that ability to mourn with the families and understand what they were going through because you lost someone important to you on that day? For any of our viewers who don't recall, a member of your White House family—a very close advisor, Warren Carmichael—died in the attacks on the Mall here in D.C."

"Thanks for the question, Lucy. We miss Warren so much. There are no words to describe how important he was as an advisor and a friend to me and to everyone here. But every single person who lost someone that day—and even people who didn't know anyone who was killed or hurt in the attacks—endured something truly shocking and terrifying. If people feel that I did a respectable job tapping into the emotions that others felt, then I think Warren would have been the first to say that's not a bad outcome."

"Madam President, your staff is giving us a sign to wrap things up. I know we'll speak again later today, but is there anything else you want to say before the event gets under way?"

"It's important to remember the families after today's ceremonies and tributes are over. For them, the pain never ends. We can all learn so much from their examples. The true character of this country is not that we avoid tragedy. It's that we find our way back. Today I plan to honor the resilience, strength, and grace of all the family members and friends of the victims, including the Carmichaels, who will be here today."

"Madam President, before we go, I want to ask you one final question. The attacks of July 31 and your administration's response to them will always be viewed as the most historic aspect of your presidency, but I wonder if you ever do any thinking, now that you're just eighteen months away from the end of your presidency and a return to life as an ordinary citizen, about the rest of your legacy?"

"I can't say that I do, Lucy," Charlotte demurred. She worried for an instant that perhaps Lucy knew about the house she'd just allowed Brooke and Mark to buy for her in their Atherton neighborhood.

"Thank you, Madam President. Until we speak again in a few hours," Richard concluded.

Charlotte waited until the cameramen moved away from their positions, and then she allowed Monty to remove the microphone from her jacket. She slid the battery pack off her skirt and handed it to him.

"Nice job," he murmured.

Charlotte smiled at Monty and Dale. "Thanks, everyone."

Charlotte left the Oval Office and walked down to Melanie's office. She sat down across from her.

"Do you ever think about what happens after this?"

"After today? I'm going to sleep for more than thirty minutes at a time."

"Not just today."

"What? Your second term?"

"Yes."

"Your presidency is farther from being over than two pregnancies."

"You have a way with words, Melanie."

"What's really going on, Madam President?"

"Lucy asked me if I ever thought about my legacy, and I hadn't thought about it much before the attacks, because I was just regaining my momentum after Tara, and I obviously haven't had time to think about it since, but I wonder if we should be doing more, you know. So that we have a handle on the things that I can work on when this is all over."

Melanie leaned back in her chair and looked at the president carefully. Charlotte could tell that she was trying to figure out if she was fishing for reassurance about the hugely important day ahead or if she actually wanted to initiate a conversation about her legacy fifteen minutes before the helicopter arrived to usher them to Air Force One for the two-day trip.

"Madam President, I've done a lot of thinking about your legacy, and I think it's something we should start talking about regularly, once we get through today."

Charlotte felt so completely understood and supported by Melanie that she had to fight an unexpected wave of emotion. She stared at the carpet for a few seconds and then met Melanie's gaze.

"That sounds like a very good plan."

The sound of Marine One landing on the South Lawn interrupted them.

"I'll meet you in the Oval in five minutes. I need to check on the baby before I leave," Melanie said.

Charlotte walked slowly back to the Oval Office and stood alone, waiting for Monty to summon her. Usually, the senior staff gathered in the Oval Office before their departure so they could all walk out together, but today there was only space for Melanie and Monty to ride with her on Marine One because Penny and Harry were accompanying her. Once Melanie arrived, Monty gave them the signal that it was time to go.

"Good luck, Madam President," Sam said.

Charlotte smiled and walked with Melanie to the East Wing, where Penny and Harry were waiting for her. She put an arm around Penny and walked out with the twins to the helicopter. Melanie and Monty waited for them to board before they walked out so that they would avoid being in the camera shot.

As Marine One lifted off the South Lawn, Charlotte watched the reporters and visitors grow smaller and the Washington Monument closer. As they flew the short distance to Andrews Air Force Base, Charlotte thought about everyone who would be with her over the next two days. Brooke and Mark would be waiting for her on Air Force One. Dale would be there, too. She'd accompanied Lucy and Richard to the airport as soon as the interview had ended. The Carmichaels would also be on board.

Charlotte leaned back and watched Harry huddle close to listen to something Monty was saying. Next to them, Melanie was examining the line-by-line schedule for the day. Penny was sitting across from her, and their chairs were close enough that their knees touched.

"What are you thinking about?" Penny asked.

"I was thinking that I'm happy that you and your brother are coming with me."

"And?"

"Why does there have to be an *and*?"

"Because you had that look that usually means that you're either about to cry or say something overly sentimental."

"I'm going to try very hard not to cry, but it's going to get harder as the day goes on. And if it would be sentimental to tell you that I'm proud of you and happy that we've spent so much quality time together this year, then yes, I'm going to be overly sentimental today. Don't tell anyone, please."

Penny did a half smile, half eye-roll. "Warren sounds awesome. I'm sorry I didn't know Warren."

"Me, too. You would have liked him a lot."

"I want to hear more about him."

"You will. We'll be with the Carmichaels. They tell some really funny stories about him when he was in high school."

"I want to hear your stories."

"My stories?"

"You should write a book."

"About what?"

"Being the first woman to be president, the attacks, getting separated from Dad, having twins in high school and college while you're president. You should write about how you juggled all of us."

Charlotte tried to hide her surprise. She stared out the window and swallowed hard to get rid of the lump that had formed in her throat. "Why don't we write it together? You could include your perspective, too. That would be more interesting," she suggested.

"Or I could interview you." Penny sounded excited.

As Marine One landed at Andrews, Charlotte gave Penny's hand a squeeze. Her heart was heavy for the sad occasion that had brought them all together, but she found immense comfort in the company of her twins. When she stepped off of Marine One, Harry held out his arm, which she accepted. He felt so sturdy, more like a man than a boy. He was nineteen, and would be twenty in a few weeks. They were starting their junior years in college. Charlotte slipped her other arm through Penny's, and the three of them walked arm-in-arm to the stairs leading up to Air Force One. The kids stopped and let her walk up alone so that the press could film her, but before she did, she turned back to look at them. She wanted to remember this day forever. Charlotte couldn't remember a single day before it when they'd felt like more of a family.

Acknowledgments

It was the privilege of my lifetime to work in the White House on September 11, 2001. The thousands of acts of humanity that I witnessed in the days and months that followed inspired much of the emotion of this purely fictional tale. Obviously, to imagine how a fictional president might act, I was inspired and informed by the heart of the man for whom I worked, President George W. Bush. He wrote in his book *Decision Points* about how the country would move on but he would never forget. I'm grateful that I had the opportunity to work for him and to know him and to understand a little bit of what it was like for him on that day.

So many people helped me remember not just the emotions, but the logistics of a day like the one detailed in *Madam President.* Thank you to my former White House colleagues who helped me tell those parts of the story. Geoff Morrell has my gratitude for his insights and for his early support of a female SECDEF. I am also grateful to my friends in the White House press corps who read drafts of this novel in its earliest stages and helped me imagine how a day like this would be experienced as a journalist.

During the most intense writing phase, my regular appearances on *Morning Joe* were my only human interactions outside of my immediate family. Joe Scarborough, Mika Brzezinski, Willie Geist, Mike Barnicle, Donny Deutsch, Mark Halperin, and Jon Meacham provided encouragement and good cheer. Dana Bash, Mark Leibovich, Bianna Golodryga, and Wendy Button provided much needed "straight talk" about early chapters. Dana Perino, Ari Fleischer, Claire Buchan Parker, Chris Edwards, and Reed Dickens helped me remember the White House as it actually was. Heather Karpas and Kristyn Keene at ICM were some of the earliest and best editors of the manuscript and I will always be thankful. Henley Old has been by my side through the process of writing all three novels and there wouldn't be a series without her. My mom read every version and always gave me honest and constructive criticism. My agent, Sloan Harris, was the first person to believe that there was an entire book to be written about a single day. I'm the luckiest writer on the planet to have an advocate and a partner like Sloan. Emily Bestler is the most nurturing editor that anyone could ever dream of working with. She made the story better and clearer and truer in every way imaginable. I'm extremely fortunate to work with the team at Emily Bestler Books. Megan Reid, Matthew Rossiter, and Lisa Sciambra are simply the best of the very best.

I'm so blessed to have a husband who supports and cherishes and cheers for the side of me that disappears into my characters and their travails for months on end. I love you. And to Liam, I love you to the moon and back.